FRANCIS FORD COPPOLA'S

Zoetrope
ALL STORY

FRANCIS FORD COPPOLA'S

Zoetrope
ALL STORY

Edited by
Adrienne Brodeur
and Samantha Schnee

Introduction by
Francis Ford Coppola

Methuen

1 3 5 7 9 10 8 6 4 2

Published in 2001 by Methuen Publishing Ltd
215 Vauxhall Bridge Rd. London SW1V 1EJ

First published in the United States by Harcourt, Inc.

Methuen Publishing Limited Reg. No. 3543167

A CIP catalogue record for this book is available from the
British Library

ISBN 0 413 76700 0

Designed by Lydia D'moch

Printed and bound in Great Britain by
Cox and Wyman Ltd, Reading

CONTENTS

INTRODUCTION

In my mind I have this dream studio in the clouds. It is a beautiful group of buildings surrounded by gardens and parks. The Writing Department is easy to spot; it has a huge yellow pencil hanging over the front door and a bar inside. On the first floor is my short-story magazine, *Zoetrope: All-Story* (next to the bar), and on the other floors are the Screenwriting Department, the Screenstory Department, and the Writers' Research Department. In the basement there's a little solitary-confinement cell, which is the Crazy Idea Department. I spend a lot of my time there cooking up ideas, *Zoetrope: All-Story* being one of them.

What happens in the Story Department is what everything else in my dream studio hinges upon. What first intrigues a director? The story. What attracts the best actors? Ditto. What are the first questions anyone involved in filmmaking asks? "What is the story?" "What is it about?" You've got a story? Then write it as a story—not a screenplay. That format exists largely so that a production manager can say,

"Oh, hmmm, that's an interior, that's an exterior, that's day, which is cheaper than night," and add it all up to estimate schedule and costs. A screenplay is designed as much to facilitate budgeting and provide some "control" as it is to convey story or emotion. Once the story is written, then we can go upstairs to the Screenwriting Department and take it to all the other departments (Budgeting, Legal, Art, Casting, Music, and so forth) that are dying to get their hands on it. The story is the foundation upon which all else is built, which is not to say that a good story alone can make a good movie. You also need collaborators, luck, money, weather, and a million other things. However, it is not possible for a good movie to exist without a good story.

This is one reason I've always been puzzled that none of the powerful, well-funded major studios make the cultivation of writing their main focus. Even though many of them own publishing companies (which they force to mimic the studios' approach to artistic creation), and base movies on successful books, none of them that I know of devote serious resources to the cultivation of *literary* work—stories from contemporary writers who help us understand our lives and our times. No other major industry ignores its most vital resources to this extent. Major oil companies spend millions on exploration, sending geologists and scientists to look for oil all over the world. Technology companies have research-and-development departments, and automobile companies have "skunk works," but the development departments for Hollywood studios tend to want to jump over the literary part and get right to the screenplay, to commence budgeting and casting and everything necessary to justify some cash flow.

So I decided a few years back that the wisest investment I could make for my own film company, American Zoetrope (which, though old and venerable, remains very small and has few financial resources), would be to take what cash we had and dedicate it to literary cultivation. I thought the best place to begin was with the short story, because it most approximates the dimensions of the average film. Novels tend to have too much material, but short stories contain all the basic elements that a film needs in one package: character, plot, and setting. Like movies, stories are to be consumed in one sitting. The good ones transport you, the great ones change you, and the bad ones—well, at least they are short.

In the old days, someone would suggest an idea, and Sabatini or Dickens or Thackeray would step in and do the job. Much of the great wealth of our literary tradition comes from commissions for periodicals. Similarly, *Zoetrope: All-Story* sometimes commissions work, just like back then, when writers needed commissions to make a living. My thought was that if occasionally we threw out an idea—a simple idea about people and the times, such as our first commission, "The Baker's Wife," by Sara Powers, whom we invited to "write a love story involving people who are having the same dreams," or our most famous commission, "The Girls' Guide to Hunting and Fishing," by Melissa Bank, whose goal was to "describe what would happen to a woman who used *The Rules* on someone who was the 'right man' for her already"—it might become a rich story.

So how it works is I'll give a simple idea to Adrienne Brodeur, our editor in chief, who, after reviewing a writer's work, will say, "Hmmm, this is an idea that this particular writer might connect with," and she will see if the writer likes the concept. From that point, the writer can then take it anywhere he wants. We're not looking for slavish execution of the idea, but for an artist to take it to heart and make it his own. That's our process when it comes to commissions, and I would say we've had some wonderful and, for the most part, successful results from this method. "Fair Warning" by Robert Olen Butler and "Her New Life" by Emily Perkins were commissioned just for this anthology. Probably neither of them thought about the assignment one week into working on it, and the stories they crafted became fully their own. All we did was give an impetus. I like the commission idea and I think artists like it. It's one thing to sit around and wonder whether you are going to write out of your soul or not; sometimes it is refreshing when someone gives you a concept to work with.

My idea in starting *Zoetrope: All-Story* was to build the world's greatest story department, and I shudder to realize that I am calling it that. I hired Adrienne Brodeur as the editor in chief because she was interested in literature and publishing and not in movies. So when we are asked if our main task is to look for stories that can be good movies, the answer is, strangely, "no." There is a logical reason for this. If we looked only for stories that could make good films, we would be excluding a giant group of writers whose work and ideas and emotions *must* be included to publish the best writing talent of the nation, the culture, the era, but whose particular stories might not be adaptable into movies. We don't want to exclude any great short story, because we want to work with the best writers and their best work, and we would miss this opportunity if we were looking only for adaptable fiction. We understand that only a few of the sto-

ries we publish will make good films, but you never know...
perhaps the contact with the work or with the writer will
eventually lead to future collaboration.

In the past it was common for a short story to be adapted
into a successful film. Did you know that the movies *All
About Eve, High Noon, Psycho, Blow-Up, The Fly,* and *It's a
Wonderful Life,* among others, all had their start as short stories? The stories these movies were based on were part of
a storytelling tradition in force in the twenties and thirties,
fueled by writers like John O'Hara, Dorothy Parker, Ring
Lardner, and F. Scott Fitzgerald, that, among other things,
inspired and taught the fine screenwriters of the forties and
fifties who produced the screenplays for these films. Well,
this heritage inspired me to take my story department out of
the clouds and make it real, in the form of a magazine.

We are, quite frankly, interested in good writing, good characters, and intriguing stories that spellbind us, but also
teach us about life, so we can face that twenty-four-hour-a-
day maw of marketing that's being aimed at us—advertising
that tries to convince us we aren't complete unless we buy
this, or look like her, or are married to him, and so on. What
are artists supposed to do? What we strive to do at American
Zoetrope: use our resources to counter the constant pres-
sures that make us feel bad about ourselves with something
alive, fulfilling, and exciting: literature.

Best,
Francis Ford Coppola

sara **powers**

THE BAKER'S WIFE

Most Friday evenings since they were married they spent on
their porch that listed steeply toward the street. They sat in
loose-limbed wooden chairs that seemed as if they might at
any moment slide off down the steps, drinking cold bottles
of beer and letting the fragrant Texas evening rise up around
them until it was night. And on one night, this night that
concerns us, they told lies, wove them into the net of conversation like tails of seaweed threading themselves through
a fisherman's seine.

"Three lies," Louis said—and she thought, *God what a
face he has: lean and freckled, red sideburns shaved to a point
under his cheekbones*—"about anything. Just drop them in
the conversation."

"That sounds dangerous," she said, half meaning it.

"Tomorrow we'll tell each other what they were." He
wore silver rings on his fingers. His hands, long and elegant,
were the hands of a musician, the hands of a snake charmer.

The conversation looped and strode; they gave each
other presents of the stories that held their past selves like

miniature scenery trapped in glass: she told him of her flir-
tation with exhibitionism, her dance before the window
with the blinds half lowered, yellow light blazing out from
behind her silhouetted hips, and a silent audience smirking
around curtains across the courtyard. He was intrigued and
excited by this, but skeptical. Not a very good liar, he
thought. And he told her about a little dog he had thrown off
a neighbor's third-story balcony when he was six; she was
horrified. "They said they'd beat me up if I didn't," he said.
"So I picked it up and threw it over the railing."

"Poor Louis," she said. "Still, I think I would have been
beaten up."

"Not me," said Louis. "I heaved the thing right over."

They had met a year and a half before, at Christmastime;
they fell in love. She was a photographer; too pretty for her
own liking, she bleached her hair white blonde and wore
boys' clothes that hung loosely over her thin frame. He was
a pastry chef and a fiddle player; shabbily elegant, he wore a
tiny row of sapphire studs in one ear. One night, several days
after they had met, they sat in a tapas bar on a dark street of
warehouses, drinking wine and ordering the small plates of
food from a doleful bartender. They speculated about him.

"Brokenhearted," Louis said. They had a bowl of olives
and a plate of sausages and manchego cheese.

The bartender was cherubic, with downturned eyes. "An
older woman just left him," she said.

"Look at the way he wipes the bar, so sadly," Louis said.
"I feel bad disturbing him."

But they were infatuated, and feeding each other olives,
tasting the olives on each other's kisses; each kiss was a
small revolution starting in their mouths. Sophie was ab-

sentmindedly running her hand up and down his thigh; she took it off to gesture at something.

Louis looked stricken. "Whatever else you do," he said, "don't stop that."

She moved her hand back; his thigh was so thin and hard under her fingers that he seemed almost breakable. She wanted to cradle him. But as he tipped back the squat bottle of Spanish beer and drank, she knew there was something fierce in him too.

"What are you thinking?"

She smiled, still kneading his leg with the heel of her palm. "I don't know if I should say it," she said. "I'm afraid to say."

Looking at her he said, "There is nothing you can't say to me. I want to hear everything." Sophie was looking at him and knew that it was true. Dorothy brought oil to the tin man and he felt that same moment of awful bliss. Louis was asking everything of her and yet only that she be entirely herself. All she could say was "All right." Then she married him.

At the Canadian border, he told her, he and the rest of his band squatted naked in a jail cell for eight hours, bare feet flat against the cold floor, while the Mounties searched the bus for drugs. She said she had her first orgasm with an electric toothbrush. He said they would have beautiful children. She told him about a famous female sculptor who had tried to kiss her, whose breath smelled of celery and garlic, whose unhappiness was like a household pet. They walked down the hill to the corner for more beer. He told her about climbing a stony mountain in Mexico with a blonde and humorless girlfriend, hiking for hours under the hot sun, and how she walked farther and farther away, refusing to talk to him, until at the top she told him she didn't want to see him anymore. Sophie told him he was her muse.

"Sophie," he said. He loved her name, the softness of it like the velvety night.

For a long time, it was like this: taxi drivers asked them if they were on their honeymoon; waitresses turned away from them with sweet tears blossoming in the corners of their eyes; the rain fell around them in sheets, shielding their kisses. Even cats followed them home.

People said, "Let's have a drink," meaning: we want to be close to you because you are radiant and drunk on each other.

They drank that evening and the stories looped outward toward the absurd, the lies were flung recklessly and dangled like shimmering strands of audiotape from the tree branches. They laughed, lost hold of lies in midtelling, caught each other and confessed.

"My uncle," she said, "was a playboy, lost it all in the crash of '29, and drove a bus in Newark for the rest of his life."

"My grandfather," he said, "was a confidence man."

"And you're not?" she asked, smiling at him. "How do I know you don't have three other wives in three other towns?"

"They're getting mad," he said. "I haven't seen any of them in a while."

"Send a card," she suggested. "No need to be rude."

"Maybe I will." He grinned.

She turned toward him and rested her bare foot on his thigh, kneading it with her toes. "I encountered a ghost once."

"Liar," he said.

"Nope. Listen," she said. "It was in Saratoga in this big old country house where I was staying. Things had happened there; I forget what: children drowned, tragedies...."

"What did it look like?" he asked.

"I didn't actually see it," she said. "I was too scared. I felt its presence. It picked up my mattress and bent it. Eleven-thirty in the morning. I was napping."

"That's what you get for being so lazy. It was the ghost of sloth coming to get you."

"Whoever it was, it was terrifying."

"So very cosmic," he said.

"Shut up, Louis," she said, going inside to the bathroom. When she came out she kissed the top of his head, loving the hard shape of his skull beneath his hair.

"So nothing paranormal has ever happened to you?" she asked.

"A weird thing did happen a few weeks ago," he said slowly. "Did I tell you this? Edwina and I had the same dream."

"Exactly the same, or sort of the same?" Pretty Edwina. She felt a brief current of jealousy run through her.

"Actually, it was really eerie. They were almost identical. We were bank robbers—"

"You and Edwina?"

"Yeah. And we got arrested and were out on bail and everybody was crying about it. You were crying. Edwina and I weren't though. We were too far gone. We didn't care."

"I wasn't crying," said Sophie. "In fact, I'm the one who turned you guys in."

"Bitch," said Louis. "I'm going back to the wife in Kansas City." He went into the house and got cold beers from the refrigerator. As he sprung the caps off with the opener, he thought of his wife's face when he'd mentioned Edwina, and wondered if he'd said too much.

When he returned she said, "I punched a drunk in a bar once. Just like this." She demonstrated, a short jab to the mouth. "He wouldn't leave me alone. I told him, 'I'm gonna punch you.' He started on some bull about how he knew karate, and bam! midsentence I hit him."

"What'd he do?"

"He put his hand to his mouth like this, and said, 'Bitch hit me!' Then they threw him out of the bar. I saw him the next week and he bought me a drink."

"Now I know you're lying."

"I swear. Then he started hitting on me again. I thought I was going to have to do it all over again."

Laughter. The moon sat on the treetops like a big yellow hen on her nest. The drunk who lived under their house roared. Soon he would turn his radio up, and the Mexican songs would battle the floorboards, dividing the night with horns.

"Louis," she said. She heard it in the creaking of the floor-boards of their crooked little wooden house, in the stretch and moan of the live oak that hovered over the porch. "Louis," the house would say sometimes when she was there alone during the day.

A couple emerged from the shadows of the old tree, wraiths holding hands.

"Pipe down," said the larger half, which turned into their friend Harry. "You two drunks."

The other half was Edwina, little Edwina with her pointed chin and her sundresses, her friendliness and her slight air of calculation, whom Harry had found somewhere in Tennessee and brought back to Austin with him.

"Fast Eddie," said Louis. "Come here."

Edwina let loose of Harry's hand and climbed the stairs, smiling at Louis, and bent and let him kiss her. She turned and kissed Sophie.

"All that laughing was making my bones hurt," she said. "What are you two up to?"

"Lying," said Sophie.

Louis agreed. "A little fibbing."

"So it comes down to that," Harry said. His shadow was immense, draped across the steps and the two in the chairs. "Married and nothing left to say to one another but lies."

"Could be fun," murmured Edwina to Louis. He winked at her.

"Harry," said Sophie. "Come here." He was a big man with broad bony hands and eyes the color of the noonday sky, and he could make music out of any instrument he picked up. She kissed his stubbled cheek.

"Where's the beer?" he asked, cupping one of his big hands over the top of her skull.

"You can have anything you want," she said, at the same time that Louis said, "Settle down, big man," and was on his feet and through the screen door. Edwina followed him in.

Harry glanced briefly at the closing door and sat on the step at her feet.

"So what's new in Sophie's world?" he asked. "How is the graven image business?"

She poked him with her big toe. "Slow. I'm not making enough money yet."

"Give it some time," he said. "You're still new in town. We're still trying to suss out the Yankee."

"I guess so," she said. "But Louis works so hard, and I know he's sick to death of baking, of getting up at the crack of dawn, of picking dough out of his hair at night. The band needs to get some kind of break."

"We all do," said Harry, but they both knew that his situation was different: his grandmother, a leathery West Texas housewife, raised seven kids and spirited spare change into a stock portfolio that she left to her favorite grandson. Harry lived modestly and knew he would never have to work.

Inside the house Edwina studied pictures of Louis and Sophie that were stuck to the refrigerator while he pulled the damp bottles from inside it.

"How old were you in this one?" she asked.

He came around behind her, frowning at the picture. "Oh, twenty-five, I guess."

"Were you wild? Look at you with that crazy hair and those eyes...."

He laughed. "Don't bring up my checkered past; you'll get me in trouble with my wife."

"She's jealous of your past?"

"Maybe just worried that I might still have atavistic habits from my former self," he said.

"Where was this taken?"

"I don't know, Eugene, Oregon, or one of those towns ... on the road somewhere. Back when I had the rock-'n'-roll life full time."

"You miss it a lot?" she said, turning to face him.

He took a step back and set the beers on the counter to get a better grip on them. "Of course," he said. "I'm so sick of baking. All I want to do is play fiddle."

She was still looking at him with a slender smile, slouched slightly against the refrigerator.

She waited.

He grabbed the bottles up. "Those people are likely to parch to death if we stay in here yakking. Here you go." He handed her a couple of the bottles and loped off through the living room.

Edwina followed, wearing her delicate smile.

Later, as they lay in bed, two heads on one pillow, Louis confessed two but not the third of the lies he had told her.

"So wait," she said. "What was the third one? You told three, right?"

"I don't know," he said. "I mean, I remember that I told three but I can't remember what the last one was."

"What do you mean you don't remember? You have to," she said. "It's not fair. Otherwise there is going to be this thing about you that I'm going to believe in that's false."

"Well, tell me yours and maybe I'll remember the other one."

"I don't want to tell you mine now," she said. "Anyway, maybe a little mystery is good for a marriage."

"Hold on," he said, laughing now but raising himself up on one elbow in the dark and looking down at her face. Eyes closed, it was a pale oval darkened by a wide slash of mouth, framed against bleached hair, white pillow. "That's not fair. I told you the two lies I remember. You've got to tell me at least two of yours."

"Guess," she said.

"Your first orgasm was not with an electric toothbrush."

"It was," she said. "Eleven years old."

"I don't believe it," he said. "You heard that somewhere." He put his face right down to her cheek. "Remember, the deal was you have to tell the truth now."

"Ha! Don't you get picky about rules, mister." She opened her eyes and grinned, rolling a half turn away from him. "I was a perverse little child."

"Precocious is more like it." He put his arm over her and pulled her around to face him. "I think it's great."

"Water, please," she said, and he handed her the glass from the bedside table. She leaned over him and drank it. His fingers traced the lobe of her breast as she drank. She put the glass back and said, "I can't believe that was a lie about your first love. What was her name...."

"Fatima Nelson," he said, hand over his eyes, laughing, "I can't believe you bought that name."

"That's a terrible thing to lie about," she said, sinking back down. "Your first love—that's a sacred thing. Fatima Nelson, oh my God...." They lay side by side giggling. "And she was fat and you were fat...."

The giggling faded and they rolled toward one another, and crooked arms and legs around each other, their breathing slowed and they slept. And they dreamed.

She started awake in the middle of the night; Louis's back was a pale comma curving away from her. He slept with his face in the pillows like a child. It had been a dream that woke her, she realized, about Edwina. Sophie and Louis had been in a dim, narrow bar, and as they stood she had looked back toward the door; through the rectangle of glass she had seen Edwina—the short black braids, the elfin, pointed chin. Edwina had leered at Sophie as their eyes had met through the door, and she had felt evil in the look, as though Edwina was some kind of corrupt spirit assigned to her. Sophie touched Louis's back, for luck or protection—his smooth cool skin her church. As she sank back toward sleep she remembered the rest of the dream: she had risen and flown right at Edwina through the small square window. Although Sophie had been terrified, bluffing as best as she could, she had not turned away, and it was Edwina who did, shrinking to the side with a grimace. Sophie had won. Then she slept again.

At six he woke, pulled back the covers, kissed her stomach, and was gone. Sophie woke up later; the sun was pushing at the back of the blinds and she felt sticky under the comforter. She threw it off her and lay there, absentmindedly running her hand down her body; she felt ripe, she thought, and wondered if her body wanted a baby. Rolling over, she smelled Louis's side of the bed; his scent was there like cloves on the sheet. He had said they would have beautiful children; she pictured them freckled and thin with that large-headed look that skinny children have. She imagined herself loving them and could almost feel it, the ferocity of love that wasn't born yet. Then she remembered the lies, and the one undiscovered lie, the snake hidden somewhere in the tall grass of the night's conversation. She frowned, her legs tangled in the sheets, and forgot about the slim little bodies of her children and thought only about the untruth that lay between her and Louis. What had he lied about? She strained to recall everything they had talked about, but the beers and the hours had stacked up one on the other and trying to grasp any one piece of the conversation was like chasing light. Her secret was that she had only told one lie; the others she had lost control of at the start, her mouth twitching as she tried to lasso a crazy grin, or had considered and discarded knowing she couldn't pull them off. But he didn't need to know that. Not now.

Louis was making *mille-feuilles*. His chef's jacket was buttoned wrong and he had a smudge of flour on his cheekbone, but his hands were nimble and delicate as he rolled dough paper thin. He was trying to recall the third of the lies he had told, was running what he could remember of their conversation over in his head. So easy for him to lie; stories rolled off his tongue as easily as the pastries bloomed lightly under his hands. He didn't want to lie to Sophie; lying belonged to his past, in the sarcophagus of all the past selves he had discarded. But it worried him slightly that he had lied with such nonchalance that he couldn't even remember it; he knew he needed to be vigilant or the habit of lying would creep back up on him.

While Louis worried about deceiving his wife, the dough fluttered from under the rolling pin; thin as leaves, silky as the surface of a still pond, it fluttered and grew across the marble counter.

She finished developing film, hung the wet and pungent strips from the shower rod, squinting at the images. There was Louis, sitting on the porch steps, hand on fist, head cranked around toward the camera, eyes directly into the lens. Doubt my sincerity, his eyes challenged her. Go ahead. She let go of the film and wandered out onto the porch. The neighbor's yellow lab limped up the walk and settled its swollen torso against the lower step. Afternoons were quiet on their street; cats lorded over the porches, curtains were drawn, and air conditioners exhaled steadily out of windows. This time of day it seemed that even the angels napped; the steady rhythm of their breathing was the heartbeat of the afternoon. She sat on the steps and let the heat wrap around the back of her neck like a hot fist. The fact was, she knew he had been a liar before she married him. In a worn, old, wooden railroad hotel out in the Hill Country, she lay on his stomach and asked him, "So, what are your faults?"

"My faults," he said. "Well, I used to be quite a fibber. Not any more though. I had to quit it like cigarettes. And, I guess I can be cruel when I'm backed into a corner."

They were quiet a moment, both considering his faults.

"What are yours?"

"Ummm," she said. "I'm mistrustful. I want to be liked too much and it makes me weak. I can be very self-absorbed." She squirmed, uncomfortable with naming her own crimes. What generosity he showed then when he ran his fingers over her ribs, around the flare of her hips, and grabbed her legs just where they swelled into buttock. All the air in her lungs released itself as she pushed her legs into his hands, and talk, of flaws and all else, was forgotten.

Sitting on the porch remembering this, she felt the first tendrils of doubt unfurl in her midsection. Who was to say, after all, that last night was the first night he had lied to her? She thought of his face, open and honest, of the steadiness of his gaze when they talked, and it seemed unlikely that underneath the man she knew there could be another, slicker man who lied; but, she thought, maybe he couldn't help himself. What could he have lied to her about? She searched back over the year for strange moments, moments of doubt or awkwardness that she had let go at the time. There were a few times when he was strangely evasive, when he had the strained voice and aggressive eye contact of a liar. One morning she had startled him on the porch—he had woken earlier and made coffee and collected the mail—reading a letter. When he heard the screen door creak his head snapped up, and as he turned to look at her, his hand creased and folded the letter.

"Hey," she said.

"Morning, doll," he said, and by then he was already

lazily seductive, his mouth carving out one of his lapidary smiles. The hand with the letter was low in his lap.

"Who'd we get a letter from?" she asked.

"Just my brother. He wrote me. He's having some girl troubles." He crooked an arm around one of her skinny legs. "I have an idea," he said. "Let's have a breakfast picnic."

He jumped up and was at it full tilt, banging open cupboards and rummaging in the refrigerator, sending her to the corner for fruit while he made crêpes; she put on her shoes and hugged him, but an after-image of his head jerking up and his hand falling away into his lap burned just below her happiness.

At the time, she had decided that it was nothing. *After all*, she had thought, *he chose me, this beautiful man*. Now she wondered.

She stared at a grackle, its feathers an oily green-black, that pecked at the cracks in the walkway. It hopped, cocked its head, and half stretched its wings, and that gesture reminded her of her dream about Edwina. Then, still staring at the bird but no longer seeing it, she remembered Louis's tale about he and Edwina having the same dream. That must be the third lie. What a strange lie, she thought. Why? Then she remembered her own jealousy at hearing the story, and she laughed out loud, scaring the grackle, who danced stiff-legged to a safer distance. Inside the dark house she picked up the phone and dialed the restaurant. It rang and rang and finally she put the receiver down. She imagined the two of them laughing about it when he got home, his shirt damp from the heat, as she poured him a glass of wine, and the relief they would both feel when there were no secrets between them. She would tease him about trying to make her jealous, and he would grab her and slyly slick the wine off her lips with his tongue.

She was giddy with relief, and knew she wouldn't be able to return to the still, stubborn images of her film. She didn't even want to stay in the house, but outside the afternoon blazed away and made it nearly impossible to do much else. She walked through the rooms of the house and settled on doing the dishes. They were nearly done when the phone rang, and she bounded for it.

"I was thinking," Edwina said. "That on a day like this the only thing to do is go to Barton Springs. Should I pick you up in a bit?"

"I'll walk over," Sophie said, impetuously.

She headed up the steep short hill their road climbed, passing crooked little wooden houses bleary with vegetation and bright splashes of flowers. Porches overflowed with flowerpots, wind chimes, rocking chairs, porch swings, tricycles, and blinking cats. Sophie loved the ramshackle and the clutter; it was her home and it was soothing to walk slowly in the heat up and down the steep narrow streets. A thread of sweat traced her spine. She walked several more blocks through the neighborhood, and then it began to change to one of Spanish-style houses with lawns and the occasional small apartment building. She kept walking, cutting across the elementary-school playing field shaded by the twisted branches of a live oak, and came out behind a small row of shops. Harry and Edwina's house was a small, one-story bungalow almost sunk in vegetation. She leaned her wet brow on the cool wood of the door—walking anywhere in midday always started out seeming like such a good idea, and ended with the blood throbbing in her neck and her body slick with moisture.

She could hear the notes falling as distinct as raindrops from Harry's mandolin in the cool interior of the house, and then the insectile trilling of the telephone interrupting it, and Harry's heavy footfall. There was a strange pleasure in being there, just beyond the source of these sounds. Sophie lingered on the porch, in no hurry to puncture her solitude. Maybe it was the echo of the telephone that made her remember, with a surge of mistrust, the morning when she woke to find Louis's side of the bed empty; when she went looking, she saw that he was out on the porch with the telephone. She had stood quietly for a second beside the screen door, but he was talking low and she could only hear the lilt and murmur of his voice, and there was something too soft in it. She turned away because it made her feel uncomfortable to stand there like that, half listening; she knew it wasn't right. Now she held that memory in her hand angrily, like it was the single screw left over after she had reassembled a broken appliance. It made the heat hotter, it broke her spell, and it made her lift her knuckles to the wooden door.

When there was no answer to her knock, she opened the door; the air conditioner was running full blast and Harry was singing softly.

Said it would rain, I made a bet. Lost my hat and my head got wet . . .

He put down his mandolin when he saw her. "Hey darlin'. She's out in the garden." Edwina worked for an organic greenhouse several days a week and spent the rest tending the garden that erupted lushly from their small backyard.

She put her hand on his shoulder as she walked by. "Keep singing," she said. Harry always made her feel good.

Sophie walked back through the kitchen and the sunporch and paused at the door. The heat of the day cast even the garden in a whitish tinge; she squinted and saw Edwina kneeling beneath a huge straw hat, tying a bean plant to a stake.

"Crazy woman," she called out. "Get out of that sun and let's go to Barton Springs."

"Hey girl," Edwina looked up. "I'm ready."

She wore her hair in short braids that made her look even younger. Louis had once called her "fetching," and the word always popped up in Sophie's mind when she saw Edwina. She had suspected sometimes that Edwina had a small crush on Louis.

Sophie stepped outside and down the few steps to the backyard, into the sun and heat and the smell of vegetation, the beans swooning away from their stakes, and the tomato plants heavy with green globes. The insect life clicked and hummed under the leaves. Edwina gathered her string and scissors and stood for a moment looking over the garden: queen of her kingdom.

"Something's eating my cucumbers," she said. "I'm going to sit out here one of these nights with Harry's gun and find out who's doing it."

"I swear it's not me," said Sophie. "Let's go."

Edwina put on her bathing suit, and they got into her truck. They turned on the air conditioning and put the windows down, letting the hot air roll across their faces, an indulgence they shared without guilt. Edwina smoked a cigarette and drove too fast; the sunlight raked the windshield.

"How's Louis?" Edwina asked.

"Baking," said Sophie. "I haven't seen him all day."

"I saw him this morning at the bakery on the corner when I was driving by. He was wearing overalls and no shirt and sipping a cup of coffee at one of the outside tables. He looked adorable. Girl, I sure wouldn't let him walk around like that if I were you, showing all that skin and his tattoos—some little rock chippy will snatch him up."

Edwina looked over at Sophie, then back at the road as they pulled into the Barton Springs parking lot.

Sophie laughed. "I can hear myself yelling, 'You ain't leavin' the house like that, boy!'"

"You two were having a great time last night. We could hear you laughing from the top of the hill. You guys always seem like you're having so much fun together." Edwina smiled. "I'm jealous."

"But you have a great man," said Sophie. "I love Harry."

"I know," Edwina said. "And I love him to death too. But we don't have fun like that."

"I have to admit I do have more fun with Louis than with anyone else I've ever met," Sophie said. Her good fortune rose in her like a charmed snake.

"Me too," said Edwina, pulling into a parking spot.

They gathered their towels and lotion and crossed the dirt and grass in the slow motion walk peculiar to summer afternoons. It was too hot to speak. They paid their money and found a spot under the live oaks where the sun and shade mottled the grass, high above the long cool rectangle of water.

They sat on the towels and looked down on the bobbing heads, the white ghosts of bodies wavering below the surface, the dogs barking and splashing below the spillway.

"Can I ask you a weird question?" Sophie asked, pulling her sunglasses down over her eyes and fiddling with the cap of the suntan lotion.

"The weirder the better," said Edwina, pulling her bathing suit straps down to rub sunblock on her shoulders.

"Have you ever suspected that Harry was lying to you?"

"Nah," Edwina said. "Harry can't lie. He's the worst liar in the world. He knows he can't pull it off, so he's smart enough to stay honest."

"Can you lie?"

"Sure. All good Southern girls can tell a fib or two." She turned and smiled at Sophie. "My mama raised me right," she said. "But the truth is good enough for me."

They sat quietly for a moment looking at the swimmers moving about in the water, as randomly elegant as the dance of ants busily crisscrossing a patch of dirt.

"So you think Louis is lying to you about something?" Edwina settled on her back and pulled her sunglasses down over her eyes.

"I don't think so," said Sophie. She wasn't sure how much to say to Edwina. "But we were playing this lying game last night, and Louis... he seemed too good at it."

Edwina thought about it and said, "Well, honey, Louis does have his slippery spots, but I'm sure he's not lying about anything serious."

"Slippery spots?"

"All men have their slippery spots, their little slick patches, their hiding places. Especially men in bands."

"Except Harry," Sophie reminded her.

"Except Harry," Edwina said. She paused. "Sometimes I almost miss it. You know what he's like? One of those streams where you look in and you can see everything on the bottom, the different colored rocks, the fish... snails...." She laughed and stood up. "Speaking of water, it is too damn hot not to be in it."

Sophie insisted they walk a little farther down the pool to a place where they were allowed to dive. She was addicted to that moment of flight; she loved to feel her body stretched taut between the poles of skull and toes, to slice into the cool, slightly silty water of the springs, and to feel the momentum push her through the water until it released her back to the surface. She felt perfect when she dove.

When they pulled themselves out and climbed lazily up the slope to their tree, Edwina said, "Go on now, what is it you think he's lying about?"

Something in Edwina's voice made Sophie hesitate. "Oh, nothing really. That game just pushed me off balance, set my imagination running where it's got no need to go."

"Everything okay between you two?" Her voice was a shade too light.

Sophie looked over at Edwina. She could not see Edwina's eyes behind the glasses.

"They're great," she said. "Can I have that sunblock?"

Edwina surprised her by laughing. "Then girl, you have an overactive imagination. It was a game. Louis loves the fuck out of you." She turned over on her stomach after she said this and rested her cheek on her arm, looking away from Sophie. Her black braids leaked water over her shoulders.

They lay without saying anything for several minutes. The locusts trilled and buzzed, singing the heat.

Dreams could leave a stain on her day, Sophie knew, and as she remembered the Edwina of her dream grimacing and cringing away from her, she wondered if this accounted for the strange, subtle tensions she felt between them.

She looked over at Edwina's small dark arms and legs, as hairless as a child's, and then she couldn't resist looking at her own pale, thin legs with their scratches and old scars. She lay back down and looked up through the tree at the mosaic of dark branches and blue sky. The color of Harry's eyes, she thought.

After a few minutes she rolled over and scratched her fingernail lightly on Edwina's arm. "Hey."

"What, lady?" murmured Edwina.

"Did you ever—excuse me if this just sounds too weird—dream the same dream as Louis?"

Edwina raised herself up on her elbows and looked first down at her towel and then over at Sophie. "The same dream?"

Then it was a lie, thought Sophie. She doesn't know about it.

"Oh, something stupid. One of the lies Louis told last night. I should have realized . . . he said he had some dream in which you and he were bank robbers and you got caught and everyone was crying and I was crying. But the weird part was that he said you had also had the same dream that same week, and somehow you both discovered it. It's too ridiculous. I don't know how I ever thought it could be true."

"Sophie," said Edwina. "We did." She looked up at Sophie. "We both did have that dream. About two, three weeks ago. It was the weirdest thing."

"Are you sure it was the same?" asked Sophie, more sharply than she meant.

"Yeah. In mine we started out robbing stores, but then it was banks, and we got caught. And I remember you—you were crying."

"How did you guys discover this?" asked Sophie. "Do you two talk about your dreams a lot?"

"Louis came by one day last week to drop off something for Harry, and we had a chat. He told me about his dream, which turned out to be almost exactly like the one I'd had a few days before. I guess he didn't say anything then be- cause . . . well, you know, it was just kind of weird."

She looked up and gave Sophie a little shrug of her shoulders.

"That is very strange," Sophie said slowly.

"I don't think it's that weird," said Edwina, sounding an- noyed. "I mean, Louis and I have always sort of thought alike."

No, thought Sophie. Louis and I have always thought alike. She rolled onto her side, facing away from Edwina. She needed to think. If the dream story were true, she thought, then there is still a lie floating around somewhere between last night and today, between her and Louis.

"It wasn't the only time," said Edwina from behind her. "It had happened once before." Sophie rolled back to face her.

"I remember it because it was New Year's Eve. We all had brunch the next day. You and I didn't know each other well at all then. I had dreamed that I kissed Louis, and I probably shouldn't have told him, but I did. I'm honest."

"And?" said Sophie stiffly.

"He had had the same dream, that he kissed me in a club." More softly, she said, "It flipped us both out a little."

"Where was I when this conversation took place?"

"We were in the kitchen."

Try as she could Sophie could not bring details of that hungover meal into focus; she remembered only a vague impression that Edwina was pretty, quiet, and crazy about Harry.

"Soph. . . ." said Edwina. "Are you upset about this?"

Sophie rolled onto her back. "It's very strange," she said finally. "I wish . . . that I had been told."

Edwina, floating face down in Barton Springs, those delicate arms spread like a bird's wings across the surface of the water. Edwina waking from sleep with the taste of Louis's dream kiss in her mouth. And the worst, Louis and Edwina, in Sophie's kitchen, gazing at each other in astonishment as they compared dreams.

Sophie was not adept at anger; it only made her feel muddled and heavy; it dulled rather than sharpened her.

"Sophie?"

She turned her head.

"They were only dreams. I don't want...." It was Edwina's turn to lose her words. It crossed Sophie's mind that Edwina might be lying.

"I'm like Harry," she interrupted. "I can't lie and I can't tell when other people are."

Edwina ran her fingers down her braids, squeezing out the water. "Well, it takes practice," she said. "Maybe that's all you need. You could tell lies if you wanted, just start with a few small ones. See how it feels."

"More lies are not what's needed," said Sophie.

"Who knows? It might make you feel better just knowing you could if you wanted to," said Edwina. "It would make you feel less vulnerable. Equalize the balance of power."

The balance of power, Sophie thought. *Cold War. Mutually assured destruction.* She was suddenly very, very tired, and she willed Edwina to shut up.

Louis was mixing batter in a bowl big enough to sit in. He watched the beaters swivel around each other in their herky-jerky dance and picked a dried crust of batter off his wedding ring and shut off the mixer. He had stopped trying to remember the lie he had told. It didn't really matter. It was an innocent tale, a fiction meant to entertain like his other concoctions: his pastries mounded with sweet fruit, his keening, soaring fiddle music. But in combing through his conscience, he hit a snag. At first he had ignored it, instead he had begun constructing a new dessert that had been taking shape in his imagination. There were elements in it which still puzzled him, and as he labored the kitchen grew hectic around him: he pulled pans from the oven, reduced sauces on the stove, dissolved gelatin, and greased molds on the counter. This chaos was his most comfortable refuge from his own conscience, but when his cakes were cooling, and his poached apples sliced and piled, he sat on his stool and treated himself, as he liked to in the aftermath of a frenzy of work, to an image of his wife, lovely and undressed. In today's version she was on the couch, reading, her hair caught up in a clip. When he gave himself this small present, though, the other image, the one that he had snagged on, floated back.

She was at rehearsal and she was at the gigs and she would stand back against the wall of the club and he thought sometimes, but couldn't quite tell, that she was staring at him. She was small and dark and somehow incredibly sexy to him, with her pointed chin and her childlike limbs. One night when he came down from the stage, sweat along his hairline, and his shirt damp with the effort of making music, she walked up and handed him a cold beer. "Thanks, Edwina," he said. Of course he knew her. She was Harry's.

He didn't kiss her then. It was New Year's Eve, when Sophie was waiting for him to arrive at a friend's party after his gig, and he was drunk on all the drinks that had been sent to the band, and they were in a narrow hallway outside the bathrooms. Harry was in New Orleans, recording with a band Louis had wanted to play with. Her mouth was sour with liquor and her tongue was short and hard; it moved insistently in his mouth. He was unexpectedly aroused by this, but he had placed his hands on her shoulders and shaken his head, and after that kiss he avoided being alone with her. He desperately did not want to be unfaithful. Sophie had come into his life like a force of nature; boyish and sharp-minded, she had saved him. Then Edwina had sent the letter. It was the most erotic letter he had ever received. He read and reread it; finally he burned it in the kitchen sink one afternoon.

"Look," he said the next time he saw her, on the porch of her house when he came to pick up Harry's equipment. "You are incredibly sexy and..." He looked out at the van and at Harry's broad back and his straw-colored hair. "And I'm very flattered by your interest, but I'm married and I love my wife and I'm faithful and your boyfriend is one of my oldest friends." There it had ended. Still, it disturbed him that he kept it from Sophie. It was not how he had envisioned his marriage.

The wall phone rang and he wiped his hand on his sleeve and picked it up.

"Raoul's."

"I'd like to speak to Louis, please," said the voice, which he recognized.

"Randy," he said. "This is Louis. What's going on?"

"I got some good news for you, my friend."

"What would that be? I've got cakes baking here."

"Martin wants you to go on tour with him this summer. West Coast, East Coast, Midwest, South, Canada. Two months."

Louis looked at the cake pans in his hands and knew that this meant the end of them. No more getting up at six. No more dough under his fingernails. No more day job. Just music and money enough to live.

"Louis?"

"Yeah, that's great. That's fantastic. When do we start rehearsing, and when do we go?"

"I'll call you in a few days with the details when we've worked them out. I just wanted to let you know. I figured you'd be excited."

"More than that, man," Louis said. "You just made my year."

After they hung up, Louis filled the cake pans again and slid them in the oven and sat back on his stool. His shoulders hunched his lanky form into a crescent. A finger to his lips, he stared at the stained apron draping his lap as if his new good fortune were gathered there. I ought to call Sophie, he thought, and then, all at once, he remembered the lie he had told. He laughed out loud on his stool to remember it. He laughed to think of his sweet and brittle wife believing him when he said that he shared a dream of robbing banks with dark little Edwina. Passing by the kitchen window, a neighborhood child saw the crazy baker laughing alone among his sugars and his pans.

She stood at the door of their bedroom, heart beating like a bird's in her chest, when she should have been printing: at the foot of the bed were his crumpled jeans and yesterday's T-shirt; a glass with an inch of water on the bedside table. She picked up the clothes in her arms and instinctively lowered her face to them, started toward the laundry hamper and then stopped, turned and lay the clothes on the bed as if they were waiting for a wearer. Louis's clothing, his collapsed hollow image, waited as she slid open a drawer of his dresser. What was she looking for? Her fingers brushed the surface of his faded fragrant shirts, she lifted the edge of one; a single narrow finger dug to the bottom. She had been thinking of petal-thin sheets of writing paper pulled from envelopes, of unfamiliar script, of nothing at all, until it drove her to this. Yet when her nail scratched the wood bottom of the drawer she pulled it away as if it were burned. She slammed the drawer and left the room, pausing to glance at the clothes on the bed, and with a quick motion she scrambled them into a pile. This was not the person she wanted to become.

I will wait until he gets home and talk to him, she thought. She would tell him how that funny episode, that drunken storytelling evening, had metastasized into this doubt and ugliness. He would reassure her that he was the person she thought he was; she would lay her worries down like a baby to a nap. That was all she wanted. She thought for a while; she rested her sleek flaxen head on her knees. But she could not rest and, wandering back to their bedroom, she lay down next to the clothes. She pulled them to her and then pushed them away, seeing too clearly Louis leaning against their kitchen wall, Edwina gazing up at him, the kiss hanging, dreamed and considered, in the air between them while Sophie drank her coffee with Harry in the dining room. A half hour later, leaving the pillows clenched like fossils of her anger and tear marks on the sheets, she got up off the bed and paced the creased wood floors, barked a rough exclamation of anger once at the ceiling, and decided what she would do.

Louis was icing his cakes when the phone rang again.

"Hey mister," Sophie said when he picked it up.

"My girl," he said.

"You coming home soon?"

"I'm almost done with my cakes. But then I've got rehearsal."

"I'll be asleep when you come in," she said. "So I'm going to tell you now."

"What's that?" he asked distractedly, thinking about how he would tell his good news.

"Louis," Sophie said, and her hand was trembling on the receiver. "We're going to have a baby. I'm pregnant."

Silence. Nothing. Nothing went through his head. He closed his eyes and opened them and tried to process this. A baby.

"Oh my God, Sophie." And then, "Oh, my love."

"Just think about it," she said. "Tonight while you're rehearsing. Imagine it. And it will be real to you by the time you come home and put your hand on my stomach."

Her hands shook for a few minutes after she put down the phone. She had thought she might practice a little first. Start small: tell him that she spent the day getting drunk with her friend Isabelle, or that she forgave him for forgetting his third lie, or that an old boyfriend had called her. She had meant to tease the game out a little longer, to find her way back to solid ground by dropping little fibs like a trail of bread crumbs. But the physical laws that govern the actions of the heart are both capricious and absolute, and they demanded from her the lie she told. She reassured herself as she stood in the living room with the late afternoon sun spilling over her shoes. There would be time later on to let him know she could lie as well as he could. They would be sitting on the porch, the beer bottles sweating slightly, and she would say. . . .

He hung up the phone and leaned his head against his arms on the wall. A kind of airlessness enveloped him. Oh, Sophie, he thought. He imagined her tender belly. He pictured her breasts getting fuller. He turned his back to the wall and slid down it. His arms on his knees, his head on his arms, he sat for a long time. Every now and then he could be heard to say his wife's name.

———

She opened a bottle of wine and had a glass, lying on her back on the couch. It tasted faintly of bananas. She had another glass. The orange hour came—it was her favorite hour—and it went, and still she lay on the couch letting the shadows form and reform around her. The drunk who lived below them turned on his music, and it came up through the floorboards and moved past her into the air above. Once she said into the room, "I am a liar," testing it. She thought it sounded pretty good.

If you had seen him play that night you would have recognized, carved in the tautness of his facial muscles, a great strained tenderness. He excused himself from the rehearsal once and made a phone call. Above the laughter, and the tuning of guitar strings, you might have caught fragments of what he said: "I'm sorry... bad timing... very much wanted to do it but it's impossible...." Returning from his phone call he took the offered beer and hoisted it. "Cheers," he said to his bandmates.

The cab of his truck was dark as he drove home, and his lights swept the darkened city. Worried about what he might say or do, he spoke out loud. "She doesn't need to know," he said.

She is dreaming when the bedroom door opens, and he comes in, his shirt and shoes off already. In her dream a large bird looms over her, as he kneels next to the bed. He pulls back the sheet and puts one long-fingered hand on her abdomen. His ring shines in the moonlight coming through the window. She senses him there and wakes just slightly, knowing there is something she has to tell him. She thinks she says, "I was just lying. Getting you back." Perhaps she hears herself say it in her dream, but all he sees is her lips twist a little in sleep, parting slightly with a small, sticky sound. A little sigh escapes.

When he takes off his jeans and gets into bed, she rolls over and pulls him close. He puts his hand between her thighs. He buries his face in her neck. A little while later, if she weren't so sleepy, perhaps she would have recognized the slight fizzing, the tiny burst of activity deep within her. Perhaps she would have known that they were making a baby.

THINNING THE HERD

"He kept spewing them out. Like rabbit turds. Who did he think he was—Trollope? They should give me a medal instead of locking me up. Don't you think?"

I nodded imperceptibly, anxious not to inflame him further. They had warned me he was prone to sudden fits of rage. That morning he had been given new medication in an attempt to stabilize his mood swings.

We were sitting in the sun-splattered visitors' room at Camarillo State Hospital for the Criminally Insane, face-to-face across a green Formica table under the vacant eyes of an armed guard. The room reeked of Mr. Clean and Haldol. I had been there for forty minutes and had already filled two microcassettes on my Panasonic tape recorder.

It was his doctor, a psychopathologist named Rayna Midori, recently arrived from Bombay, who had decided that talking to a writer might be therapeutic. His court-appointed lawyer gave permission with the proviso that I wouldn't publish anything until all the appeals were exhausted.

"That could be twenty years," I pointed out.

"I sincerely doubt it," the lawyer replied, in a tone of voice that indicated just how much confidence he had in his case.

In any event, I was not rushing into print. I had no deadline. I didn't even have an assignment. What I had was a curiosity to learn what motivated a forty-six-year-old Culver City computer programmer to murder five writers on five successive Tuesdays in the late summer and early autumn of 1993.

Warren David Warren, dubbed "The Scribe Slayer," "Son of Shakespeare," etc., by the tabloids, had chosen me to tell his story from a large pool of applicants for the job. It was never explained to me, or to anyone else for that matter, why he picked me, and when I asked Warren the question during our first interview, he simply replied, "You were far enough down the line."

Just how far down the line I would never know, but I found myself wondering about it. *Was I before or after Updike? What about John Irving? Anne Tyler?* Certainly those people deserved it more than I did, given the basic premise that Warren David Warren articulated to me during our very first interview.

"I was merely thinning the herd," he said.

He took a sip of coffee from a styrofoam cup and settled as comfortably as he could in the uncomfortable molded-plastic chair.

"It was a question of ecology. Do you understand?"

I nodded. Carefully. Gingerly.

"Everywhere you go," he continued, in a measured voice that, for the moment, was devoid of emotion, "someone's writing something. Your sister-in-law, your accountant, even your gardener. They're all taking writing classes, working on novels, sending outlines and sample chapters to publishers.

Every day the herd gets bigger and bigger, chewing up all the grazing land, denuding the landscape. Soon it'll be dried up entirely. And then what?" He stopped and looked at me for confirmation. I gave him a perfunctory nod. It wasn't until that evening, however, when I was home transcribing the interview, that I was able to admit to myself that Warren David Warren had articulated feelings that were not entirely foreign to me.

The following day he described a vision that was eerily close to one of my own recurring nightmares.

"It's like somewhere in a warehouse in Palmdale," he said. "You've chained two thousand monkeys to computers, and each time they type a page you give them a banana, and then you take these pages and rearrange them in random samples, which you send out indiscriminately to publishers."

In my own particular nightmare you had students from all the writing schools everywhere hot-wired to an on-line brain scanner, and at night, while they slept, the contents of their brains were downloaded directly onto the hard disks of publishing houses. In the morning, the publishing houses remitted checks into the liquid money-market accounts of the writing-school graduates.

"As far as I was concerned," Warren explained, "Jamison was the head monkey. His books were on the bestseller list for forty, fifty weeks at a shot. You couldn't even go to the supermarket without seeing twenty different-colored copies of his latest book staring at you from the checkout stand next to the *Enquirer.*"

Murray Jamison had been garroted with the interface cable that ran between his computer and his printer on August 31, 1993, while working on the galleys of his fifteenth novel, published posthumously and now in its eighty-fourth paperback printing.

It was reported that the killer had broken into Jamison's San Clemente house from the beach side, using the mandated public access to the beach to get inside the compound. This revelation revived the controversy about public access to beaches in California. Jamison's widow went on television claiming that her husband would be alive today, if there hadn't been public access.

"She didn't know what she was talking about," Warren claimed. "I went right in the front. There was a eucalyptus tree next to the wall. They showed his house on *Lifestyles of the Rich and Famous*. I freeze-framed on my VCR, magnified the image through the digital scanning device, and read the number.

"While I was disconnecting the cable I told him what I thought of *The Furrier*. The *Times* actually gave it a good review. They said it was vintage Jamison. It was vintage monkey drivel was what it was. I read the book standing up in Barnes and Noble."

When on the following Tuesday a second writer was found dead in Century City, the police had not drawn any immediate connection with Jamison. Vera Vruma was defenestrated from her penthouse condo, splattered on the roof of the building's heating and air-conditioning unit off Pico Boulevard. It wasn't a pretty sight. A reporter for one of the eleven o'clock news remote teams tossed her cookies in the van before doing a stand-up, white-faced and shaky, beside the bloodstained chalk outline of the body. Though there was no note, the initial assumption was suicide.

Vruma wrote erotic thrillers about complex women with vaguely bisexual longings. Two of her books had been turned into high-grossing movies and a third was under option.

"She was nothing more than a literary pornographer,"

Warren David Warren said. "Just because she used semi-colons, people thought she was Anaïs Nin."

The police still didn't think Vera Vruma was murdered until Lorenzo LaCivita's body bobbed up from the bottom of the Lake Hollywood Reservoir on a Friday night ten days later. The medical examiner put the murder three days earlier, on a Tuesday night—exactly a week, as it happened, after Vera Vruma took her involuntary swan dive and two weeks after Murray Jamison's air supply was shut off in his San Clemente study.

Actually, it wasn't the police but a reporter from *Hard Copy*, a young almond-eyed Asian woman by the name of Lilian Wong, who first speculated in public about the connection among the three dead writers. She went on the air with a special report called "Writer-Killer on the Loose: Terror at the Typewriter."

"I had been wondering what was taking them so long," Warren David Warren told me. "The whole point was being lost. There are so many random murders in Los Angeles that it takes a while for people to see the connection. The fact was, until that *Hard Copy* reporter went on TV with her story I couldn't get arrested.

"LaCivita could have been top on my list, but I saved him for third because he wasn't taken seriously. The *Times* didn't even review his books. Did you know that *The Windless Journey of the Soul* was on the hardcover nonfiction list for 196 consecutive weeks? I mean, have you ever read it?"

I shook my head.

"That man should have been declared a public health nuisance years before I killed him. I got him jogging around the lake at dusk. Bludgeoned him with a cement garden sculpture, then tied him to it and sent him off to the bottom of the lake. I read somewhere it's a hundred feet deep. If I had tied him better he wouldn't have come up for years. Talk about a windless journey...."

To be perfectly honest, I hadn't mourned for Lorenzo LaCivita. I'm sure I wasn't the only writer who breathed a furtive sigh of satisfaction in anticipation of the additional bookstore window space that would be freed up by his retirement from the field.

But I admit that I felt a frisson of anxiety nonetheless when the *Hard Copy* reporter did her "Son of Shakespeare" story. Three murders. Three successful writers. Three Tuesdays in a row. Though we were still perhaps a murder or two short of a full-blown serial killer, things were looking trendy.

I remember waking up the following Tuesday with a tight little spot of anxiety in my gut. I remember thinking about the fact that it was Tuesday. I remember trying to calm myself down with the thought that I was not a bestselling author. Far from it.

I did my morning exercises and allowed the routine of the day to reassure me. I was calm, benumbed in the quotidian. I wrote my five pages, had a martini with lunch, took a nap, then made the mistake of turning on the TV.

Barb Papilla, the ebullient Latina anchorwoman on the Channel 9 *Early Evening News*, announced that a fourth writer had bought the ranch.

Anticipating my false sense of security, Warren David Warren had chosen a mid-list writer this time. Xavier Dionne, a French Canadian novelist, had written a thriller about the murder of a noted separatist politician in Rimouski. *Cul de Sac*, or *Dead End* as it was called in its English translation, had been dismissed by the critics, and his American publisher was trying to counteract the lukewarm press with a twelve-city book tour.

"I got Dionne right after he did *Good Morning, L.A.,*" Warren told me, by now less guarded if not completely forthcoming with me.

"They had him in the Holiday Inn on Highland. Cheap publisher. They wouldn't put Joyce Carol Oates in the Holiday Inn. I got his room number off the house phone and then slipped in and hid in the closet while the chambermaid was getting more towels.

"When he walked in the door and saw me sitting there with a copy of his book in my hands, he said, 'I'm sorry. The signing is at Brentanos at eleven.' When I didn't answer, he asked me who I was.

"What I should have said was that I was the angel of death come to dispatch him. But I didn't think of it at the moment. *L'esprit de l'escalier.*

"Instead I read him a passage from his book—a long, redundant, turgidly written paragraph, one of many—and asked him how he could possibly have written that.

"For a moment he didn't say anything. He just stood there looking hurt. And then, and this really takes the cake, he started to defend himself. He said it was a bad translation. The man had less than a minute to live and he was blaming things on the translator.

"I used a 9mm Beretta with a silencer. Got him right in the larynx. Then I took the copy of *Dead End,* underlined the egregious paragraph, and left it beside him, open to that page."

On Wednesday night Lilian Wong had a camera crew in the room at the Holiday Inn. The underlined paragraph was printed as a graphic on the screen over footage of the crime scene. It caused a sensation. There were debates on the literary merits of the paragraph and discussions of whether writers should pay the supreme price for bad writing.

But mostly there was fear. We all wondered where "The Scribe Slayer" would strike next. Writers took precautions. They hired security guards. Some writers even left town.

"You were certainly getting press after Dionne," I said to Warren.

"It was about time. But they still weren't talking about the issue. Nobody was talking about the need to cut back the herd. That's why I sent the letter to the *Times*."

Warren's letter to the editor was studied by forensic experts at the LAPD before being printed in the Monday edition of the *Los Angeles Times*. In it he spoke about the "ecological imbalance" caused by the "exponential increase" in the number of writers in the world. He explained that he had nothing personal against writers, that he himself was a writer, albeit unrecognized, but that in the absence of self-discipline or the appropriate Darwinian forces coming into play, the problem was only getting worse. He blamed computers, writing schools—which he called a "nefarious cottage industry"—and the poor taste of the publishing industry. It will not be long, he predicted, before a Grisham's Law of Literature will take over with bad writing, driving good writing out of the market.

"It really pissed me off," said Warren, "when those idiot psychologists started showing up on *Larry King* with my letter and spouting off that serial-killer garbage. They thought I was just some sort of crackpot whacking writers because I had nothing better to do.

"And then when they started to say that I chose Tuesday because it was the day on which something traumatic must have happened to me... I mean, really...."

"Why *did* you choose Tuesday?"

He looked at me the way a schoolteacher looks at a star

pupil who asks a question to which he would have known the answer if he had been paying attention.

"I thought you got it."

"I really do get it. The whole ecological thing. Neo-Malthusian theory, and so forth. But I don't know why you couldn't thin the herd on Monday or on Wednesday."

He smiled. It was not a particularly pretty smile. He had been undergoing extensive work in the prison dental clinic and was flashing a lot of amalgamated silver. Then he leaned forward, out of earshot of the guard, and whispered something that sounded to me like "Egg McMuffin. "

My face must have registered a blank because he started to raise his voice. "The thing that it's about but it isn't. Don't you see? Like the *Maltese Falcon*. That movie's not about a stuffed bird. It's about human greed. For Christ's sake."

When he started shouting and spitting, the guard had him removed by orderlies wearing protective clothing, even though I protested that he was not going to harm me.

I woke up at four that morning, wide awake, and realized that the word he was trying to tell me was "McGuffin." So Tuesday was a McGuffin. Great. I got the answer that no one else was able to get during the trial and afterward. But it didn't make me any happier.

You see, I desperately needed to believe that Warren David Warren was a lunatic and not a revisionist literary Darwinian, as he claimed to be. The implications of the latter theory were unthinkable for someone whose last book sold 1,124 copies. Frankly, I'm surprised I wasn't higher up on Warren's hit list, considering the fact that there were 3,876 unsold copies of my book that were considered too worthless to be recycled on the remainder tables. I was an ecological menace.

Number five, as it happened, was even less successful than I was. She had only one thin volume of abstruse poetry, which had been published by a Midwestern university press with a print run of 500 copies.

"She reviewed a book of poems for *The New York Times Book Review,*" Warren explained. "*Interstices* or *Interlinear* or something. I don't remember. I hadn't read the book. But the review was so pretentious I almost threw up. She used the word *ineluctable* three times. After I read that review, she moved right up to the top of the list."

Joanna Taubman-Lully presumably never saw it coming. She had not been grazing on a lot of prime land. On the contrary. You couldn't even find her book, *Birdsong,* in a bookstore, let alone in the window. You had to order it from the university mail-order catalogue.

It was perhaps fitting, then, that her end came through the mail. Warren sent her a fan letter with an autograph sticker and a self-addressed, stamped envelope. She was to sign the sticker and mail it back to him. The letter arrived on a Tuesday, of course, and she signed the sticker, put it in the envelope, and licked the flap without knowing that the flap had been treated with a tasteless and odorless compound that became a slow-acting poison when combined with saliva.

According to Lilian Wong on *Hard Copy,* Taubman-Lully, 47, was dead seven hours after licking the envelope and dropping it into the mailbox on the corner of Ocean Park and 17th Street in Santa Monica, where she shared a small rented house with her lover, Jocelyn Brautman, 29, who found her on the kitchen floor when she came home from work—by which time the evidence had already been picked up and sorted in the Santa Monica post office for next-day delivery to Warren David Warren.

"They said I wanted to get caught. All those TV shrinks with their theories of unconscious guilt and self-hatred. That's not why they caught me. They were lucky.

"There was no way I could have known that Gerry Kim was going to show up to clean Gavin Frobisher's pool on Tuesday, between four and five in the afternoon. I had scouted it out, and I knew that the pool man came on Wednesdays and Saturdays. This particular week he decides to come on Tuesday. He said on *Geraldo* that he couldn't come on Wednesday that week because his brother-in-law needed him to help carry lawn fertilizer in his truck because the brother-in-law's truck was getting new engine mounts.

"Everything else I had covered. I had a way into the yard. I knew that Gavin Frobisher worked outside in the late afternoon. They said in *Vanity Fair* that he liked to work in the nude and jump in the pool every ten pages.

"You can imagine the look on his face when I climbed over the tool shed, carrying a copy *of The Bridge to No-where*—that piece of shit they're making into a movie with Michelle Pfeiffer.

"He grabs a towel and looks at me, figuring me for some sort of fan. Though he's not thrilled that I've snuck into his yard, he sees the book in my hand and smiles. Jesus. What an ego. His head is in the guillotine, and he's asking the executioner if he wants him to sign a copy of his book before he drops the blade?

"'Look, I don't mind signing books,' he says, 'but you shouldn't have come in like that. It's an invasion of privacy.'

"I hold his book up and I say, 'This... *this* is an invasion of privacy.'

"Suddenly there's fear in the man's eyes. He figures he's dealing with a nutcase. He reaches for the portable phone, and I dropkick it into the pool.

"When he gets up, his towel falls off, and he's standing there naked, his scrotum shriveled up like a dried apricot. He backs away toward the house, as I take the *bindlestich* out of my pocket. . . ."

I sat there, fascinated, wrapped up in his story. Even though I knew how it ended, I was captivated. Warren David Warren was, as they say on the book jackets, a born story-teller. If only he had been given a little more grazing room, I found myself thinking as he told me that a *bindlestich* is a Swiss shoe-repairing tool, a sharp, two-pronged instrument used to pull the stitches out of leather.

We never got to find out just how Warren was planning to use the *bindlestich* on Gavin Frobisher because Gerry Kim walked in the gate at that moment to clean the pool. The sound of the gate closing distracted Warren David Warren long enough for Gavin Frobisher to open the sliding glass door, run inside his house, and call 911.

Gerry Kim told Geraldo that he just went about his business checking the chlorine-pH balance of the pool as Warren walked right past him out the gate, and Frobisher, looking out his front window, got the plate number off Warren's 1989 Honda Civic.

They picked Warren David Warren up three hours later at his apartment in Culver City as he sat eating a burrito and watching a rerun of *I Love Lucy*. He surrendered without a struggle to the LAPD SWAT Squad, who had cordoned off the entire street and posted armed snipers on neighboring roofs.

Lilian Wong was among the first on the scene. As they led Warren out of the building and the public got their first look at him, she told her viewers, "I am here on a quiet Culver City street where suspected writer-killer Warren David

Warren is being led away by members of a combined LAPD-FBI task force...."

"If only the pool man's brother-in-law's truck didn't need motor mounts," Warren uttered wistfully, "I could have nailed Frobisher...."

It was late in the afternoon, and the sun was starting to drop behind the mountains. In a few minutes they would come and take him back to the ward. He would disappear behind the locked door, to be sedated and parked in front of the TV with the others, and I would never see him again.

That afternoon when I arrived, I had been informed by Dr. Midori that this was to be my last interview with Warren David Warren.

"Frankly, I believe these sessions are now contraindicated," she had said to me, sitting behind the gunmetal gray desk underneath her University of Bombay Medical School diploma. "I had hoped that by talking to you he would begin somehow to understand the wrongness of his acts, but we seem to be faced with the contrary. If anything, he appears more agitated after speaking with you than he is before."

"Really?" I said, raising an eyebrow.

"Yes. His dementia is such that he thinks that you somehow approve of what he did."

"Incredible."

So as I sat there that afternoon with Warren David Warren in the dwindling daylight, I tried to tie up one or two loose ends.

"How were you going to use the *bindlestich* on Frobisher?" I asked him.

The last flickering embers of Haldol lit the corners of his eyes.

"How do you think?"

"Down his throat?" I ventured.

"All the way," he grinned. "As far as I could go."

I looked at him and nodded. There was a moment of perfect understanding between us.

"When you had gotten down the list as far as me," I said, "how would you have done it?"

"Elegantly," he said.

"I would have expected no less."

"When I get out of here, I'm coming after you," he promised, with conviction.

"Of course. I'll write fast."

Just before the guard took him away, he whispered, "Get Frobisher."

"No problem."

A half hour later, as I was driving south on 101, I heard an interview on NPR with a TV star who had just written his third bestseller. There was a first printing of 500,000 copies, and they were going back to press. The bookstores couldn't keep the book in stock. I decided to move him up the list. Right after Frobisher.

THE GATES ARE CLOSING

Help me.

I slid my hands up the legs of Jack's shorts to stroke the top of his thigh and he lost his grip on the paint roller. A hundred tiny drops flew through the air at me. Thoroughly speckled, squinting to keep the paint out of my eyes, I stroked higher under his boxers, right up the neat, furry juncture of his crotch.

"Jesus," he said. "It's not like I have any balance anyway." Which is true. He has Parkinson's, and if it weren't for the fact that he's been house painting for twenty-five years and is the synagogue president's husband, no sensible group of people would have him painting their religious institution. I volunteered to help because I'm in love with Jack and because I like to paint. I lay down on the dropcloth and unbuttoned my shirt.

"Want to fool around?"

"Always," he said. There has never been a sweeter, kinder man. "But not right now. I'm pretty tired already."

"You rest. I'll paint."

I took off my shirt and bra and painted for Jack. I strolled up and down with the extra-long paint roller. When the cracks in the ceiling lost their brown, ropy menace, I took the regular roller and did the walls. I poured Jack tea from my thermos and I touched my nipples with the windowsill brush.

He sat up against the *bimah*, sipping my sweet milky tea and smiling. His face so often shows only a tender, masked expressiveness, I covet the tiny rips and leaks of affect at the corner of his mouth, in the middle of his forehead. His hand shook. He shakes. Mostly at rest. Mostly when he is making an effort to relax. Sometimes after we've made love, which he does in a wonderfully unremarkable, athletic way, his whole right side trembles and his arm flutters wildly, as if we've set it free.

I told a friend about me and Jack painting the synagogue for Rosh Hashanah, and this woman, who uses riding crops for fun with strangers and tells me fondly about her husband's rubber fetish, got wide-eyed as a frightened child and said, "In *shul*? You made love in *shul*? You must have really wanted to shock God." I said no, I didn't want to shock God (what would have shocked God? two more naked people, trying to wrestle time to a halt?), it was just where we were. And if someone had offered me the trade, I would have rolled myself in paint and done dripping off-white cartwheels through the entire congregation for more time with Jack.

Rosh Hashanah and Yom Kippur are my favorite holidays; you don't have to entertain anyone or feed anyone or buy things for anyone. You can combine short, skipping waves of kindly small talk with deep isolation and no one is offended. I get a dozen invitations to eat roast chicken the night before and a dozen more invitations to break the fast, including the one to Jack and Naomi's house. I think her name was Nancy until she went to Jerusalem in eleventh grade and came back the way they did, lean and tan and religious and Naomi. Jack thinks she's very smart. He went to Catholic school and dropped out of Fordham to run his father's construction business. Mouthy Jewish girls who can talk through their tears and argue straight through yours, myopic girls who read for pleasure, for Jack, this is real intelligence. And Naomi Sapirstein Malone totes him around, her big converted prize, the map of Ireland on his face and blue eyes like Donegal Bay, nothing like the brown eyes of the other men, however nice their brown eyes are, not even like our occasional blue-eyed men, Vilna blue, the-Cossack-came-by eyes, my mother used to say.

My mother still couldn't believe that I'd even joined a synagogue. Two bar mitzvahs when I was thirteen set off an aversion to Jewish boys that I have only overcome in the last ten years. And if I must go, why not go someplace nice, with proper stained glass and a hundred brass plaques and floral arrangements the size and approximate weight of totem poles? There, you might be safe. There, you might be mistaken for people of position, people whom it would be a bad idea to harm. When my brother Louis had his third nervous breakdown and they peeled him out of his apartment and put him in a ward with double sets of locking doors and two-way mirrors, the doctors tried to tell me and my mother that his paranoia and his anxious loneliness and his general relentless misery were not uncommon in children of Holocaust survivors. My mother was not impressed and closed her eyes when Lou's psychiatrist spoke.

We went out for tuna fish sandwiches and I tried to tell her again, as if it was only that she didn't understand their zippy American medical jargon. I counted Lou's symptoms on my fingers. I said that many young men and women whose families had survived the Holocaust had these very symptoms. I don't know what I thought. That she would feel better? Worse?

"Well, yes, of course, they suffer. Those poor wretches," she said, in her most Schoenbrunn tones.

"Like us, Meme. Like us. Daddy in Buchenwald. Grandpa Hoffmann in Ebensee. Everyone fleeing for their lives, with nothing. The doctor meant us."

My mother waved her hand and ate her sandwich.

"Please. We're very lucky. We're fine. Louis has your Uncle Morti's nervous stomach, that's all."

Louis recovered from his nervous stomach with enough Haldol to fell an ox, and when he got obese and shaved only on Sundays and paced my mother's halls day and night in backless bedroom slippers, this was Uncle Morti's legacy as well.

> *Your might, O Lord, is boundless.*
> *Your loving-kindness sustains the living.*
> *Your great mercies give life to the dead.*
> *You support the falling, heal the ailing, free the fettered.*

How can you say those prayers when your heart's not in them, Jack said. My heart is in them, I said. I don't think belief is required. I put my hand out to adjust his yarmulke, to feel him. I never saw anything so sweetly ridiculous as his long pink ears anchoring that blue satin *kippah* to his head.

You could wear a really dashing fedora, I said. You have that sexy Gary Cooper hat. Wear that. God won't mind. God, I said, would prefer it.

Naomi's break fast was just what it was supposed to be: plat-
ters of bagels, three different cream cheeses in nice crystal
bowls, roasted vegetables, kugels, and interesting cold salads. There was enough food so that one wouldn't be ashamed
in front of Jews, not so much that one would have to worry
about the laughter of spying goyim.

I helped Jack in the kitchen while Naomi circulated.
Sometimes I wanted to say to her, *How can you stand this?
You're not an idiot. Doesn't it make you feel just a little ridiculous to have gone to the trouble of leaping from Hadassah president to synagogue president in one generation and find
yourself still in your mother's clothes and still in your mother's
makeup and even in her psyche, for Christ's sake?* I didn't
say anything. It was not in my interest to alarm or annoy
Naomi. I admired her publicly, I defended her from the men
who thought she was too shrill and from the women who
thought their husbands would have been better presidents
and therefore better armatures for them as presidents' wives,
sitting next to the major donors, clearly above the *bala-
bostas* at God's big dinner party. We'd had forty years of men
presidents, blameless souls for the most part, only the occasional embezzler or playboy or sociopath. Naomi was no
worse, and she conveyed to the world that we were a forward-
looking, progressive congregation. I don't know how forward-
looking Jews can actually be, wrestling with God's messenger,
dissolving Lot's wife, wading through six hundred and thirteen rules for better living, our one-hundred-and-twenty-
year-old mothers laughing at their sudden fertility and our
collective father Abraham, willing to sacrifice his darling boy
to appease a faceless bully's voice in his ear.

Jack and I were in charge of the linguine with tomato cream
sauce, and we kept it coming. He stuck his yarmulke in his

back pocket and wrapped Naomi's "Kiss Me, I'm Kosher!" apron around me. On the radio, an unctuous reporter from NPR announced that people with Parkinson's were having a convention, that there was an ACT UP for Parkinson's sufferers. ("I'd like to see that, wouldn't you?" Jack said.) The reporter described the reasonably healthy people, the leaders, naturally enough, angry and trembling but still living as themselves with just a little less dopamine, and he interviewed the damned, one worse than the next, a middle-aged classics professor, no longer teaching or writing, his limbs flying around him in mad tantric designs; a young woman of twenty-five, already stuck in a wheelchair, already sipping from the straw her mother held to her lips while they roamed the halls of the Hilton looking for the sympathetic ear that would lead to the money that would lead to the research and the cure before she curled up like an infant and drowned in the sea of her own lungs.

"Morris Udall, respected congressional leader for thirty years, lies in this room, immobile. His daughter visits him every day, although he is unable to respond—"

This is endless heartbreak. I don't even feel sorry for Mo Udall, God rest his soul, he should just die already. There is no reason for us to listen to this misery. I want to plunge my tongue down Jack's throat, pull gently on his chest hairs, and knot my legs tightly around his waist, opening myself so wide that he falls into me and leaves this world forever.

We look at each other while the radio man drones on about poor Mo Udall, his poor family, all of his accomplishments mocked (which is not the reporter's point, presumably) and made dust by this pathetic and terrible disease. Jack looks away and smiles in embarrassment. He listens to this stuff all the time, it plays in his head when there is no radio on at all; he's only sorry that I have to listen too.

It's better to cook with him and say nothing, which is what I do. I want to hold him and protect him; I want to believe in the possibility of protection. Growing up in the Hoffmann family of miraculous escapes and staggering surprises (who knew Himmler had a soft spot for my grandfather's tapestries? who knew the Germans would suddenly want to do business and fulfill their promises?), I understood that the family luck had been used up. I could do well in life, if not brilliantly, and if my reach did not exceed my grasp, I would be all right. My grasp included good grades, some success as a moderately good painter, and lovers of whom I need not be ashamed in public.

> *We abuse, we betray, we are cruel.*
> *We destroy, we embitter, we falsify.*
> *We gossip, we hate, we insult.*
> *We jeer, we kill, we lie.*

One can recite the *Ashamnu*, beat one's breast for hours in not unpleasant contemplation of all one's minor and major sins, wrapped in the willing embrace of a community which, if it does very little for you all the rest of the year, is required, as family is, to acknowledge that you belong to them, that your sins are not noticeably worse than theirs, and that you are all, perverts, zealots, gossips, and thieves, in this together.

"This girl from one of the art galleries wished me happy Yom Kippur," I said to Jack.

"Hell, yes. A whole new Hallmark line: Happy Day of Atonement. Thinking of You on This Day of Awe. Wishing You the Best of *Barkhu*."

We had all risen and sat endlessly through this second holiday, and my own silent prayers got shorter and shorter

as those of a few *alter kockers* and two unbearably pious
young men lengthened, making it clear that their communi-
cations with God were so serious and so transporting they
had hardly noticed that the other three hundred people had
sat down and were waiting to get on with it. The faintly
jazzy notes of the *shofar* had been sounded the correct number of times, and I had the pleasure of hearing last year's
president say Jack's name. John Malone. Not Jack. In the
shul, Jack sounded too sharply Christian, so clearly not part
of us. *Jack Jack Jack,* I thought, and I would have shot my
hand up to volunteer to rebuild the back steps with him, but
I myself always questioned the motives of women volunteer-
ing to help on manual labor projects with good-looking
men. I didn't think badly of them, I just couldn't believe they
had so little to do at home, or at the office, that the sheer
pleasure of working with cheap tools on a Sunday afternoon
was what got them helping out my darling Jack, or Henry
Sternstein, the best-looking Jewish man, with dimples and
beagle eyes and, according to Naomi's good friend Stephanie
Tabnick, a chocolate-brown beauty mark on his right buttock, shaped very much like a Volkswagen.

> Open for us the gates, even as they are closing.
> The day is waning, the sun is low.
> The hour is late, a year has slipped away.
> Let us enter the gates at last.

Jennifer, their daughter, came into Naomi's kitchen to
nibble. I smiled and put a dozen hot kugel tarts, dense
rounds of potato and salt and oil, to drain on a paper towel
near her. Jack was fond, and blind, with Jennifer. She was
tall and would be lovely, smart, and softhearted, and I think
that he could not stand to know her any other way, to have

her suffer not only his life, but hers. When Jennifer succeeded in the boy venues, Naomi admired her extravagantly and put humiliating tidbits in the synagogue newsletter about Jennifer's near miss with the Westinghouse Prize or her stratospheric PSATs; when Jennifer failed as a girl, Naomi narrowed her eyes venomously. Fiddling with her bra strap, eating too many cookies, Jennifer tormented Naomi, without meaning to. She sweated through her skimpy, badly chosen rayon jumper, built to show off lithe, tennis-playing fourteen-year-olds, not to flatter a solid young woman who looked as if in a previous world she would have been married by spring and pregnant by summer. And Naomi watched her and pinched her and hissed at her, fear and shame across her heavy, worried face.

I loved Jennifer's affection for me; that it was fueled by her sensible dislike of her mother made it better, but that wasn't the heart of it. The person who was loved by Jennifer and Jack was the best person I have ever been. My mother's daughter was caustic and cautious and furiously polite; my lovers' lover was adaptable, imaginative, and impenetrably cheerful. Jennifer, I said to her at her bat mitzvah, surrounded by Sapirstein cousins, all with prime-time haircuts, wearing thin-strapped slip dresses that fluttered prettily around their narrow thighs while Jennifer's clung damply to her full back and puckered around the waistband of her panty hose, Jennifer, your Hebrew was gorgeous, your speech was witty, and you are a really, really interesting young woman. She watched her second cousin toss long, shiny red hair and sighed. Jennifer, I said, and when I pressed my hand on her arm she shivered (and I thought, *Does no one touch you?*), Jennifer, I know I don't know you very well, but believe me, they will have peaked in three years and you will be sexy and good-looking and a pleasure to talk to forever.

She blushed, that deep, mottled raspberry stain fair-skinned girls show, and I left her alone.

Now, when I dropped by as a helpful friend of the family, she brought me small gifts of herself and her attention, and I even passed up some deep kisses with Jack in the garage, "getting firewood," to give enough, and get enough, with Jennifer.

Jack put one hand on Jennifer's brown curls and reached for a piece of kugel. I looked at him and Jennifer laughed.

"Oh my God, that's just like my mother. Daddy, wasn't that just like Ima? I swear, just like her."

Jack and I smiled.

"You know, about what Daddy eats. She read that he should eat a lot of raw vegetables and not a lot of fat. Like no more quesadillas. Like no more of these amazing cookies. You are now in Fat-Free Country, folks, leave your taste buds at the door." She grabbed four chocolate lace cookies and went into the backyard.

I had read the same article in *Newsweek*, about alternative treatments, and I dropped gingko powder into Jack's coffee when I couldn't steer him completely away from caffeine, and sometimes, instead of making love, I would say, I would chirp, *Let's go for a swim! Let's do some yoga!* and Jack would look at me and shake his head.

"I already have a wife, sweetheart. Andrea, light of my life. Darling Mistress. I don't need another one."

"You should listen to Naomi."

"All mankind, all humankind, should listen to Naomi. I do listen and I take good care of myself. It's not a cold, D.M."

I wanted it to be a cold, or even something worse, something for which you might have to have unpleasant treatments with disturbing, disfiguring side effects before you got better, or something that would leave scars like train tracks or leave you with one leg shorter than the other or even leave you in a wheelchair. Treatments that would leave you still you, just the worse for wear.

Jack had come back to my house after we painted the synagogue. There are a million wonderful things about living alone, but the only one that mattered then was Jack in my bed, Jack in my shower, Jack in my kitchen. His eyes were closing.

"D.M., I have to rest before I drive home."

"Do you want to shower?"

"No, I'm supposed to be painty. We've been working. I'm not supposed to go home smelling of banana-honey soap and looking..."

His head snapped forward, and I put a pillow under him, on top of my kitchen table. He slept for about twenty minutes, and I watched him.

Once, early on, I washed his hair. His right side was tired, and I offered to give him a shampoo and a shave. I leaned his head back over my kitchen sink and grazed his cheeks with my breasts and massaged his scalp until his face took on that wonderful, stupid look we all have in the midst of deep pleasure. I dried his gray curly hair and I buffed up his little bald spot and then I shaved him with my father's thick badger brush and old-fashioned shaving soap. My father was a dim, whining memory for me, but I put my fingers through the handle of the porcelain cup and I thought, *Good, Papa, this is why you lived, so that I could grow up and love this man.*

People came in and out of Naomi's kitchen, and Jack and I passed trays and bowls and washed some more dairy silver and put bundles of it into cloth napkins. I set them out on the dining room table.

Naomi put her hand on my shoulder.

"He looks tired."

"I think so," I said.

"Will he lie down?"

I shrugged.

"Everyone's got enough food. My God, you'd think they hadn't eaten for days. Half of them don't even fast, the *trombeniks*."

I started picking up the dirty plates and silverware, and Naomi patted me again.

"Tell him we're done with the pasta. I'm serving the coffee now. He could lie down."

"He'll lie down when they go home."

Naomi looked like she wanted to punch me in the face.

"Fine. Then we'll just send them all home. Good *yontiff*, see you Friday night. They can just go home."

I dragged Naomi into the kitchen.

"Jack, Naomi's dying here. They're eating the houseplants, for God's sake. The bookshelves. Can't we send these people home? She's beat. You look a little pooped yourself."

Jack smiled at Naomi and she put her head on his shoulder.

"You're full of shit. Naomi, are you tired?"

"I am, actually. I didn't sleep last night."

I am grateful for sunny days, and for good libraries and camel's hair brushes and Hirschel's burnt umber, and I was very grateful to stand in their kitchen and bear the sight of Jack's hand around Naomi's fat waist and thank God that he didn't know how his wife slept.

We threw six plates of *rugelach* around and sent everyone home. I went in the middle of the last wave, after they promised they wouldn't even try to clean up until the next day. There was a message from my mother on my machine.

"Darling, are you home? No? All right. It's me. Are you there? All right. Well, I lit a candle for Daddy and Grandpa. Your brother was very nice; he helped. It's pouring here. I hope you're not driving around unnecessarily. Call me. I'll be up until maybe eleven. Call me."

My mother never, ever fell asleep before two A.M., and then only in her living room armchair. She considered this behavior vulgar and neurotic, and so she pretended that she went to sleep at a moderately late hour, in her own pretty, pillowed queen-size bed, with a cup of tea and a gingersnap, like a normal seventy-eight-year-old woman.

"Hi, Meme. I wasn't driving around looking for an accident. I came right home from Jack and Naomi's."

"Aren't you funny. It happens to be terrible weather here. That Jack. Such a nice man. Is he feeling better?" My mother had met him at an opening.

"He's fine. He's not really going to get better."

"I know. You told me. Then I guess his wife will nurse him when he can't manage?"

"I don't know. That's a long way off."

"I'm sure it is. But when he can't get about, I'm saying when he's no longer independent, you'll go and visit him. And Naomi. You know what I mean, darling. You'll be a comfort to both of them, then."

I sometimes think that my mother's true purpose in life, the thing that gives her days meaning and her heart ease, is her ability to torture me in a manner as ancient and genteelly elaborate as lace making.

"Let's jump off that bridge when we come to it. So, you're fine? Louis is fine? He's okay?" I don't know what fine would be for my brother. He's not violent, he's not drooling, he's not walking into town buck naked. I guess he's fine.

"We're both in good health. We watched a program on Mozart. It was very well done."

"That's great." I opened my mail and sorted it into junk, bills, and real letters. "Well, I'm pretty tired. I'm going to crawl into bed, I think."

"Oh, me too. Good night, darling. Sleep well."

"Good night, Meme. Happy Day of Atonement."

I didn't hear from Jack for five days. I called his house and got Jennifer.

"My dad's taking it easy," she said.

"Could you tell him—could you just bring the phone to him?"

I heard Jack say, "Thanks, Jellybean." And then, "D.M.? I'm glad you called. It's been a lousy couple of days. My legs are just Jell-O. And my brain's turning to mush. Good-bye, substantia nigra."

"I could bring over some soup. I could bring some rosemary balm. I could make some gingko tea."

"I don't think so. Naomi's nursing up a storm. Anyway, you minister to me and cry your eyes out, and Naomi will what? Make dinner for us both? I don't think so."

"Are you going to the auction on Sunday?" The synagogue was auctioning off the usual, tennis lessons, romantic getaways, kosher chocolates, and a small painting of mine.

"I'm not going anywhere soon. I'm not walking. Being the object of all that pity is not what I have in mind. I don't want you to see me like this."

"Jack, if I don't see you like this and you're down for a while, I won't see you, period."

"That's right. That's what I meant."

I cry easily. Tears were all over the phone.

"You're supposed to be brave," he said.

"Fuck you. You be brave."

"I have to go. Call me tomorrow, to see how I'm doing."

I called every few days and got Jennifer or Naomi, and they would hand the phone to Jack and we would have short, obvious conversations, and then he'd hand the phone back to his wife or his daughter and they'd hang up for him.

After two weeks, Naomi called and invited me to visit.

"You're so thin," she said when she opened the door.

My thinness and the ugly little ghost face I saw in the mirror were the same as Naomi's damp, puffy eyes and the faded dress pulling at her hips.

"I thought Jack would enjoy a little visit, just to lift his spirits." She didn't look at me. "I didn't say you were coming. Just go up and surprise him."

I stood at the bottom of the stairs. "Jack? It's me, Andrea. I'm coming up."

He looked like himself, more or less. His face seemed a little loose, his mouth hanging heavier, his lips hardly moving as he spoke. The skin on his right hand was shiny and full, swollen with whatever flowed through him and pooled in each reddened fingertip.

"I can't believe she called you."

"Jack, she thought it would be nice for you. She thinks I am your most entertaining friend."

"You are my only entertaining friend."

I sat on the bed, stroking his hand, storing it up. *This is my fingertip on the gold hairs on the back of his right hand. This is my fingertip on the protruding blue vein that runs from his ring finger to his wrist and up his beautiful forearm.*

"If you cry, you gotta go."

"I'm not."

"D.M., I may want something from you."

I put my hand under the sheet and laid it on his stomach. *This is my palm on the line of brown curling hairs that grow like a spreading tree from his navel to his collarbone. This is the tip of my pinkie resting in the thick, springy hair above his cock, in which we discovered two silver strands last summer.* His cock twitched against my finger.

Jack smiled. "You're the last woman I will ever fuck. I think you are the last woman I will have fucked. You're the end of the line."

I was ready to lock the door, step out of my jeans, and straddle him.

"I had a very good time. D.M., I had a wonderful time with you. My last fun."

Naomi stuck her head in. "Everything all right? More tea, Mr. Malone?"

"No, dear girl. We're just having a wee chat." I never heard him sound so Irish. Naomi disappeared.

"Well, *Erin go bragh.*"

"You've got an ugly side to you," he said, and he put one stiff hand to my face.

"I do. I'm ugly sides all over lately."

"When it gets bad," he said, "I'll need your help. I seem to have taken a sharp turn for the worse this time."

I put my face on his stomach, which seemed just the same beautiful stomach, hard at the ribs and softer below, thick and sweet as always, no wasting, no bloating.

"And when I'm worse yet, and I want to go, you may have to help."

I saw Jack's face smeared against the inside of a plastic bag.

"That's a long way away. We all want you with us. Jennifer needs you, Naomi needs you, for as long as you're still, you know, still able to be with them."

Jack grabbed my hair and pulled my face to his.

"I didn't ask you what they wanted. I didn't ask you what you want. I can't ask my wife. I know she needs me, I know she wants me until I can't blink once for yes and twice for no. She wants me until I don't know the difference. You have to do this for me."

I put my hands over my ears, without even realizing it until Jack pulled them away.

"Darling Mistress, this is what I need you for. I can't fuck you, I can't have fun with you." He smiled. "Not much fun anyway. I can't do the things with you that a man does with his mistress. There is just this one thing that only you can do for me."

"Does Naomi know?"

"She'll know what she needs to know. No one's going to prosecute you or blame you. I've given it a lot of thought. You'll help me and then you'll go, and it will have been my will, my hand, my choice."

I walked around the room. With a teenager and a sick man and no cleaning lady, Naomi's house was tidier than mine on its best day.

"All right? D.M.? Yes?"

"What if I say no?"

"Then don't come back at all. Why should I have you see me this way, see me worse than this, sweet merciful Jesus, see me dumb and dying, if you won't save me? Otherwise, you're just another woman whose heart I'm breaking, whose life I'm destroying. I told you when I met you, baby, I already have a wife."

———

Avinu Malkenu, inscribe us in the Book of Happiness.
Avinu Malkenu, inscribe us in the Book of Deliverance.
Avinu Malkenu, inscribe us in the Book of Merit.
Avinu Malkenu, inscribe us in the Book of Forgiveness.
Avinu Malkenu, answer us though we have no deeds to
  plead our cause; save us with mercy and loving-
  kindness.

"You're a hard man," I said.
"I certainly hope so."

I am waiting. I have cleaned my house. I paint. I listen.

salman **rushdie**

MIDNIGHT'S CHILDREN:
A SCREENPLAY
IN SEARCH OF A MOVIE

This is the story of a production that never was: a five-episode television adaptation of my novel *Midnight's Children*, a project on which two writers, three directors, at least four producers, and a whole passionately dedicated production team worked for over four years, and which foundered for political reasons when everything was in place.

Midnight's Children was first published in 1981, and after it won the Booker Prize that autumn there was some talk of making it into a movie. The director John Amiel, who was pretty hot at the time because of his television success with Dennis Potter's series *The Singing Detective*, was interested, but the project never got off the ground. I was also approached by Rani Dube, one of the producers of Richard Attenborough's multi-Oscared *Gandhi*. She professed herself very keen indeed to make a film of my book, but went on to say that she felt the novel's crucial later chapters—dealing with the excesses of Indira Gandhi's autocratic rule during the so-called Emergency of the mid-seventies—were really unnecessary, and could easily be omitted from any film. Unsurprisingly, this approach, of which Mrs. G. would no doubt have heartily approved, failed to find favor with the book's author.

Ms. Dube retreated, and after that things went quiet on the movie front. I put all thoughts of a film or television adaptation out of my mind. To tell the truth, I wasn't too bothered. Books and movies are different languages, and attempts at translation often fail. The wonderful reception that had been accorded the novel itself was more than enough for me.

Twelve years passed. Then, in 1993, *Midnight's Children* was named the "Booker of Bookers," in the judges' opinion the best book to have won the prize in its first quarter-century. This great compliment attracted the attention of not one but two television channels, and within weeks I was in the fortunate position of being wooed by both Channel Four and the BBC. It was a close thing, but in the end I chose to go with the BBC, because, unlike Channel Four, it was able to fund and produce the serial, and because of the reassuring presence of my friend Alan Yentob at the corporation's creative helm. I trusted Alan to steer the project safely through whatever troubles might lie ahead.

Not long afterward, Channel Four signed up *A Suitable Boy*, by Vikram Seth, and then there were two "India projects" on the go. I was heartened to think that British television was willing to invest so much time, passion, and money in bringing to the screen these two very different contemporary novels that take place far away. We might offer a welcome change, or so I hoped, from the many costume-drama adaptations of the English literary canon that came out every year.

From the outset I made it clear to Alan Yentob and the original producer, Kevin Loader, that I would prefer not to write the adaptation myself. I had already spent years of my life writing *Midnight's Children*, and the idea of doing it all over again was both daunting and unappealing. It would feel, to borrow Arundhati Roy's memorable condemnation of the act of rewriting, "like breathing the same breath twice." Besides, I had no experience of writing large-scale television drama. What we needed, or so I argued, was a television professional who would be sympathetic to my book but able to reshape it to fit the very different medium it was now preparing to enter. We needed, in short, an expert translator.

We first approached the highly regarded Andrew Davies, who reread *Midnight's Children*, thought about it for a while, but eventually turned us down, saying that while he was an admirer of the novel he didn't have enough of a feel for India to be confident of success. Then Kevin Loader proposed Ken Taylor, the adapter of Paul Scott's *Jewel in the Crown*. I readily agreed to the suggestion. I was not an admirer of the so-called "Raj Quartet," but had thought the TV adaptation, with its high production values, brilliant acting, and finely crafted scripts, to be a marked improvement on the original. And, of course, as a result of his work on *Jewel*, Ken knew a good deal about India.

At our first meeting, it became clear that Ken, while evidently attracted to the project, had worries about the nature of the text to be adapted. Television drama has long been dominated by naturalism, and Ken's own inclinations and dramatic instincts were strongly naturalistic. How, then, was he to approach a novel with such a high content of surreal and fabulistic material? What was he to make of hypersensitive noses and lethal knees, of optimism diseases and decaying

ghosts, of humming men and levitating soothsayers, of
telepaths and witches, of 1,001 magic children, indeed of the
novel's central conceit: that Saleem Sinai, a boy born at the
instant of Indian independence, had been somehow "hand-
cuffed to history" by the coincidence and that, as a result, the
entire history of modern India might somehow be his fault?

I told him that however highly fabulated parts of the
novel were, the whole was deeply rooted in the real life of the
characters and the nation. Many of the apparently "magical"
moments had naturalistic explanations. The soothsayer who
seems to be levitating is in fact sitting cross-legged on a low
shelf. Even Saleem's "telepathic" discovery of the other "magic
children" can be understood as an extreme instance of the
imaginary friends invented by lonely children. Saleem's idea
that he is responsible for history is true for him, I said, but
it may or may not be true for us. And all around Saleem is
the stuff of real Indian history. Interestingly, on the novel's
first publication, Western critics tended to focus on its more
fantastic elements, while Indian reviewers treated it like a
history book. "I could have written your book," a reader flat-
teringly told me in Bombay. "I know all that stuff."

Somewhat reassured, Ken agreed to undertake the task.
It's easy to be wise after the event, but I now think it was
quite wrong of me to "sell" Ken this naturalistic version of
my book. I suppose I thought it would allow him to pull the
dramatic structure of the serial into shape, and if the scripts
needed an injection of "unnaturalism," that could be added
later. Unsurprisingly, it turned out to be much more complicated than that.

Who would direct the scripts? Much too early to think
about that, I was told; script first, director later. And would
there be difficulties in gaining approval to film from the Indian government? I hoped not; after all, the novel itself had

always been freely available throughout India, so what logical reason could there be for objecting to a film of it? In those early days, it was easy to shelve such matters until later.

Ken went punctiliously to work on a seven-episode screenplay, and I went back to my own writing. In these years I was finishing *The Moor's Last Sigh*, beginning *The Ground Beneath Her Feet*, and co-editing *The Vintage Book of Indian Writing*, so most of my attention was elsewhere. There followed a long phase in which Ken beavered away; Kevin Loader left the BBC; producers came and went; an Indian production company was signed up, one of its major tasks being to secure government approval; and concerns grew about how much the project was going to cost. Meanwhile, over at Channel Four, *A Suitable Boy* bit the dust. It's an ill wind, and so on, and there was a small ignoble feeling of relief at our end—we would no longer be competing for the same actors, the same sources of co-financing, the same audience—but we were also saddened, and chastened. The Seth cancellation was a bad omen for us, too.

I was abroad when a director was finally signed up: Richard Spence, a young filmmaker with a reputation for visual flair. At much the same time, it was decided that seven episodes were too many; could we compress the story into five? In the end we agreed to a feature-length opener followed by four fifty-minute episodes. Two hundred ninety minutes instead of 350: a whole hour less.

When I got back to England, I met Richard and was impressed by his ideas. We talked for hours, and I began to feel that we had the makings of something exciting. Richard's imagination would build on the solid foundations of Ken's work.

It soon became apparent, however, that the working relationship between Ken and Richard was deteriorating.

When I heard that Richard was asking Ken to make further drastic cuts in the storyline—in particular to the hero's childhood years—I began to worry. *Midnight's Children* without children? The original impulse for the novel had been to write a story growing out of my memories of growing up in Bombay; were we really going to make a TV version which cut all that out?

There was a crunch meeting in Alan Yentob's office at the BBC. For a moment it seemed as if the whole project might founder there and then. I tried to mediate between Ken and Richard. Ken was right that the childhood sequence was essential, and was in his serious way acting as the faithful guardian of my book. But Richard was right that Ken's draft scripts needed revision, to inject exactly that quality of imagination and magic which I'd hoped the involvement of a director would add. By the end of the meeting it seemed we might have hammered out a way forward.

But within days it became plain that Ken and Richard couldn't work together. One of them would have to go. In Hollywood the decision would have been simple and ruthless; whoever heard of a director being fired because the writer couldn't work with him? But this was England, and Ken had been working on the project for a long time. The BBC backed him. Richard was disappointed but graceful, and took his leave.

By now, I had begun to worry about the scripts, too. We had lost our director, the financial powers that be at the BBC were not green-lighting the production, and I heard that the scripts we had were not attracting other directors or inspiring confidence in the BBC's corridors of power. I myself was now sure that the scripts did need a lot of work, I had all sorts of ideas about how they might be revised, and Ken and I had long telephone conversations about what might be done. But the changes made were minimal. We were going nowhere fast.

It was around this time that Alan Yentob asked me if I'd consider taking over as scriptwriter. I had begun to think this might be the only way forward, but my fondness for Ken and respect for his efforts stopped me from agreeing. Also, I would have to set aside work on my new book, and I wasn't at all keen to do that.

Meanwhile, Gavin Millar had expressed an interest in directing, but had radical ideas about script revisions. In a document entitled "A Modest Proposal," he offered up a series of provocative thoughts, the most extreme being his idea that we should change the narrative sequence of the story. Instead of beginning, as the novel does, with the story of the narrator's grandparents and then parents, Gavin suggested that we should plunge into Saleem's own story, and then tell the other tales in a series of flashbacks that went further and further back in time.

Gavin's note provoked in me a sort of "lightbulb moment." I suddenly saw with great clarity how to write the scripts. I saw how to make his "Modest Proposal" work, and beyond that, how to change the architecture of the screenplay into something much freer, more surrealist. (Later, I would decide to abandon Gavin's time-scrambling ideas and go back to the novel's original, simpler time line. I'm sure it was right to do so, but I'm also sure that Gavin's iconoclastic intervention had freed my imagination, and without it I might never have worked out how to proceed.)

I think that Gavin's note caused an equal and opposite reaction in Ken. It made him feel enough was enough; it made him dig in his heels, and stand by his drafts as if they were shooting scripts. At this point I understood that if anything was ever going to happen, I would have to take over, and after the passage of so much time and effort I wasn't prepared to let the project founder.

So I agreed to do it. The moment I started work I saw that little or nothing of the existing screenplays could survive. The entire manner of the scripts would be different now, the episodes would start and finish in different places, the selection of material from the novel and the internal arc of each episode would be different. All the two versions had in common was the dialogue taken directly from the book.

I asked the production team to make it plain to Ken that what had started as a rewrite had become an entirely new piece of work. There was no nice way of saying this, but it needed to be said. Unfortunately, the executives concerned delayed telling Ken, which meant that the human mess was eventually much worse than it need have been. Ken was hurt and angry, I was upset, our friendship was damaged, there were accusations and counteraccusations. In the end, Ken withdrew, like the dignified man he is. I only wish it had all been handled better.

For a while I worked with Gavin, but in the end, like Andrew Davies, he backed out, too, on the grounds that he didn't have the "feel" for India that the films required. I had been writing feverishly, convinced that the scripts could be made to work, and Gavin's withdrawal, coming after everything else, felt like a sledgehammer blow.

All this coming and going had delayed us by over a year, but the delay did give us one lucky break. Tristram Powell, who had earlier been unavailable to direct, was now available. In 1981, when *Midnight's Children* was first published, it had been Tristram who made the Arena documentary about it. He professed himself keen to make the series, but only on the basis of my new approach.

I began a mad writing burst. In five weeks, in November

and December 1996, I finished a draft of the entire five-episode screenplay. I gave myself Christmas Day off, but otherwise was hardly ever away from my desk. As I have already suggested, I had a great time. I was much less respectful of the original text than Ken had been. His fidelity to the novel, his sense of himself as my representative, had constrained him. Perhaps nobody would have felt free to make the kind of changes I made so guiltlessly. Out went long sequences—the sojourn in the valley of Kif, the war in the Rann of Kutch. Out went some of the novel's more fanciful notions (a politician who literally hummed with energy) and peripheral characters (the snake-poison expert who lives upstairs from the Sinai family). In came new devices, such as the idea of allowing the peep-show man, Lifafa Das, to introduce each episode as if it were a part of his peep show, and occasional "unnaturalist" moments at which the narrator, Saleem, remembering his past life, is able to step into the bygone moments and watch the action unfold.

Storylines were altered to suit the requirements of episode structure and dramatic form. For example, Saleem's visits to Pakistan were reduced and condensed, and indeed now take place at somewhat different points in the story, to avoid the problem of yo-yoing back and forth at high speed between Bombay and Karachi. Also, in the novel, Saleem's uncle General Zulfikar is murdered by his embittered son. In the screenplay, however, it seemed absurd to introduce a different Pakistani general later in the story, at the end of the war in Bangladesh. So I kept Zulfikar alive until then, and arranged for him to be bumped off in quite a different way.

Perhaps the most significant changes in the plot have to do with the central duo of Saleem and Shiva, the two babies who are swapped at birth and thus lead each other's lives. In the book, Shiva never learns the truth about his parentage, and it doesn't matter, because the reader is aware of it throughout. On the screen, however, so large a plot motif simply insists on a climactic confrontation, and so I have provided one. There is a part of me that thinks that the version of events in this screenplay is more satisfactory than the one in the novel.

The new scripts were well received. There followed a period of several months in 1997 during which Tristram Powell and I worked on the text, refining, clarifying, adding, subtracting. Tristram was so sharp, so helpful, so full of suggestions and improvements, and so completely in tune with the novel that I was sure we had found the ideal director for the job. The two of us worked together easily, and the scripts grew tighter by the day. Even when we had to change things purely because we couldn't afford them, we found solutions that didn't compromise the spirit of the work. For example, all the shipboard scenes in the screenplay now take place in dock; we didn't have the cash to go to sea, but it doesn't matter. More significantly, the Amritsar Massacre of 1919 now happens off camera. To my mind, the horror of this famous atrocity is actually increased by suggesting rather than showing it.

The production's other problems began to surface. The BBC's bizarre bureaucracy—there were no fewer than five layers of "suits" between the producer and the controller of BBC2—made it virtually impossible to get any definite decisions. Also, it became clear that we were competing for our budget with other drama projects, notably *Tom Jones*. And the money the BBC was putting up was simply not going to be enough. We needed outside investors.

We found them, in the form of an American-based ex-banker and a businessman, both of Indian origin, both fired by patriotic pride. And so, finally, the sums added up, and the long sessions in which Tristram and I worried away at the scripts had produced a screenplay which everyone involved was excited by. We did three casting read-throughs in London, and the quality of the British Asian actors we saw impressed me greatly. At the time of the original publication of *Midnight's Children,* there would have been very few such actors to choose from. One generation later, we were able to audition a diverse and multitalented throng. I was touched and moved by the actors' feelings for my novel and their professional excitement at reading for roles other than the usual corner-shop Patels or hospital orderlies that came their way. The only snag we encountered was that some of the younger actors, born and raised in Britain, had difficulty pronouncing Indian names and phrases!

Not all the parts were cast in this way. Some of the senior Indian actors—Saeed Jaffrey, Roshan Seth—were approached and offered their choice of roles. There were also casting sessions in Bombay, and it was in Bombay that we found our Saleem, a brilliant young actor called Rahul Bose. Other "discoveries" included Nicole Arumugam as Padma and Ayesha Dharker as Jamila (whose sensational voice stunned us all when, in the middle of one readthrough, she burst into unaccompanied song), and it is intensely frustrating that we were not able in the end to give them the opportunity they so richly deserved.

For when the "green light" moment was finally upon us, the Indian government simply refused us permission to film, giving no explanation at all, and no hope of appeal. Worse still was the discovery that the BBC's Indian partners had been told months earlier that the application would be refused. They had not informed us, perhaps believing they could get the decision changed. But they couldn't.

I felt as if we'd nosedived into the ground at the end of

the runway. I also felt personally insulted. That *Midnight's Children* should have been rejected so arbitrarily, with such utter indifference, by the land about which it had been written with all my love and skill, was a terrible blow, from which, I must say, I have not really recovered. It was like being told that a lifetime of work had been for nothing. I plunged into a deep depression.

But now the new producer, Christopher Hall, and the rest of the team made a heroic effort to save the project by relocating it in Sri Lanka. And Sri Lanka did indeed give us approval to film. (In writing.) President Chandrika Ranatunga herself said she was strongly behind the project. Because of the Indian refusal, and the continuing controversy surrounding *The Satanic Verses*, she met with Sri Lankan Muslim MPs to reassure them about the content of our screenplay and to tell them that the project was economically important for Sri Lanka.

So it was all on again. The hurt at my treatment by India remained unassuaged, but at least the film would be made. We found locations (in some ways Sri Lanka was actually an improvement on India in this regard), offered work on the crew to many local people, and cast a number of Sri Lankan actors in featured roles. The spirit of cooperation we encountered was a delight. (The Sri Lankan army offered to help us stage the war scenes called for by the script.) We set up a Colombo production office and planned to start filming in January 1998.

Then it all went wrong again. An article appeared in the *Guardian*, written by a journalist named Flora Botsford who was also attached to the BBC in Colombo, and who, in the view of Chris Hall and the production team, used her inside knowledge of the problems we'd had to stir up a controversy. Local Muslim MPs who had previously made no objection to the filming now ascended their high horses. It seems too that this article alerted the Iranians, who then brought pressure on the Sri Lankan government to revoke permission. The entente cordiale that we had worked so hard to establish was breaking down.

At this point the Sri Lankan government was engaged in trying to get sensitive devolution legislation through its national assembly, and to do this it needed the support of opposition MPs. This meant that a tiny handful of parliamentarians were able to demand political concessions in return for their votes. And so, although the Sri Lankan media were strongly in favor of our project, and Muslim as well as non-Muslim commentators wrote daily in our support, permission was in fact revoked, abruptly and without warning, just one day after we had been assured by the government ministers that there was no problem and that we should just go right ahead and make our film. All our bright hopes came to nothing. Like Sisyphus, we had to watch the undoing of all our work, as the great rock of our production ran away downhill into a Sri Lankan ditch.

For me, the rejection of *Midnight's Children* changed something profound in my relationship with the East. Something broke, and I'm not sure it can be mended. This is the story of a failure, then. But publication is always an act of optimism. What has once been thought cannot be unthought, Friedrich Dürrenmatt wrote. Nothing stays the same. Governments change, attitudes change, times change. And a film brought into half-being may yet manage, somehow, to get itself born.

THE GIRLS' GUIDE
TO HUNTING AND FISHING

My best friend is getting married. Her wedding is only two weeks away, and I still don't have a dress to wear. In desperation, I decide to go to Loehmann's in the Bronx. My friend Donna offers to come with me, saying she needs a bathing suit, but I know a mercy mission when I see one.

"It might be easier if you were bringing a date," Donna says in the car, on the Major Deegan Expressway. "But maybe you'll meet somebody."

When I don't answer, she goes on. "Who was the last guy you felt like you could bring to a wedding?"

I know she's not asking a question as much as trying to broach the subject of my unsocial life. But I say, "That French guy I went out with."

"I forgot about him," she says. "What was his name again?"

"Fuckface," I say.

"That's right," she says.

At the entrance to the store, we separate and plan to meet in an hour. I'm an expert shopper, discerning fabric content by touch, identifying couture at a glance. Here at Loehmann's, on Broadway at 237th Street, I'm in my element—Margaret Mead observing the coming of age in Samoa, Aretha Franklin demanding R-E-S-P-E-C-T in Motor City.

Even so, I search for a whole hour without finding a single maybe, until I see it, my perfect dress, a black Armani sheath—but only in an ant-sized 2 and a spider 4.

I think, *A smarter woman than I am bought my 10 at Saks or Barneys weeks ago, knowing it would never find its way to Loehmann's. She knew her dress when she saw it and didn't hesitate. That woman is zipping up her sheath right now, on her way to meet the man she loves.*

But in the communal fitting room, Donna hands me the black Armani sheath in a 10—the one that almost got away. I take this as an omen.

Is the dress perfect? It is so perfect.

I say, "You're my fairy godshopper," and sit on the fitting-room bench, holding the sheath in my arms while Donna tries on bathing suits. She adjusts the straps of a chocolate maillot and frowns at herself in the mirror. She doesn't know how beautiful she is, especially her sultry, heavy-lidded eyes; she says people stop her on the street and tell her to get some rest.

"No wonder I'm single," she says to the mirror. "Even I don't want to get into bed with these thighs."

I say that getting married isn't like winning the Miss America Pageant; it doesn't all come down to the bathing suit competition.

"What do you think it comes down to?" she says.

I say, "Baton twirling."

———

Afterward, we celebrate our purchases over turkey burgers at the Riverdale Diner. In a put-on silky voice, I say, "I am a woman who wears Armani."

"Clothes are armor," she says.

"I don't need armor," I tell her; "I'm happy for Sophie and Max."

"I hate weddings," she says. "They make me feel so un-married. Actually, even brushing my teeth makes me feel unmarried."

She stops doing her shtick, and suddenly she does look tired; her lids practically cover her eyes. She tells me she's been reading a terrible book called *How to Meet and Marry Mr. Right.* "Their main advice is to play hard to get. Basi-cally, it's a guide to manipulation."

I'm thirty-four, but wisdom-wise, I don't have any idea how to date, myself—or, that is, I only know how to date myself—but I say that maybe she should stop reading it.

"I know," she says, only half agreeing. "But it's like I've been trying to catch a fish by swimming around with them. I keep making myself get in the water again. I try different rivers. I change my strokes. But nothing works. Then I find this manual that tells me about fishing poles and bait, and how to cast and what to do when the line gets taut." She stops and thinks. "The depressing part is that you *know* it'll work."

I say, "I hate fish."

The wedding is held at a restored mansion on the Hudson. I come up here sometimes on Sundays. If there isn't a wed-ding going on, you can pay admission to tour the house and grounds, but I pay my $4.50 just to sit in an Adirondack chair and read the newspaper and look at the river. It's a spot so idyllic it makes you feel you're in a painting—a Seurat, maybe—and for a while I kept hoping a gentleman in shirtsleeves and a boater would dot-dot-dot over to me. Then I overheard a guard say that this place was just for the pinks and grays—wedding parties and senior citizens.

I arrive in the rainy late afternoon to help Sophie dress. I'm directed upstairs to the first door on the left, where I expect an old-fashioned bedroom with lace curtains, a vanity, and a four-poster bed, but I find Sophie and her friends in a conference room with stacked plastic chairs and a slide projector. She's up at the lectern, clowning in her bra and stockings.

I go up to her and the words "blushing bride" come to mind, though she is, in fact, an almost constant blusher—from sun or wind, laughing, crying, anger, or wine. Now she actually appears to be glowing, and I kiss her and say, "Hello, little glowworm."

Her hilarious friend Mavis pours me a big glass of wine; she's pregnant and says that I have to drink for two now.

After I help Sophie on with her off-the-shoulder ivory gown, she asks me to put on her makeup, though she knows I don't really know how. It's for the ritual of it; I brush a tiny bit of pale eye shadow on her lids and put on barely-there lipstick. She blots her lips with a tissue.

Mavis says, "Jesus, Sophie, you look like a whore."

The photographer knocks to tell Sophie it's time for pictures, and the rest of us follow. Mavis and I stop in the bathroom, and from the stall she tells me she didn't realize for a long time that she was pregnant; she thought she was just getting fat and becoming incontinent. "So the pregnancy was really good news."

Since I have nothing to add about pregnancy, I tell her I read that Tiny Tim wore Depends in his final years. He wasn't incontinent, just thought they were a good idea.

Downstairs, we join Mavis's husband and the other guests. We take our seats in the room where the ceremony will be held. It has a river view, but all you can see now is fog and rain and wet grass.

I ask Mavis what her ceremony was like and she says that instead of "The Wedding March," she chose K.C. and the Sunshine Band's song "That's the Way—Uh-huh, Uh-huh—I Like It" and danced herself down the aisle.

Her husband does a deadpan "Uh-huh, uh-huh."

The music plays. We wait. Mavis whispers that she has to go to the bathroom again. I say, "Think how much better you'd feel if you had a Depends on right now." This is what I'm saying when Max and Sophie walk down the aisle.

The reception kicks off with a klezmer band doing their bloop-yatty-bloop, and Sophie and Max are hauled up on chairs for the Jewish wedding version of musical chairs. I was raised as an assimilationist, but it's not my confused identity that prevents me from joining in; I've got the spirit, but I can't clap to the beat.

Finally, we go to our tables. I'm at One, sitting between Mavis and Sophie, and I know everyone at the table except the man taking his seat at the opposite end. He's tall and gangly with olive skin, a high forehead, and big eyes; cute, but that doesn't explain what comes over me. I haven't had this feeling in so long that I don't even recognize it; at first I think it's fear. My hair follicles seem to individuate themselves and freeze; then it's like my whole body flushes.

He smiles over at me and mouths, "I'm Robert."

I mouth, "Jane."

When I come out of my swoon, Mavis is telling the table that my Depends comment made her pee in her pants. She tells me I should work Tiny into my toast, and only now do I remember that I'm supposed to give one.

I try to think of it during dinner, but I'm also trying not to stare at Robert, and I'm shaky and not exactly prepared when it's my turn to go up to the microphone.

"Hi," I say to the crowd. I wait for something to come to me, and then I see Sophie and it does. I say that we met after college in New York, and that over the years we had a succession of boyfriends but weren't so happy with any of them. We were always asking each other, "Is this all we can expect?"

"Then," I say, "there was our sea-horse period, when we were told that we didn't need mates; we were supposed to make ourselves happy just bobbing around in careers.

"Finally, Sophie met Max," I say, and turn serious. I look over at him. I think, *He has a nice face.* And I say this into the microphone. "He gets how funny and generous and wholehearted she is. He understands what a big person she is, and yet he doesn't want to crush her." I get some blank stares here, but Sophie's laughing. I say, "Max is the man Sophie didn't know if she could hope for."

When I sit down, Robert stands, I assume to give his toast, but he walks over to my side of the table and asks Mavis if she'll trade seats with him.

She says, "No," and waits a moment before relinquishing her chair.

Robert sits beside me and says, "I loved your toast."

I linger over the word "love" coming out of his mouth about something of mine.

He tells me that he knows Max from freshman year—roughly twenty years—and I remember that a huge number of Oberlin friends are here and ask what bonds them all for life.

He says, "No one else will be friends with us."

Then another toaster picks up the microphone.

Toast, toast, toast; Robert and I can only talk during the intermissions in hurried exchanges: I learn that he's a cartoonist, and I have to tell him that I work in advertising. "But," I say, and don't know what to say next, "I'm thinking of opening a dog museum."

Toast.

"A dog museum?" he says. He's not sure if I'm kidding. "For the different breeds?"

"Maybe," I say. "Or else it could be a museum that dogs would enjoy. It could have interactive displays of squirrels dogs could chase and actually catch. And a gallery of scents."

Toast.

He tells me he's just moving back to New York from L.A. and is staying with his sister until he finds an apartment. I tell him I live in the huge ancient apartment complex nicknamed the Dragonia for its gargoyles. Almost everyone knows someone who has lived there—an ex-girlfriend or masseuse, a cousin—and Robert does, too, though he doesn't specify whom.

Toast.

Will I check on vacancies for him? I will.

Sophie's father goes up to the microphone for the last toast, a position of honor he's requested. He reads a rhyming poem:

> *I despaired at my spinster daughter*
> *though I thought her awfully fair.*
> *Then came Maxie, praise the Lord,*
> *from the heavens, I had scored.*
> *But Max, like Sophie, makes documentaries,*
> *how are they going to pay their rentaries?*

Sophie's shaking her head; Max is trying to smile at his father-in-law. Robert leans over and whispers to me,

Dad is trying awfully hard,
but this guy is no one's bard.

Max and Sophie go table to table to talk to their guests, and as soon as Robert and I have the chance to talk without interruption, a statuesque beauty in a drapey gown interrupts.

"Jane," Robert says, "this is Apollinaire."

I'm about to say, "Call me Aphrodite," but realize in time that he's not kidding.

"Have a seat," he tells her, nodding to the one next to me, but she gracefully drops down beside him, as though to fill her urn, forcing Robert to turn his back to me. It occurs to me that I may not be the only butterfly whose wings flutter in the presence of his stamen.

After she glides off, Robert tells me that she composes music for movies and has been nominated for an Oscar. I think of my only award, an Honorable Mention in the under-twelve contest to draw Mr. Bubble.

"I like her toga," I say, confusing my ancients.

We talk, we talk, and then Robert announces to the table at large that it's time for us to prepare the newlyweds' get-away car.

Outside it's drizzling. Robert retrieves two grocery bags from the bushes and leads us to Max's car.

Mavis shaving creams smiley faces on the windows.

"Trés droll," her husband says, looking on.

I don't spray a word. I hold my shaving cream poised but nothing comes out. I say that I'm blocked.

Robert, tying cans to the bumper, says, "Just pretend you're spraying in your journal."

As we walk away from the parking lot, he says, "I'm pretty sure that's his car."

Inside, Sophie says she's bummed a cigarette and we go out to the patio. The tables and chairs are wet, but we manage to hike up her dress so it's just her underpants against the seat, and her big skirt swooping up and over the arms of the chair. She reminds me of a swan.

We have so much to say to each other that only quiet will do. We pass the cigarette back and forth, as we have done a thousand times, until her little niece and nephew run outside and shout, "Everyone's looking for you!"

Sophie hands me the cigarette, and as she gets up, she says, "Watch out for Robert." Before I can ask why, the little ones drag her inside.

Inside, someone is calling out, "Unmarried women! Maidens!" Most of Max and Sophie's friends are single, and a big crowd gathers by the staircase; for the first time in my wedding-going life I stand among them. Sophie appears at the top of the steps. Her eyes widen when she sees me. Trusting nothing to chance, she doesn't even turn her back to the crowd; she tosses the bouquet to me, and I catch it.

Then kissing and rice throwing, and the newlyweds are off to Italy for three weeks.

It's time for me to go, and I want to say good-bye to Robert, but he's talking to Apollinaire. I catch his eye, and wave, and he excuses himself and comes over.

"You're leaving?" he says.

He walks me out the door and down the path to the

parking lot. For the moment the rain has stopped, though the sky hasn't cleared and the trees are full of water.

"This is my car," I say. It's an old VW Rabbit with so many scratches and nicks it looks like it's been in a fight.

He stands at the passenger door; I'm at the driver's. He seems to be waiting for something, and I say, "I'd like to invite you in, but it's a mess."

The front seats are covered with old wet towels because the convertible top leaks, and the floor is littered with fast-food wrappers from the last dozen road trips I've taken. I tell him that the garbage and rags discourage thieves. "If the trash doesn't deter them, there's the wet poodle smell."

"You have a poodle?" he says.

"A standard," I say. "Jezebel."

He grew up with standard poodles and loves them, and what color is mine? I think, *I have found the only straight man in the world who loves poodles.*

He tells me he has a cat.

"A cat?" I say. "How can you do that?"

"I love her," he says. "But we both know she's just a place holder."

Then there's a rush of drops—at first I think it's from the trees, but it's real rain, total rain, and Robert pulls his jacket up over his head and runs over to my side, kisses my cheek and gallops back to the mansion, presumably into Apollinaire's widespread wings.

I sit on the wet rags, and try not to feel like a wet rag myself.

Then he's knocking on my window. I roll it down. He asks, "Can I call you?" and I answer "Sure" so fast that my voice overlaps the rest of his sentence "about the Dragonia?"

"Sure," I say again, pretending I didn't say it the first time. "I'm in the phone book," I say. "Rosenal."

"Rose'n'Al, Rose'n'Al, Rose'n'Al," he says fast, and disappears.

He doesn't call on Sunday.

Monday, between writing lines like, "Call now for your free gift," and "There's never been a better time to call," I call home to check my answering machine. I feel elated dialing, despondent when I hear the inhuman voice say, "No new messages." Then I call again.

Donna calls to ask about the wedding, and I tell her about Robert. It feels good just to say his name, like he's still a clear and present danger. Then I have to say, "But he hasn't called."

She says, "Why don't you call him?"

I don't answer.

My devoted friend says, "I don't think you could have felt so strongly if he didn't feel the same way about you."

I say, "How do you feel about Jeremy Irons?"

When I get home, the machine's red light is blinking. I say, "Please be Robert." It is. His voice is low and shy, saying he's on his way out and will call back.

I play the message again and watch Jezebel's face. "What do you think?" I ask her.

She looks back at me: *I think it's time for my walk.*

We go around the block and are almost home when we run into a dog we haven't met before, a beautiful weimaraner. Jezebel goes right up to him and licks his mouth. The weimaraner jumps back. "He's a little skittish," his owner says, led away by Herr Handsome.

"I can't believe you just walked up and kissed him," I say to Jezebel, "without even sniffing his butt first."

I make a salad. I try to start another Edith Wharton novel, but I can't concentrate in the silence of the phone not ringing.

Then I think, *What if he does call? I'll just mess it up.* The only relationships I haven't wrecked right away were the ones that wrecked me later.

I don't admit to myself what I'm doing when I put my bike helmet on and ride over to the Barnes & Noble a few blocks away. I pretend that maybe I'm just getting another Edith Wharton novel.

But I bypass Fiction and find Self-Help. I think, *Self-Help?—if I could help myself I wouldn't be here.*

There are stacks and stacks of *How to Meet and Marry Mr. Right*s, the terrible book Donna told me about, terrible because it works. I take my copy up to the counter, as furtively as if it were a girdle or vibrator.

There isn't a photograph of the authors, Faith Kurtz-Abromowitz and Bonnie Merrill, but after only a few pages, I see them perfectly. Faith is a reserved blown-dry blonde; Bonnie, a girly-girl, a giggler with deep dimples. I have known them my entire life: in gym class, playing volleyball, they were the ones clapping their hands and shouting, "Side out and rotate—our team is really great!" In college, Bonnie was my Secret Santa. In personnel offices, when I joked about my application phobia, Faith was the one who said, "Just do the best you can."

Now I am turning to them for guidance.

Still, they promise that if you follow their advice, "You will marry the man of your dreams!" And I read on.

Their premise is that men are natural predators, and the more difficult the hunt the more they prize their prey. In other words, the last thing you want to do is tap a hunter on the shoulder and ask him to shoot you.

Half of me has to make fun of the book, if only because I've broken all of their rules—"vows," they call them; the other half is relieved that I haven't broken any with Robert yet I read the book from bold blurb to bold blurb until I get to **Don't be funny!**

I think, *Don't be funny?*

"Right," I hear smooth, stoical Faith say. "Funny is the opposite of sexy."

"But I'm attracted to funny men," I say.

Bouncy Bonnie says, "We're not talking about who *you're* attracted to, silly! Go out with clowns and comedians if you want to! Laugh your head off! Just don't make any jokes yourself!"

"Men like femininity," Faith says, crossing her legs. "Humor isn't feminine."

"Think of Roseanne!" Bonnie says.

"Or those fat, knee-slapping girls from *Hee Haw*," Faith adds dryly.

"What about Marilyn Monroe?" I say. "She was a great comic actress."

"That's probably not why there's a new lingerie line named after her," Faith says.

I say, "But Robert likes me because I am funny."

"You don't know why he likes you," Faith says.

Bonnie says, "You looked terrific in that sheath!"

I hate this book. I don't want to believe it. I try to think what I do know about men. What comes to mind is an account ex-

ecutive at work saying, "Ninety-nine percent of men fanta-
size about having sex with two women at once."

My mother hardly ever gave me advice about men, and
I only remember asking her once, in fifth grade. I'd dis-
patched a friend to find out if the boy I liked liked me. "Bad
news—" my friend reported, "he hates you."

My mother kept saying, "What's wrong, Puss?" I couldn't
tell her. Finally, I asked how you got a boy you liked to like
you back. She said, "Just be yourself," which seemed like no
advice at all, even then. At a loss, my poor mother suggested
I jump on my bike and ride around the block to put roses in
my cheeks.

My brother calls inviting me to a benefit for a theater company Friday night—his girlfriend, Liz, knows the director.
"It's a singles event," Henry says.

"Singles?" I say. I think of individually wrapped American cheese slices.

"There's some theme," he says.

"Desperation?" I suggest.

He holds the phone and asks Liz what the theme is.

I hear her say, "It's a square dance."

"A square dance?" he says, in a you're-kidding tone.

"Don't say it like that," she says. "Let me talk to her." She
gets on the phone. "Jane?" she says.

"Hi."

"It sounds dorky," Liz says, "but I went last year and it
was really fun!"

It occurs to me that I might not like fun.

"You want to meet men," Faith says.

Bonnie says, **"Say yes to everything you're invited to!"**

"What else were you going to do Friday night?" Faith

says calmly. "I think we're talking about Edith Wharton—am I right?"

I'm getting the address of the party when my call waiting beeps. It's Robert. "Hi," I say, flustered. "I'm on another call."

Faith says, "Say you'll call him back."

But I'm confused—isn't this my fish on the line?

"Not yet," Faith says. "He's just a nibble."

I ask Robert if I can call him back.

He says that he's at a pay phone.

"So what?" Bonnie says. "It's a quarter!"

But I say, "Hold on a sec," to Robert and tell Liz I'll see her at the hoedown.

Robert and I talk about how much fun the wedding was. I'm distracted, trying to follow the vows or at least not to break any, but the only ones that come to mind are: **Don't say "I love you" first! Wear your hair long! Don't bring up marriage!**

He tells me he's in the Village, he's been looking at apartments, and asks if I want to meet for coffee.

Bonnie says, **"Don't accept a date less than four days in advance!"**

I stall, asking him how the apartments were, until the recorded voice of an operator comes on the line, requesting another nickel or our call will be terminated.

He adds a nickel. "Terminated sounds so permanent," he says. "So final."

I think, *Not if you believe in the aftercall.* But Faith says, "No jokes."

"So," he says, "do you want to get some coffee?"

I make myself say, "I can't."

"Good girl," Faith says.

"Oh," he says. Pause. Then he asks if I want to have dinner Friday.

"You have plans." Faith says, "Say it."

"I can't Friday," I say.

He goes right by it and asks about Saturday.

"Fine," Faith says.

"Okay," I say to Robert.

Then the operator comes on again, asking for another nickel.

He says, "Listen to her pretending that she didn't interrupt us before."

I am fizzy with elation.

After therapy, I'm on the elevator when Bonnie says, "That was great!"

"What?" I say.

"You kept the vow **Don't tell your therapist about the guide.**"

"Because I want her to think I'm improving," I say. "I'm hoping that one day she'll say I'm all better and don't need to come back anymore."

"And one day your dry cleaner will recommend hand washing," Faith says, brushing her hair.

Thursday night, Robert leaves a message with his sister's phone number; I copy it down and pick up the phone to call him back.

"Not yet," Faith says. "Make him wonder a little."

"Isn't that rude?" I say.

"No," Faith says, "rude is not writing that thank-you note to the gay couple who had you out to Connecticut three weeks ago."

"I don't know why you hang out with them anyway!" Bonnie says, looking up from a big bowl of popcorn. "Gay men hate women."

"Excuse me?" I say.

"It's true," Faith says.

"Why am I listening to you?" I ask.

Faith says, "Because you don't want to sleep with Edith Wharton for the rest of your life?"

I call Robert back from work.

"Eight o'clock okay?" he says.

I agree, barely able to keep the thrill out of my voice.

Bonnie points to her little watch and in a singsongy voice says, "Hang up!"

I say, "Look, I have to go."

After I hang up, Bonnie say, "Short conversations! And you be the one who gets off the phone first!"

Faith nods. "Make him long for you."

The square dance is way on the East Side, in the Twenties, just a gym with a caller in braids. I spot Liz, adorable in overalls, and Henry, still in his suit.

"Howdy-do," I say.

I stand with my brother and Liz. Here I am at a party on a Friday night and I have a date tomorrow. I think, *I am a dater; I am a snorkeler in the social swim.*

Faith says, "Feels good, doesn't it?"

It does.

Much clapping and stamping and yee-hawing. I can't clap, of course, but I'm about to let out a yee-haw when Faith shakes her head.

"I was just having a good time," I say.

Faith reminds me that that's not what I'm here for.

"This is a singles dance!" Bonnie says, clapping right in time.

Liz says that we should be dancing, and when I agree, she takes it upon herself to find a partner for me.

The guy she brings back is Gus, the stage manager, a big teddy bear with a fuzzy face and teeth so tiny they make him appear not to have any.

He's aware of performing a kindness; he seems to regard me as poor, plain Catherine from *Washington Square* or poor, sick Laura from *The Glass Menagerie*.

He takes my hand and leads me danceward.

"Bow to your partner," Braidy says. "Ladies, curtsy."

When Gus and I promenade, he smiles encouragement at me, like I'm Clara from *Heidi* and he's teaching me how to walk. But I suddenly remember square dancing in gym circa third grade, and it's the nine-year-old in me swinging my partner and do-si-doing.

"Great!" Bonnie says.

Faith offers up a restrained "Yee-haw."

After dancing, I'm about to say *I'm parched as a possum*, but Faith interrupts: "Say, 'Let's get something cold to drink,'" and those are the words I say.

"Sure," Gus says.

We go to the beer-sticky bar, and Faith says, "Ask him what a stage manager does."

"Men love to talk about themselves!" Bonnie says.

So I ask, and he says, "I do what no one else wants to do."

I'm told to smile as though captivated.

Sipping a beer herself, Faith says, "Now let him do the work."

I am only too happy to oblige.

Bonnie says, "Let your eyes wander around the dance floor!" But this seems unkind.

"He's a prospect," Faith says, "not a charity."

I look around, and Gus, trying to regain my attention, asks me if I'd like to dance again.

Bonnie says, "One dance per customer."

Instead of saying a jokey *Much obliged, but I should join my kin,* I anticipate Faith and say, "It was nice meeting you, Gus."

Like a caller herself, Bonnie says, "**Circulate!**" And I do.

Faith says, "Do not establish eye contact."

"Really?" I ask.

"You think that's the only way to get a man to notice you, don't you?" she says.

"You poor lamb!" Bonnie says.

I've never acknowledged this even to myself. I sound pathetic.

"Yes," Faith says, "especially because nothing is more compelling to a man than a lack of interest."

To my astonishment, she's right. Men appear out of nowhere and glom on to me. Bonnie and Faith tell me what to do, and I obey: I refuse a second dance with a man I'm actually attracted to; I don't enter the pie-eating contest; I ask questions like "What kind of law do you practice?"

By the end of the night, my phone number is in a half-dozen pockets. "This never happened to me before," I tell Faith.

She says, "I know I should feign surprise."

When my brother and Liz walk me to my bike, he says, "Who were those guys you were talking to?"

"Who knows?" I say, giddy with the freedom to make jokes. "I feel like the belle of the ball."

He says, "The ho of the hoedown."

"You know what just occurred to me?" I say, laughing. "I went to a singles square dance in a gym, to meet men."

When Liz says, "You can't think that way," I'm reminded of Faith in personnel saying, "Just do the best you can."

I wonder if my brother is going to marry her.

Right before Robert arrives, Bonnie says, "Don't be too eager!" When I look in the mirror, my smile is huge and my eyes bugged out with anticipation. I tell myself to think of death. When that doesn't work, I think of yesterday's brainstorming session to name a new auto club for frequent drivers.

Robert buzzes. I open the door and he looks as excited as I did a moment before. He sees Jezebel and gets on his knees and rubs her haunches. "Jezzie," he says.

"Do you want a glass of wine?" I ask.

He does.

He follows me into the kitchen. He's still in apartment-hunting mode, he says, and do I mind if he looks around?

"Go ahead," I say, and he goes.

He asks if I've had a chance to check on vacancies in my building, and I'm reminded of Erich von Stroheim in *Sunset Boulevard* saying, "It wasn't Madame he wanted, it was her car."

"I'm sorry—I haven't," I say, and if I were in one of his cartoons, there would be icicles hanging from my balloon.

Maybe he hears it, because he's quiet a moment. He walks around my living room and stops at the table with my little cardboard barnyard animals on their wooden stands. He picks up each one—the bull, the lamb, the pig, the cow—and reads the breed information on the back. I say that I found them at a flea market in upstate New York; I pictured little farm kids coming in from their chores to play with their cardboard cows and lambs. I'm about to explain what I find moving and also funny, but I see that I don't have to.

He goes to my bookshelves and notices my portable typewriters from the fifties. He whispers their names, SILENT and QUIET DELUXE, which is what I did when I first saw them.

Over dinner, at a goofy little French place in the neighborhood, he asks how I got into advertising.

Bonnie says, "**Don't be negative!**"

"It started as a day job," I say. I tell him that I thought I'd write plays or novels or appliance manuals at night. But advertising made my I.Q. go down; every night I had to work just to get it back up to regular.

"What did you do?" he asks.

I got rid of my TV, I tell him, and read classics.

"Like which ones?"

"*Middlemarch* was the first," I say.

He laughs. "You say it like you're not sure I've heard of it."

We keep talking books, and when I tell him that *Anna Karenina* is my favorite, it seems to have the effect "I'm not wearing any underwear" has on other men.

I say, "The good thing about reading is that you never get blocked—and every page is really well written." He smiles, but seriously, and I can tell he hears what I'm saying.

I ask about his work, and he says that it's hard to describe cartoons—you wind up just saying the plot, and his cartoons never have one. "I'll show them to you," he says.

When I ask him why he left L.A., he tells me that it was the loneliest place on earth. "Especially when you're hanging out with people," he says. "Everybody smiles at your jokes."

He loves New York, he says. "It's like Oberlin—it's where people who don't belong anywhere belong."

Only when Faith tells me to stop gazing do I realize that I am. I look down at his hand on the table. I see the indent where he holds his pen, which is slightly darkened from ink he couldn't wash off.

Bonnie says, "Ask if he uses a computer."

"You don't use a computer?" I say, which seems like the most mundane question I could ask.

"Just for the animation," he says. "I'm a Luddite, like you on your—" he whispers, "—QUIET DELUXE."

I don't know what a Luddite is, but Bonnie won't let me ask.

When the check comes, Faith says, "Don't even look at it."

"Let him pay!" Bonnie says.

"What are you thinking about?" Robert asks, putting his credit card in the leatherette folder. "$87.50 for your thoughts."

"Be mysterious!" Bonnie says.

"Excuse me," I say, and go to the ladies' room.

"The red wine stained your teeth a little," Bonnie says, handing me a tissue. "Just rub the front ones."

"Listen," I say to them, "I appreciate what you're trying to do for me, but I think I'm better off on my own with Robert."

"Last night wasn't a fluke," Faith says.

"But Robert's different," I say.

"The only difference is that you want him," Faith says.

Bonnie says, "Which is why you need us more than ever!"

On the way home, Robert takes my hand in his, not lacing our fingers, but really taking ownership of my whole hand.

"Let go of his hand first," Faith says.

I love holding hands. In my entire dating life I have never let go first.

"You can do it," Faith says, and I make myself.

At my door, instead of asking if he can come in, Robert asks if he can take Jezebel out with me.

"On our first date?" I say.

"If you let me," he says, "I'll respect you even more."

Outside, he meets the neighborhood dogs—and says what I always do: "Can I say hello to your dog?" His favorites are my favorites—Flora, the huge bulldog; Atlas, the harlequin Great Dane,

I think, *You love dogs as much as I do.*

Back at my apartment, I take Jezebel off her leash, and in my mini-vestibule, he leans toward me and we kiss.

"The date ends now," Faith says. "It's not going to get better."

"Okay," I say in my love daze. "Good night, Robert."

His eyes look disappointed, and I want to touch his hand or pull him toward me, but Bonnie says, "**Keep him guessing!**" And I do.

He calls the next morning while I'm walking Jez. "Hi, girls," his message says. "I wondered if you wanted to go to the dog run."

There's nothing I want to do more, but I know that I can't.

Bonnie actually gives me a hug.

"I want to see you," Robert says when he calls later.

My whole body hears these words.

He asks when we can get together, and though I think, *Right now is too long to wait,* I say, "Friday?"

"Next Friday?" he says, crestfallen.

"High five," Bonnie says, and slaps hands with Faith.

Robert says, "Do you like me at all?"

"Yes, I like you."

"A lot?" he asks.

"Pause before answering," Faith says.

"Yes," I say.

"Good," he says. "Don't stop."

Bonnie sings the Mary Tyler Moore theme song, "Who Can Turn the World On with Her Smile?"

Robert calls me at the office and calls me at home. He calls just to say good morning and good night.

One night, he calls to tell me he thinks he's found an apartment only a few blocks from mine and wants me to see it.

I tell Robert I wish I could. I want to so badly it hurts. I wonder when I can be normal again.

"You're normal now," Faith says.

"You were screwed up before!" Bonnie says.

Faith says, "If you were being your normal self, he wouldn't even be calling you now."

"All right," Robert says. "I guess I'm going to sign the lease." Then: "You don't feel like I'm stalking you, do you?"

I meet Donna for a drink and admit that I read the book she told me about—the fishing manual.

"Isn't it the worst?" she says.

"I know," I say.

"All those exclamation points," she says. "It can't apply to New York."

"The thing is," I say, "it's working."

"You're actually doing it?" Then she says, "I don't know why I say it like that—I tried it myself." She tells me that she kept pretending to be aloof, but men didn't seem to notice. "Maybe it was the men I was meeting," she says. "Cab-drivers," and she imitates herself nonchalantly giving an address.

I tell her about my date with Robert and that now he's calling me all the time and he's actually moved into my neighborhood.

"No!" she says, mocking my distress.

"But it's like I'm tricking him into it," I say.

She says, "Well, what about all those guys who act like they're in love with you to get you into bed? Like Fuckface."

"But," I say—I'm having trouble saying what I mean, "I want this to be real."

She says, "Was it more real when he wasn't calling you?"

I'm getting ready for my date with Robert when Faith says, "Try not to make so many jokes this time."

"Listen," I say, "funny is the best thing I am."

Faith says, "Making jokes is your way of saying *Do you love me?* and when someone laughs you think they've said yes."

This gives me pause.

Faith says, "Let him court you."

Bonnie hands me my deodorant. "You can be as funny as you want *after* he proposes!"

Robert arrives early, saying he wants to take me to a play. He has brought a stick for Jezebel to chew, and she gives him the loving look I wish I could.

I pour a glass of wine for him and go back to the bathroom to finish drying my hair. "Now this is a real date!" Bonnie says.

I say, "Your idea of a real date probably ends in a carriage ride through Central Park."

"Her point is that it started with asking to meet for coffee," Faith says. "Now he's trying to win you."

Through the motor of my blow-dryer I hear the phone ring, and when I come into the living room Robert's staring down at the machine, frowning. Gus is asking if I'd like to go out for dinner next week.

Robert looks over at me. "She can't," he says to the machine. "Sorry."

We go to *Mere Mortals*, a collection of one acts by David Ives, the best of which is about two mayflies on a date; they watch a nature documentary about themselves and discover their life span is only one day long—after mating, they'll die.

Leaving the theater, Robert and I are both dazzled and exuberant, talking at once and laughing, and we spontaneously kiss.

He says, "I want to mate with you and die."

We have a drink at one of those old-fashioned restaurants in the theater district. Robert says the mayflies play is what every cartoon he draws aspires to be—beautiful and funny and sad and true.

"I want to see them," I say.

"Okay," he says, and takes out a piece of paper.

It's a pen-and-ink drawing of Jezebel, and I think, *You are the man I didn't know I could hope for.*

"Relax," Faith says. "It's a sketch."

Back at my apartment, we begin to mate with our clothes on, lying on the sofa on top of shards of chewed-up stick.

At first Faith's voice is no more than a distant car alarm. But it gets louder and I hear her say, "No."

"Yes," I say to her.

"You don't want to lose him," she says, in the voice you'd

use to talk someone on acid out of jumping out a window. "The way you've lost every man you've really wanted."

I sigh inwardly and pull back.

"What?" he says.

I tell him that I'm not ready to sleep with him yet.

"Okay," he says, and pulls me back to him. We go on kissing and touching and moving against each other for another few minutes, and then he says, "Are you ready now?"

Here is a man who can make my body sing and make me laugh at the same time. "Which is why you don't want to lose him," Faith says.

Over the phone, he tells me that his ex-girlfriend called him today. I picture Apollinaire.

I want to ask who she is and how he feels about her, but Faith practically takes the phone from me. Instead, I ask how long ago he went out with her.

Almost a year ago and she's why he left New York. "She sort of decimated me." He asks if I'd mind signing a non-decimation pact.

I'm choosing which of my decimation experiences to relate, but Bonnie says, "He doesn't need to know about that!"

We meet for a drink at the café between our apartments. He asks what I wish I could do instead of advertising.

I think, *I'd like to make pasta necklaces and press leaves; I didn't really appreciate kindergarten at the time.* But I just shake my head.

He says, "Let's make a list of what you think would be fun to do."

"No," Faith says. "Don't let him think you need help."

"I do need help," I say.

"He'll think you're a loser!" Bonnie says. With her thumb

and index finger she makes an L, pinches it closed and opens it fast: the flashing Loser sign.

He doesn't call the next morning, afternoon, or night, and, needless to say, I can't call him.

Friday night, we go to the movies as planned, but he doesn't hold my hand in the dark theater, doesn't kiss me on the cab ride home. I want to ask him what's wrong, but Faith says not to. "It shows how much you care."

When the cab pulls up to the Dragonia, he tells me he's tired. He doesn't ask if I have plans for Saturday night.

Saturday night, I read until midnight. When I take Jezebel out for her last walk I go all the way to his street, down the dark side. He and Apollinaire are sitting on his stoop.

I am shaking when I get home.

Sunday, when the phone rings I run for it. But it's a crush from college, Bill McGuire—nicknamed "Mac." He lives in Japan and says he'll be coming to New York next weekend and wants to take me out for dinner Saturday.

I hesitate.

Bonnie says, **"Get out there!"**

"I've been out there," I say. "Now I want to stay in with Robert."

"He's not staying in!" Bonnie says.

"I don't know that," I say.

"You saw them!" Bonnie says.

"They could just be friends," I say.

"Friends?" Bonnie says.

"He went to Oberlin!" I say.

"Regardless," Faith interrupts, "hunters like competition. It tells them that what they want is worth having."

"But I would feel terrible if he went on a date with someone else," I say.

"And you're trying to set an example?" Faith says.

"It doesn't work like that!" Bonnie says.

I agree to dinner, but as soon as I hang up, I say, "This feels wrong."

"It's right," Faith says, unzipping her dress. "It's just unfamiliar."

"No," I say. "It feels wrong."

She's wearing a slinky, champagne silk slip with spaghetti straps. "Aren't you being pursued the way you always wanted to be?" Faith says.

"I was," I say.

"This'll help," Faith says decisively.

"I hope you're right," I say. "That's a pretty slip."

"You should get one!" Bonnie says.

The day after Sophie gets back from Italy, we meet for coffee at a café in the Village. Before she tells me about her honeymoon, she asks what's going on with Robert.

I tell her that I don't know. "I think maybe he's seeing someone else."

She says, "What?"

"I saw him with that statue from your wedding," I say. "Apollinaire—the goddess of NASA."

"Apple's a lesbian, okay?" she says. "Besides, he's in love with you. The question is, are you in love with him?"

I nod.

"So, why are you making him so crazy?" she says. "He's not even sure you like him."

I hesitate before breaking the vow **Don't talk to non-guide girls about the guide!** Then I tell her everything. For a second she looks at me like I'm someone she used to know. "Are you serious?"

"I know how it sounds," I say. I try to think how to explain. I borrow Donna's swimming-vs.-fishing analogy. "I realized I didn't know anything about men."

She says, "You didn't know about manipulation."

I say, "Tell me I haven't wrecked every relationship I've ever been in."

She says something about the unworthiness of my ex-boyfriends.

"I don't want to wreck it with Robert," I say.

"You won't," she says, "if you cut this shit out."

I admit that I don't think the book is all wrong.

"What's it right about?" she says.

"Well," I say. "Max made the first move, right?"

"Right," she says. "Max is a slut."

"And he pursued you," I say. "You didn't even return his calls."

"I thought he was insane," she says.

I persist. "And he said, 'I love you' first."

"On our first date," she says. "He's like you—or how you used to be—"

I say, "Well those are all vows from the book."

"Vows?" She shakes her head. "You need deprogramming."

She bums a cigarette from our waitress, and I remember to ask her why she warned me about Robert.

She hesitates. "I thought of him as a commitment-phobe. But now I'm more worried about you. You have to stop reading that book."

"I haven't read it in weeks," I say. "I internalized it—you know how susceptible I am." I remind her of the time I borrowed an ancient typing manual from the library; I kept typing a practice exercise about the importance of good grooming in job interviews. I say, "Every time I go on one I still think 'Neatly combed hair and clean fingernails give a potential employer—'"

She interrupts me. "You need an antidote." She suggests Simone de Beauvoir.

I'm reading *The Second Sex* when Faith says, "My husband was a total commitment-phobe!"

"Really?" Bonnie says.

"Lloyd didn't have a girlfriend the whole four years he was in medical school."

I say, "Maybe he was studying all of the time."

"Yeah," she says, "studying pussy."

Bonnie's nose wrinkles. "Faith!"

"The point is," Faith says, "the guide is about getting commitment-phobes to commit."

"I'm trying to read," I say.

"Did you ever read her letters to Sartre?" Faith says. "Pathetic."

I ignore her.

She says. "You'll notice that she never became Madame Sartre."

"Look," I say, "I'm not thinking about marriage any-more. I just want to be with Robert."

"You sound just like Simone," Faith says.

Friday, Robert takes me to dinner at the Time Café, a hipster restaurant, and we're seated across from a table of models.

He doesn't even seem to notice them, and against Faith's protests, I tell him with my eyes how I feel.

I can see he's surprised—he practically says, "Me?"

I say, "You."

"Me, what?" he says.

I say, "Will you make love to me after dinner?"

Bonnie says, "I can't believe you."

Faith gets the waitress and orders a double martini.

Robert moves the table and comes over to me on the sofa, and we kiss and don't stop until our salads come.

He eats his with theatrical speed. "Let's take Jezebel and go to the country tomorrow."

"Yes," I say.

Robert tells me that Apple invited us to her girlfriend's place in Lambertville, and all he has to do is call them.

Bonnie says, "You have a date tomorrow, kiddo."

I taste the vinegar in my salad.

Once our plates are cleared, I excuse myself and go to the phone.

I dial Information. I feel bad canceling on Mac, but when the operator asks, "What listing, please?" I feel even worse. I don't know where he's staying.

During dinner I try to convince myself that I could just not show up for the date. But I know I'm incapable of this.

"Robert," I say finally, closing my eyes. "I can't go away with you."

"Why?" he says.

I can't make my mouth form the words. I start to. I say, "I have . . ." and Robert says, "You have a date."

He shakes his head for a minute. Then he signals for the waitress. While he signs the credit-card slip, I blather on about how the guy is from Japan, and I would cancel but I don't know—he interrupts me with a look.

"Two stops," he says to the cabdriver.

Faith says, "Nice going."

———

In the morning, I call Robert, but his phone rings and rings. I take Jezebel to the dog run at Madison Square Park. It is the first true day of summer, but the clear sky and strong sun make New York seem gritty.

Even the sight of Jezebel prancing around doesn't cheer me up. I feel like the old whiny beagle none of the dogs will play with.

"I know how hard this is," Faith says. "But if Robert is so easily discouraged, he's not right for you anyway."

I say, "If Robert did this to me, I'd try to forget about him."

"You're putting yourself in his place," Faith says.

"But you're not Robert!" Bonnie says. "You're not a man!"

"I'm a dog," I say, "and you're trying to make me into a cat."

I wash my hair. Dry it. I put on a dress and sandals. Drop lipstick in my bag. I do it all as perfunctorily as if I were preparing for an appointment with my accountant.

Bonnie says, "Look at your nails! You could repot a geranium with what's under there."

"What is it with you people and nails?" I say irritably.

I put on my bicycle helmet.

"You're not riding your bicycle," Bonnie says. "He'll think you're a weirdo."

"I am a weirdo, Bonnie."

"Well," she says, "you don't have to wear it on your sleeve or whatever."

I see Mac before he sees me. He's tall with broad shoulders and wavy blond hair, aristocratic in a blue blazer and white shirt. His strange features—beady eyes, thin lips, and pointy chin—somehow conspire to make him attractive, though I feel none of the electricity of yesteryear.

"Jane Rosenal," he says, and as he kisses my cheek, I realize that for all of our flirting we never kissed.

He looks down at my helmet. "Bicycle?"

"Yup," I say.

"Isn't it dangerous?" he says.

I nod.

"Do you mind eating outside?" he asks.

We follow the maître d' upstairs to an exquisite roof garden with candles and flowers, flowers everywhere. It's breezy and the sky is full of billowy clouds, and for a moment I am not sorry to be here. Then I remember Robert and the cost of this dinner.

"Do you want a bottle of wine?" Mac asks.

"I think I'll have a drink-drink," I say, and when the waiter comes I order a martini. Mac says he'll have the same.

"So," he says and begins to ask the questions you'd expect. He speaks and then I do, his turn then mine; it's less like a conversation than a transatlantic call.

He says that he lives in a residence hotel for businessmen, which is convenient and luxurious; and it isn't until he adds, "Home, sweet residence hotel, I guess," that I realize he's funny, dry, and deadpan, his own straight man.

"By the way," he says, "you can call me Mac if you want to, but I go by William now."

I say, "I go by Princess Jane. If we get to know each other better, I may let you call me just Princess."

He laughs. "That's what I remember about you," he says. "You were so funny."

"See?" I say to Bonnie and Faith.

"And it only took him fifteen years to call," Faith says.

After two martinis and a bottle of wine with dinner, I realize I better order coffee if I want to walk down the steps.

During dessert, Mac asks if he can call me Princess, and I say, "Yes, William."

He tells me that he plans to come back from Asia before long; he wants to teach in Morristown, New Jersey, the horsey suburb where he grew up.

"What would you teach?" I ask.

"Anything but gym," he says. "What about you, Princess? Can you see yourself growing old in the suburbs?"

I know what he's asking, and the Faith and Bonnie in me is glad to hear it. But I say, "Only if it's a choice between the suburbs and setting myself on fire."

Outside, he suggests we go somewhere to get a drink or hear music.

"No, thank you," I say. I tell him that I have to walk my bicycle, and if I start now I'll just make it home before sunrise.

"Can I kiss you?" he asks.

I shake my head. I'm about to say that my lips are spoken for, but with a pang I realize that they are not. I say, "You can unlock me," and I hand him the key.

He unlocks my bicycle, and says, "We'll put it in a cab."

He hails one, and manages to get my bicycle into the trunk.

I get in the cab and thank him for dinner. He nods. "My pleasure."

I say, "You have a nice personality." Then I give the driver my address.

No messages on the machine. I take Jezebel out and walk her to Robert's building. I look up at the windows and try to guess which are his.

"Go home, pumpkin," Bonnie says.

I sit on the stoop. Jezebel maneuvers herself so she can lie beside me, and puts her head on my lap.

To the tune of "Why can't a woman be more like a man?" I whisper, "Why can't a man be more like a poodle?"

"You've had too much to drink," Faith says. "If you want to, you can call him in the morning."

I say, "You're just saying that so I'll go home."

In the morning, there's still no answer at Robert's.

In the afternoon, when the phone rings I run for it. "Princess?" Mac says. He tells me he had a great time.

"Same here," I say.

After we hang up, Bonnie pats my knee. "Isn't it nice just to hear the phone ring?"

I picture Robert in the country with Apollinaire and her girlfriend. "Robert, please," she's saying. "The woman's in advertising, for Christ's sake."

Maybe they've invited a date for Robert, a straight, statuesque Oscar nominee.

"You're losing it!" Bonnie says. "You're the one who had the date!"

In the evening, I call Robert again, and this time he picks up the phone.

I say, "Aren't you supposed to be stalking me?"

"I went away," he says, and his voice is flat.

I ask if he'll meet me at the outdoor café between our apartments, and he agrees.

After we hang up, I go to the mirror, and Bonnie hands me my lipstick. Faith sits on the ledge of the tub and reaches for an emery board. She files her nails, stops and looks up at me. "This is the deciding moment in the hunt," she says.

"The hunt!" I say. "This is New York—nobody hunts!"

"You don't have to get snappy," Bonnie says. "It's just an analogy."

"No more hunting or fishing," I say.

Faith says, "Just being yourself, is that it?"

"No!" Bonnie says, frowning so hard her dimples show.

"Yes," I say.

"You're going to lose him, Jane," Faith says.

"I won't."

"Yes," Faith says. "You will."

"Okay, but I'll lose him my way," I say.

"That's the spirit," Faith says.

I close my eyes. "I want you to go now."

Faith says, "We're already gone," and when I open my eyes they are. The bathroom is suddenly empty and quiet. I am on my own.

At the café Robert is sitting outside, looking at the menu.

He half rises and kisses my cheek, as though we've already broken up and are starting a friendship, which throws me.

"How are you?" I say.

"Fine," he says. "You?"

I nod.

We both order red wine. I say, "Where'd you go?"

He doesn't answer right away. "I went to New Jersey. To my parents' house," he says, sounding like he wishes he could say any place else.

"How was it?" I say.

"The usual," he says. "I watered the lawn, argued with my father, regressed, and aged."

I smile, which he doesn't seem to see.

Our wine comes, and he takes a sip and then another.

"Your mouth's purple," I say.

"Listen," he says. "This isn't going to work out."

"No?" I say.

He shakes his head and looks down at Jezebel, who lifts her head to be scratched, and he reaches down.

"Don't pet my dog," I say. "If we're breaking up, you can't touch either of us."

"We can't break up," he says. "You're going out with other people."

"Other person," I say. "From Japan," I add, as though it proves something.

"Whatever," he says.

I say, "I don't want to go out with anyone else." I feel relieved saying these words, until I see that they have no effect on him.

"It's not that," he says.

"What is it?"

He takes a deep breath. "I fell in love with someone else," he says.

"Oh," I say. "Well." I once heard someone describe jealousy as ice water coursing through your veins, but in mine it's more like vomit.

"It's not that you're not great—you are great," he says. "I just thought you were different."

"What do you mean?" I say.

He says, "At the wedding, you seemed different from . . ." he hesitates, "from who you turned out to be."

It takes me a second to realize—he means he fell in love with me! Then I realize he also means he fell out of love with me.

My voice is so low that even I can't hear it when I say, "Who did I turn out to be?" I have to repeat myself.

He shakes his head; I see that he doesn't want to hurt

me, which hurts even more. "No," I say, "really, I want to know who I turned out to be."

"Like someone from my high school," he says.

I think of Faith and Bonnie in gym.

"Or I felt like I was in high school and I was going after you," he says. "Like I had to earn you or win you or something."

"Yeah," I say.

"We were dating," he says. "I don't even know how to date."

"But I don't either," I say.

He doesn't react. He can't hear me anymore; he's decided who I am, and that I am not for him.

"I know I'm weird," he says, "but for me our relationship started when I met you at the wedding."

"Same," I say.

"You're not the same, though, Jane," he says, and his voice is careful again. "You let me know that I had to ask you out, with notice, for dates. Datey dates."

"Datey dates," I say, though he has no way of knowing this is an expression I use myself.

"It's not that you did anything wrong," he says. "I mean, you're the normal one."

I am not normal, I say to myself.

"I'm sorry," he says, and he means it.

"Who did you think I was?" I say. "At the wedding."

He shakes his head.

"Tell me," I say.

He looks at me as though I'm a good friend, and he lets himself reminisce about the person he was in love with. "You were really funny and smart and open," he says. "You were out there."

"I was out there," I say.

His voice is sad. "Yup."

"Listen," I say. He's sympathetic but I can tell he's wondering how long this will take, and I have to fight myself not to say good-bye and stand. "I got scared," I say.

He seems to hear me, but I don't know which me— maybe just the friend he hopes I will turn out to be.

"I felt the way you did at the wedding," I say. "But I'm bad at men."

He laughs for the first time in a long while.

"You get all these voices about what a woman is supposed to be like—you know, feminine." I do not want to continue. "And I've spent my whole life trying not to hear them. But..." I steel myself to go on, "I wanted to be with you so much that I listened."

He nods, slowly, and I can tell he's starting to see me, the me he thought I was and am.

Still, it takes all of my courage to say, "Show me your cartoons."

On the way to his apartment, I tell him that he can hold Jezebel's leash if he wants to, and he does.

I follow him up the steps to his building, climbing over the ghost of me from last night, up to his apartment on the top floor. Jezebel and I wait outside while he closes the cat in his bedroom. Then he leads us to his study, which has big dormer windows, all of them open, facing the backyard. He asks if I want a glass of wine, and I say yes.

One wall is covered with taped-up cartoons in black ink and watercolor.

I find the gallery of scents from my dog museum. Sea horses bobbing. I see cartoon him up there pining for cartoon me.

He hands me my wine. And I tell him that his cartoons are beautiful and funny and sad and true.

He smiles.

I ask him what else the review of his dreams says about him. He likes this question. He thinks. Then he says, "Robert Wexler is a goofball in search of truth."

I think, *I'm a truthball in search of goof,* and I realize that I can say whatever I want now. And I do.

Instead of laughing, he pulls me in. We kiss, we kiss, we kiss, in front of Jezebel and all the cartoons. There is no stopping now. Both of us are hunter and prey, fisher and fish. We are the surf'n'turf special with fries and slaw. We are just two mayflies mating on a summer night.

ᴀdam ʜaslett

NOTES TO
MY BIOGRAPHER

Two things to get straight from the beginning: I hate doctors and have never joined a support group in my life. At seventy-three, I'm not about to change. The mental-health establishment can go screw itself on a barren hilltop in the rain before I touch their snake oil or listen to the visionless chatter of men half my age. I have shot Germans in the fields of Normandy, filed twenty-six patents, married three women, survived them all, and am currently the subject of an investigation by the IRS, which has about as much chance of collecting from me as Shylock did of getting his pound of flesh. Bureaucracies have trouble thinking clearly. I, on the other hand, am perfectly lucid.

Note, for instance, the way I obtained the Saab I am presently driving into the Los Angeles basin: a niece in Scottsdale lent it to me. Do you think she'll ever see it again? Unlikely. Of course, when I borrowed it from her I had every intention of returning it, and in a few days or weeks I may feel that way again, but for now forget her and her husband and three children who looked at me over the kitchen table like I was a museum piece sent to bore them. I could run circles around those kids. They're spoon-fed Ritalin and private schools and have eyes that say, *Give me things I don't have.* I wanted to read them a book on the history of the world, its immigrations, plagues, and wars, but the shelves of their outsized condominium were full of ceramics and biographies of the stars. The whole thing depressed the hell out of me and I'm glad to be gone.

A week ago I left Baltimore with the idea of seeing my son Graham. I've been thinking about him a lot recently, days we spent together in the barn at the old house, how with him as my audience ideas came quickly, and I don't know when I'll get to see him again. I thought I might as well catch up with some of the other relatives along the way. I planned to start at my daughter Linda's in Atlanta, but when I arrived it turned out she'd moved. I called Graham, and when he got over the shock of hearing my voice, he said Linda didn't want to see me. By the time my younger brother Ernie refused to do anything more than have lunch with me after I had taken a bus all the way to Houston, I began to get the idea that this episodic reunion thing might be more trouble than it was worth. Scottsdale did nothing to alter my opinion. These people seem to think they'll have another chance, that I'll be coming around again. The fact is I've completed my will, made bequests of my patent rights, and am now just composing a few notes to my biographer, who, in a few decades, when the true influence of my work becomes apparent, may need them to clarify certain issues.

—Franklin Caldwell Singer, b. 1924, Baltimore, Maryland.
—Child of a German machinist and a banker's daughter.

—My psych discharge following "desertion" in Paris
was trumped up by an army intern resentful of my
superior knowledge of the diagnostic manual. The
nude-dancing incident at the Louvre in a room full
of Rubenses had occurred weeks earlier and was of
a piece with other celebrations at the time.

—B.A., Ph.D., Engineering, The Johns Hopkins University.

—1952. First and last electroshock treatment, for
which I will never, never, never forgive my parents.

—1954–1965. Researcher, Eastman Kodak Laborato-
ries. As with so many institutions in this country,
talent was resented. I was fired as soon as I began to
point out flaws in the management structure. Two
years later I filed a patent on a shutter mechanism
that Kodak eventually broke down and purchased
(then–Vice President for Product Development Arch
Vendellini *was* having an affair with his daughter's
best friend, contrary to what he will tell you. Notice
the way his left shoulder twitches when he is lying).

—All subsequent diagnoses—and let me tell you, there
have been a number—are the result of two forces,
both in their way pernicious. 1) The attempt by the
psychiatric establishment over the last century to
redefine eccentricity as illness, and 2) the desire
of members of my various families to render me
docile and if possible immobile.

—The electric-bread-slicer concept was stolen from
me by a man in a diner in Chevy Chase dressed as
a reindeer whom I could not possibly have known
was an employee of Westinghouse.

—That I have no memories of the years 1988–90 and
believed until very recently that Ed Meese was still

the attorney general is not owing to my purported paranoid blackout but, on the contrary, to the fact that my third wife took it upon herself to lace my coffee with tranquilizers. Believe nothing you hear about the divorce settlement.

When I ring the buzzer at Graham's place in Venice, a Jew in his late twenties with some fancy-looking musculature answers the door. He appears nervous and says, "We weren't expecting you till tomorrow," and I ask him who *they* are and he says, "Me and Graham," adding hurriedly, "We're friends, you know, only friends. I don't live here, I'm just over to use the computer."

All I can think is I hope this guy isn't out here trying to get acting jobs, because it's obvious to me right away that my son is gay and is screwing this character with the expensive-looking glasses. There was a lot of that in the military and I learned early on that it comes in all shapes and sizes, not just the fairy types everyone expects. Nonetheless, I am briefly shocked by the idea that my twenty-nine-year-old boy has never seen fit to share with me the fact that he is a fruitcake—no malice intended—and I resolve right away to talk to him about it when I see him. Marlon Brando overcomes his stupor and lifting my suitcase from the car he leads me through the back garden past a lemon tree in bloom to a one-room cottage with a sink and plenty of light to which I take an instant liking.

"This will do nicely," I say, and then I ask him, "How long have you been sleeping with my son?" It's obvious he thinks I'm some brand of geriatric homophobe getting ready to come on in a religiously heavy manner, and seeing that deer-caught-in-the-headlights look in his eye I take pity and disabuse him. I've seen women run down by tanks. I'm not about to get worked up about the prospect of fewer grand-children. When I start explaining to him that social prejudice of all stripes runs counter to my Enlightenment ideals— ideals tainted by centuries of partial application—it becomes clear to me that Graham has given him the family line. His face grows patient and his smile begins to leak the sympathy of the ignorant: poor old guy suffering from mental troubles his whole life, up one month, down the next, spewing gran-diose notions that slip like sand through his fingers to which I always say, you just look up Frank Singer at the U.S. Patent Office. In any case, this turkey probably thinks the Enlight-enment is a marketing scheme for General Electric; I spare him the seminar I could easily conduct and say, "Look, if the two of you share a bed, it's fine with me."

"That drive must have worn you out," he says hopefully. "Do you want to lie down for a bit?"

I tell him I could hook a chain to my niece's Saab and drag it through a marathon. This leaves him nonplussed. We walk back across the yard together into the kitchen of the bungalow. I ask him for pen, paper, and calculator and begin sketching an idea that came to me just a moment ago— I can feel the presence of Graham already—for a bicycle capable of storing the energy generated on the downward slope in a small battery and releasing it through a handlebar control when needed on the uphill, a potential gold mine when you consider the aging population and the increase in leisure time created by early retirement. I have four pages of specs and the estimated cost of a prototype done by the time Graham arrives two hours later. He walks into the kitchen wearing a blue linen suit with a briefcase held to his chest and seeing me at the table goes stiff as a board. I haven't seen him in five years and the first thing I notice is that he's got bags under his eyes and he looks exhausted. When I open my arms to embrace him he takes a step backward.

"What's the matter?" I ask. Here is my child wary of me in a strange kitchen in California, his mother's ashes spread long ago over the Potomac, the objects of our lives together stored in boxes or sold.

"You actually came," he says.

"I've invented a new bicycle," I say, but this seems to reach him like news of some fresh death. Ben hugs Graham there in front of me. I watch my son rest his head against this fellow's shoulder like a tired soldier on a train. "It's going to have a self-charging battery," I say, sitting again at the table to review my sketches.

With Graham here my idea is picking up speed, and while he's in the shower I unpack my bags, rearrange the furniture in the cottage, and tack my specs to the wall. Returning to the house, I ask Ben if I can use the phone and he says that's fine, and then he tells me, "Graham hasn't been sleeping so great lately, but I know he really does want to see you."

"Sure, no hard feelings, fine."

"He's been dealing with a lot recently... maybe some things you could talk to him about... and I think you might—"

"Sure, sure, no hard feelings," and then I call my lawyer, my engineer, my model builder, three advertising firms whose numbers I find in the yellow pages, the American Association of Retired Persons—that market will be key—an old college friend who I remember once told me he'd competed in the Tour de France, figuring he'll know the bicycle-industry angle, my bank manager to discuss financing, the

Patent Office, the Cal Tech physics lab, the woman I took to dinner the week before I left Baltimore, and three local liquor stores before I find one that will deliver a case of Dom Pérignon.

"That'll be for me! " I call out to Graham as he emerges from the bedroom to answer the door what seems only minutes later. He moves slowly and seems sapped of life.

"What's this?"

"We're celebrating! There's a new project in the pipeline!"

Graham stares at the bill as though he's having trouble reading it. Finally, he says, "This is twelve hundred dollars. We're not buying it."

I tell him Schwinn will drop that on donuts for the sales reps when I'm done with this bike, that Oprah Winfrey's going to ride it through the halftime show at the Super Bowl.

"My dad made a mistake," he says to the delivery guy.

I end up having to go outside and pay for it through the window of the truck with a credit card the man is naïve enough to accept and I carry it back to the house myself.

"What am I going to do?" I hear Graham whisper.

I round the corner into the kitchen and they fall silent. The two of them make a handsome couple standing there in the gauzy, expiring light of evening. When I was born you could have arrested them for kissing. There ensues an argument that I only half bother to participate in concerning the champagne and my enthusiasm, a recording he learned from his mother; he presses play and the fraction of his ancestry that suffered from conventionalism speaks through his mouth like a ventriloquist: your-idea-is-fantasy-calm-down-it-will-be-the-ruin-of-you-medication-medication-medication. He has a good mind, my son, always has, and somewhere the temerity to use it, to spear mediocrity in the eye, but in a world that encourages nothing of the sort the curious boy becomes the anxious man. He must suffer his people's regard for appearances. Sad. I begin to articulate this with Socratic lucidity, which seems only to exacerbate the situation.

"Why don't we just have some champagne," Ben interjects. "You two can talk this over at dinner. "

An admirable suggestion. I take three glasses from the cupboard, remove a bottle from the case, pop the cork, fill the glasses, and propose a toast to their health.

My niece's Saab does eighty-five without a shudder on the way to dinner. With the roof down, smog blowing through my hair, I barely hear Graham, who's shouting something from the passenger's seat. He's probably worried about a ticket, which for the high of this ride I'd pay twice over and tip the officer to boot. Sailing down the freeway I envision a lane of bicycles quietly recycling power once lost to the simple act of pedaling. We'll have to get the environmentalists involved, which could mean government money for research and a lobbying arm to navigate any legislative interference. Test marketing in L.A. will increase the chance of celebrity endorsements, and I'll probably need to do a book on the germination of the idea for release with the first wave of product. I'm thinking early 2001. The advertising tag line hits me as we glide beneath an overpass: *Making Every Revolution Count.*

There's a line at the restaurant and when I try to slip the maître d' a twenty, Graham holds me back.

"Dad," he says, "you can't do that."

"Remember the time I took you to the Ritz in that Rolls-Royce with the right-hand drive and you told me the chicken in your sandwich was tough and I spoke to the manager and we got the meal for free? And you drew a diagram of the tree fort you wanted and it gave me an idea for storage containers. "

He nods his head.

"Come on, where's your smile?"

I walk up to the maître d', but when I hand him the twenty he gives me a funny look and I tell him he's a lousy shit for pretending he's above that sort of thing. "You want a hundred?" I ask, and am about to give him an even larger piece of my mind when Graham turns me around and says, "Please don't."

"What kind of work are you doing?" I ask him.

"Dad," he says, "just settle down." His voice is so quiet, so meek.

"I asked you what kind of work you do."

"I work at a brokerage."

A brokerage! What didn't I teach this kid? "What do you do for them?"

"Stocks. Listen, Dad, we need—"

"Stocks!" I say. "Christ! Your mother would turn in her grave if she had one."

"Thanks," he says under his breath.

"What was that?" I ask.

"Forget it."

At this point, I notice everyone in the foyer is staring at us. They all look like they were in television fifteen years ago, the men wearing Robert Wagner turtlenecks and blazers. A woman in mauve hot pants with a shoulder bag the size of her torso appears particularly disapproving and self-satisfied, and I feel like asking her what it is she does to better the lot of humanity. "You'll be riding my bicycle in three years," I tell her. She draws back as though I had thrown a rat on the carpet.

Once we're seated it takes ten minutes to get bread and

water on the table, and sensing a bout of poor service, I
begin to jot on a napkin the time of each of our requests and
the hour of its arrival. Also, as it occurs to me:

—Hollow-core chrome frame with battery mounted
  over rear tire wired to rear-wheel engine housing
  wired to handlebar control/thumb-activated accelerator; warning to cyclist concerning increased
  speed of crankshaft during application of stored
  revolutions. Power break?
—Biographer file: Graham as my muse, mystery
  thereof, see storage container, pancake press, flying
  teddy bear, renovations of barn for him to play in,
  power bike.

Graham disagrees with me when I try to send back a
second bottle of wine, apparently under the impression that
one ought to accept spoiled goods in order not to hurt anybody's feelings. This strikes me as maudlin, but I let it go for
the sake of harmony. Something has changed in him. Appe-
tizers take a startling nineteen minutes to appear.

"You should start thinking about quitting your job," I
say. "I've decided I'm not going to stay on the sidelines with
this one. The power bike's a flagship product, the kind of
thing that could support a whole company. We stand to
make a fortune, Graham, and I can do it with you." One of
the Robert Wagners cranes his neck to look at me from a
neighboring booth.

"Yeah, I bet you want a piece of the action, buddy," I say,
which sends him back to his endive salad in a hurry. Graham listens as I elaborate the business plan: there's start-up
financing for which we'll easily attract venture capital, the
choice of location for the manufacturing plant—you have to

be careful about state regulations—executives to hire, designers to work under me, a sales team, accountants, benefits, desks, telephones, workshops, paychecks, taxes, computers, copiers, decor, water coolers, doormats, parking spaces, electric bills. Maybe a humidifier. A lot to consider. As I speak, I notice that others in the restaurant are turning to listen as well. It's usually out of the corner of my eye that I see it and the people disguise it well, returning to their conversations in what they probably think is convincing pantomime. The Westinghouse reindeer pops to mind. How ingenious they were to plant him there in the diner I ate at each Friday morning, knowing my affection for the Christmas myth, determined to steal my intellectual property.

—Re: Chevy Chase incident, look also into whether or not I might have invented auto-reverse tape decks and also therefore did Sony or GE own property adjacent to my Baltimore residence—noise, distraction tactics, phony road construction, etc.—and also Schwinn, Raleigh, etc., presence during Los Angeles visit.

"Could we talk about something else?" Graham asks.

"Whatever you like," I say, and I inform the waiter our entrées were twenty-six minutes in transit. Turns out my fish is tougher than leather, and the waiter's barely left when I have to begin snapping my fingers for his return.

"Stop that!" Graham says. I've reached the end of my tether with his passivity and freely ignore him. He's leaning over the table about to swat my arm down when the fellow returns.

"Is there a problem?"

"My halibut's dry as sand."

The goateed young man eyes my dish suspiciously, as though I might have replaced the original plate with some duplicate entrée pulled from a bag beneath the table.

"I'll need a new one."

"No he won't," Graham says at once.

The waiter pauses, considering on whose authority to proceed.

"Do you have anything to do with bicycles?" I ask him.

"What do you mean?" he asks.

"Professionally."

The young man looks across the room to the maître d', who offers a coded nod.

"That's it. We're getting out of here," I say, grabbing bread rolls.

"Sit down," Graham insists.

But it's too late; I know the restaurant's lousy with mountain-bike executives. "You think I'm going to let a bunch of industry hustlers steal an idea that's going to change the way every American and one day every person on the globe conceives of a bicycle? Do you realize what bicycles mean to people? They're like ice cream or children's books, they're primal objects woven into the fabric of our earliest memories, not to mention our most intimate connection with the wheel itself, an invention that marks the commencement of the great ascent of human knowledge that brought us through printing presses, religious transformations, undreamt-of speed, the moon. When you ride a bicycle you participate in an unbroken chain of human endeavor stretching back to stone-carting Egyptian peasants, and I'm on the verge of revolutionizing that invention, making its almost mythical power a storable quantity. You have the chance to be there with me, 'like stout Cortéz when with

eagle eyes he stared at the Pacific—and all his men looked
at each other with a wild surmise—silent, upon a peak in
Darien.' The things we'll see!"

Because I'm standing as I say this a quorum of the
restaurant seems to think I'm addressing them as well, and
though I've slipped in giving them a research lead I can see
in their awed expressions that they know as I do, not everyone can scale the high white peaks of real invention. Some—
such as these—must sojourn in the lowlands where the air
is thick with half measures and dreams die of inertia. Yes! It
is true.

"You'll never catch up with me," I say to the gawking industrial spies.

This seems to convince Graham we indeed need to
leave. He throws some cash on the table and steers me by
the arm out of the restaurant. We walk slowly along the
boulevard. There's something sluggish about Graham, his
rounded shoulders and bowed head.

"Look, there's a Japanese place right over there, we can
get maki rolls and teriyaki, maybe some blowfish, I can hear
all about the brokerage, we might even think about whether
your company wants to do the initial public offering on the
bike venture, there could be an advantage—"

He shakes his head and keeps walking up the street, one
of whose features is a truly remarkable plenitude of shapely
women, and I am reminded of the pleasures of being single,
glances and smiles being enjoyed without guilt and for that
matter why not consummation? Maybe it's unseemly for a
seventy-three-year-old to talk about erections, but oh, do I
get 'em! I'm thinking along these lines when we pass what
appears to be the lobby of a luxury hotel convention-center
kind of place, and of course I'm also thinking trade shows

and how far ahead you have to book those things so I turn in and, after a small protest, Graham follows (I tell him I need to use the bathroom).

"I'd like to talk to the special-events manager," I say to the girl behind the desk.

"I'm afraid he's only here during the day, sir," she replies with a blistering customer-service smile, as though she were telling me exactly what I wanted to hear.

"Well, isn't that just wonderful," I say, and she seems to agree that yes, it is wonderful, wonderful that the special-events manager of the Royal Sonesta keeps such regular hours, as though it were the confirmation of some beneficent natural order.

"I guess I'll just have to take a suite anyway and see him in the morning. My son and I will have a little room-service dinner in privacy, where the sharks don't circle!"

Concern clouds the girl's face as she taps her keyboard.

"The Hoover Suite is available on nineteen. That's $680 a night. Will that be all right?"

"Perfect."

When I've secured the keys I cross to where Graham's sitting on the couch. "Dinner is served," I say with a bow.

"What are you talking about?"

"I got us a suite," I say, rattling the keys.

Graham rolls his eyes and clenches his fists.

"Dad!"

There's something desperate in his voice.

"What!"

"Stop! Just stop! You're out of control," he says. He looks positively frantic. "Why do you think Linda and Ernie don't want to see you, Dad, why do you think that is? Is it so surprising to you? They can't handle this! Mom couldn't handle this! Can't you see that? It's *selfish* of you not to see a doctor!" he shouts, pounding his fists on his thighs. "It's *selfish* of you not to take the drugs! *Selfish!*"

The lobby's glare has drained his face of color and about his unblinking eyes I can see the outlines of what will one day be the marks of age, and then all of a sudden the corpse of my son lies prostrate in front of me, the years since we last saw one another tunneling out before me for some infinite distance, and I hear the whisper of a killing loneliness travel along its passage as though the sum total of every minute of his pain in every spare hour of every year was drawn in a single breath and held in this expiring moment. Tears well in my eyes. I am overcome.

Graham stands up from the couch, shaken by the force of his own words.

I rattle the keys. "We're going to enjoy ourselves."

"You have to give those back to the desk."

By the shoulders I grab him, my greatest invention. "We can do so much better," I say. I take him by the wrist and lead him to the elevator, hearing his mother's voice behind us reminding me to keep him out of the rain. "I will," I mutter. "I will."

Robert Wagner is on the elevator with Natalie Wood but they've aged badly and one doesn't take to them anymore. She chews gum and appears uncomfortable in tight clothing. His turtlenecks have become worn. But I figure they know things, they've been here a long time. So I say to him, "Excuse me, you wouldn't know where I might call for a girl or two, would you? Actually what we need is a girl and a young man, my son here's gay."

"Dad!" Graham shouts. "I'm sorry," he says to the couple, now backed against the wall as though I were a gangster in one of their lousy B movies. "He's just had a lot to drink."

"The hell I have. You got a problem with my son being

gay?" The elevator door opens and they scurry onto the carpet like bugs.

For a man who watched thousands starve and did jack shit about it, the Hoover Suite is aptly named. There are baskets of fruit, a stocked refrigerator, a full bar, faux rococo paintings over the beds, overstuffed chairs, and rugs that demand bare feet for the sheer pleasure of the touch.

"We can't stay here," Graham says, as I flip my shoes across the room.

His voice is disconsolate; he seems to have lost his animation of a moment ago, something I don't think I can afford to do right now: the eviction notices in Baltimore, the collection agencies, the smell of the apartment... "We're just getting started," I say quickly.

Graham's sitting in an armchair across the room, and when he bows his head, I imagine he's praying that when he raises it again, things will be different. As a child he used to bring me presents in my study on the days I left for trips and he'd ask me not to go; they were books he'd found on the shelf and wrapped in Christmas paper.

I pick up the phone on the bedside table and get the front desk. "This is the Hoover Suite calling. I want the number of an agency that will provide us with a young man, someone intelligent and attractive—"

Graham rips the phone from my hand.

"What is it?" I say. His mother was always encouraging me to ask him questions. "What's it like to be gay, Graham? Why have you never told me?"

He stares at me dumbfounded.

"What? What?" I say.

"How can you ask me that after all this time?"

"I want to understand. Are you in love with this Ben fellow?"

"I thought you were dead! Do you even begin to realize? I thought my own father was dead. You didn't call for four years. But I couldn't bear to find out, I couldn't bear to go and find you dead. It was like I was a child again. I just hoped there was an excuse. Four years, Dad. Now you just appear and you want to know what it's like to be gay?"

I run to the refrigerator, where among other things there is a decent chardonnay, and with the help of a corkscrew I find by the sink I pour us two glasses. Graham doesn't seem to want his, but I set it down beside him anyway.

"Oh, Graham. The phone company in Baltimore's awful."

He starts to cry. He looks so young as he weeps, as he did in the driveway of the old house on the afternoon I taught him to ride a bicycle, the dust from the drive settling on his wetted cheek and damp eyelashes, later to be rinsed in the warm water of the bath as dusk settled over the field and we listened together to the sound of his mother in the kitchen running water, the murmur of the radio, and the stillness of evening in the country, how he seemed to understand it as well as I.

"You know, Graham, they're constantly overcharging me and then once they take a line out it's like getting the Red Sea to part to have it reinstalled but in a couple of weeks when the bicycle patent comes through that'll be behind us, you and Linda and Ernie and I, we'll all go to London and stay at the Connaught and I'll show you Regent's Park where your mother and I rowed a boat on our honeymoon circling the little island there where the ducks all congregate and which was actually a little dirty, come to think of it, though you don't really think of ducks as dirty, they look so graceful on the water but in fact—" And all of a sudden I don't believe it myself and I can hear my own voice in the room, hear its dry pitch, and I've lost my train of thought and I can't stop picturing the yard where Graham used to play with his friends by the purple lilac and the apple tree whose knotted branches held the planks of the fort that I was so happy for him to enjoy never having had one myself. He knew me then even in my bravest moments when his mother and siblings were afraid of what they didn't understand, he would sit on the stool in the crumbling barn watching me cover the chalkboard propped on the fender of the broken Studebaker, diagramming a world of possible objects, the solar vehicles and collapsible homes, our era distilled into its necessary devices, and in the evenings sprawled on the floor of his room he'd trace with delicate hands what he remembered of my design.

I see those same hands now spread on his thighs, nails bitten down, cuticles torn.

I don't know how to say goodbye.

In the village of St. Sever an old woman nursed my dying friend through the night. At dawn I kissed his cold forehead and kept marching.

In the yard of the old house the apple tree still rustles in the evening breeze.

"Graham."

"You want to know what it's like?" he says. "I'll tell you. It's worrying all the time that one day he's going to leave me. And you want to know why that is? It's got nothing to do with being gay. It's because I know Mom left *you*. I tell you it's selfish not to take the pills because I know. Because I take them. You understand, Dad? It's in me too. I don't want Ben to find me in a parking lot in the middle of the night in my pajamas talking to a stranger like Mom found you. I don't want him to find me hanged. I used to cast fire from the tips of my fingers some weeks and burn everything in my path and it was all progress and it was all incredibly, incredibly beautiful. And some weeks I couldn't brush my hair. But I take the pills now, and I haven't bankrupted us yet, and I don't want to kill myself just now. I take them and I think of Ben. That's what it's like."

"But the fire, Graham? What about the fire?"

In his eyes, there is sadness enough to kill us both.

"Do you remember how you used to watch me do my sketches in the barn?"

Tears run down his cheeks and he nods his head.

"Let me show you something," I say. Across the room in the drawer of the desk I find a marker. It makes sense to me now, he can see what I see, he's always been able to. Maybe it doesn't have to end. I unhook a painting from the wall and set it on the floor. On the yellow wallpaper I draw the outline of a door, full-size, seven by three and a half.

"You see, Graham, there'll be four knobs. The lines between them will form a cross. And each knob will be connected to a set of wheels inside the door itself, and there will be four sets of hinges, one along each side but fixed only to the door, not to the frame." I shade these in. Graham cries. "A person will use the knob that will allow them to open the door in the direction they want—left or right, at their feet or above their heads. When a knob is turned it'll push the screws from the door into the frame. People can open doors near windows without blocking morning or evening light, they'll carry furniture in and out with the door over their heads, never scraping its paint, and when they want to see the sky they can open it just a fraction at the top." On the wall I draw smaller diagrams of the door's different positions until the felt nib of the pen tatters. "It's a present to you, this door. I'm sorry it's not actual. You can imagine it,

though, how people might enjoy deciding how to walk
through it. Patterns would form, families would have their
habits."

"I wanted a father."

"Don't say that, Graham." He's crying still and I can't
bear it.

"It's true."

I turn back to the desk and, kneeling there, scrawl a
note. The pen is nearly ruined and it's hard to shape the letters. The writing takes time.

> —Though some may accuse me of neglect, I have been
> consistent with the advice I always gave my chil-
> dren: never finish anything that bores you. Unfor-
> tunately, some of my children bored me. Graham
> never did. Please confirm this with him. He is the
> only one that meant anything to me.

"Graham," I say, crossing the room to show him the
piece of paper, to show him the truth.

He's lying on the bed, and as I stand over him I see that
he's asleep. His tears have exhausted him. The skin about his
closed eyes is puffy and red and from the corner of his
mouth comes a rivulet of drool. I wipe it away with my
thumb. I cup his gentle face in my hands and kiss him on
the forehead.

From the other bed I take a blanket and cover him,
pulling it up over his shoulders, tucking it beneath his chin.
His breath is calm now, even. I leave the note folded by his
hands. I pat down his hair and turn off the lamp. It's time
for me to go.

I take my glass and the wine out into the hall. I can feel
the weight of every step, my body beginning to tire. I lean

against the wall, waiting for the elevator to take me down. The doors slide open and I enter.

From here in the descending glass cage I can see globes of orange light stretching along the boulevards of Santa Monica toward the beach where the shaded palms sway. I've always found the profusion of lights in American cities a cause for optimism, a sign of undiminished credulity, something to bear us along. In the distance the shimmering pier juts into the vast darkness of the ocean like a burning ship launched into the night.

nicola **Barker**

INSIDE INFORMATION

Martha's social worker was under the impression that by getting herself pregnant, Martha was looking for an out from a life of crime.

She couldn't have been more wrong.

"First thing I ever nicked," Martha bragged, when her social worker was initially assigned to her, "very first thing I ever stole was a packet of Li-lets. I told the store detective I took them as a kind of protest. You pay 17½ VAT on every single box. Men don't pay it on razors, you know, which is absolutely bloody typical."

"But you stole other things, too, on that occasion, Martha."

"Fags and a bottle of Scotch. So what?" she grinned. "Pay VAT on those too, don't you?"

Martha's embryo was unhappy about its assignment to Martha. Early on, just after conception, it appealed to the higher body responsible for its selection and placement. This caused something of a scandal in the Afterlife. The World Soul was consulted—a democratic body of pinpricks of light, an enormous institution—which came, unusually enough, to a rapid decision.

"Tell the embryo," they said, "hard cheese."

The embryo's social worker relayed this information through a system of vibrations—a language which embryos alone in the Living World can produce and receive. Martha felt these conversations only as tiny spasms and contractions.

Being pregnant was good, Martha decided, because store detectives were much more sympathetic when she got caught.

Increasingly, they let her off with a caution after she blamed her bad behavior on dodgy hormones.

The embryo's social worker reasoned with the embryo that all memories of the Afterlife and feelings of uncertainty about placement were customarily eradicated during the trauma of birth. This was a useful expedient. "Naturally," he added, "the nine-month wait is always difficult, especially if you've drawn the short straw in allocation terms, but at least by the time you've battled your way through the cervix, you won't remember a thing."

The embryo replied, snappily, that it had never believed in the maxim that Ignorance Is Bliss. But the social worker (a corgi in its previous incarnation) restated that the World Soul's decision was final.

As a consequence, the embryo decided to take things into its own hands. It would communicate with Martha while it still had the chance and offer her, if not an incentive, at the very least a moral imperative.

Martha grew larger during a short stint in Wormwood Scrubs. She was seven months gone on her day of release. The embryo was now a well-formed fetus, and, if its penis was any indication, it was a boy. He calculated that he had, all things being well, eight weeks to change the course of Martha's life.

You see, the fetus was special. He had an advantage over other, similarly situated, disadvantaged fetuses. This fetus had Inside Information.

In the Afterlife, after his sixth or seventh incarnation, the fetus had worked for a short spate as a troubleshooter for a large pharmaceutical company. During the course of his work and research, he had stumbled across something so enormous, something so terrible about the World Soul, that he'd been compelled to keep this information to himself, for fear of retribution.

The rapidity of his assignment as Martha's future baby was, in part, he was convinced, an indication that the World Soul was aware of his discoveries. His soul had been snatched and implanted in Martha's belly before he'd even had a chance to discuss the matter rationally. In the womb, however, the fetus had plenty of time to analyze his predicament. It was a cover-up! He was being gagged, brainwashed, and railroaded into another life sentence on earth.

In prison, Martha had been put on a sensible diet and was unable to partake of the fags and the sherry and the Jaffa cakes which were her normal dietary staples. The fetus took this opportunity to consume as many vital calories and nutrients as possible. He grew at a considerable rate, exercised his knees, his feet, his elbows, ballooned out Martha's belly with nudges and pokes.

In his seventh month, on their return home, the fetus put his plan into action. He angled himself in Martha's womb, at just the right angle, and with his foot, gave the area behind Martha's belly button a hefty kick. On the outside, Martha's belly was already a considerable size. Her stomach was about as round as it could be, and her navel, which usually stuck inward, had popped outward, like a nipple.

By kicking the inside of her navel at just the correct angle, the fetus—using his Inside Information—had successfully popped open the lid of Martha's belly button like it was an old-fashioned pillbox.

Martha noticed that her belly button was ajar while she was taking a shower. She opened its lid and peered inside. She couldn't have been more surprised. Under her belly button was a small, neat zipper, constructed out of delicate bones. She turned off the shower, grabbed hold of the zipper, and pulled it. It unzipped vertically, from the top of her belly to the middle. Inside, she saw her fetus, floating in brine. "Hello," the fetus said. "Could I have a quick word with you, please?"

"This is incredible!" Martha exclaimed, closing the zipper and opening it again. The fetus put out a restraining hand. "If you'd just hang on a minute I could tell you how this was possible."

"It's so weird," Martha said, closing the zipper and getting dressed.

Martha went to Tesco's. She picked up the first three items that came to hand, unzipped her stomach, and popped them inside. On her way out, she set off the alarms—the bar codes activated them, even from deep inside her—but when she was searched and scrutinized and interrogated, no evidence could be found of her hidden booty. Martha told the security staff that she'd consider legal action if they continued to harass her in this way.

When she got home, Martha unpacked her womb. The fetus, squashed into a corner, squeezed up against a tin of Spam and a packet of sponge fingers, was intensely irritated by what he took to be Martha's unreasonable behavior.

"You're not the only one who has a zip, you know," he

said. "All pregnant women have them; it's only a question of finding out how to use them, from the outside, gaining the knowledge. But the World Soul has kept this information hidden since the days of Genesis, when it took Adam's rib and reworked it into a zip with a pen knife."

"Shut it," Martha said. "I don't want to hear another peep from you until you're born."

"But I'm trusting you," the fetus yelled, "with this information. It's my salvation!"

She zipped up.

Martha went shopping again. She shopped sloppily at first, indiscriminately, in newsagents, clothes shops, hardware stores, chemists. She picked up what she could and concealed it in her belly.

The fetus grew disillusioned. He reopened negotiations with his social worker. "Look," he said, "I know something about the World Soul which I'm willing to divulge to my Earth Parent Martha if you don't abort me straight away."

"You're too big now," the social worker said, fingering his letter of acceptance to the Rotary Club which preambled World Soul membership. "And anyway, it strikes me that Martha isn't much interested in what you have to say."

"Do you honestly believe," the fetus asked, "that any woman on earth in her right mind would consider a natural birth if she knew that she could simply unzip?"

The social worker replied coldly, "Women are not kangaroos, you cheeky little fetus. If the World Soul has chosen to keep the zipper quiet then it will have had the best of reasons for doing so."

"But if babies were unzipped and taken out when they're ready," the fetus continued, "then there would be no trauma, no memory loss. Fear of death would be a thing of the past. We could eradicate the misconception of a Vengeful God."

"And all the world would go to hell," the social worker said.

"How can you say that?"

The fetus waited for a reply, but none came.

Martha eventually sorted out her priorities. She shopped in Harrods and Selfridges and Liberty's. She became adept at slotting things of all conceivable shapes and sizes into her belly. Unfortunately, the fetus himself was growing quite large. After being unable to fit in a spice rack, Martha un-zipped and addressed him directly. "Is there any possibility," she asked, "that I might be able to take you out prematurely so that there'd be more room in there?"

The fetus stared back smugly. "I'll come out," he said firmly, "when I'm good and ready."

Before she could zip up, he added, "And when I do come out, I'm going to give you the longest and most painful labor in Real-Life history. I'm going to come out sideways, doing the cancan."

Martha's hand paused, momentarily, above the zipper. "Promise to come out very quickly," she said, "and I'll nick you some baby clothes."

The fetus snorted in a derisory fashion. "Revolutionar-ies," he said, "don't wear baby clothes. Steal me a gun, though, and I'll fire it through your spleen."

Martha zipped up quickly, shocked at this vindictive little bundle of vituperation she was unfortunate enough to be carrying. She smoked an entire pack of Marlboros in one sitting, and smirked when she unzipped just slightly at the coughing which emerged.

The fetus decided that he had no option but to rely on his own natural wit and guile to foil both his mother and the forces of the Afterlife. He began to secrete various items that

Martha stole in private little nooks and crannies about her anatomy.

On the last night of the thirty-sixth week, he put his plan into action. In his arsenal: an indelible pen, a potato, a large piece of cotton from the hem of a dress, a thin piece of wire from the supports of a bra, all craftily reassembled. In the dead of night, while Martha was snoring, he gradually worked the zipper open from the inside and did what he had to do.

The following morning, blissfully unaware of the previous night's activities, Martha went out shopping to Marks and Spencer's. She picked up some Belgian chocolates and a bottle of port, took hold of her zipper, and tried to open her belly. It wouldn't open. The zipper seemed smaller and more difficult to hold.

"That bastard," she muttered, "must be jamming it up from the inside." She put down her booty and headed for the exit. On her way out of the shop, she set off the alarms.

"For Chrissakes!" she told the detective, "I've got nothing on me!" And for once, she meant it.

Back home, Martha attacked her belly with a pair of nail scissors. But the zipper wasn't merely jammed, it was meshing and merging and disappearing, fading like the tail end of a bruise. She was frazzled. She looked around for her cigarettes. She found her pack and opened it. The last couple were gone, and instead, inside was a note:

Martha, I have made good my escape, fully intact. I sewed a pillow into your belly. On the wall of your womb I've etched and inked an indelible barcode. Thanks for the fags.

Love,
Baby

"But you can't do that!" Martha yelled. "You don't have the technology!" She thought she heard a chuckle, behind her. She spun around. On the floor, under the table, she saw a small lump of afterbirth, tied up into a neat parcel by an umbilical cord. She could smell a whiff of cigarette smoke. She thought she heard laughter, outside the door, down the hall. She listened intently, but heard nothing more.

GEORGE MAKANA **clark**

THE LEOPARD GANG

I was kissing Madota behind a pile of sandbags when the war of liberation came to Manicaland, working my hand beneath the blouse of her school uniform, touching the cotton of her brassiere for the first time. The war didn't arrive in jeeps, their fenders, bonnets, and running boards covered with rebels come to drag us out of our beds and shoot us on the lawns of our homes in the harsh light of our own security lamps. That story happens later. War came to us instead with the growl of a dog, and a cry of pain and fear that made Madota sit up and button her blouse.

I clambered over the sandbags to witness a grim tug-of-war. A guerrilla soldier clung stubbornly to our clothesline pole, his foot trapped in the maw of my father's security dog, a Ridgeback. The dog dragged the rebel earthward by degrees. Because the Rhodesian Security Forces tracked the terrs by the figure-of-eight patterns on their soles, the intruder was barefoot, his combat boots strung over his shoulder. The links of the dog's choke collar rattled with each shake of its head as it separated flesh from anklebone. A poet might have seen in the man a sort of backward Christ, his face pressed against the pole, arms wrapped around the crossbar, but there's no poetry in a fifteen-year-old boy determined to lose his virginity, and I saw only an old man screaming.

Behind me, Madota tucked her blouse into her waistband. I'd spent the better part of an hour opening the garment one-handed, my thumb and forefinger working the mother-of-pearl through starched buttonholes as my other hand stroked the pleats of her plaid skirt. In opening her shirt, I had exposed a swell of brown flesh against the bleached whiteness of her secret undergarment. Two silver rings hung from a thin metal chain around her neck. We both understood that a new line had been drawn between us, that the next time I coaxed her to the sandbags, this open blouse would be my entrenched position. My assault on Madota's maidenhead was glacierlike, unrelenting and slow and inevitable. I meant to become a man, there with Madota in the dirt behind the sandbags, before my sixteenth birthday.

"Leave off," I said, pulling at the choke collar, but the dog refused to release the rebel soldier. My father had bought the Ridgeback from a trainer in Umtali, a red-faced Afrikaner who beat his animals with his fists, then turned them loose on a dummy whose head and hands were painted dark. No one felt comfortable petting the nameless dog, and Madota would only come onto our property if I escorted her.

It was the dog that had prevented the Shona lorry driver and his turnboy from delivering the sandbags to our door a week earlier. Instead they stood in the bed of their lorry and tossed sandbags and nervous glances at the Ridgeback as it paced the edge of our property line with a show of hackles and teeth and black gums. Afterward, I wheedled and coaxed Madota behind the bags heaped on the shoulder of the road, and there, for the first time, I kissed the face and neck of my childhood friend and worried at her school uniform, a haze of dust floating in the late afternoon sun, her brown fingers against my freckled wrist, caressing, restraining.

"Give it up!" I commanded, but the trainer had never bothered to teach his animals to release the painted dummy, and the Ridgeback held fast to the guerrilla's foot. I stepped back and pointed to my feet. "Sit!" I said, and the Ridgeback let go of the terr and obediently sat before me, fixing its flat stare on my throat.

The terr climbed from the pole, his weight on his un-damaged foot, and regarded us impassively. In me, he saw a pale *murunge* boy who seduced Shona girls for sport, and in Madota, he saw the sort of girl who made poor choices. The rebel was stooped and white-bearded, like Madota's father when he was alive, and she cast her eyes at the ground as she brushed the dirt from the seat of her skirt. The Shona are a proper people, as were the ancient sisters who ruled the native school and orphanage, members of the withered and for-gotten missionary order of Saint Agnes, from whose care Madota sometimes managed to escape in order to join me behind the sandbags against all rules of accepted behavior.

The terr turned his back on us and began to hobble to-ward my house to wait for the police to take him away to prison, there to await his execution. To give him over to our security forces would be to accept his assessment of us. Madota's hand rested on my sleeve, and in this gesture I felt a silent plea. There had always been an unspoken language of touch between us, though in the matter of sexual inter-course I refused to listen.

"No, this way," I called to his back. I motioned to the

tangle of wild vegetation behind our house the way a toddler might wave a loaded pistol, or an informant point to a neighbor with whom he'd just quarreled, a spurious gesture with no regard for consequences. I would help the terr because I felt sorry for him, tattered and bleeding, old and disoriented, and this was the Christian thing to do. Or because I'd become fed up with oppression, and I loved Madota, and so on, the sort of rot that comes early in the story when everybody's still looking for reasons. I draped the rebel's arm around my neck so that I could take his weight. "There's a place you can hide," I said, and with this, I stepped into the story that had carelessly rambled into my yard.

The old terr looked at me suspiciously, almost annoyed that he would now be forced to reappraise me. I held my breath, and Madota squeezed my hand; here was a breach in the solidarity between the white people of our country, the cement that held Rhodesia together, and there followed a break in the story to accommodate the enormity of the moment.

That evening, Madota climbed from the window of the crowded barracks she shared with sixty-four other Shona girls, all wards of the church, and she gapped it from the sisters of Saint Agnes. She slowed to a walk when she reached an ancient mahogany whose roots had thrown up a section of the brick wall surrounding the convent—a place, the story goes, where the nuns in their distant youth had met with their Shona lovers. Madota stepped respectfully over the rubble of gnarled roots and broken masonry. It was a sacred tree.

She skirted a desolate plot of ground that on certain days of the year was anonymously decorated with lilies and orchids from the sisters' hothouse, and sped down the kopje, her bare feet holding the path in the darkness, silver wedding rings jangling on the chain around her neck, until she reached the garden shed. In this way, bringing only her spare school uniform, a picture Bible, and a leather case containing her toiletries, Madota left the care of the sisters of Saint Agnes and joined the rebellion.

Her first duty was to tend to the guerrilla's foot, washing the punctures and tears and applying ointments and fresh bandages that I pilfered from my father's large stockpile of first aid supplies. The terr called himself Granma, after the yacht that smuggled Castro, Che, and a small cadre of revolutionaries into Cuba. Granma had trained for thirteen weeks on the Caribbean island, most of it in the mountains of the Oriente. He'd returned to Rhodesia with bulging calf muscles, a working knowledge of map reading and Soviet-manufactured light weaponry, and a ceramic coffee mug. Granma fell into a dream in which an enormous dog held his foot fast in its muscled jaws, and we left him, motionless and sweating, on the dirt floor of the garden shed, which was hidden by a dense tangle of undergrowth, outside the territory the Ridgeback had marked with its urine.

I led Madota behind the sandbags and removed her shirt. This had become a struggle between us, and we took no enjoyment in it. I succeeded in unhooking her brassiere before the dawn brought its truce, and we lay on our sides, not looking into each other's faces, each frustrated with the other, the sandbags hard against our hips and shoulders.

That weekend, while my father and I shifted the sandbags into our house to shore the perimeter walls against gunfire and shrapnel, Madota nested in the old gardener's shed, clearing a small patch of the weedy tangle that had once been a brilliant garden in the days before my father grew too frightened to hire Shona servants. Her breathy

voice sounded like pan pipes as she sang and planted, sometimes a strange and unknown hymn, for the sisters of Saint
Agnes were secret psalmists, but more often a bit of non-
sense her father had sung to her in her childhood: *There was
once a girl, there was once a girl, there was once a girl, let's go
to Zinjanja!* Madota planted matinal and nocturnal flowers,
and in the late afternoon hours we witnessed showers of
purple morning glories wilt on the vine while moonflowers
spread their white petals beneath the darkening sky, and her
song floated on their scent, *Who went to fetch firewood, who
went to fetch firewood,* and hundreds of species of butterflies
sent representatives to the congress that convened in the
constant bloom of her garden, *who went to fetch firewood,*
and the wind jostled chimes suspended from threads—
shards of dutchware blue from Indonesia, stemless champagne flutes, chipped glass napkin rings, and silver spoons
pounded flat, an orchestra that swelled and fell away behind
Madota's voice as if her breath animated them, *let's go to
Zinjanja!* This was not a rebel hideout she was preparing—
this point has been clarified in the retellings—but rather a
home for the two of us. She planted mint in paraffin tins and
set them on the sill of our only window so the mountain
wind would rustle it on its way into the shed, and it would
always smell cool and fresh inside, until the hot month of
November, when the wind chimes fell quiet and Granma's
foot began to go septic.

Granma was nearing sixty, stooped but muscular, and he
clung to the old Shona belief that all things were woven together into the fabric of the universe. For this reason he
never took more than one cup of instant coffee and chicory,
though he clearly enjoyed it over any other beverage. "If I
take too much, someone will have to stoop longer in the sun
to pick more beans in exchange for the right to remain on

their ancestors' land," he explained. Granma polished his ceramic drinking cup after his daily coffee, wrapped it in an undershirt, and placed it carefully in his ruck, out of respect, he told me, for the Cuban who'd been in charge of his weapons training. The revolutionary had been a potter in the days of Batista, and the factory owner would not allow time for the cups to cool before the workers removed them from the kiln. The man's fingertips, Granma told us, were like mushrooms.

Granma nursed his daily coffee and watched his foot gray like aged steak, and Madota planted her garden and fetched water and changed the bandages that wrapped his rancid foot, and my father and I stacked the sandbags against the papered walls of the bungalow until the heather print was completely obscured. My father had shipped the wallpaper, along with my mother, from Scotland twenty years earlier, and the African climate had been cruel to both. We piled the sandbags in rows of twenty, floor to ceiling, each tier staggered for cohesion in case any stray rockets managed to clear the towering mesh fence my father planned to erect around the house.

My father and I ate from tins in the dark kitchen, my mother in her room. The kitchen window was left unblocked to help me better see the sink where I scrubbed our dishes, but the mesh cover allowed little light, and we grew used to finding particles of dried food on our china and flatware. There were eleven interior doors in our bungalow, most of the rooms with two and three entrances, giving occupants the impression of many choices. But my father had sealed the kitchen door and covered the windows with mesh, and when our rebel executioners finally came to wake us from our dream of security, they would lead us out the front door.

Granma's foot prevented him from leaving the shed, so he sent Madota in his stead to rendezvous with the surviving rebels who had crossed with him into Rhodesia. Granma had designated the ancient mahogany at Saint Agnes's as the rendezvous point in the event the cadre became separated, because the tree was prominent on the crest of the kopje, and it was sacred, and for other reasons we would later discover. One of their cadre had been lost during the river crossing, drowned or taken by a crocodile, Granma couldn't say. He had turned to pull his comrade onto the bank, but there was only the black, swirling water of the Zambezi. A mounted patrol of Grey's Scouts fell upon the exhausted and wet guerrilla band, and many surrendered without a fight. Granma threw down his rifle and hid in a tree while the scouts executed their captives, and yet there was no bitterness in his voice as he reached this place in his story. "What would you have them do, nephew? Arrest my comrades, feed them, give them dry clothes?" he asked. "That way we could all fight this war forever, and with clear consciences."

Madota returned with a stooped man and an emaciated boy, not much older than myself, both weaponless, the only members of the decimated cadre to make the rendezvous. October Twenty-Five had been trained in the Soviet Union and took his name from the date of their Great Revolution. He had worked in the refinery in Umtali until the birth of his twelfth child. The other guerrilla had adopted the name Zhanta, after the legendary Shona warrior of the Rebellion of 1897. Like Granma, the two guerrillas had taken revolutionary names to bolster their morale and, in the advent of capture, to shield their villages and families from reprisals.

Zhanta followed Madota into the shed, his left eye welling, its cornea bleached white. The eye blinked and teared constantly, as if trying to rid itself of the naked pupil that floated on its surface like a bit of blown ash. As a child, he'd been taken away from his village to work in the dip tanks because his parents couldn't afford to pay a tax. *"Mhoro,* comrade," he said to Granma, looking at me with his leaking eye, and I caught the faint scent of harsh toxins. I imagined that the dead parasites he rinsed from the cattle at the dip tank had become, for him, a metaphor for the Europeans who infested his homeland.

"Ahoi," Granma replied, then lowered himself onto the dirt floor of the shed, his damaged leg stretched before him. October Twenty-Five squatted silently. Of the thirty-seven members of their cadre who crossed the Zambezi into Rhodesia, only the three remained alive, each uncomfortable with his survival. No one introduced me, and I stood outside their circle, unsure if I was a comrade or an enemy. Granma spread his outdated survey map over a battered trunk, the only piece of furniture in the shed. When I dragged this trunk from the crawl space in the bungalow to our shed, chips and fragments of glass and delft and porcelain and china glaze and longing and heart's desire had shifted like musical sand in the ullage of its depths.

Madota made her chimes from the detritus she found inside the trunk, a coffin-sized steamer lined with rotted toile depicting Napoleon's Egyptian campaigns. Its contents smelled of Scottish mildew and stone, and spindrift, and stevedores' spilt beer, and untreated crate wood, and alien scents of faraway cargo, the wafture of seas and continents. The trousseau had accompanied my mother on her sea journey from Scotland, a hopeless chest filled with the sort of frippery that quickly disintegrates in Africa. Because Granma was the only rebel who had previous experience as a guerrilla soldier, we elected him our leader, and we circled

around the trunk that would become our dining and campaign table, and so convened the first meeting of the Leopard Gang.

Place, rather than time, is the stitch that weaves African stories together, and when Granma told us he knew where a
cache of weapons could be found, it seemed foreordained
that they'd be buried near the sacred mahogany that tow-
ered over Saint Agnes's, on a patch of desolate ground scattered with dead and fresh flowers. The previous owners of
the weapons, the story goes, were a cadre of rebels who,
in the early days of the war, infiltrated into Rhodesia with
neither reconnaissance, nor planning, nor any local support
from the villagers, whom the police alternately bribed and
bullied for information. They suffered three weeks of star-
vation and exposure before they finally buried their weapons
and money and uniforms and made their way south across
the Botswanan border. Only one member of the cadre,
Granma, would return to Africa to resume the *hondo*.

Granma's foot had prevented him from joining us, so
there was a childish excitement among the Leopard Gang
when we broke ground beneath the waxing crescent moon,
playing pirates after treasure. At times Madota's shoulder
touched mine as we put our weight to the spades, and an
acute awareness of her flooded me, and I felt myself swell
against the fabric of my trousers. Although the beleaguered
guerrillas had buried the weapons shallowly in their haste to
be rid of them, the dry season had turned the mound of
earth into the crown of a great skull, and the romance
quickly evaporated as the tips of our shovels scratched and
scraped against the hardpan.

As we dug, I told October Twenty-Five and Zhanta about
the twelve lay Catholics, all young Shona men under the

direction of a Swiss Bethlehem priest, who had built the chapel, convent, native school, and orphanage during such a dry season. A mother superior and twenty-four young novices came with the rains, and the chapel sank and canted beneath their feet. After the Swiss Bethlehem father returned to Umtali, the Shona men erected a temporary barracks at a discreet distance from the convent and, according to the story, continued to serve the sisters, first installing blair toilets and a donkey boiler, then a runoff channel to direct the rainwater down the kopje. The laymen stayed on after there was nothing left to build, repairing all imperfections, save the breach in the wall forced by the mahogany's roots, which provided secret access to the compound.

There was a mandatory hanging clause in the Law and Order Act for anyone found guilty of terrorist activity. Possession of a firearm constituted such an offense, and in our fatigue it was easy to imagine that the hole we dug was, in a way of speaking, our own grave. October Twenty-Five shuddered and climbed out of the shallow pit to smoke a cigarette beneath the mahogany, and Zhanta threw a shovelful of dirt at him. "Why do you stand there breathing through your nose while we work so hard? Granma says, 'Where one rests, another works double.'"

"Granma's always talking. Zzzz, zzz, zzz. Where's he now? Who's working double for him?" October Twenty-Five spat. He had little use for ideology. "Granma also says he'll take on all the sins of our country." Granma was a sinnerist who believed he could save people from evil by committing their transgressions for them. October Twenty-Five thought Granma was *vuta*, full of airs.

Zhanta's colorless eye glared. He believed Granma was a holy man. Madota and I continued to dig, uneasy in our growing fear that we would exhume the fine bones of smothered infants. It was widely known that the nuns had buried their unwanted babies here, marking the anniversary of each interment with a spray of hothouse flowers. At a depth of four feet, we uncovered a bed of sticks that the rebels had spread over the weapons. I trained my penlight into the shallow pit while October Twenty-Five inventoried the cache: five Chinese AK automatics, seven grenades, one land mine, several thousand rounds of ammunition, stacks of ZANU pamphlets, straps of South African and Rhodesian money, camouflaged uniforms, two TNT demolition slabs, a military radio, a PPSH Russian submachine gun, piles of Mao's *Little Red Book*, and discarded uniforms.

We reburied the pamphlets and books, as well as the radio—the Rhodesian Security Forces occupied so many frequencies that it wasn't safe to use it. Madota and I shook out two sets of camouflaged uniforms to take home and wash for ourselves. My fatigue shirt had a bullet hole in the shoulder, and when we returned to the shed Madota sat close and taught me how to sew it shut, my hands in hers, looping the needle in small, even stitches, the cooking fire hot on our faces, the smoky chicory from Granma's coffee in our nostrils.

That same night, a leopard visited Granma in a dream, and she told him we would be invisible at night if we kept off the crest of hills where the stars and moon would silhouette us, and she warned us that we must put aside our selfish interests or fail in our rebellion. The leopard was the spiritual animal of Granma's family, and she advised and warned him in his dreams.

We called ourselves the Leopard Gang in honor of Granma's dream, and we broke off the front and back sights on our weapons to prove we would kill close in the night, and we called each other "comrade" and fired our empty rifles point-blank at life-size soldiers cut from butcher paper and taped to the rocks. The night wind made our enemies writhe under our imaginary fusillade. On Granma's strict orders, we aimed dead-center mass, like they teach in Cuba: "Humans are too hardheaded, and sometimes the bullet will turn against the skull. Better to hit the belly or chest. That way, you remove three soldiers from the fight—the soldier you shoot, and the two who carry him away." The mountain wind swallowed the hollow tick of our dry fire, and our silent target practice went unheard by the sticks of police and soldiers who patrolled the highlands, nor did it reach my father as he paced the bungalow's perimeter with the Ridgeback, checking locks, testing mesh window coverings, nor did it penetrate my mother's bedroom, where she kept my father's loaded service revolver within arm's reach at all times. Whether she planned to use this weapon as a last-ditch defense against the terrs who would one night burst into her room, or whether she intended at that final moment to turn it on herself, is beyond my ken.

In September, when the Leopard Gang was still new, we cleared Granma's maps from the steamer trunk and laid on a feast: Granma peppered rusks of stale bread with cinnamon, and we immersed them in his ceramic mug until they were soft with instant coffee and chicory; October Twenty-Five fried beetles that Zhanta rooted from the bark of dead flame trees that had once grown in the garden; I bought scuds of beer and takeaways of fried meat; and Madota stewed a pot of fresh vegetables that had been delivered to us anonymously. Though the Leopard Gang stayed clear of the Shona in a nearby trust land, we had awoken that morning to find gem squash, tomatoes, cucumbers, maize, pumpkins, papaya, mangos, and courgettes piled outside the shed door. "There are brothers and sisters everywhere," Granma told us.

Madota said a simple grace, "Keep us well, Father," and I wondered which "father" she meant: the Christian God of the Sisters of Saint Agnes, as illustrated in her book of Bible stories; Mhondoro, the great tribal spirit of the Shona people; or the spirit of her own dead father. Granma told me to hang some meat outside the shed, and I reckoned this to be some sort of spiritual offering to facilitate the healing of his foot, which I suppose, in a sense, it was.

"Have more, brother," Zhanta pressed Granma.

Granma refused. "If I take too much, someone else goes without."

October Twenty-Five had no such qualms and accepted another scud of beer, then sang the song of the absent lover for his wife who waited in the trust lands for his return. *Faraway mountains hide you from me*, the shed's solitary window above him framed the emptiness of the night sky, *while closer mountains throw their shadows at me*, and here he made a fist, for dramatic tension maybe, or some feeling for his woman that had welled up inside him, *Would that I had my war club*, or perhaps this was how the song was sung, with balled fists, *I would smash the near mountains*, and he brought the fist down on the table softly so that it would not disturb his beer, *Would that I had bird wings*, and he made as if he were going to rise, but instead settled back on his haunches, *I would fly over the far mountains*.

His song conjured a buried memory of my parents singing behind the closed door of my mother's room, their harmonies perfectly blended, proof that this was something they'd done often in the long ago, before my father brought his bride to Africa. It was an ancient air, mournful and Scottish. They never sang again in my hearing, and so I'm unable to weave the lyrics of their song into this narrative, nor provide details from behind that closed door to establish a scene, leaving this bit a curious digression to be edited out, perhaps, in the next telling.

No one spoke at the close of October Twenty-Five's song, and he laughed at my surprise. "I know how you like to tell stories, nephew," he said to me, "and that you say I joined the revolution to get away from my wife and all those children." Outside the shed, the flies hummed around the meat I'd hung out for Granma. "Now I'll tell you the truth. My wife's a small woman. When she birthed our twelfth child, the *nganga* told us she wouldn't live through another; if I went with her again, the result might kill her. I had to go somewhere, so I joined the liberation movement."

"*Ehe!* Why not use a condom, man?" Zhanta asked.

"A condom can fall off, or sometimes they break holes. No, I'm a patient man. There's no quick end to our revolution, and she hasn't so many childbearing years left."

It took more than a day for the flyblown meat to cultivate maggots, which Madota applied to Granma's gangrenous wound to eat away the poisoned flesh. While Granma screamed into a knotted rag stuffed into his mouth, Madota and I resumed our struggle, hidden in the thicket that surrounded the shed. I had progressed to the point where Madota was naked to the waist, but despite my coaxing and petting, she refused to yield to me. "Why do we do this?" she asked. The contest might have lasted all night had October Twenty-Five not discovered us when he left the shed to relieve himself. "This sort of thing endangers everyone," he muttered, and returned with a full bladder to watch over Granma.

That morning, Madota burned out the maggots with a glowing stick, and Granma fell into a deep sleep that lasted two days. When he awoke, he refused to take any of the instant coffee we'd made for him, and he gave his ceramic mug to Madota, and he told us his dream. "In my sleep, the leopard told me our first target. We attack the sisters at Saint Agnes tonight."

Zhanta's eye stared at Granma, and Madota seemed to sink into herself. I retreated further away from the circle of rebels. Up to this point, it had all been playing soldiers and talking.

"They're only old women, comrade," October Twenty-Five said.

"Those old women with their Jesus. He's more dangerous than soldiers." Granma's foot appeared smaller beneath the bandages. "A proper savior would commit our sins for us, so that we might be spared."

Madota rose. "Is this what we trained and planned for? Soldiers are supposed to die in combat, but nuns!"

"Just so!" Granma thumped the chest, and its contents shifted musically. "How many such acts can we stomach? It's time for a new war, one so ugly nobody can face it. The old one's gone on too long."

"They aren't hurting anybody," I said. It had been my practice to remain silent at these meetings, and my voice sounded thin and childish in my ears.

Granma settled back on his haunches and stared at me. "When I was a small boy, a messenger from the Ministry of Lands informed my family that our ancestral homestead had been designated as white and our cattle would be confiscated to make room for their convent and orphanage. No one's blameless, nephew." And here was the reason his story kept circling round to the ancient mahogany tree atop the kopje.

Zhanta's bleached eye wept in its socket. Shortly after his release from the dip tanks, guerrillas had come to his village and promised his mother they'd send her son to England to study so he could become a leader when majority rule came. They took him across the border into Zambia, where they gave him a khaki shirt and trousers and a new name and sent him to Algeria for training. Each night, Zhanta pictured the faces of his family and fought to remember the exact position of each house in his village. "We'll never go home," he said miserably.

"This is something you've just now realized?" Granma said sharply.

"I didn't join the liberation movement to kill nuns," October Twenty-Five said.

Granma placed his hand on October Twenty-Five's shoulder. "No worries, comrade. I'll take their deaths upon myself." In these last days, Granma spoke with gravity and portent, as if he were reading scripture.

I collected water in buckets from the bungalow's faucet and we ritually cleansed ourselves in preparation for the attack, lathering and rinsing our genitals and armpits, and no one else stared when Madota joined us. But I couldn't look away from her nakedness, the water that ran down her belly and off the hair between her legs, and I quickly rinsed and covered my hardness. We dressed and drew leopard spots on each other's faces with burnt sticks, and we set off together to Granma's new war, because we were too frightened to face it alone.

I'd like to cut away this part of my narrative, but over years the bones of stories turn to stone, and it becomes difficult to break one away from the rest. The Leopard Gang moved through the breach in the brick wall, toward the unlit chapel where the old nuns, it is said, danced slowly in each other's arms, their eyes closed, remembering. Madota and I took our place with the submachine gun behind the rubble of bricks thrown up by the mahogany tree. From here we could watch the road that wound up the kopje and provide covering fire for our comrades. The white walls of the convent shone against the moon like the gates to heaven in Madota's picture Bible. This story was supposed to be about how I lost my virginity and became a man, but somehow Granma had turned it inside out until now it was all about killing nuns, and there was no longer any time for coming-of-age. My blood was up when I raised the submachine gun and trained it between Granma's shoulder blades. Perhaps Madota read my intent, for she unbuttoned her fatigue shirt and let it drift to the ground. The silver wedding bands that hung from her neck shone against her skin. The larger ring had belonged to her father, who raised her, the smaller ring to the mother who had died outside her memory. Granma limped into the darkness, and I sighed as I lowered the weapon, and the mountain wind swept away my breath.

Madota raised her arms and I removed her undershirt, humming inside with satisfaction as I kissed her face and neck and breasts and nipples. Madota showed me how to arrange her body beneath me and, after a few misguided thrusts, guided me into her. Below us, an armored car wound its way up the kopje followed by a five-tonner filled with soldiers who sat on sandbags to protect their testicles from land mines, and I wondered who in the Leopard Gang had betrayed us. I tried to roll over to the submachine gun, but Madota pulled me back to her. I couldn't find my breath, her beauty and the moment stretched out before me. I heard the squeak of axles as the vehicles moved closer, and the rustle of dead petals from the nuns' hothouse flowers beneath us. Perhaps Madota relented not because she loved me, but rather so she could cease to love me, or maybe there, lying on her fatigue shirt beneath the immense moon-shadow of the mahogany, she imagined herself in the marriage bed we would never share.

The first report of Granma's rifle came to us from the convent. The nuns, some say, recited in unison as they were exterminated, *The Lord is my shepherd, I shall not want,* and it has been reckoned that the interval between each shot was precisely the amount of time it took Granma to hobble over to the next kneeling sister, *He maketh me to lie down in green pastures,* and with each line another voice fell away, *He leadeth me beside the still waters,* until only one sister was left to deliver the final line of their dwindling psalm, *and I will dwell in the house of the Lord for ever.*

The rattle of the armored car and the five-tonner continued to grow closer, Granma fired his final shot from inside the convent, my flesh was overwhelmed, and here was the reason I joined the war of liberation, to bring Madota to this moment of selfishness, and I rutted and roared and shut out the rumble and clatter of vehicles and soldiers and gunshots, my eyes closed to her impassive stare so as not to spoil this beautiful moment when I became a man.

Exhausted, I listened to the crack of the soldiers' FN rifles and the deeper pop of the Leopard Gang's Chinese assault rifles as they returned fire. I could barely lift my head to see October Twenty-Five catch it on the lawn of the chapel. A bullet in the chest turned him to face his executioners, a second in the neck, a third in the groin. He must have rejoiced at this last wound, for he was no longer a threat to his own wife, and he lay on his side and bled into the ground, and he sang the song of the absent lover until there was no more breath to carry the words to the trust lands where she waited for him. Zhanta's dying silhouette moved between the trees amid the wink of the soldiers' flash suppressors, the restless, bleached eye now sightless, his arms and legs dancing crazily as he fell, only to miraculously rise again in his village where, it was said, he was seen by his mother and her cousin. There was no sign of Granma during this brief skirmish outside the chapel, and the news service would report only two bodies recovered.

I closed my eyes and dreamed of Madota in some future, faraway place where I could never find her. She cradled an infant in her arms, a girl child that looked like her mother, but with blue eyes and a ginger cast to her hair. I reached out to touch my lost family, but their skin was as rough as the wool of Madota's fatigue shirt, and my fingers came away sticky with blood in the place where she had lain, but now was gone. If the mahogany had not sunk its roots deep into the earth over the centuries, it would have turned away as I ran into the darkness of the forest, having seen enough.

The branches of the sacred tree now support an epilogue to this story—chimes made from broken rifle sights, silver wedding rings, and broken bits of a ceramic coffee mug, a sign, perhaps, that Madota refused to drink from Granma's cup. The caretaker of the empty convent bought the chimes, she recalled, at a *musika*, before the police shut down the native market and scattered the vendors, from a woman who carried on her hip a colored child with ginger hair. I received my call-up notice on the second anniversary of the Leopard Gang's attack on the sisters, and was given two weeks to report for induction into the Rhodesian Security Forces.

My father, worried that the underbrush might provide the terrs with cover, hired a bulldozer to level the ground between the bungalow and the security fence. Some nights, I crossed the floodlit area between the sandbagged walls of

our house and the mesh fence, past the Ridgeback that patrolled the broken ground, the stump of its docked tail stiff
and unwagging, and through the surrounding tangle of new
growth and deadfall to the place where the Leopard Gang
had once sat and planned around my mother's hope chest,
the shed now dark and the roof collapsed. The crepuscular
moonflowers still opened their white petals, though, and the
wind continued to gather hollow notes from the chimes, and
these were reasons enough to draw me there.

The Portuguese had lost Mozambique, and the new government there welcomed the boys of the *hondo* to operate
from behind the closed frontier that bordered the eastern
highlands of Rhodesia. From their new base camps, the
terrs could easily cross the free-fire zone into Manicaland on
foot, or even come to us in the night, crowded onto the running boards and bonnets of jeeps.

The sound of their engines woke me, and I heard them
shoot our security dog, and still I didn't leave my bed. The
eleven doors in our bungalow offered only illusory escape
routes—our only exit was through the heavy front door,
spotlighted with security lamps.

Neither my father nor mother registered any shock at
the sight of the hooded rebels who had crowded their
dreams since they landed together in Africa. The terrs set
fire to the bungalow and we all fell back before its heat. My
father would go to his death ahead of us, neither courageous
nor cringing, but resigned, as if he hadn't any place in this
new world where it was no longer a good thing to be white.
My mother followed him passively—perhaps her pistol had
clattered to the floor when she reached for it, and they found
her scrabbling on her knees in the darkness. Or she had
placed the barrel in her mouth but could not make herself
pull the trigger. Regardless, the pistol was useful only to

ward away night fears, like the Ridgeback that lay motionless beside the burning house, its tongue lolling.

They shepherded us away from the house and made us
lie down on broken soil where they would bring us to still
waters. This was the path of righteousness, and though we
lay in the shadow of the valley of the Vumba Mountains, I
feared no evil, for Granma stood there before us, terrible
and deathless, with his walking stick and his Chinese assault
rifle, and I took such comfort as I could in his presence.

Granma stood above my father, the barrel of his rifle
pointed dead-center mass, and he retreated a step to avoid
the backsplash of gore. My mother took my father's hand
and he squeezed back, the only sign of affection between
them I would ever witness. At least they would have this, the
dying together. My father bounced as the bullets *thupped*
into his back, and my mother wailed as she fully realized for
the first time since my birth that she was in Africa, a rend-
ing ululation that resonated even after Granma took her
death upon himself.

I buried my face in my arms as Granma's uneven footsteps grew closer, and I shuddered at the touch of his rifle
against the back of my head. A breath of wind filled the hol-
lows of the valley like pan pipes, and from somewhere
within the foliage outside the security fence, Madota's bric-
a-brac chimed like bells for a wedding, *There was once a girl,*
and I wanted to marry her and hold our daughter in our
arms, *there was once a girl,* and my story no longer belonged
to me, any more than the ancient sisters of Saint Agnes
could lay claim to the tales I'd invented of their Shona lovers
and smothered children.

Certainly there followed the staccato of automatic gunfire, but only muted sounds penetrate such moments and reg-
ister on the memory. The soft tangle of music from Madota's

wind chimes, *let's go to Zinjanja!* The crackle of flames that burned away the covers of the sandbags, melting their contents into walls of opaque glass. Granma broke training and pushed his rifle against my head, hard enough to make the barrel slide at an oblique angle, and the first bullet turned my skull without penetrating it, as he always warned us might happen if we didn't fire dead-center mass, and the rest streamed harmlessly into the ground. My shoulder settled against my father's, and my mother's dead fingers touched the wetness of my anointed head as I fell into darkness, and now that the rebels had finally come, we were a family, my father, my mother, and I.

At this point, a Shona storyteller might conclude simply with "Day breaks"; or a child with the rote "The end"; or, in the psalmody of the sisters of Saint Agnes, "Amen." But endings sometimes go and come without the story taking notice. Granma's story, I suppose, is still alive with atrocities committed so others will be spared, and Madota's story flows with her breast milk into our daughter, while the story of my father and mother continues along a path this earthbound narrative cannot follow. My own story invariably circles round to the night when Granma spared me to answer my call-up notice and become a soldier on the other side of the same fight, his disciple in the new war, a storybook of fresh offenses open before me.

john **nichols**

TO MAKE
A LONG STORY SHORT

Years ago I was sitting in a Hollywood restaurant surrounded by a half dozen executives from Columbia Pictures
and Johnny Carson Productions. We were talking about my
novel *The Nirvana Blues*. They were considering the book
for a film project with myself attached as writer. "If you
were doing the screenplay," one gentleman asked, "how
would you go about it?" I quickly said, "Well, first of all I'd
buy the book, then throw it away and make a movie." I understood this to be a well-known industry shibboleth. And
although I tendered it in a rather smarty-pants manner, I
was being deadly serious, thinking that for sure my wise approach would land me the gig.

The Nirvana Blues wasn't optioned by those guys, and
nobody hired me to do the screenplay.

Live and learn.

Hard to believe, but at the time I was not an utter neo-
phyte. For Alan Pakula, in 1966, I had done several drafts of
my own novel *The Sterile Cuckoo*. I'd written a script for another of my fictions, *The Wizard of Loneliness*, that reached

the silver screen in 1988. Robert Redford and Moctesuma Esparza had hired me to adapt my book *The Milagro Bean-field War*. The Costa-Gavras film *Missing*, for which I did several rewrites, had earned a screenplay Academy Award in 1982 (I was arbitrated out of a credit). And I had written scripts for both Karel Reisz and Louis Malle.

Not to imply I belonged in the whiz-kid-with-discipline category, but during my strictly accidental film-writing career up until that moment, I had to have learned *something* from Pakula, Reisz, Redford, Malle, and Costa-Gavras.

Since then my adventures in the screen trade have included bouts with Ridley Scott, a CBS miniseries about Pancho Villa, a sequel to *Midnight Express* entitled *Midnight Return*, and another tussle with one of my own novels, *American Blood*. That the scripts have rarely been shot is perhaps my fault, though I'm also aware that these frustrations are basically the luck of the draw in a difficult métier.

I love movies, and it's been a hoot to work on them. The economic punch line, here, is that I have always been paid for my failures: that is, I never wrote a screenplay on spec. I remember Karel Reisz once throwing up his hands in delight, exclaiming, "My God, John, isn't it *wonderful* that people pay us exorbitant amounts to play like little boys with elaborate toys in this crazy medium!"

Yet, though I've earned a living from Hollywood since 1980, over all those years I've only spent about forty-eight hours actually *in* Los Angeles, where I've never even driven a car, been invited to the Playboy mansion, or seen a human being toot cocaine. All my scripts post-1980 were written in my hometown of Taos, New Mexico...whenever I could take a modest break from trout fishing, alpine hiking, and irrigating my small but voluptuous garden. Maybe I don't know beans about the politics and infrastructure of Hollywood, but I am a happy screenwriter. Granted, this flouts the norm, but—hey—*somebody* has to be happy.

Am I an impostor? Maybe. I never looked for a job in pictures, nor asked for one: they all just fell out of the sky. But because of the people involved, and the excitement of their projects—how could I refuse? Nevertheless, I've always considered myself a novelist by trade, an essayist occasionally, a photographer into the bargain. In fact, it seems to me that movies are so impossible to get off the ground that only a hardened criminal would accept money for writing them. Hence, I've tended to feel guilty when deranged producers pay me top dollar for options on my own novels ... and then hire me to butcher them.

I mean, aren't movies supposed to be short stories? Usually they're about two hours long, max. A film script is almost always between 110 and 120 pages long, and most of that is air. You can't play too much with the structure because of the limitations. Movies are not like epic poems, they're like sonnets—same number of lines every time. The story has to be told with great economy. If the plots are too complicated, the machine breaks down, and the audience becomes lost. If too many characters are involved, there isn't time to flesh them out, so they become very thin and the story doesn't work.

Thus, hiring a novelist like me to write a screenplay of his own book would seem to be begging the question. I say this because some of my works are enormous, with a cast of thousands inhabiting a grotesque panoply of incident, rumination, and complicated plot folderol that meanders all over the map. If anyone actually tried to develop a movie that was faithful to one of these epics, it would be a twenty-hour megadrama in the Chinese operatic tradition, and nobody would buy a ticket.

Yet I have been engaged repeatedly by savvy practition-ers of the producing or directorial game to work on my own novels, or on other projects of enormous bulk and scope and complexity that would seem to lie way outside the purview of cinematic possibility.

Having said that, I'll admit that my first novel, *The Ster-ile Cuckoo*, was ideally suited to film. There were only two main characters involved in this simple college love story. It was the first picture that Alan Pakula directed, and I believe he chose it for the simplicity. What better way to get his feet wet than by translating what was essentially a short story onto the screen?

God knows why Alan hired me to write a script. I was twenty-five, full of pep, at the top of my game... and a total rube. By way of introducing me to the medium, Alan sug-gested I buy a published copy of Horton Foote's script for *To Kill a Mockingbird*, a movie Alan had produced. I read that piece in shock because it was so pared down and "simple" compared to the novel. Unfortunately, I couldn't figure out how to emulate Horton Foote, so eventually Alan got an-other writer, Alvin Sargent, whose version of my college ro-mance reached theaters across America with Liza Minnelli in the title role.

Years passed, fourteen of them to be exact, before I be-came seriously involved in movies again by rewriting the Costa-Gavras film *Missing*. When a producer named Eddie Lewis phoned to ask if I wanted to meet Costa, I thought it was a crank call. Lo and behold, two days later I stumbled off a train at 8 A.M. in Los Angeles, a chauffeur handed me a script, and I was driven in a limo to the Marina Pacific Hotel (a Venice flophouse), where a ruggedly handsome European asked me in somewhat tortured English, "Vell, John—wot you tink?" Turns out I spoke lousy French better than Costa spoke rotten English, so we mostly palavered in Napoleon's idiom for a couple of days. Then I returned to Taos and in three weeks rewrote the script that became a film that received four Academy Award nominations. I thought, "Gee, this is like filching candy from a baby. A really *helpless* baby."

Around that time, Moctesuma Esparza took an option on *The Milagro Beanfield War* and gave me the task of doing an adaptation. No doubt Mocte hired me because I came cheap; the financing had commenced as a diminutive grant from the National Endowment for the Humanities to do a small film for PBS. After a year had passed, Redford arrived on the scene and, perhaps just to be polite, he saw me through two more drafts. At one point I was teamed with Frank Pierson, the noted author of *Cool Hand Luke* and *Dog Day Afternoon*, and we futzed with the structure a lot. Inevitably, I was cashiered so that David Ward could take over. Yet, two years further down the road, I was rehired by Bob and Mocte for another run-through shortly before principal photography commenced. I heard that during the shoot more rewriting occurred on a daily basis. How the final version emerged in its wifty, affectionate, and loving shape is a mystery to me. It's as if thousands of nuts, bolts, and cherry bombs were tossed into an enormous Waring blender and the result was a delicious smoothie.

By the time Redford entered the equation on *Milagro,* I had concluded that my job as a writer was to labor very hard to realize the director's vision. Of course, understanding that vision is a major piece of psychodrama. I remember long afternoons when Costa and I just stared at each other, speechless, trying to come up with an idea. On other occasions I ranted about overthrowing the capitalist system while Costa kept patiently explaining to me that I should be more charitable toward America's democratic traditions.

Redford would often act out scenes that seemed totally incoherent to me, then I would torture myself at night for being unable to understand my notes. Karel Reisz *talking* the movie was exquisitely articulate about every scene, the overall story, the slightest important nuance. But when finally I asked him why he didn't write the script himself, Karel answered: "Because the second I put down a single word on paper, everything turns to shit."

Well, back on *Milagro*, our worst problem was the unwieldy novel and its cast of thousands. Yet from day one all the seers agreed: "This must be an ensemble piece." "Ensemble" means billions of featured actors, not just two or three or four. Of course, an ensemble piece limited to two hours' running time, max, means the "appearance" of billions of featured actors, and those must be drawn in a *serious* shorthand. Unfortunately, that sort of shorthand in such a limited structure guarantees that those actors will come across as caricatures. So the first thing that had to be done with *Milagro* was to throw the book away big time.

They bought the novel and I helped throw it away by cutting 80 percent of the story material and 90 percent of the characters. Truth to tell, at the start I posited a brilliant idea to the appropriate pooh-bahs: Why not tell the tale exclusively from the point of view of Joe Mondragon, the fiesty little guy who illegally irrigates a bean field, thus opening the floodgates of state retribution, which is promptly answered by indigenous revolution. "By focusing on just one person," I explained, "*Milagro* will become simple and clean."

The pooh-bahs stared at me, horrified. They were hankering for *War and Peace in Northern New Mexico*, not *Enrique Meets Selena*. But that was like cramming a battleship into a perfume bottle. Never one to argue in vain, however, I floundered through the process of cutting out many characters and merging others while crafting an ensemble piece. Soon enough David Ward took over, then I was invited to retweak his version. In retrospect, I'll never complain that a movie was made, but my gosh, the *contortions* it took to get there.

When I sat down to adapt my novel *The Magic Journey* for Louis Malle, I had a similar problem. Two hundred characters, thirty principal players, a massive story covering forty years of development in a small New Mexico town. The novel's first three hundred pages—an "introduction"—fulsomely described the years between 1930 and 1970, leading eventually to the main action of my fable, which was contained in the last four hundred pages. Not exactly the stuff of sonnets.

Right off the bat, I needed a shtick to convey the extended Dickensian intro in a single scene. I pulled it off brilliantly (I thought), but when you are required to produce that kind of belt-tightening, you do tend to wonder: Why, in the name of DeMille, Bertolucci, and Bondarchuk, are films made from huge books that are by definition unsuitable to the medium?

Also (on second thought), if I were being totally honest today, I'd probably have to admit that on-screen my beautifully compacted opening to *The Magic Journey*'s film version might have resembled a tattered constellation of confused stars that had just been gulped by a black hole. The proof in the pudding was that Louis read my first-draft screenplay ... and immediately went south.

On the other hand, my excellent adventure with Karel Reisz was a blissfully simple story set in 1981. Some Haitian boat people are shipwrecked on a tiny key in the Bahamian island chain, and neither Haiti, Cuba, the Bahamas, nor the United States will touch them. The refugees are all doomed to expire of famine and thirst until an American Coast Guard captain, goaded to make a courageous decision by his own estranged and outraged son, rescues the benighted boat people. But in the process he breaks international law, and his moral act superceding that law costs him his career.

For background information I read thick histories of Haiti, also reams of news coverage about the boat people. In Miami and Key West, Karel and I interviewed many Haitians as well as members of the Coast Guard. Still, our premise was simple, our cast small, and our plot ridiculously straightforward.

A snafu developed, however. Karel wanted the Haitians to be rescued off their sand spit during a major tropical storm. This meant that terrified Haitians lashed into bosun's chairs would be hauled across angrily tossing waters onto a Coast Guard cutter pitching and heaving in enormous sea swells. I kept trying to write *down* the storm, but Karel insisted on *more* pyrotechnics. When I balked, Karel complained in his aristocratic London accent, "Oh John, I *do* wish you'd quit trying to de-James-Bondify my film." Our producer muttered that Warner's would never fund a picture that had to be shot in a tank on Malta, and our failure to get it made perhaps proved him correct. Too bad, because Karel was the most delightful, articulate, down-to-earth, and gentlemanly fellow I ever worked for in films: our brief collaboration was a treat.

Midnight Return, a sequel to the Alan Parker/Oliver Stone film *Midnight Express*, which I worked on between 1996 and 1999, also seemed like a pushover for the screen. The original 1978 film ended when Billy Hayes escaped from a Turkish prison after being incarcerated for five years. For the sequel, all I had to do was get Billy across the Sea of

Marmara in a rowboat, then whisk him around Asia Minor and through Thrace to the Greek border: a piece of cake, no? *Run, Billy, run!* Of course, I read two books by Billy himself, and schmoozed with him into the bargain. Half a dozen Turkish guidebooks fell to my inquisitive probing. I also watched movies set in the region, including *Yol*, by Yilmaz Guney, and Elia Kazan's *America, America*. Then I read several studies of internal strife within Turkey at the time of Billy's escape. But the finished story was easy as pie, swiftly moving, straight to the point. There was a built-in clock, a structure as simple as *The Fugitive*, and an exotic setting: I merely filled in the blanks.

You don't believe me? Here's the cover evaluation of my script from the first company that considered it:

> An excellent, tightly written script with great characters, excellent dialogue and superb pacing. The story begins with intense action, plunging us directly into the nightmare of Billy Hayes's final moments in Sagmalcilar prison, then the equally perilous prospect of "freedom" in a hostile country. Once you're out, what do you do? The action has several well-placed pauses throughout, and measured crosscutting to the excellent ancillary characters, all of whom are well drawn and interesting in their own right. The dialogue is also superb, always natural and to the point, never clumsy or over the top. Harvey in particular has some great lines, making him a welcome, believable comic foil to the almost unbearable tension that's created in this hair-raising odyssey. While the story sometimes seems to go out of its way to paint Billy as heroic—something that's perhaps difficult

under his circumstances—the actual escape is quite credible, and his determination and intelligence are certainly impressive. I can't wait to see this film.

So why is the project still looking for a director almost a year after I completed it? Ah, that is one of those Hollywood mysteries that I know absolutely *nothing* about.

Of course, my most recent effort, *Che and Fidel* (1999), penned for Peter Davis and Bill Panzer, is back in the Subject-Matter-Not-Exactly-Tailored-for-the-Movie-as-a-Short-Story realm. But given my leftist politics and radical history, *Che and Fidel* is the love story I was born to write. Those guys are my heroes, and I don't care who knows it. Fidel has to be one of our century's most extraordinary men. Yet we're clearly not talking here about a Simple Little Movie: this is Panorama, in spades. My Che/Fidel bibliography is thirty books long, and I have many articles, speeches, and documentary films besides. But I suspect (duh!) that my Marxist-Leninist sympathies for Che and Fidel guarantee that the picture will never get made. I don't even know at this writing if I'll be retained on the job. No matter, the educational process was a fascinating spiritual and political journey that went like so:

1. I read somewhere that the adolescent Che worshipped Mahatma Gandhi, so I devoured a book on Gandhi.
2. Hugh Thomas's monumental history of Cuba was worth the trip alone.
3. To review the revolutionaries' economic philosophies, I reread Robert Heilbroner on Adam Smith, Malthus, Ricardo, Marx, and John Maynard Keynes.

4. Fidel's letters from prison were mega-inspirational.
5. Che's *Motorcycle Diaries*, about his early travel adventures in South America, were succinct and more fascinating than Kerouac or William Least Heat-Moon.

In short, learning about Che and Fidel was one of the great adventures of my life.

It's too bad Guevara and Castro were both anti-American mad-dog socialists, because who in their right mind in Hollywood is going to eagerly finance *that* political perspective? And, again: How do you sculpt a precisely structured limited masterpiece out of such complicated historical material?

Still, hope beats eternal, and I rarely dwell on the negatives. It's a fact that nobody can take away the pleasures I've gleaned from writing for the movies. Here I am, pushing sixty, still in love with the process. Who knows if I'll ever land another gig in L.A.? That thin air the jobs have always fallen from is becoming an ever more rarefied ether. Nevertheless, I plod on, always alert to the possibility, convinced that one day in the not-too-distant future, some well-dressed barbarian with a tattered soul and a few bucks in his or her pocket will hand me Balzac's entire *La Comédie humaine* and ask, "John, can you make a movie from these novels?"

In a New York minute I'll reply, "Of course, pal. Just buy the books and let me throw them away."

Then I'll create yet another panoramic and convoluted ensemble piece... that all of us will pretend is a short story.

chris **spain**

SCARING
THE BADDEST ANIMAL

Blind school and school school are still out for summer, the summer Tigre Velez is still going to be champion of the world, the summer Piggy Garcia still reads books. Piggy and Tigre, two-fifths of the 141st Street Bad Bengalis, are flat on their backs, sticky with sweat, stuck to the stoop steps like kicked-over colas. It's so hot Piggy's got his helmet off, that New York Giants helmet he wears in the out-of-doors to keep his big brain inside his head.

"Too hot for fighting flyweights," says Tigre, still breathing from the gym.

"Hobbes going to be dying today," says Tigre. "Wishing he was hanging with the penguins."

"I already said I was sorry," says Tigre.

"She wants to see a movie and the phones was all broke and we just went," says Tigre.

"Didn't even get any, a waste of money, a stupid night," says Tigre.

"You still not talking?" says Tigre.

Piggy, his world written all over with Tigre smells of gym

sweat and glove leather and some Claudia something that smells like lemonade, decides not.

Piggy is called Piggy because in seventh grade his favorite book was *Lord of the Flies,* and he's got curly hair and can't see. Sometimes they call him Piggy and sometimes they call him Book. Today Piggy's fingers are parked on the page, melting down the dots. He's not reading because he already knows too much. The worst thing he knows is yesterday Tigre dissed him hard, went to the movies without calling, left him sitting on the stoop steps half the night. No, that's not the worst thing.

Tigre Velez, the baddest Bad Bengali, coughs his little nose cough, something he got from catching one too many punches. Tigre Velez, who has never been knocked down, not once, even when skinny and fighting guys twice as big, big guys like World Trade. Tigre's got his *mochila* full of all the tricks: *relámpago* hands, dancing feet, a good-luck tiger, and, most important, an assassin's heart. Tigre is going to be champion of the world and make ten million pesos and buy a house in Piermont and get the Bad Bengalis out of this shitty place. The worst thing Piggy knows is he's in love with Tigre, always has been.

"What you reading?" asks Tigre.

Piggy's not falling for that one. And he's not forgiving Tigre.

Pluto scrapes down 141st as if he's been in the ring himself, beat to death, and is just looking for a place to fall. Pluto because of a mile-long nose, and because he still watches cartoons all Saturday morning.

"Pluto coming," says Tigre.

"From over there I'm thinking you guys been whacked," says Pluto.

He drops. Like the sound of folding clothes.

"Why we parked here?"

"Piggy locked us out," says Tigre.

"Yo, Piggy, what you do that for?"

Because all the Bad Bengalis are coming over to watch *Gladiators* on Piggy's mom's large screen. Because *Gladiators* is Tigre's favorite show.

"He's not talking," says Tigre. "He's pissed."

"Tigre try to call," says Pluto. "I saw. The phones was broke."

"I think he's in love," says Tigre.

Piggy's blood stumbles over the hurdle of his glass heart.

"In love?"

"With Claudia."

"No *911*?" says Pluto. "No *Gladiators*? Now what?"

The book Piggy's not reading is all Darwin and evolution and survival of the fittest and from where did we get our big brains. About carnivores having bigger brains than herbivores. About how hunting takes more brains. About how maybe from hunting, from having to kill, comes love and grief and all the rest.

"Hot," says Pluto.

"My pops says Vietnam War weather," says Tigre.

"What's he know?" says Pluto.

"He's been there. Monsoons and shit."

What Piggy aches to read is Tigre. To hold him in his hands. To run Tigre skin through his fingers. To write chapters of himself in the book of Tigre. He breathes in when Tigre breathes out. He breathes the air of Tigre. He breathes Tigre, and hunts his big brain for how to punish him more.

August leans on the city like a dying King Kong. Like some kind of thick jungle air, heavy with expectation and violence. Like the blood-soaked weather at the top of the food chain. The last two-fifths. Tuna unheads his headphones, spilling tinny baseball speak up and down the street. Angel smells like a hamburger and large fries.

"He lock us out again?" says Angel. "I knew it. I almost didn't come."

"Yo, Piggy, should be you feeling bad for Tigre," says Tuna. "He spend seven-fifty, didn't even get any elbow."

"Piggy's not talking," says Pluto.

"Where's Hobbes's McNuggets?" says Tigre.

Hobbes is the Bengal tiger at the zoo. Angel always brings home a nine-piece so Tigre can feed Hobbes just before close time. When Tigre is champion of the world, he's gonna buy Hobbes a new house, too, break him out of that shitty cement.

"Man, you got to quit feeding that tiger McNuggets," says Pluto. "You gonna give him a heart attack."

"My moms won't let us touch that stuff. She says it's a plot to kill black people."

"Right, Tuna, like they couldn't just drop a bomb on us."

"You ain't black," says Tuna.

"I ain't white," says Pluto.

Tigre comes up on his elbows, hurts the cement. Never a time Piggy isn't aware of the space Tigre's body takes. Every Tigre touch written in permanent ink on Piggy's skin.

"So where's the McNuggets?" asks Tigre.

"I quit," says Angel. "*Pendejo con* a *pistola* want ice cream.

I trying to give him money and he nearly shoot me 'cause he don't want money, he just want ice cream."

"Who was that? You know him?"

"Angel, you got to quit that McDonald's shit, you should work White Castle. They got bulletproof over there."

"He already quit. You deaf, didn't you hear him just say?"

"Square hamburgers," says Tuna. "That shit would not happen in California. People way too hip for square hamburgers. My moms is crazy is what. Crazy to come here. Get me killed."

"Tuna, you just a feto ambulante."

"What did he call me?"

"He say you an ambulant fetus."

"A walking abortion."

"That fucking tiger gonna starve to death, no more Mc-Nuggets."

Trains lurch out of the city's arteries, spill messages of fight or flight. The sun gone from Piggy's skin and the air thicker, more liquid, a better conductor of sound. Girl laughs. You can hear them from half a block. Maybe Roxy. Claudia. Claudia for sure. She smells like lemonade. Love and grief and all the rest.

"Hey, Tigre, your paleta," says Angel.

"Lick her," says Pluto.

"Freeze your tongue off," says Tuna.

Tigre staggers to his feet as if to beat a ten count, steps off the stoop steps, crosses the street. Does she want to go to a movie? Only if he pays. The silver sound of Tigre emptying his pockets. A streetlight chatter it's hard for Piggy to hear over. Then Tigre shuffling back.

"Strike three," says Pluto.

"Shit," says Tigre.

He boots the lip of the bottom step, sits, closer, for a minute forgets to breathe. Piggy almost ready to forgive him, almost ready to fall in love again.

"And my *Gladiators* happening right now," says Tigre.

"Probably already Eliminator."

"Gemini, he's the baddest."

"Gemini, nothing. Take Nitro over Gemini any day."

"You guys all faggots," says Tigre. "Take Ice, let her crack me in half."

Glass breaking somewhere. Maybe Piggy's heart.

Tigre has said he is sorry, Piggy knows he is sorry, but Piggy needs him to be something more than that.

"They're not even real," says Piggy.

"Ha!" says Tigre. "You talked."

"What?" says Pluto.

"It's just a stupid TV show," says Piggy.

Humming air, buzzing lights.

"Real gladiators," says Piggy. "They fought against each other with swords. Two guys with swords. Or one guy with a sword against one guy with a net and spear, or against a lion or a bear. "

The 141st Street Bad Bengalis, who are never given pause, are given pause again. Anyone else but Piggy they would call a liar.

"Why?" Pluto finally asks.

"Sometimes slaves," says Piggy. "Or rich men who lost everything, only way to get it back. Or for glory. For the glory of who was the baddest."

"Slaves? Like America?" asks Tuna.

"But who wins?"

Electricity arcs across an insulator, pops.

"The one that doesn't die."

Then Piggy turns to Tigre, to the space he knows holds Tigre. His naked elbows and his breathing.

"And the winner, the winner could have any woman he wanted."

A boom box booms, giving the air a heartbeat. Piggy feeling like he's in the middle of a four-way intersection, and something big is coming, only he's not sure which direction it's coming from.

"Do or die," Tigre finally says, as if he's found an answer.

Sometimes just Tigre's voice spills the air out of Piggy like that.

"What?" asks Tuna.

"Stand on the tracks, see who stay the longest," says Angel.

"That's played, that's tired," says Pluto.

"Grab the third rail, do a Sparky just to put me out of my misery," Pluto says.

"What's a Sparky?" asks Tuna.

"He's dead, he's cooked."

"Not on the tracks," Tigre says.

"Not on the tracks?"

Piggy, not yet sure why, not breathing.

"It's who gets in the cage," says Tigre. "That's the man."

"What cage?"

"The zoo cage. Like Piggy said, we're the gladiators. We find the baddest animal, see who badder. Who get their props."

"You're crazy."

"Snakes. Snakes the baddest," says Angel.

"Fuck snakes, I ain't getting nowhere near no snakes."

"Snakes don't count," says Tigre. "They lock them up."

"Cheetah bad. One hundred kilometers an hour."

"Book, how much miles is that?"

"Like it's not dangerous enough already?" says Tuna. "Like we might not get shot for breathing?"

Piggy dangles on the zoo wall, his drumming heart drowning out a river of cars on the avenue. The bricks radiate heat like something alive. Everybody else already gone from the air around him, everybody else already kicked over. Piggy the only one who knows the way at night. He can still turn them back.

"Stupid dark."

"Mad cool."

"Book," says Tigre. "Throw yourself, I'll catch you."

The air blurs on Piggy's fingertips. To a bump and a big Tigre laugh. Piggy sitting right on top of him.

"What happened, what?"

"Where's Piggy at?"

"Tigre finally been knocked on his ass," says Tigre. "By a blind man."

"Okay," Tigre says. "We're even."

Tigre laughs buzzing up Piggy's legs and thighs.

The air hangs on them like wet towels, and there is a dripping, as if someone wrings out the ends. Just their footsteps. Just their breathing. And the dripping night. Piggy runs his fingers over exhibit markers, tells them what they're not seeing. They are at the elephants. They have to go past Asia and World of Darkness and Jungle World. It's behind that.

"What's up if they catch us?"

"Nothing, like a parking ticket."

"If the crocodile don't eat you."

"What crocodile?"

"The one they let out to guard at night."

"You shitting me, right?"

"How else you think they don't get everything stole?"

"If there's crocodiles, I'm not going."

"Tuna, there's no fucking crocodiles."

Raspy breathing from across wrought iron and dead water. As if someone files down a piece of metal on the dark. And still that steady dripping; drip, drip, the night is bleeding.

"Hear him," says Tigre.

"Hey, puss, puss."

"Something is stank. Something stank bad."

"Hobbes got bad breath is what he got."

"Hey, brush your teeth mister fucking tiger."

"Shhh, don't make him mad."

Piggy takes his helmet off. The flick and flaring of Pluto's lighter. Listening to them see.

"His ass is kicked is what. Just like ours. Too fucking hot to get up."

"Put that shit out."

The light leaving. Just Hobbes's breathing. And their own breathing. And the leaking light.

"Got to swim," says Pluto. "Only way to get across."

"I ain't getting in that shit. That shit probably kill you."

"Otherwise you go, right, Tuna?"

A spill of bootlace. The drag of shirt cloth off shoulder skin. Tigre's zipper run down tooth by tooth.

"Hold this," says Tigre.

The warmth of Tigre in the shirt and jeans. The smell of Tigre. As if Piggy is holding part of him.

"Tigre?" says Piggy. "You're not really."

"Loco," says Pluto. "Fucking nuts."

A pop of ligament and muscle. Air spilling from Tigre's mouth. The soft drop to the other side.

"Tigre?"

"Can you see him?"

"Don't talk, don't say nothing," says Tigre.

"You want light?"

"No light."

A splash, like a rock in a puddle. Then a second dripping, a dripping behind the dripping that was already there.

"Yo, he's really doing it, he is. Yo, shit."

"That Hobbes better of ate already."

Piggy lifts the jeans and shirt to his face. The heat already gone. As fast as that. He turns his head one way, then the other. His own skin tight on the night, waiting to tear. The space between his heartbeats closing in.

"Tigre," Piggy hears himself say. "Tigre, come back."

When it happens, it's such an explosion that Piggy can't put together any kind of sound picture. There is a grunt, and a yell, a Tigre yell, must be, and air rushing into lungs, and air rushing out, and something sharp dragging across cement, and Pluto's lighter falling, and Piggy's helmet hitting the ground, like a skull cracking open, and something running, and over it all a guttural noise, an erupting volcano, a sound from the center of the earth.

The wrought iron rusts through in Piggy's fingers. Echoes off of everything.

"Tigre?" says Piggy.

A breathing something. It's at the water, at the bars, coming over the fence.

"Tigre?" Piggy says.

"What is it? What?" says Pluto.

"Run!" yells Piggy. "Run!"

They trip over each other, go down in a tangle of Bad Bengali arms and legs. Piggy throws his hands out in front of his face. Drops like rain on his prickly skin. Blood is all he can think. Then a big Tigre laugh.

"Pussies," says Tigre. "Pussy faggots."

"Tigre?" says Pluto.

"You thought Hobbes was coming to get you?" says Tigre. "Ho, ho, ho!"

"Who's the baddest?" says Tigre. "Who?"

"You touch him?" asks Tuna.

"Touch him? I pull his tail."

Piggy listens to Pluto and Tuna and Angel dance a circle around Tigre, slap the bare skin of Tigre, the brave skin of Tigre.

"You touch the fucking tiger! You touch the baddest animal. Shit, shit, shit!"

"Man, you large. You fucking large!"

"You hear him roar? He was pissed man, pissed."

All of Piggy's skin beating, like a heart, ticking, like time.

"Piggy?" says Tigre.

Tigre's okay. Everything's going to be okay.

"Where you at?" asks Tigre.

Piggy wipes his face with his sleeve. All the heat has run out of this place.

"Piggy?"

Piggy listening harder.

"Piggy, what?"

"I'm not hearing him," says Piggy.

"What?"

"I'm not hearing Hobbes."

"Hearing him what?"

"Breathing."

Their own breathing dropping away.

"Maybe he went inside. There's an inside."

"Something fell," says Piggy. "Something went down hard."

Pluto finds his lighter. Piggy at their shoulders, peering with the skin on his face. Quiet except the burning air. As clear a picture as his blind eyes have ever seen.

"Hobbes sleeping?"

"Twisted funny-like. Like awkward."

"Hey, Hobbes, get up!"

"That fucking tiger ain't moving, he's dead."

"Dead?" says Tigre.

"Probably a fucking heart attack, all those McNuggets."

"Dead?" says Tigre again.

"Fucking McHeart attack for sure."

Piggy has fallen off the edge of a flat earth, into a darkness he has never known. He stumbles with his hands out in front of him, as if groping toward the end of his life. He kneels, to hold Tigre, to not fall over.

"I'm sorry," says Piggy.

"I love that Hobbes," says Tigre.

"I'm sorry," says Piggy again.

"What am I going to do with no Hobbes?"

As if seeing himself for the first time. The taste of his own teeth in his mouth. Piggy, who already knew too much, knows more. We are the baddest animal, thinks Piggy. The baddest animal is me. The summer Tigre is still going to be the champion of the world, the summer Piggy still reads books.

Emily **perkins**

HER NEW LIFE

Here, then, was Abby Turner's new life. She woke alone each morning in her cousin Felicia's white, low-ceilinged apartment on the Upper East Side, drank tea out of Felicia's mug, surrounded by Felicia's anonymous catalog furniture, and dressed in one of her own few work outfits.

She took the subway to the corner of Eighth and Twenty-third. Thirty soliciting letters out before lunchtime, a sandwich and a flick through magazines at the local café, filing and photocopying in the afternoon. Pizzazz, the video-production company where Abby worked, was third, even fourth rate. Her boss was a moron.

After work, she took the subway to SoHo, or Chelsea, or the park, and walked. She had grown up with these locations, blown up on a screen or reduced to video, but always contained within a slot-shaped oblong of film. Now she was in the frame. Ignoring the advice of her small-town parents—"Don't look up at the skyscrapers, you'll get mugged"—she stared in awe at the heights, the scale, the architectural detail. She gazed up above the gleaming

points of the Chrysler Building at the clouds scudding west
and imagined them in black-and-white, racing away over
the city to the world outside, a world that had all but disappeared.

Abby wanted to eat everything, hear everything, do everything. She stood in the back of East Village poetry read-
ings, sat in the courtyard at the Frick, and made herself walk
through Washington Square Park alone even though she
was scared. She imagined every one of those things captured on film, but she did them all alone.

And then, on this day, Abby's new life turned again. A famous television producer was reading from his autobiogra-
phy at a bookstore on West Broadway. Abby had spent the
weekend in the Museum of Television and Radio, watching
tapes of his documentaries from the archive, making notes.
When the second hand at last ticked to six, she switched off
her word processor and went to the bathroom to brush her
hair. She came out to see her boss standing by the desk, a
pile of papers in his hand. It was 6:45 before she got out of
there.

So this was Toby Wright's first sight of Abby: from a seat at
the back of the crowded bookstore, he saw a blonde girl
enter the room, late. She looked undaunted, although four
or five faces had swiveled to see who the latecomer was. He
saw her strangely bright eyes, the jut of her chin, her arched
collarbone, and her wide, amused mouth. She sat at the end
of his row and stared intently at the producer, drawing a
notebook and pencil from her bag. After the audience had
applauded politely and been invited to buy copies of his
memoir, the producer sat at a trestle table, ready to sign.
Toby stood behind him, watching Abby wait in line. She
held the book as though she were a naughty schoolgirl.

What Abby noticed as she stood in line was the great liver-spotted head of a man bent over copies of his book and behind that a young man, not much older than herself, staring at her through heavy glasses, almost as if he knew her. She smiled, and raised an eyebrow. He blushed. She had never seen such a good-looking boy blush before, and stared down at her hands, her pulse quick.

"Your name?" The producer had a bored, booming voice.

"Abby," she replied, and looked up again, straight into the boy's large green eyes. His face was open, his nose lightly freckled, his hair a messy brown. "Abby Turner. I really love your work."

"My work? Aren't you a little young to be familiar with my work?"

Abby reddened. "I go to the radio and television museum. To the archive? I watched your documentaries there. I really like the one about Ellis Island."

"Hear that, Toby?" the producer said, craning his neck back to the young man. "You're not my only underage fan. Don't just stand there. Get this girl a glass of water." He made a flourishy gesture over the title page with his pen and handed her the book. "Go tell each other how much you respect me. Start a club."

Abby followed Toby to the doorway, where he offered her a cigarette. "I like his work," he said. "Shame about the book. It's kind of long."

"How do you know him?" Abby exhaled. "Thanks."

He pushed at the bridge of his glasses in a self-effacing way. "I work at Whittington Studios; Paul's on the board. I'm just here to demonstrate company support."

"Whittington? Where Lucia Clarke works?"

"Yeah." Toby smiled. "You know her?"

"I—"

"Toby!" A bellow from inside the store. "Back here!"

He grinned. "Oh, the glamour. Hey, come to dinner with us. Please. It's just me and Paul and the publishing idiots." Toby jerked his head toward a preppy-looking man and a woman in a neck brace. "Save me, okay?"

The restaurant was cool and modern. White brick tiles lined the walls, and the seats were white, too, with purple velvet cushions. A tall waitress showed them to a table where the young man and the neck-brace woman were waiting. They each worked for the publishing house doing something Abby didn't quite catch. On the wine list she saw a bottle that cost the same as her week's rent. Discreet-looking couples, women with gold hair and men in well-cut suits, occupied the other tables. Abby imagined a camera on a dolly, going from table to table, eavesdropping. She hoped no one could tell that her blouse was from a discount store.

"So," Toby asked when there was a gap in the conversation, "how do you know Lucia Clarke?"

Paul looked up. His eagley eyebrows met in a frown.

"Oh, I don't," Abby said. "I did an essay for an ethics paper on the effects of her living with her subjects, you know, like she did in Borders."

"That's my favourite documentary of all time."

"All her work is incredible. What's she like?"

"Underrated. Smart. And a dyke," growled Paul. "It's a fucking loss to mankind. She's the sexiest woman in this fucking business." He turned to the publishing girl. "What the hell happened to your neck?"

Toby lowered his voice. "She's kind of private. Everyone at Whittington worships the ground she walks on. Where did you go to college?"

"You haven't heard of it, it's pretty low rent. We had scholarships sponsored by local dried-goods manufacturers."

"What, like the Dehydrated Mash Millennium Masters' Program?"

"You're looking at last year's Pot Noodle Graduate."

Toby burst out laughing, then stopped. "Oh my God," he said. "You're not joking."

"I do think," the publishing man announced to the table, "excepting a work as wonderful as yours, Paul, the genre of memoir has had its day."

Toby leaned close in to her. "Let's give Paul a few minutes of torture. You want a cigarette at the bar?"

He asked her things nobody had asked her since she'd arrived in New York. "My job sucks," she said. "There's this receptionist who's kind of sexy, but real thick. She's about it as far as human contact goes. I'm subletting my cousin Felicia's apartment while she's in Europe. That's a kind of soulless place, too. But," she said, her eyes shining, "you know what? I don't care. It could be a hundred times worse and I would still love it. When I walk down the street, or get a cup of coffee, it doesn't matter what the day is like, or the garbage, or the smells—I'm here. There's a guy on the subway that wears a cat outfit and plays a trumpet accompaniment to 'Part-Time Lover.' Do I sound stupid?"

"No. Are you always like this?"

She put a hand to her mouth. "Like what? No. Yes. Like what?"

He smiled. "Tell me more about the city."

"I love the mix, the different areas, the languages, you can walk down a street and not hear English spoken for blocks. You wouldn't believe how vanilla milk shake it is where I come from. God." She took a drag on her cigarette.

"You know how many contrasts there are here? How the city has this clean geometry, this three-dimensional grid, and then there's all the crazy flotsam messing it up? I like the flotsam. If I was going to film the city I'd try to capture that movement, that mess."

"You like mess."

"Not in real life," she smiled. "I don't know a lot about it, in real life." *Shut up*, she told herself. "I'm rambling," she said, and laughed. "I'm drunk."

Toby reached for a paper napkin and wrote something down. "Um, if you want to come look around Whittington at all. Call me. Okay?"

"Okay." Abby started to smile at him, but her face felt naked with excitement. She had to turn away.

At the end of the evening Abby walked home from her subway stop and her life seemed transformed again. With drunken eyes she gazed out at the night, at the blue shadows and yellow streetlights, the city like a faded dress, frayed and stained but scattered with sequins. She glimpsed her reflection in a shop window and stopped, amazed that she didn't look more different. A quantum leap had occurred. She had been picked up—plucked, was how it felt—from the hot, dirty street, and set down in a parallel universe, somewhere similar but quite, quite new.

Toby got her a position at Whittington with astonishing ease. Though he was still a researcher after three years, he had some sway. At first she had thought she couldn't afford to work as an unpaid intern. Then it seemed that she couldn't afford not to, although it would eat away at her meager savings. She would just have to budget carefully. It was a coup to be here, as much as it felt like starting college over again.

"I heard these studios only take graduates from places like, you know, *Amherst,*" she said to Toby, putting on a snotty accent.

"Hmm," he'd answered, "I don't know, maybe, I guess."

"Where did you go to college?" He looked sideways at her.

"Amherst."

"Oh." Abby laughed. He laughed too.

Young people in scruffy, fashionable clothes walked through the Whittington buildings fast, like there was always somewhere else to be. Every now and then two or three of them stood together in a corner or doorway, talking in intense and rapid sentences punctuated by knowing laughter. If Abby hadn't had Toby around, she would have been lost. Behind glass office partitions, on telephones or at computer terminals, the next echelon operated: development people whose meetings took place in separate rooms or over lunch tables in a nearby restaurant. The young researchers and trainees, the technical crew, and the administrative minions ate lunch together in the first-floor cafeteria. A boom operator never sat with a production assistant, who never sat with an accounts manager. It would be interesting, Abby thought, to force them to mix up, to film them trying each other's jobs for a day, to see how long the bitching and buck-passing would last.

She ate with Toby, who gradually introduced her to the paid interns, the style-conscious, self-conscious group that made up the entry-level employees at Whittington. If you ignored the in-jokes and the overbearing confidence, they were all right, but she liked it better when it was just him and her. One day she had a glimpse of Lucia Clarke running from the elevators into a taxi, a cafeteria paper bag in her hand, dark hair and red shoes. She looked younger than the press photograph used by the industry papers. Abby glanced around, eager to see if anyone else had noticed her, but they were all carrying on with their lives, moving happily along their gridded paths.

She was assigned to a magazine show about decorating and Toby gave her tips, told her the best places to go for materials and how to get stuff for free. They needed a certain type of consumer for the program. Abby inquired through design shops, conducted interviews, and made recommendations. One afternoon, as she stood in the designer's office waiting to show him some samples, she caught a snatch of conversation just outside the open door: "I don't know why you're not giving her the usual tasks." The whiny voice belonged to Heather, a researcher a year or two older than herself. "We need query letters answered, we need the parking organized for the shoot, there's a whole stack of filing."

"She's too smart for that shit," Toby's voice came back in reply. "It'll get done anyway. She's got us some terrific interviewees. Total television. There's this one couple—"

"Forget it," Heather said. When Toby came into the office he was on his own.

Whittington was on Hudson, a three-train journey from Felicia's apartment, but Abby didn't mind the time. On the way home, she stood straphanging in the crush, her head leaning on her raised arm, and thought about Toby. He hadn't mentioned a girlfriend. They hadn't really spoken about anything but work. He was self-contained in a way, but easy with his information. Over the past few weeks he had made the work seem manageable, clearly and patiently. He must be good with children. "Oh, shut up," she told herself out loud. Nobody looked at her. She closed her eyes, and swayed with the other bodies to the rhythm of the train, and imagined taking Toby's glasses off and kissing him. By the time she opened her eyes again she had missed her stop.

He couldn't protect her from the worst of it, though: the incessant demands for coffee runs, the lunch orders, the cleaning and moving when they were finished with a particular location. Heather appeared on set one day with the producer's daughter, a wriggling, red-faced toddler. "Here," she said, handing her to Abby. "You're not busy, are you? Her au pair's sick or she's got measles or something. Just look after her till the end of the day. Don't let her get in the way." And Abby watched open mouthed, the surprisingly strong child squirming in her arms, as Heather sauntered off, exchanging some flirtatious banter with the camera assistant and swinging her chickeny hips as she went.

It was three months before the inevitable happened. One lonely Saturday Abby went to the cash machine to find that she had forty-one dollars left in her account. The rent was due at the end of the next week. She ran back to the apartment and checked Felicia's cupboards. Three cans of salmon and a jar of peanut butter. No friends. No food. No money. After checking down the back of the sofa—there wasn't a penny there—she sat on the bed with her palms pressed over her mouth, trying not to panic.

On Monday morning she was hurrying along the corridor, her head down, when she collided into Toby. Papers hit the floor. He scooped them up and grabbed her arm. "Hey. Are you okay?"

She waved the fax in her hand and looked at him with despairing eyes. He dragged her through a fire door and into the stairwell, and she told him that she couldn't work there anymore. "I'm broke," she explained. "I've been so stupid, I have no savings, I should never have left Pizzazz." She tried to smile, but her mouth wobbled. "I'd better get this fax to Ivor."

Toby's hand was still on her arm. Her skin tingled where he held her. It was hard to focus on what he was saying. "Look, if you're short of cash I can get you a coat-checking job. It's a fancy place, not far from here. Go see them to-night, okay?"

"Thanks. Thank you." They stared at each other. Abby felt breathless, but it wasn't from running. Toby put his hand to his glasses, as if to adjust them. "Ah, who's that fax for—Ivor? You'd better get it to him."

She started at the restaurant that weekend. It was a linen-tablecloth-and-real-silverware place, expensive and stuffy. The maître d', Stefan, was a friend of Toby's brother. "Younger or older?" she asked Stefan as he studied the ros-ter. "Grant's older," he said. "He used to work here, too, until that thing with his eyesight." His sight? Abby wanted to ask, but Stefan kept talking. "I can give you four nights," he said.

The work was easy, and tips plentiful. Some evenings Abby could make upwards of a hundred dollars. But still she went home alone each night, out of the subway, past the dry cleaner's and the diner, up in the elevator to the blankness of the sublet studio. If the red light on the answering machine ever blinked, it was only a friend of her cousin's wondering if Felicia was back. Most evenings Abby crawled into bed ex-hausted without turning on a light.

Two Saturdays later there was a message waiting when she got to the restaurant. It was from Toby. Adrenaline rushed through her and she felt dizzy. She'd never asked him what he did on weekends, for fear that he'd then ask her, and she'd have to say "Window-shopping." The message read, *Party at Heather's. Call if you want to come.* She called straightaway. "I'll swing by," he said, "and pick you up."

She bounced up and down, chewing her thumb when no one was looking, impatient for the night to end, for the night to begin. When it was nearly time she pulled on the green velvet jacket she'd bought that morning and applied lipstick in her small silver hand mirror. Toby was coming to pick her up. It was almost a date. She stood out the back of the kitchen, by the door to the yard where cats and rats fought over food scraps, and smoked one cigarette after another. Finally, he arrived.

The party was crowded. There were faces Abby recognized from Whittington and a lot she didn't. She felt nervous; she didn't know what to do with her hands.

"Hi," said Heather, giving Toby an enthusiastic hug. "So great you could make it."

"Hi, Heather," said Abby. "Nice place."

Heather looked at her, perplexed. "Hi..."

"You know Abby," Toby said. "New at Whittington."

"Oh yeah," Heather said, as if she were saying, No, actually, I don't. "Hello. There's drinks over there, and you can dump your coats on the bed—you know where it is, right?" This last was over her shoulder to Toby, as she disappeared back into the crush. *Oh*, thought Abby, *I see.*

"Ignore her," Toby said. "Give me your coat and let's get a drink."

Abby stood at the table laden with wine and vodka bottles and rice crackers and felt the music pounding through her chest. Across the room, through the animated, shiny heads, she could see Toby being stopped by a young man who began talking at him with an urgent expression. In the nearest corner a trio of girls were greeting each other with kisses. "We were just at the screening," one of them said, "of the new film by Lucia Clarke." Abby strained to listen. A girl she had seen frequently with Heather was rolling her eyes. "Her usual lecture about falling standards..." "But her work's so amazing," another one of them said, "and I *love* her new haircut."

Ordinarily, Abby would have looked at this scene and wondered how it could be filmed. But the newness of it all overwhelmed her and she couldn't think straight, couldn't find enough distance. By the stereo, several guys she had seen at Whittington argued about which CD to play next. Other people were dancing, or standing around nodding with serious expressions on their faces. Toby had made his way closer, but now Heather was dancing around him and laughing. Abby poured herself a second shot of tequila. "Hi," she said to the next person to approach the bar, a smooth-looking guy in a T-shirt bearing the title *Borders*, from Clarke's Mexican documentary. "Did you work on that?"

"Er, no." He sloshed some tequila on the table. "My friend did, though. Want to meet him?"

"Uh, okay," said Abby. "Sure."

She was following T-shirt boy through the group of dancing people when Toby took hold of her elbow. "Where are you going?" he shouted.

"To talk with some guy," Abby shouted back. "What about you?"

A girl tripped and pushed Toby forward so his face was only inches away from Abby's. She blinked, and stared at his mouth. "I'm going to get a drink," he said in a voice that she could hear perfectly clear below the music, "so I can work up the courage to ask you to leave. Now. With me."

His apartment was small. There was no door between the living room and the interior bathroom—to open one would have used up too much space. Instead there was a graying curtain, a faded Hawaiian maiden dancing up one side of it. One wall of the living room housed a sink, a counter, and a small oven. Off that room two further curtains opened onto bedrooms—one a decent size and the other, Toby's, just big enough for a double futon. The next morning Abby lay on the bed beside him, the heat of his hand on her stomach, the warmth of his breath brushing her neck. Out in the living room someone put a record on. Toby groaned and turned in toward Abby, his lips against her cheek.

"I share with this girl," he explained later, after the music had stopped and the door outside had slammed. And he had brought her a cup of tea in bed. "Teresa Yo. She's crazy and she goes out with this horrible French restaurateur, but it keeps the rent cheap. How're you feeling?"

"Good." Abby smiled, slowly. "Great."

"You are incredibly, unbelievably beautiful."

She ducked her head. "Ah, no."

"I want to look at you all the time. Since the bookstore. It's been driving me insane at work. I keep making up new things to tell you so I can just stand there and stare. Did you notice? Do you mind me saying so? Am I creeping you out? Jesus, Abby, Abby, I'm going to have to get stronger prescription glasses." She laughed, and reached to kiss him again.

They tried to keep it secret at work, but that didn't last. They were in the first flush of lust, when everything about the other seemed wonderful and strong, when their similarities were causes for celebration and their differences to be marveled at. Toby was unlike any boy Abby had known. He was confident without being aggressive, as though he had come to some realization about himself and had nothing to prove.

He loved, he said, to see the city through her eyes: together they roamed the East Village; they dressed as cheesy tourists and took the Circle Line around the island; they borrowed a DV camera from work and he taught her how to use it. Lucia Clarke had pioneered DV documentaries, and on rainy Saturday afternoons they sat side by side in the Whittington archive, watching her work and pointing out to each other why it was so good to enter a particular scene here, or leave another one there. "You idolize that woman," Abby said to Toby. "It goes, your mother, your sister, Lucia Clarke, me."

"You forgot the Virgin Mary," he said, and she punched him.

For the next few months, after she had finished coat-checking, she would take a taxi to his place and they'd hide in his room from Teresa Yo and her condescending boyfriend, drinking rum and fooling around and laughing, laughing. Before long they were asking each other the inevitable questions: who, when, how.

"College romance. Well," she said late one autumn night, looking straight into the video camera, "first there was Andrew . . . and then there was Elizabeth."

"Elizabeth?" Toby sat beside her like a talk-show host, but he looked at the camera, too, as though he were seeing them both reflected in a mirror.

"And Andrew." She smiled. "Not at the same time."

"Oh," he said. "I see."

Another time, after Toby had absorbed this new information, they talked about relationships again. He asked if she remained friends with her exes and she said no, but that was circumstance, that the breakups had always been amicable enough. He asked if she had ever been hurt. "No," she said after thinking for a minute. "Not badly. There's a lot I don't know. Sometimes I feel as though life is out there, that there are these things, these possibilities, these truths that float just outside my periphery, just beyond my reach. Do you know what I mean?"

"I think so," he said. "I guess."

The leaves fell; the nights lengthened; the gray of the river thickened with cold. "Are you going home for Thanksgiving?" Toby asked Abby.

"No. I can't face it."

A smile crept over his face. "Teresa's going to Vermont with her boyfriend. Do you want to stay here with me?"

She felt suddenly shy. "You know what else it is?"

He nodded. "Our six-month anniversary."

They roasted potatoes and burnt a chicken and opened two bottles of red wine. Abby gave Toby a copy of *Masters of Light*; he gave her underwear. *It was*, she thought, *like a British television play from the sixties*. She imagined living here with him, making a home. Having a baby.

"Tell me," she said over the flickering candle flame, a potato halfway to her mouth, "you're so good at what you do, how come they haven't made you an AP?"

Toby sighed, tipped his head back, and adjusted his glasses. He looked anxious but almost relieved, as though an inevitability had come to pass. "I haven't been around full-time for the last three years. I've had to spend several months away."

"Where?"

"Baltimore. Hospital. And afterward I go to my parents' place upstate." He stood up. "Where's the ashtray?"

She followed his progress around the small apartment. She felt scared, whether for herself or for him it was hard to tell. "What was wrong with you?"

He leaned over and kissed her cheek. "Do you feel like coming for a walk?"

The evening was cold and still. They walke
hour, looking at the Christmas displays going
lights and the magic-workshop kitsch of departi
decorations. It was like a dream sequence, Abby
the strange silence and the glowing colors against the
They sat on benches by the park and Abby watched
dreds of tiny bulbs light up, one by one, while Toby told
There was a history of blindness in his family. "It's not nec
essarily hereditary," he explained, "my parents are just a bad
genetic combination, it seems." His older brother's vision
was down to 20/400 and there were no surgical procedures
available. "We're taking part in a yearly survey at Johns
Hopkins. That's why I have to spend time away," he said.
"The prognosis is always the same, but the length of time
left isn't." He turned away from the silhouetted shapes of
trees and wrought iron to face Abby. "I only told you this,"
he said, and his voice was fierce, "because I love you. If it's
going to make you behave differently toward me, I don't
want to see you anymore. Okay?"

She took his hand. "Toby..."

"Of course, sooner or later I won't be able to see you at
all." He laughed, and brushed a strand of hair back over her
ear with his cold fingertips. "Bad joke we white-stick people
get to make. But I mean it. You promise?"

She stared at him, scared. "Promise."

"It's not necessarily hereditary," he said again, taking
her face in his hands. "You know what I'm saying, don't
you?"

"Yes." Blinking in hot tears she kissed his cheeks, his
lips, his neck, his hair.

He pulled back, and managed a smile. "So guess what.
Teresa's moving out. Now you know the worst, what do you
think about moving in with me?"

That night Abby dreamed of walls. She could hear his ·oice. *It starts with night blindness,* he had said, *and I'll lose my peripheral vision.* She woke to find him staring at her as though he was memorizing every inch.

Toby sat in Ivor's office, waiting for him to get off the phone. He picked at his thumbnail and tried to look as though he wasn't listening. At last Ivor hung up. He blinked at Toby. "Ah," he said eventually. "Toby Wright."

"Yes. You wanted to see me."

"Indeed. Very exciting. New Lucia Clarke documentary. Family roots, ethnicity. American preoccupations." This was how Ivor talked, dispensing with pronouns and verbs wherever possible. "Frankly, too fucking esoteric. But she writes her own brief these days. Researcher. Position. Starts next week."

Many of the researchers were intimidated by Ivor's manner. Toby wasn't one of them. "Are you offering me the job?"

"Ha. Yes." Ivor looked down at some papers on his desk, then back up at Toby. "Good. That's all."

A Lucia Clarke documentary. Toby Wright, researcher. A grin spread wide over his face. This was what he'd joined Whittington for. But the timing couldn't have been worse. "Ivor, this is my dream job. But I can't take it. I'd really like to. More than anything. But you know I have this cone-rod dystrophy..."

"You what?"

"The eye thing."

"Oh." Ivor looked displeased. "The eye thing."

"I have to go to Baltimore for another set of tests next week. I wrote you a memo about it last month." Visiting specialist, they had said, there may be a new possibility. We don't want to get your hopes up but we think it's worth it.

The evening was cold and still. They walked for over an hour, looking at the Christmas displays going up, at the lights and the magic-workshop kitsch of department-store decorations. It was like a dream sequence, Abby thought, the strange silence and the glowing colors against the dark. They sat on benches by the park and Abby watched hundreds of tiny bulbs light up, one by one, while Toby told her. There was a history of blindness in his family. "It's not necessarily hereditary," he explained, "my parents are just a bad genetic combination, it seems." His older brother's vision was down to 20/400 and there were no surgical procedures available. "We're taking part in a yearly survey at Johns Hopkins. That's why I have to spend time away," he said. "The prognosis is always the same, but the length of time left isn't." He turned away from the silhouetted shapes of trees and wrought iron to face Abby. "I only told you this," he said, and his voice was fierce, "because I love you. If it's going to make you behave differently toward me, I don't want to see you anymore. Okay?"

She took his hand. "Toby..."

"Of course, sooner or later I won't be able to see you at all." He laughed, and brushed a strand of hair back over her ear with his cold fingertips. "Bad joke we white-stick people get to make. But I mean it. You promise?"

She stared at him, scared. "Promise."

"It's not necessarily hereditary," he said again, taking her face in his hands. "You know what I'm saying, don't you?"

"Yes." Blinking in hot tears she kissed his cheeks, his lips, his neck, his hair.

He pulled back, and managed a smile. "So guess what. Teresa's moving out. Now you know the worst, what do you think about moving in with me?"

That night Abby dreamed of walls. She could hear his voice. *It starts with night blindness,* he had said, *and I'll lose my peripheral vision.* She woke to find him staring at her as though he was memorizing every inch.

Toby sat in Ivor's office, waiting for him to get off the phone. He picked at his thumbnail and tried to look as though he wasn't listening. At last Ivor hung up. He blinked at Toby. "Ah," he said eventually. "Toby Wright."

"Yes. You wanted to see me."

"Indeed. Very exciting. New Lucia Clarke documentary. Family roots, ethnicity. American preoccupations." This was how Ivor talked, dispensing with pronouns and verbs wherever possible. "Frankly, too fucking esoteric. But she writes her own brief these days. Researcher. Position. Starts next week."

Many of the researchers were intimidated by Ivor's manner. Toby wasn't one of them. "Are you offering me the job?"

"Ha. Yes." Ivor looked down at some papers on his desk, then back up at Toby. "Good. That's all."

A Lucia Clarke documentary. Toby Wright, researcher. A grin spread wide over his face. This was what he'd joined Whittington for. But the timing couldn't have been worse. "Ivor, this is my dream job. But I can't take it. I'd really like to. More than anything. But you know I have this cone-rod dystrophy . . ."

"You what?"

"The eye thing."

"Oh." Ivor looked displeased. "The eye thing."

"I have to go to Baltimore for another set of tests next week. I wrote you a memo about it last month." Visiting specialist, they had said, there may be a new possibility. We don't want to get your hopes up but we think it's worth it.

"Oh. Dystrophy. Time off. Pity."

"Yes. I'm sorry. I really wish this could have worked out."

"Well. All right." Ivor returned to his papers, ready to shuffle.

"Ivor—if I might suggest—there's an intern who's been here about nine months now. She's fantastic, got a lot of initiative. Abby Turner?"

The producer's head snapped up again, turtle-like. "Bright girl. Yes. Know her. Yes."

The first thing she wanted to do was tell him. Abby ran along the Whittington corridors, down the stairs—too impatient for the elevator—down, down to the basement picture archive where he had said he would be that afternoon. When she pushed open the heavy door, breathless, the only person at the microfiche table was Heather.

"Hi," Abby panted. "Have you seen Toby?"

Without lifting her eye from the viewfinder, the other girl shook her head.

"Okay—thanks." Turning away, Abby let the door clang shut and ran back up the stairs. She had to find him, she had to say—everything was different for her now, everything. She could leave the restaurant, she could be free, she was going to work with the most incredible—but there he was, coming down the long concrete-walled hallway toward her, light from the overheads glinting off his glasses.

"Toby! Toby! Guess what!" Her bag and her folders fell to the ground as she raced full-tilt into his arms.

Lucia Clarke had started her career as a photographer. Her first break came young, when a SoHo gallery gave her a solo show at twenty: she hung large, formal portraits of her family alongside pictures of strangers in the same poses. Though each shot was carefully composed there was always a random, unexpected detail, a hint of unpredictability, of mess. Her style, unforced and haunting, was quickly acclaimed. Advertising companies began to call; she made a few high-profile music videos. Her music work had the same aesthetic as her photography—beautifully constructed scenes with chaos at the edges. She was given to bold statements: "I'll make five videos then get out," she was quoted as saying. "MTV is a young man's game." By then she was twenty-two.

Now she was twenty-nine. She had made a television drama about nineteenth-century nuns; it won an Emmy for direction. She had also made documentaries on computer bugging and on life in a Mexican border town. Critics praised her breadth of interest and her fresh, contemporary style. She was credited for revitalizing television as a serious form of entertainment. But the magazine interviews were never allowed to go too deep. The only subjects that she could be quoted on were her own heroes: Gus Van Sant, Errol Morris, and David Lynch. Beyond this, her life was private.

It was the morning of the first production meeting. Abby had been awake since six. It was hard to even believe that she was a fully paid researcher at Whittington Studios working with Lucia Clarke. And now an intern was bringing in a tray of coffee, and she was taking one, nodding—thank you—trying not to show that she surely did not deserve this, that only yesterday she had been serving the coffee herself. And there, across the shiny oval table, sat the woman she had caught glimpses of, as an elevator door was closing, or getting into a taxi outside the studio building. She was here, in the same room, at the same table. She sat down, and Lucia smiled at her and spoke: "You must be Abby," she said. *Yes*, she had thought, unable for a moment to reply. *Yes, I must.*

The documentary was about the effect on Czech immigrants of the 1989 revolution and the links that were being re-established between the American community and those back home. "In a way it's intended as a companion piece to Paul Wolff's documentary on Ellis Island, which I urge you all to watch. What fascinates me," said Lucia at that first meeting, "are our self-imposed borders, how they affect in-between people, what a family means, or a community, distance and similarity. I've got several ideas about where this might go, but as you know"—she laughed—"Ivor has very kindly given us free rein. So it'll be a new process. Whatever we unearth will inform our next move. There's a fantastic guy at Columbia I want to talk to, so let's call him now and get up there with a DV as soon as we can. Abby? Can you set this up?"

In the young academic's dusty study, filming while Lucia conducted the preliminary interview, Abby was as nervous as she'd ever been in her life. After an hour they took a break while the professor made a couple of phone calls. Abby's hands were shaking. "Are you sure you don't want the whole crew in here?"

"The room's too small and they're too intrusive. You're great with the camera," Lucia said. "Most young women are intimidated by it."

Abby smiled. "My friend taught me. Toby Wright?"

Lucia nodded. "I've heard good things about him."

That night Abby relayed this back to Toby. "Isn't that great? She's heard of you."

He kissed her. "She praised *your* camera skills."

She bit his arm. "Which *you* taught me."

"Come here." He pulled at her wrists so she fell on top of

him, giggling. "Face it. She loves us. She worships us. We're her heroes."

From the start, Lucia spoke to Abby as if she were an equal. "Television is full of hierarchical shit," she said. "People treat those beneath them one way and their supposed superiors another. It makes me sick." Abby thought of Heather, obnoxious to the interns and other researchers, bowing and scraping before Ivor or any executive. "It's all about fear," Lucia said another time, when they were having a coffee break between watching video interviews with recent immigrants. "There's no such thing as working in TV without it, these days. But you know something? You can ignore the fuck out of it if you really try. Hey, have you got a cigarette?"

Abby knew the public facts about Lucia. Anything else she'd heard was water-cooler gossip between researchers and interns. But as they worked together she found out more. Lucia was single. Her last important relationship had ended two years ago. It had hurt. She struggled with self-doubt and her worst fear was mediocrity: at the end of each day she would review the work done and ask if it was good enough. One evening she and Abby sat watching rushes. At a tiny kitchen table an Orthodox priest talked about faith. "In the end," he said, "it's a daily choice." "God," Lucia murmured, "you know, that's true." *She's kind of private*, Abby remembered Toby saying, and wondered why this did not seem to be so.

Early one morning Lucia came in to find Abby already at her desk, a stack of books in front of her. Pulling a thermos out of her cycle bag, she offered a cup to Abby. "I hate the coffee in this place. So tell me. Are you enjoying this project?"

"I love it."

"Good. The last of Lucia's Handy Hints: only ever take

work on projects that inspire you. Be poor, waitress, whatever you need to do, but don't fall for the tyranny of mediocre television. Enough people are doing that already. They don't need your help."

Abby took a sip of coffee. It was rich and sweet. "This is good."

Lucia grinned. "Why thank you, Miss Turner."

She was going to blush. The sexiest woman in this fucking business. Where had she heard that? She had to look away.

Toby got up in the night for a glass of water. Abby, deep in exhausted sleep, did not stir. He stood beside the window to the fire escape and pressed his forehead against the cool glass. She was so charged, so full of energy these days. She raced around, he knew, from library to newspaper archive to university lecturer's office, compiling as much information as she could. And she spent the evenings reading, on the Internet, or on the phone. But still some nights she could come home to find him, to lead him to the bed and tell him how much he was loved. Outside a siren started up. There's a spark in her, Abby said of Lucia, a fire. It's contagious. He listened, and smiled, and told her the truth: that he was happy for her. He didn't tell her another truth: that when she described Lucia she might have been describing herself. Toby sat at the kitchen table and looked around him. Without his glasses the room was an incomprehensible blur.

Whittington gave everyone the week off for Christmas. "I have to go back to Dullsville," Abby said. Snow fell quietly: they were in the location parking lot, waiting for a generator truck to turn around. She stamped her feet. "I'll last until the day after Christmas, then forget it."

Toby touched the soft skin of her palm through a hole in her mittens. "Come back early. Meet my parents."

They kissed. She said, "I can't. I've got to work."

Lucia's place was a top-floor loft on Crosby. Abby climbed the three flights of stairs, squeezed past the bicycle leaning in the deceptively small doorway and tried and failed to say anything intelligent for five minutes. The loft was fronted with an enormous living room that led into a kitchen space, with a large scrubbed table and shelves and shelves full of books. There was a bedroom in the back, ending in ceiling-high warehouse windows that opened onto a scrappy courtyard below. The rooms were suffused with light, a worn parquet floor gleamed underfoot, and the smells of cinnamon and coffee hung in the air. "Wow," she said. "This is—"

"I know," said Lucia, drawing on a cigarette. "I can't really afford it. Sometimes I wake in the night, panicking. But it's fun to pretend for a while."

"I brought those books."

"Thanks. I really appreciate your doing this. How was your Christmas?"

"Well, it's over."

They looked at each other and smiled.

After the work was done they drank coffee and talked, and as they talked Abby caught herself noticing the way the locket around Lucia's throat rose and fell with her words, her slim hands as she lit a cigarette, the contrast between her dark hair and the smoothness of her skin. The heaviness of her thickly lashed eyelids. "I really should go." She got up to leave.

"You know what?" said Lucia. "There's this industry thing next Friday. It'll be kind of stiff, but I'd like you to meet some people. Will you come with me?" She explained that it was a major awards party. "I've been nominated for the doc-umentary prize." *And you're asking me?* Abby thought. *Is this, like, a date?* She didn't know how that made her feel, aside from confused. She didn't know what to say.

Toby and his brother, Grant, walked through a park near their parents' house. Grant had a dog with him, a young Labrador from the Blind Foundation.

"If Lucia were a guy," Toby said as the snow squeaked underfoot, "I'd ask Abby straight out if she liked him. It'd be easy to make a joke of it, and I could tell from her response what she really felt. But this way, even knowing what I know about Abby's past, I can't. Jesus, I'm repressed."

"She has a past?"

"Kind of. She's had relationships with girls—but some-times . . . it's weird."

"Are we coming up to the swings yet?"

"They're over on the left." Toby took his brother's arm. "Everything here is the same as when we were kids. Exactly the same."

"I shouldn't go," Abby said, lying on their futon, her head against his chest, listening to him breathe. "It's our last Fri-day together before your trip to Baltimore." Your trip, that was what they called it, not the specialist, or hope.

"Don't be crazy. Sweetie, you've got to. It'll be amazing, huh? And you can come back and tell me everything."

She turned her face up toward his, to try and read him. His eyes were closed. "But I want to go to it with you."

"No." He kissed the top of her head. "I've got a hot date at the Laundromat. Hate those hospital PJs. Oh, go ahead, honey, you've got to say yes. Even if it's only to make Heather sick with envy."

"Open your eyes," Abby said, "so you can see how much I love you."

It was impossible to guess how big the room was because of the crush of people, but it seemed as though it might go on forever. Chandeliers blazed and reflected from enormous mirrors; ivory pillars supported the high, high ceiling; there was the strong, stately smell of lilies. Abby imagined a camera looking down on it all, catching the shifting configurations of people like a subtle code, an Elizabethan dance. She took a glass of champagne from a passing waiter and, led by Lucia, pushed her way through the crowd. Everywhere, coiffured men and women were chattering, gesturing, stretching their bejeweled necks, laughing.

Lucia turned to smile at Abby again. "You really look great." Abby blushed and tugged at the neck of the black antique dress she'd found in a thrift store. At first it had been fun dressing up, alone in the apartment, pinning back her hair as though she were a woman mysterious to herself, uncertain of what the night would hold. Toby had come home early, surprising her. A lurch of guilt had risen in her stomach. She did not understand why. He'd watched as she'd smoothed new stockings over her legs, and asked her in a strange new voice, "Who are you dressing up for?" "Myself," she'd replied. "Everyone knows women dress for themselves." But she'd answered the question too quickly, and she knew it. Maybe Toby knew it too.

Whoever Lucia had dressed for, it was hard to look at anyone else in the room. She was wearing a long red dress, red lipstick, and red toenail polish on her sandaled feet. "I want you to meet someone," she said. When Abby saw where they were headed, she grabbed Lucia's hand in excitement. "That's Paul Wolff."

"You know him?"

"No." Abby laughed, and shrugged. "I saw him read, once."

The old man was leaning on a column, holding court like a Roman senator. When he saw Lucia he stepped forward, his face creased with pleasure. "Hello, star," he rumbled. "Look at you."

Lucia kissed him. "Paul, this is Abby Turner. She's going to be the next."

Abby ducked her head. "Hi."

The producer frowned. "I know you."

"We had dinner—your book had just come out. I loved it, by the way," she said, and blushed again.

"Of course, of course." He looked from one to the other of them, and laughed. "My God, you're both going to make some men jealous tonight."

The three of them circulated together for a while, meeting actors and presenters and writers and producers. Abby was standing next to people she had read about, or seen on-screen, or whose work she loathed or admired. If that had been all she was doing—standing there, watching and listening—it might not have been unlike a dream. But to all these people Lucia, and soon Paul, said the same thing: "Tremendously talented. Keep your eye on her." And the actor or presenter or writer or whatever would look closely, as if they were really taking notice, and shake her hand. "Pleasure to meet you, Abby." They would drink from their constantly replenished glasses of champagne, and somebody would say something funny, and they would all laugh. Before long, eyes followed them as they moved around the room, and stared when they stopped, and more than once she heard, "Abby Turner. An associate of Lucia's. Tremendously talented."

Then it was time to sit down and the presentations began. "Are you nervous?" Abby whispered, and Lucia nodded. "Sure. It's all very well saying these things mean nothing, and in my heart I believe that, but I also really want to win."

Underneath the table they gripped hands. It's just friendly, Abby told herself, I'm just being supportive. But her breath was shallow with tension. And when Lucia's name was called out—when she stood, and ran lightly to the stage, and smiled her truthful, open smile to the room—"I'd like to thank everybody involved"—nobody clapped harder.

She let herself into the apartment hoping two things: first, that he was asleep, and second, that she didn't smell of wine,

"Hi," he called as the door shut behind her. Well, maybe he wouldn't notice the wine. She sat on the edge of the bed and told him, "You didn't miss much. It was stuffy. Pretty boring really."

"Did Lucia win?" His voice was sleepy.

"Yeah, she did."

"That must have been exciting."

She forced a yawn. "Yeah. I guess it was."

"Abby . . ." His voice was not so sleepy. There was an edge to it that she did her best to ignore.

"Mmn?"

"I don't want you to—"

"What?"

"Nothing. I'm glad you had a good time."

A good time? She had spent the evening in a different world. She had been paid all sorts of ridiculous attentions. And later, in a downtown bar, Lucia had said to her, "A lot of that talk is bullshit. But I meant what I said to people about you. You've got an eye, and instinct. It's special. Don't ignore it." How could she explain to Toby that the most spangled, exhilarating, glittering night of her life so far had not been spent with him, whom she loved, but with Lucia?

"I'm going to take a shower," she said. When she came back to bed he was asleep. Or at least pretending.

On Monday Ivor rang her extension and said, "Prague. Filming. Brought forward. Next week. Skeleton crew. Want you to go. Passport?"

"Yes," she said. Her head felt clouded. "Yes. I have one."

"Depart Tuesday."

Two days before Toby was leaving for Baltimore. She couldn't possibly go. She had promised him she'd be there, in their apartment, waiting. Abby replaced the receiver and stared blindly into the middle distance.

Later in bed, Toby summoned up the courage to ask her about Prague. "You're leaving for Baltimore; I want to be with you," Abby replied.

"Abby." He touched the side of her cheek. "I'll be busy having lights shone in my eyes, I won't know what's going on. How long is the Prague shoot, a week?"

"Ten days."

"By the time you get back I'll be home. And they'll know whether or not there's a chance."

"Toby?" She curled into him, small.

"Mn?"

"I'm scared."

He tilted her chin up so he could make out, at least, the shape of her face. "Don't be scared for me."

I'm not, she wanted to say, *I'm scared of myself.* "I'll call you, though," she said instead. "I'll call you every day."

———

It was snowing in Prague. They stayed in a hotel just off Wenceslas Square. Abby stared out her bedroom window onto the white, Gothic beauty below, following clouds of snow spiraling around lampposts and building spires, the entrances of cobbled alleys and glowing globes of street lanterns fading, muted by the feathery dust. There was a light knock on the door. "It's me." Lucia.

They left everyone else unpacking and walked through the snow, leaning angled into the sheltered side of buildings, laughing as each fresh swipe of wind pushed them back into one another. The watercolor artists were scrambling to clear up along the Charles Bridge; underneath them, the river stirred forceful and dark. Snow dropped as though inevitably toward its surface and melted like powder. "Come on," Lucia cried as the temperature fell and the air around them thickened. "Let's find a bar."

It was three days before it happened. The schedule was tight, and they rushed from location to location in run-down taxis, views of the city—the bleak suburbs, the old town, the institutional high-rises—smeary through the dirty car windows, through the snow. All of it was beautiful to Abby, though the skies were a breakless gray and the slippery sidewalks the color of damp ash. Since she had met Lucia, she had begun to notice the delicacy of shadows, the play of light and dark in bare tree branches, or in puddles, or cast from uneven stones in the walls of old buildings. The world was a more detailed place, threaded with complexities, intriguing, enigmatic, and alive.

At the end of the third day, after a difficult shoot in bitter weather outside the cathedral, Lucia asked if she wanted to get something to eat. "I need to go over some of tomorrow's plans with you," she said. "Do you have to go back to the hotel?"

Abby snapped her folder shut and jammed it into her bag. She hoped the color in her cheeks just looked like cold. "No."

After dinner they went to a bar, and then to another, and then to a cabaret. People sat in smoky clusters; the songs were in Czech; they couldn't understand a word. Together they giggled, and smoked, and let the evening's wine take over and lull them into a slow, untranslatable reverie. At some point Abby found herself reaching for Lucia's hand, turning it over in her own and stroking the inside of her wrist. Lucia looked at her. A pulse beat fast in the base of Abby's throat. Lucia reached across the table and with one finger traced the outline of Abby's mouth. Nothing was said. They kissed. Still neither of them spoke, not in the cold, windy street where they kissed again, or in the taxi, kissing, back to the hotel, or in Lucia's room, where they kissed and kissed with ferocity, and fell onto the bed, and then the floor.

The morning came fast. Then they talked: "When did you—" "How—" "I wasn't sure—" "I can't believe—" Lucia called for breakfast and they ate rolls and drank mugs of hot chocolate, wrapped in the starchy hotel sheets, staring at one another in astonishment. "God," Lucia laughed, "you. You. It's like—" She took Abby's hand and placed it on the hot, pulsing skin over her heart.

Abby laughed, too. "I know."

"Maybe this is the ultimate in narcissism."

"What about work?" Abby asked.

"We'll be discreet." Lucia looked suddenly vulnerable. "This isn't just an out-of-town fling for you—is it?"

"No. No. It's much more than that."

———

That night she called Toby in Baltimore. At the sound of his voice a cold rush of guilt washed over her. "It's me."

"Abby." It was a bad line. They could hear their own words echoed back to them.

"How are you?"

"I'm fine. But they're not going to know for a while—the day you get back. What's it like there?"

"Beautiful. Cold. Listen, I won't be able to call as often as I said. The hotel—"

"That's all right. Don't worry about me. I love you."

She looked around the lobby. "Love you too."

For the next week, Abby hardly slept. In the evenings she and Lucia explored the old town in search of bars unpopulated by other Americans, eating sausage and bread and cheese, drinking vodka and smoking cigarettes until they collapsed, going back to Lucia's crumpled bed, talking, laughing, making love. Then the long chilly days, the dark mornings and dark afternoons. Interviews, establishing shots, montages of the city flew by like so many pages from Lucia's imagination. The hours and the cold meant nothing to Abby. As long as she could watch Lucia. It was the times they were apart that were hard.

During breaks in filming she thought of Toby, back in New York, waiting for the specialist's results, waiting for her. If only the tests would find something, and he would at least have his sight, his independence, perhaps then she wouldn't worry so much for him. Or—what if something went wrong? An aftereffect of new drugs, say, or a household accident. What if he—what if Toby died? He would never know, then, that she had betrayed him. Sitting on a bench on Petrin Hill, under a broad, leafless plane tree, Abby let herself envision the worst. While the crew unloaded equipment around her, she pictured Toby clean, untouched, unscarred in death.

This thought—this almost-hope—became so vivid in Abby's mind that after a few more days she could nearly believe it had happened. Toby lay comatose in a hospital bed while his parents decided to let him go. She called him again, two days before her return to New York, and felt a physical shock when he came to the phone.

"Any news?"

"No."

"You all right?"

"Yeah. You?"

"Yeah."

"You sound different."

"It's probably the line."

New York seemed thin, two-dimensional, slick, after Prague. That Friday night Abby sat at the scuffed kitchen table in Toby's apartment, idly pushing his mail in and out of small piles. She was tired from the flight and the room felt more like his than ever. After a minute she stopped, pressed her fingers to her temples, and let tears fill her eyes. She thought back to a time before she had left New York, to a night before Prague, before the awards ceremony, before Lucia. New Year's Eve. She and Toby had been to a bad party held by some Whittington colleagues in an East Village bar. The place tried hard to be divey: the ripped pool table and the leaking toilets didn't sit well with the price of the drinks. Heather was screaming around, cackling, making a show of ignoring them both. None of these things had mattered. After some cursory conversation with other people they'd settled into a quiet booth and played with each other's hands across the cracked Formica. "It's been a good year," Toby said. "The best in my life," she answered. And it was true. Stupidly, innocently, she couldn't imagine anything better. "What do you wish for this year?" he asked, and she had squeezed his hand and said, "I wish for things to be like this."

And now they weren't. "I don't know what to do," she said to the silence of the empty room. Looking around she saw that the apartment was familiar, tangible, there. Life couldn't be a movie anymore. She was here, and Lucia was real, and Toby, too. Everything was painfully, messily real. That night she slept on top of the bedcovers without undressing, the television flicking lurid, silent colors over her darkly dreaming form.

In the morning she took the bus upstate to see Toby. His parents lived in a wooden house on a gentle, snow-lined street. He was in the living room, by the fire. Her heart jolted at the sight of him, at his wide green eyes. He stood and they kissed like two people unaccustomed to one another. His mother brought them coffee and closed the door behind her. There was something new in the room between them.

"Hey," she said. "You look great."

He smiled. "It seems longer than ten days."

"I know." She sat down next to him and took his hand. "I missed you."

He pulled her toward him. "It's not so bad," he smiled.

"What isn't?" What did he know?

"I can still see you the same." He stroked her face with the back of his hand. "Crazy, for some reason I thought you might've gone blurry on me."

She laughed. It sounded nervous. "I'd never go blurry on you."

"There's nothing they can do." He glanced away. In the fireplace logs cracked and split, sending a rush of embers up the chimney bricks. Abby put her hands on his knees; the breath stuck in her throat.

"Toby. God. I'm so sorry."

"It was only ever a small chance. I haven't actually lost anything." He reached for her fingers but couldn't meet her eye. "Have I?"

The next day was colder still, a deep February cold that hung damply in the air and shadows. In the guest room at Toby's parents' house, Abby hadn't slept. Before anyone else was awake she dressed and walked through the chilly streets to a pay phone. Lucia answered.

Abby said, "It's me."

"How's it going up there?"

"I don't know. I think I'm jet-lagged."

"Me too. You want to have dinner tomorrow night?"

"Yes."

The soft, low sound of Lucia's voice was still in her ears as, back at the house, she waited for Toby to get his coat. It played under the silence that fell over them as she drove to the park. When they got out of the car, the grass was wet; there were chestnut husks still on the ground and through the misty air came the faded charcoal-and-newspaper smell of a dying bonfire.

He spoke first. "How's Lucia?"

Did he know she had called her? "She's fine."

"How was the shoot?"

"Fine."

He walked ahead a little, then stopped. A trio of birds flew noisily from a naked tree. "Don't make me ask, Abby," he said.

Tears came into her eyes and she swallowed hard, staring at the green sweater she'd given him for his birthday.

"What?" His voice was loud. "Ask what, isn't that what you're supposed to say? Aren't you supposed to be, I don't know, confused, not know what I'm talking about?"

"I—"

"What am I talking about?" Breath clouds puffed hot from his mouth. His voice cracked. "You tell me, Abby, what the hell am I talking about?"

She shook her head, her face crumpling. "I'm sorry, I'm so sorry. I didn't know—I didn't know this was going to happen. Nothing like this has happened to me before."

Toby laughed, once, and turned away from her. In his navy coat his back stood narrow but rigid against the gray sky. "Nothing like this has happened to me, either."

She went to him. She pressed her head against his chest. "Please, Toby."

Looking up, she saw his face as it twisted. She stared helpless at the anger in his eyes. "No," he said. And then he pushed her away.

They saw each other one last time, at Whittington, when Abby went in to pick up her paycheck. One of the interns—a new face she didn't recognize—told her he was out back, waiting for a delivery. As she pushed open the hydraulic doors and walked around the corner into the asphalt bay, she saw him signing a form for a bike messenger, holding the envelope up in farewell.

"Toby," she said. "Hello."

An ambushed expression crossed his face. She waited. He didn't smile. "Hello."

"I was just—I wanted to say hi. See how you are."

He nodded. "Fine. Busy, fine. You?"

She shrugged. "Same, I suppose." His hair was slightly longer. She remembered the smell of it. "Fine."

"Well—Abby." He put his head to one side and squinted. His voice was final. "These things, they—" For a second he wavered—she thought he was going to reach for her, she held her breath—but he looked away and his jaw hardened again. "These things happen."

He was going to go. And what was she going to say? I'm researching my own documentary. Lucia is developing a drama series. We meet up after work at a bar on Elizabeth Street and tell each other stories about our days. When the spring comes, we'll go on a holiday somewhere—drive to Texas, maybe, or fly to Buenos Aires. We have people over, writers and other directors, and we watch videos and dance and cook and we went to see the revival of that Odets play and it's all wonderful, wonderful, only every now and then— every day...

She saw it now. As she stood there in the loading bay and watched him turn, watched him walk away, she saw the new reality that would never be filtered through a lens. She saw that every day she would think of Toby, would see him sitting on that bench under the Christmas lights, or lying on the futon in his tiny, cramped room, or falling toward her at that very first party, before they had kissed. These things happen. Every day she would wonder how he was feeling now; how much he could see. These things. Every day she'd think of him and every day she would feel the small, tender, hurting place that nothing, no thing in her new life could ever seem to fill.

LUCIA NEVAI

STEP MEN

We'd seen the body. Now we wanted to see the car.

The mortician's wife gave us directions. There are only
two stoplights in this town, she said. She said to go left at
the second light—we'd see the car one block up.

We climbed into the big blue van: me, my son Roddy,
and his stepfathers, two of my three exes. Within moments,
we were barreling east on the Arizona interstate, free of the
town. Four lanes of gleaming eighteen-wheelers surrounded
us. The interstate felt like a giant existential amusement
park ride: we were all connected, our wheels were spinning,
we were going nowhere. Straw-colored scrub grass stretched
for miles to the north, miles to the south. A dry, sinister
wind was blowing. Intermittently it gathered steam and
slammed the van, wrenching the steering wheel away from
Jacques, ex number two. Our son, Neil, was dead.

"We missed it." Roddy stated the obvious with a gentle-
ness and resignation that calmed all three of us. I was proud
of Roddy. Gone were the days of the angry shaved head, the

endless scowl. Gone was the hiss that passed for an answer
to a yes-or-no question. At twenty-four, Roddy looked and
acted like a matinee idol from the coming millennium, all
groomed and glamorous with black fingernails and thrift-
store seventies hoodlum polyester. His anger went into his
music now, screaming free jazz that a few people liked.

The van was a rental with plush velour seats. The arm-
rests were adjustable, the back seats swivelled. There were
drink holders here and there. Roddy and I flew out to
Phoenix from New York and rented the van from Avis. I
thought we might need a lot of room. I had called all the
fathers—Jacques in Vermont, Howard in L.A., Sol in Nai-
robi—and left messages on their machines, telling them to
meet us in Phoenix at the Avis lot between twelve and one.

Howard, ex number three, was there waiting for us at
the Avis lot. His jaw looked tan beneath his Armani sunglasses. His haircut made him look rich. He was doing well.
When we split up, he changed his name from Howie to
Howard and moved from New York to L.A. His movie was
finally being made. He and Roddy shook hands, then he
hugged me. His back was shivering. His back always shivered when he was upset.

Jacques showed up next, same wild mass of hair he'd
had in the sixties, the same cocky, menacing air. Jacques was
a brawling French-Canadian Hell's Angel, still masquerad-
ing as a counterculture type. He was now making a go of it
as an exorcist.

Roddy was sitting in the driver's seat. Jacques told him
to move over. I freaked out. "I want Roddy to drive," I said
three times. Jacques had wrecks. He lost an eye in Mexico.
He lost the top half of his left ear in Maine. He felt hormon-
ally obligated to terrorize his passengers with theatrical

displays of traffic-related agility. I was prepared to wrestle
Jacques for the keys, to walk the fifty miles to the mortuary
in the scorching Arizona sun alone if Jacques won.

"It's all right, Mom," Roddy said. "It's going to be fine."
He got out, handing the keys to Jacques. I climbed into the
back of the van to lie down. Roddy sat next to me. Howard
rode shotgun, his back shivering madly.

"Don't wait for Sol," Roddy said wisely. His father, ex
number one, was fanatical and obsessive, a man who was so
busy saving the world that he missed his son's birthday
party ten years in a row. When he lived three blocks from us
in Manhattan, he never showed up for family occasions.
Why would he now that he lived in the Serengeti? Still, we
called him. Roddy left urgent word with his guide: where to
meet us, why, and when. That was Roddy's genius, always to
give Sol the information, but never to publicly allow himself
to hope Sol would actually show.

Now Jacques was looking for a U-turn. He eased the van
across three lanes and onto the shoulder. To do it safely took
ten miles. Jacques had become a reasonable driver. We crept
along the shoulder toward the U-turn, the van shuddering
and jumping sideways with each passing tractor-trailer.
Howard was petrified, but he didn't try to take over. He
didn't even say a word. His tan jaw was flexing aerobically
beneath his Armani sunglasses. Of the three, he had loved
me the most.

Jacques came to a full stop on the median. It was calm,
quiet, and strange there. The sound of the wind blended
with the sound of the traffic in a serene New Age hum. I was
glad we were all in shock. It was pleasant: death's free sedative. Here were four former big-time antagonists, neutered
of agenda, purged of history, simplified and tranquilized,
people who overshot a stoplight.

Jacques took a deep breath, gearing up to inch his way onto the westbound shoulder. Roddy crouched on the backseat facing out the rear window, watching hard for a break in traffic. Ahh. I felt sick with sorrow. He used to sit like that on car trips when he was ten. Neil used to poke him in the bottom. Roddy had lost his brother, his only sibling, the sole being who shared his childhood.

Slowly, Jacques brought the car up to speed on the shoulder. Roddy provided regular updates. "Not yet. Not yet." Howard closed his eyes. "Now!" Roddy said, and Jacques yanked the van hard into the fast lane, gunning the accelerator as he was born to do. We were caught up safely in the fleet again, tonnage roaring west, engines whining, truck drivers to our left and right bald-eyed on uppers, pushing ninety.

"Well done," Howard said, opening his eyes.

So the step men knew how to behave after all. Why hadn't they all along? Why had they waited to cooperate until Neil was dead?

Back in town, we followed the directions backward. We took a right at the first light. We went one block. On the left was a beauty parlor. Wanda's Hair World. No one wanted to get out of the car to ask Wanda anything.

Just in case the mortician's wife was off by a light, we went back to the main road, drove to the second light, and took a right. On the left, there was a gas station. We all felt better. At least a gas station had something to do with cars.

We rolled in and waited. A young man in a striped golf shirt and khaki pants came out. He had a very small nose. Jacques rolled down his window. "We're looking for the green Chevy that was in the accident with the bus," Jacques said.

"It used to be here," he said. He looked at us without curiosity as if there was no connection to be made between a

blue van full of strangers from out of town and a dead boy
who made headlines by setting fire to his motel room, then
driving his car head-on into a Greyhound bus. "It's not here
anymore," he said. "It's in the county yard." He gave us directions. None of us heard him very well.

"Did he say to pass a school?" Jacques asked.

"He said something about passing two motels," Howard
said.

I felt totally confused. Everything in this town looked
like a motel. The sheriff's office was in the Budget vein. The
mortuary was more Ramada. How could we tell if we were
passing real motels?

Jacques crept forward. All four of us were watching
hard out the windows on both sides of the van, eyes trained
violently on the façades, façades with numbers missing, sur-
faces painted blank with Arizona light, blanker than seemed
possible, like camouflage, taking information from us without giving any. I was afraid the town would soon be over and
we would be barreling west toward Las Vegas again in the
unavoidable company of several hundred tractor-trailers.

"School," Roddy announced. We watched it go by, sunlight strobing hypnotically on windowpanes, paper tulips
scotch-taped to the glass. "Motel," Roddy said. Then again,
"Motel."

I saw it, I saw the car. Alone in knee-high grass behind
twelve-foot-high chain link. Neil's Chevy, a beautiful metallic
color, the blue green of the water in the Caribbean. I had expected a twisted, mangled mess, a stomach-turning dish of
steel spaghetti splashed with glass and blood, a frozen 3-D
interstate battle scream. True, the entire front half of the car
was now in the backseat, but it seemed to me more whole
than it should be, given what happened—just as his body

had seemed to me more whole than it should be. Given what happened.

We had gone in to see the body one at a time. I was elated. My darling, my darling. He wasn't shredded or disfigured. He wasn't charred or amputated. He was whole. His shoulders were cold to the touch, but they yielded when I hugged him—as if he were waiting for me to get there before he went into rigor mortis. I lifted the creepy cloth the mortician used to cover the body to look at his feet. I loved his feet. Our feet look alike. Our big toes jut out where they connect to the bone at the ball of the foot. "Neil, Neil," I said, "Do you have any message for me?"

Be kind to Dad, I felt him say.

My hands were clutching the chain link so hard my fingers and thumbs hurt. A tall, potbellied Hawaiian man in a cowboy hat came up to the gate with a key. His face looked a little like a wreck itself. He unfastened the padlock and dragged the gate open. "Take your time," he said, and he meant it. He leaned back against the gate to light a cigarette.

The car was loaded to the gills with Neil's stuff, things as sweet and familiar to me as the special clean smell of his skin: the red-and-black Navajo blanket, the sub-zero sleeping bag, the green nylon tent, the folding spade, the water purifier. He'd been driving across America for a year, camping out in conditions of extreme heat and cold. I had in my pocket the postcard he'd just sent from the Grand Canyon. It came in the mail yesterday, after I got the call from the Coconino County Sheriff's Office. Detective Stu Lansberry told me what happened. He told me Neil, or someone they believed was Neil, had driven up and down the interstate shooting at the driver of a Greyhound bus—and missing. He said no one was hurt but Neil, and Neil was dead.

I took the postcard with me. On the plane, I kept reading and rereading it, looking for clues, but there was only
one—Neil signed it "love." Neil and I had been through a lot
in the last two years. Like it or not, you have to respect
someone who loses their mind. You can be sure they would
have preferred not to. As with any out-of-control molecular
process, it was surely packed with indescribable terror and
required a great deal of bravery.

There were some unfamiliar things in the car, too. Guns.
A gas mask. A night-vision scope. An unused U.S. Navy
arctic-weight jumpsuit, so new it still held the crease marks
from being in the mail-order box. Neil was on the way to
Alaska when he changed his mind and killed himself.

The wind picked up. "What's today?" I asked. Roddy put
his arm around me. "It's Thursday, Mom," he said. The way
he said it calmed me. I had asked him this before, perhaps
five times. My throat was lurching toward a sob that would
never end. Jacques saved me, handing me a smudge stick.

"Wild desert sage," he said, lighting the tip.

"Thank you," I said.

I had freaked out in the mortuary when the mortician
asked us what were our "wishes." I said burial at sea. I said
Neil had read a Chekhov story and told me burial at sea was
the best kind of burial. Jacques had gently overruled me,
recommending cremation. Then when I refused to leave the
body, Jacques distracted me, gently again, saying we all had
something important to do. We had to purge the car. And
here we were, purging the car. How strange. When Neil was
alive, Jacques had terrible ideas for family events. His ideas
for how to spend birthdays, holidays, and Christmas always
involved too much travel, too much waiting, and too many
people he'd just met along for the ride.

A silvery ribbon of soothing, pungent, herbal smoke curled off the tip of my sage stick.

"Eagle feathers," Jacques said, handling several long, strong, formidable feathers to Howard. "These are holy."

Howard accepted them as if they were.

To Roddy, Jacques presented a strange rattle made of skin and shells and hair. "For demons," he said. "The last time I tried to exorcise Neil, he had around eighteen demons."

Jacques himself was holding a large, lavender quartz crystal on a sacred-looking pillow sewn of wine-colored velvet, which looked suspiciously like a pillow I had sewn of wine-colored velvet for his mother twenty years ago.

"We're going to walk around the car—clockwise," Jacques announced. "Glenda will lead. We want to release the fragments of Neil's spirit which are still attached to this site."

I walked the way we walked in choir in junior high school, a slightly labored, solemn, swaying processional. Roddy stepped into line behind me shaking the rattle in 11/8 time.

"What do I do with the feathers?" Howard asked with no hint of sarcasm.

"Raise them to the sky," Jacques said. "To give wings to the spirit fragments." This I had to see, Howie raising eagle feathers to the sky. I looked over my shoulder, but before Howard could attempt it, Roddy stopped everything by yelling, "Dad!"

There he was, ex number one, climbing out of a yellow taxicab in his African bush khakis and pith helmet, walking toward us with mild indignation, saying, "Where were you? I was there. At one. You said between twelve and one."

Sol gave me a quick, covetous once-over—apparently I looked better than his current lady friend—and said, as if

I'd only been away an hour instead of twenty-five years, "You cut your hair."

"Jacques," Roddy said, "do you have something for Sol?"

Jacques fished around in his backpack. "Aroma scent," he said, presenting Sol with a small, very blue bottle topped off with a Victorianesque atomizer. "It purifies negativity," Jacques said. Sol seemed to accept this along with the bottle.

I started up the processional again, clockwise around the car through the knee-high grass, my sage stick lacing the air with its heavy merciful scent, lacing my brain with the scent I would forever after link with spiritual freedom. Howard clasped the quill ends in his hands and in an impressive abandonment of inhibition, raised the feathers high over his head, sweeping them across the sky to the beat of Roddy's rattle. Sol followed, spritzing the Chevy. Jacques fell in behind Sol.

We marched and swayed, marched and swayed. I assumed Jacques had some spiritually efficacious number of circuits in mind and that he would alert me when the number had been reached. Each time I looked at the Hawaiian man smoking at the gate, he had changed. He went from a scarred-up, alcoholic motor-head type to a gentle gatekeeper, neutral yet benign, a witness to our ceremony. The magic number of circuits turned out to be eighty-one—nine times nine—we found out eventually when Jacques let us stop. Jacques often made the mistake of explaining too much about his magic. We were all happier. When we gave Jacques back his things, we took turns hugging. It was three o'clock. Neil was burning. We had a few more hours to kill before it was time to pick up his ashes and drive to the Grand Canyon to scatter them—another good idea of Jacques's.

Jacques was wrapping our ritual objects in sacred silks and packing them carefully in his backpack. "What should we do now?" I said, and I looked at Howard. It was his cue. He overcame his speechlessness and rose to the occasion as he had every time I'd been hungry in a crisis during the ten years of our marriage.

"Let's eat," he said, and raised his arms to include us all.

JON **Billman**

CUSTER ON MONDAYS

sunday was a battle

Sunday, June 25th, was a battle. The last of the smoke
cleared in the afternoon, the dust settled in the barley field,
and the Sioux, Arapaho, Cheyenne, Crow, and Seventh Cavalry called the horses, picked up the arrows, dusted themselves off, and headed downtown together for cold beers at
The Mint. Most of the chiefs and officers had planes to
catch in Billings, but the group got on without them. They'd
pick up the Indian wars again at next year's Reenactment of
Custer's Last Stand.

On Monday morning, June 26th, the day after the big
battle, Owen Doggett came home from The Mint to find he
was now trespassing on the dirt half acre he used to almost
own. Everything the actor now owned formed a crude
breastwork ten yards from the chipped cinder-block front
step that led to the single-wide he also used to almost own.
A buckskin shirt. A few T-shirts. Some socks. A faded union
suit. A broken A.M. radio with a coat-hanger antenna. His
Sage fly rod. An empty duffel bag. A brick of pistol rounds,
and the title to the '76 Ford Maverick.

Charlie Reynolds, the basset hound, was off chasing rabbits in the cheatgrass; he belonged solely to Owen Doggett now. Owen Doggett banged on the window of the locked trailer house with his gloved fists and yelled, "Sweetheart, I'll make you eggs!"

His wife had already begun her day's work, tying flies for an outfitter in Sheridan. Her fly patterns are intricate, exacting, and hold the subtle variances of nature usually reserved for spiderwebs, mud dauber nests, and snowflakes. Through the cloudy window of her workroom, Sue Doggett looked up from her vise and out at her husband in his riding boots and dirty wool tunic. She mouthed, "Read my lips: I am not acting."

THE SIOUX

Mr. and Mrs. Owen Doggett were married three years ago on a moonlit Monday midnight in Reno, Nevada, after meeting at a Halloween party and dating for exactly sixteen days. The engagement lasted an afternoon and a dinner. They took the red-eye out of Billings and stayed drunk for the entire two-day trip. They married in the same clothes they met in—his custom-made Custer buckskin, her star-spangled Wonder Woman bustier. The wedding cost exactly twenty-seven dollars, bourbon and snapshots included.

Sue is a full-blooded Crow. Owen Doggett calls her "The Sioux." And sue is what she is doing; she's suing the trooper for all he's worth. No negotiations. Owen Doggett isn't worth much. Sue gave him an old government Colt revolver as a wedding present. She wanted the valuable relic back. "Indian giver!" he called her. He cannot afford a lawyer.

the colonel

Owen Doggett and Ben Fish are locals, extras, privates. But Owen will tell you he's a trouter by heart, an actor by trade, and he has faith he will one day soon be the hero, the star, the colonel in the Hardin, Montana, Reenactment of Custer's Last Stand. "Call me Colonel," he'll tell you. He is rehearsing. "I'm an actor from Hollywood. Bred-in-the-bone." Right now he, his trouting buddy, and Charlie Reynolds are on their way east so Owen Doggett the actor can audition to be the *Black Hills Passion Play*'s substitute Pontius Pilate. Colonel will not tell you he is only a private. He will tell you he may soon be cast as Pontius Pilate in a large-scale production of the second-greatest story ever told, the story of Jesus' last seven days in South Dakota. He will not tell you he is from Hollywood, Pennsylvania, and that he has to rent a nineteen-year-old grade horse when he wants to ride.

Hardin's current Custer is a Shakespearean-trained actor from Monroe, Michigan. He looks like Colonel George Armstrong Custer, owns a white stallion like Custer's, pulls a custom four-horse trailer, does beer commercials for a brewery out of Detroit, and calls his wife "Libbie." It will not be easy. Colonel is torn between what he wants to do, what his heart tells him—goddamnit, you're an actor!—and what is to be done. "History is the now of yesterday," he says. In his own recent history, Colonel has caught some nice fish, drunk a few beers, cheated on his wife, and watched some movies. He sees himself on the big screen—not in a factory, not in an office. He hasn't paid many bills, but "Hell," he says, "we don't have a satellite dish and we don't get cable. That's a big savings right there."

Libbie Bacon Custer wanted her husband to be President of the United States of America. Sue Doggett wanted Colonel to get a not-have-to-always-tenderize-a-cheap-cut-of-beef job. Not full-time necessarily, just something where the trooper worked more than one day every two weeks. But that would mean giving up a few Mondays—and Tuesdays, Wednesdays, and the like—of sore-lipping fish.

"Do I not bless you with much fish and bread?" Colonel asks his wife.

"Whitefish and Wonder Bread every day isn't my idea of heaven," says Sue.

THE PRIVATE

Colonel calls his trouting buddy, Ben Fish, "Private." They might be knocking back a few Rainiers at The Mint. They might be boning up on the Black Hills Expedition of '74 over morning coffee at the B-I. It might be Monday, when they're casting the Little Bighorn River for browns and rainbows. They might be, like right now, rumbling down U.S. 212, on their way only a few hours after dawn, with Charlie Reynolds in the middle and Private riding shotgun. Just the three of them in the old oil-burning baby-blue Maverick, their forage caps cocked back on their heads, spitting the hulls of sunflower seeds out the windows. For Private this trip is a chance to scout some new country, cast some new water.

Private is a teacher. He has stitches in the back of the head where the heel of his pregnant ex-wife's cowboy boot caught him from point-blank range. He, too, has come home from work to find his earthly belongings on the front yard, in the kind of rain that is almost snow. He has lived in a U-Store-It shed for an entire January. Private has slept in libraries and eaten ketchup soup and melba toast for breakfast. He has talked with lawyers he couldn't afford. He has lived in Wyoming.

Private is learning not who he is but where he needs to be. It's a process of elimination. Sue gives him flies for simply appreciating them and showing her the little spiral-bound steno pad in which he logs which fly caught which fish under which conditions. Private is growing older, which means to him that it's harder to have fun.

"One week," he tells Colonel. "One week and you'll have to find another couch to sleep on."

Hardin, Montana

Every now and then responsibility picks up an ax handle and knocks Colonel into government service. He delivers mail on a substitute basis. It's a job, he would tell Sue. It's a job. He works about once every two weeks. Right now it is good to be getting out of town to see about some acting, to see about some fishing.

Hardin is a tough town because it is one thing but also another. Most of it is not part of the reservation. But some of the town, across the Burlington Northern tracks, rests on the reservation. You can see cattle over there graze through the front and back yards of the trailer homes and government prefabs that are a little more in need of things—a window that isn't cardboard, siding that doesn't slap in the wind. The roads are mostly gravel and dust. There is the beef-packing plant where many townspeople, mostly Crow, work. The Crow kids go to school where Private, Mr. Fish, teaches history: Hardin Intermediate. The Bulldogs.

Every May the Bulldogs take a field trip to the Little Bighorn Battlefield. The Little Bighorn draws people from all over the country, from all over the world. Some of the students live less than ten miles from the national monument, and they've never been to it. Mr. Fish wears his wool

Seventh Cavalry uniform, riding boots and all, and acts as if he were there on June 25, 1876, taking fire from all sides.

"Company dismount!" he calls, and the students file off the bus. "Form a skirmish line on the west flank of the bus and hold your ground. Any horseplay and you'll be back in second-period study hall so fast your head will spin."

Mr. Fish and the campaign-hatted guides lead the students around the grounds amid the signs that read WATCH FOR RATTLESNAKES and METAL DETECTORS PROHIBITED. The spring wind whips their hair and makes it difficult to hear, though they understand. There are many questions. Sharp notes fill the afternoon like gun smoke as Mr. Fish bugles the students back on the bus. They talk motives and strategy, treaties and tactics on the short bus ride back to Hardin.

Colonel doesn't get called to work much. Private has summers off and many sick days during the year. On Mondays they go fishing. Sometimes to the Tongue River down in Wyoming. Sometimes the Powder River over in Broadus. Sometimes the Bighorn. But most often the Little Bighorn. They take sandwiches and keep a sharp eye out for rattlesnakes, Indians, and landowners. And it's often hot. Very hot. They fish other days, too, but always Mondays.

A sunday drive through custer's montana

By driving east—going backwards—down U.S. 212, over the Wolf Mountains, through Busby and Lame Deer, Colonel, Charlie Reynolds, and Private study through the yellow-bug-splattered windshield where Custer and his men camped on their way to the last campaign from Fort Abraham Lincoln, Dakota Territory. It's probably how the outfit would have retreated.

"If you were captured by the Sioux, the idea was to

shoot yourself before they had a chance to torture you." The actor steers with his knees, making finger pistols in the air over the steering wheel. "Troopers kept one round, their last round, for just that purpose. Shoot yourself in the head before they could cut your heart out while you watched."

The road is rough here and cuts through the charcoal remains of a forest fire that burned most of the salable Northern Cheyenne Indian Reservation, but it gets better when they get to Ashland and back into everyone's Montana.

"Private," says Colonel, not shouting over the rattle and thunk of the car so that his words are lost in the noise and it appears that he is just moving his lips, "know what the slowest thing in the world is?" The warm July wind rushes through the open windows and the gaps in the brittle rubber gasket surrounding the windshield. Private is used to this Maverick lip-reading.

"Besides us right now?" says Private. The muffler and tailpipe have a few holes in them, like tin whistles, and the sunflower seeds taste like exhaust. "It's either us right now or a reservation funeral procession with only one set of jumper cables," says Private. The speedometer needle is shaking at around fifty-one miles an hour.

Private isn't laughing. Charlie Reynolds isn't laughing. Colonel's eyes glass over at the humble recognition of having told a joke everyone heard many campaigns ago. But as you get older—he is forty-one, nearly past his Custer prime— you forget. Everything turns to history with daguerreotype eyes and brittle, yellowed edges.

"BUGS"

Charlie Reynolds stands on Private's lap and sticks his nose into the fifty-one-mile-an-hour prairie wind. Private lets his palm ride on the stream of air and dreams of becoming a scout. The Colonel talks numbers. Bag limits. Length, girth, weight. Hook size. Tippet strength. Rod action. He talks of the beefiest brown in Montana, the heftiest rainbow in Dakota Territory. "Pleistocene man used shards of bone for hooks," he says. "Indians used rock-hard spirals of rawhide until we traded steel hooks with them. Custer used steel hooks."

What is different about Sue's flies, different from the flies tied by hundreds of nimble-fingered Western women for pennies apiece, is that they are tied for fish, not for fishermen, aesthetics. Unless, that is, they are true fishermen and know the difference deep inside them, like right and wrong.

There is something of the ancient in them. From her ancestors on the frontier, as well as from evolution: her Darwinian ancestors, the fish. Sue tests her flies in an old aquarium in her workroom. The aquarium is stained, filled with the murky water of the Little Bighorn. With a pair of fencing pliers, she cuts the hook off at the bend and ties it onto a length of leader attached to a two-foot-long willow branch and flings it into the tank from across the small room. Weight. Aerodynamics. Flight. She is looking for balance. In the aquarium are several small rainbow and brown trout. She gets on her back, crawls underneath the aquarium stand, and studies the trouts' reactions to the new insects through the tank's glass bottom.

After only a week she throws the burlap water bag over her shoulder and walks to the river to turn the trout back into the Little Bighorn. "Thank you," she tells them, "thank you. Good-bye." She then unfolds the little pack rod from her day pack and ties on one of her new and experimental flies. She casts and catches new fish to help her with her work. Though it rarely happens, if she does not catch new helper fish, she walks back to the trailer with the empty burlap bag, thinking about how she is going to adjust the new patterns. She enjoys being outsmarted now and then.

What matters is what an imitation looks like on the water, in the water, not warm and dry in a tackle shop that smells like chicken livers and epoxy. Sue's workroom smells like old wool, spruce, and duck feathers. Damp dog, river water, coffee. She rendezvouses with Ben Fish at the river and bails the aquarium out once a week, trout or no trout.

If it is late and he is drunk, Colonel may tell you Sue ties the most beautiful, most perfect trout flies in the Louisiana Purchase. The Colonel calls them "bugs."

тhe тreaty

Mr. and Mrs. Owen Doggett celebrated their three-year anniversary by getting a six-pack of Heineken instead of Rainier and toasting the event at home while watching *She Wore a Yellow Ribbon* on video.

A week later, that belly-dancing night at The Mind, Sue said only this: "Three strikes, you're out." The faraway look in the Colonel's eyes was a sure sign he knew she meant it and he didn't shoot back, didn't ask about strike one, strike two.

Sue calls the legal papers "the treaty." She'll get the waterbed and the microwave. The banana boxes of Harley-Davidson parts. The eight-track player and turntable. The veneer bedroom set. The Toyota Corolla and the single-wide.

The straw that broke the camel's back is named Salome.

salome on saturdays

Real live camels. Salome told Colonel and Private about them on her breaks at The Mint. She is an actress. She works the *Passion Play* during the week and The Mint most Fridays and Saturdays. She also told the Colonel she could arrange a private audition for him because she happened to know for a fact that Pontius Pilate was moving to Florida and the director owed her a few favors that she'd probably never get a chance to cash in on anyway.

Belly dancing is hard work, she also said. So she took lots of breaks. She was not taking a break when Sue walked in after one of the battles to find her Colonel. Sue found him. The Colonel pleaded with her that it was all part of the act and about how belly dancing was an art form going back to biblical times and that it should be respected.

Horses, too, they have horses. Doves. Sheep. Donkeys.

The Black Hills Expedition of 1995

They stop in tiny Alzada for Cokes, oil, gas, beef jerky for Charlie Reynolds, brake fluid, more sunflower seeds. Colonel says to Private, "You want to scrub them mustard bugs off the windshield?" It is Sunday afternoon when they cross the twenty or so miles of the townless northeast corner of Wyoming. Yes, Colonel is trying out for Pontius Pilate, but they will fish, too.

"Nothing between this car and the North Pole but a barbed-wire fence," Private tells Colonel.

"Nothing between this car and the South Pole but Mount Rushmore and a fistful of gold mines," Colonel tells Private.

They cross the Belle Fourche River and see the Black Hills, the sacred land the Indians were afraid of.

"They heard thunder in there and thought it was the Everywhere Spirit," says Colonel.

"Maybe they were right," replies Private. "This wind does blow."

SPEARFISH, DAKOTA TERRITORY. The sign at the edge of town has a trout with a spear sticking through it. "Trout are not indigenous to the Black Hills," Colonel says to Private and Charlie Reynolds. "They were stocked, all of them. The Indians speared chubs and suckers. That's all there were."

The sun is shining and the summer-school coeds are not wearing much. "Welcome to Calvary," says the Colonel.

The Colonel tells Charlie Reynolds to stay in the car. The dog jumps onto the gravel parking lot of the Shady Spot Motel (phone, free coffee) and high-tails it to a bush, which he immediately sniffs, then waters. Private tackles him and lugs the hound back to the car.

The Shady Spot rests between the *Passion Play* amphitheater and the city park Spearfish Creek runs through. Families here enjoy the steady increases in the value of their ranch-styles and don't mind the flash and rumble of the Crucifixion and Ascension three nights a week. There are coffeehouses and bookstores and no bad neighborhoods in Spearfish. No railroad tracks. No reservations.

"Reservations?" asks the elderly desk clerk, looking them over in their forage caps, Bermuda shorts, T-shirts (Colonel's ROLLING STONES VOODOO LOUNGE TOUR, Private's BAGELBIRD), and sandals.

"Yup. Doggett."

"You fellas with the *Passion Play*?" asks the desk clerk.

"We're Texas Rangers in town on a pornography bust," says Colonel. "You rent by the hour, too?" The desk clerk does not think this is funny, is frowning. Private nods. "Yes, we're here for the *Passion Play*. There a discount for that?" One dollar.

Colonel then pays the two-dollar surcharge for Charlie

Reynolds after the desk clerk says, still looking down at his reservation book, "I see you brought a dog."

THE BOY COLONEL

Her flies are small miracles. Tiny damsels, Daisy Millers, opulent caddis flies in all colors and sizes. Shiny Telico nymphs. Little Adams. Noble royal coachmen. Muddlar minnows and grasshoppers. Bead-heads. Streamers. Hare's ears. Stone flies, salmon flies. Woolly buggers, black gnats, and renegades. She even invented a fly she calls the Libbie Bacon, tied with the soft hair from Charlie Reynolds's belly.

"It's a shame that you'll now have to buy them, pay for them," Private tells Colonel. But their fly boxes are still worlds of insects: peacock hurl, elk hair, chicken hackle, and deer tail, rabbit fur and mallard feather woven to life around a gold hook.

"And you won't?" asks the Colonel.

Sue gave Private a full fly box as a Christmas gift the first year he moved to Hardin from Wyoming. Sometimes at night, when he's alone—most every night—and cannot sleep, he opens the box under his reading light and gently touches the flies and his heart speeds up a bit. When he would lose a fly—on a large willow, a snag in the river, maybe a fish—Sue would replace it with one of the same kind but yet different, one thing but also something else. None of her flies are exactly alike. Private pointed this out to Colonel, who still called them "bugs."

Private started keeping the fly journal the first day he fished with the flies Sue tied for him, the morning of the day after Christmas. It was bitter cold and the guides on the rod kept freezing so that he would have to dip the graphite shaft into the water to de-ice the rod before each cast. Yet he caught more trout than ever in his life.

Private looks through his fly box while Colonel ties fresh leader and tippet material onto his line. Their plan is to take in tonight's *Passion Play* (free tickets) and do some fishing tomorrow after the ten o'clock audition. From the motel room window, they can see Calvary, the sturdy cross as big as a pine tree, up the hill to the east of the amphitheater. "Welcome to the Cavalry," says Colonel.

They were trying to have children—if not directly trying to prevent them is trying. Sue would often say, "I already have my hands full taking care of one boy. I don't need any more." This concerns the Colonel still. Even more so now. His mustache weighs at his lip when he thinks about it too hard.

scouting

Spearfish Creek runs strong and clear through the *Passion Play* neighborhood. Today you can stand on any bridge in town and peer down at fish feeding against the current. Many healthy rainbows and browns. Colonel's eyes widen as the men count the black silhouettes of trout feeding on the insects that wash their way. Heartbeats quicken. He calls this creek a "river."

The detachment of three—a colonel, a private, and a basset hound scout—set out into the afternoon sun from the Shady Spot to scout the holes, the "honey buckets," they will fish tomorrow. There are many of these honey buckets running through the backyards of the people who don't mind living in the New Testament neighborhood.

As they patrol the creek, the troopers wave to the grillers and the gardeners and the fertilizers and waterers, crossing now and then through the cool, calf-deep water in their sandals, though only some of the neighbors wave back; some sheepishly from behind their gazing balls and ceramic deer; some annoyed from behind their smoking Webers; some taken aback with beers in their hands, as if to say, *Honey, I think Colonel George Armstrong Custer in a Rolling Stones T-shirt and his basset hound just waded through our backyard.*

the color of sunday

Salome did not tell them about this: the hatchery! How could she have left this out? The creek runs under a stonework bridge, and they wade out from the shadow of the bridge and peer through the chain-link and barbed wire NO TRESPASSING fence of what the sign heralds as the D. C. BOOTH FISH HATCHERY, EST. 1896. And for whole moments, minutes, they are old men outside the chain-link of the city swimming pool, Seaworld, Marineland, staring in.

Tall cottonwoods, oaks, and spruce trees, as well as the flowers that have been planted around each of the three stone-and-concrete rearing pools, reflect off the green-gray water. Two lovers and a family with a stroller and children walk along the boardwalk and gaze into the pools. You can, for a quarter, buy a handful of trout meal from the gumball machine bolted to the railing. Many signs: NO FISHING.

A young woman in a khaki uniform sows trout meal from a tin bucket. The water boils with feeding fingerlings. Her auburn hair catches the late-afternoon light and is the color of Sunday. She is singing to the fry as she feeds them. Her hand dips into the bucket and she bows slightly and releases the meal. "I will make you fishers of men, fishers of men, fishers of men." Charlie Reynolds chases a butterfly at the edge of the shallow water running over their feet, never catching it, as the men watch, mouths slightly closed, hearts racing. "I will make you fishers of men, if you follow me."

The lovers and the family stop to lean over the railing and look down into another pool, a larger pool. The father buys a handful of trout food and gives it to the young boy, who flings it all at once. The water explodes with trout, trout as big— bigger—than the Colonel and Private and Charlie Reynolds have ever seen. "Good Lord, will you look at that! Did you see the size of those fins?" asks the Colonel. "Those tails!"

"Yes, she is beautiful," says Private in a dry-mouthed whisper.

sunday in jerusalem

The *Black Hills Passion Play* draws people from all over the country, from all over the world. Colonel and Private have never been here. Young Christians in purple tunics direct cars, sell tickets, sell programs. An official program costs as much as it costs Charlie Reynolds to stay at the Shady Spot, where he is now. Outside the ticket office/gift shop there is a rather graceless statue, *Christ Stilling the Waters*, by Gutzon Borglum, the artist who blasted four presidents into a mountain just south of here. The Christ of the sculpture looks less like he's stilling waters than waving to friends.

The evening is cool. The tickets Salome gave them are not excellent, not VIP tickets. The troopers are in the center, the fifty-yard line, but back fifty rows, back far enough to wonder how much real weight Salome pulls around here. But they can see downtown Jerusalem. They can see Calvary. They can see the tall cottonwoods that surround the trout hatchery a couple of blocks away. The troopers stand and remove their forage caps and place them over their hearts for "The Star-Spangled Banner." There is a sliver of moon, not yet a quarter. There is an evening star in the west. The fanfare ends. A blond angel appears in the Great Temple and recites the prologue, "O ye children of God...."

"It's going to be a long night—look at this program— twenty-two scenes," says Colonel.

"That which you will experience today, O people, treasure well within your hearts. Let it be the light to lead you— until your last day." With that the angel disappears and the streets of Jerusalem fill with asses, sheep, armored centurions on white stallions, and laughing, running children.

"Private, did you see the size of those dorsal fins?" says Colonel.

When the play ends, the troopers are not besieged with passion, which is a little disappointing to both of them. An hour and a half of Sunday left. The actor has an audition in eleven and a half hours. Pontius Pilate is a muscular, tan, deep-voiced man. No long dirty-blond curls to his shoulders. No bushy handlebar mustache. It will not be easy.

Fins the size of prairie schooner sails

"Private, you awake?" asks the Colonel at a quarter to midnight.

"Yes," replies Private. "Thinking about Sue?"

"No."

"The audition tomorrow?"

"No." Those fish. "Private, did you see those dorsal fins?"

custer's last stand

They are out the door at midnight with an electric beep of Colonel's Timex Ironman, waders on, vests heavy with tackle, wicker creels, rods in hand, Charlie Reynolds in the lead, scouting his way up the creek. They wade through the same backyards, which are now dark except for a few dim yard lights and the electric blue of hanging bug lights and TVs through a couple of windows. Walking, wading slowly, it is enough light to see by. They do not cast, do not hit the honey buckets they mapped in their heads earlier. "Just where are we going?" asks Private. The troopers are advancing.

They stop under the bridge. Charlie Reynolds is up ahead, rustling through some willows along the bank. They take the lines from the reels and thread them through the guides on their graphite rods. Colonel reaches into a vest pocket and pulls out a tin fly box. He opens it and the insects come to life in the dim glow of a streetlamp. Gold bead-heads, hooks, and peacock hurl shine in the low light. Colonel selects a size ten delta-wing caddis fly, threads his tippet through the eye, cinches down a simple Orvis knot, and slicks the insect up with silvery floatant to keep it on top of the water.

"Fishing dry, huh," says Private.

"I'm not yet sure what these Dakota fish like for breakfast," says Colonel.

Private ties on a humble Libbie Bacon in a size fourteen that will sink maybe a foot below the surface in still water, but no more.

Upstream, Charlie Reynolds finds a low spot where he ducks under the fence and into the D. C. BOOTH FISH HATCHERY. The troopers watch the basset hound's silhouette as he sniffs around the ponds and lunges at the bugs ticking under the floodlights. "How the hell did he get in?" asks Private. "Let's advance along the fenceline," says Colonel.

They find the high spot in the rusty cyclone fence.

Colonel goes to his knees and reaches his fragile rod under the sharp steel mesh. "Just how low can you go?" says Colonel. He then commences to crawl under on his soft neoprene belly, careful not to rip the three-millimeter-thick waders. He stands erect, brushing the dirt from his waders and vest. "Private, why don't you check that flank over there?" says Colonel, motioning with his rod toward the tree-lined fencerow at the south end of the hatchery. The rearing ponds are lit from the bottom and they glow in the night.

"Colonel," says Private, his rod leaning against the fence, both hands grasping the fence like a tree sloth, still outside the hatchery, still looking in. "Colonel, I can't go in there."

"Why in heaven's name not?" asks the Colonel, nervously adjusting the drag on his reel between glances at the pools after the occasional light smack of a fish on an unfortunate insect.

"Because it's trespassing," says Private.

Colonel looks at him, his mustache arched in disbelief.

"Because... I'm sorry. I know we've trespassed plenty of times before, but this is different," says Private. "And right now, I'm sorry, I haven't always, but right now I have just a little more left to lose than you."

"For one?" says the Colonel.

Says Private, "A job, for starters."

Colonel reaches into his wicker creel and pulls out the crow-black government Colt. He tucks it back under the fence, handle first, and says, "Here, there's one round in it. You know what to do if we're ambushed."

"You want me to shoot myself?" cries Private.

"Chrissakes, no. Fire into the air, warn me." Colonel leaps atop the stone wall and his rod is at once in shadowy motion, the graphite whip whistling in the still summer night. False

cast, follow through, false cast, follow through—the fly stays
suspended throughout the series of false casts, back and
forth, not landing but rehearsing to land. Sploosh! The moment the delicate caddis kisses the surface of the pool a giant
rainbow trout engulfs it, bowing the rod at a severe angle
while Colonel arches his back and sets his arms to play
the fish.

The rainbow breaks water and skips a few beats across
the surface, tail dancing in the night, its fat belly reflecting
white from the floodlights. Colonel plays out the line, careful not to overstress his leader and tippet. The reel drag
screams as the furious trout takes more line, across the
short pool, around its smooth sides, down, back to the surface, down again.

Private watches this from underneath a willow tree, sen-
tinel duty. Minutes go by and he watches with his mouth
slightly open, jaw set, palms sweating against the cork
handle of his fly rod. He can hear Colonel's heavy adren-
alined breathing and the high-pitched din of monofilament
leader and tippet, taut as a mandolin string.

Two slaps at the water near the Colonel's feet and he
sticks a thumb into her mouth, grasps the lower jaw and
raptures the fish out of the water and into the night air. She
is heavy with eggs, heavy with flesh and fins and bone. Upwards of twelve pounds and easily the largest fish Colonel,
or Private, has ever played, ever captured. Her gills heave as
he stuffs her head-first into his dry day pack that flops and
smacks the concrete sidewalk with the jingle of zippers and
buckles. Colonel reties another caddis where the tippet is
gnawed and stretched. He tosses the old fly on the sidewalk—bent hook, frayed elk hair, and hackle.

"Colonel, let's get out of here, I think a car is coming,"
whispers Private as loud as he can from a copse of ironwood

that runs along the outside of the hatchery's southern length
of fence. Fingers of one hand grasp his expensive fly rod, the
other fingers curl around the smooth hardwood handle of
the government Colt. But Colonel is in the moment, back on
the stone wall, casting in a hyper-necessary, frantic motion
that causes the tippet and leader to jerk and the fly to land a
moment after the heavy slap of the line on the water. Maybe
the car will cruise on by. Maybe whoever is driving will not
see Colonel playing a big fish under the floodlights of the
hatchery. Maybe whoever it is will not hear the gun crack
and echo in the peaceful night. "Goddamnit, Colonel, a car
is coming!" yells Private, the scout.

Another large trout takes the fly just as the million-
candlepower spotlight pans the hatchery like a movie pre-
miere and backs up quickly to light Colonel on the wall,
balancing against the fish, eyes filling with the realization
that his stand on the wall is about to come to an abrupt end.
He looks at the dark water, then up to the blinding light,
back to the water, yells "Ambush!" looks at his expensive rod
and reel, up at the spotlight, back at his rod and reel before
dropping them in the water with the trout still attached to
the business end. He leaps from the wall and runs for Charlie Reynolds's high spot in the fence.

Sploosh!

The government Colt lands in the rearing pond and
sinks to the well-lit bottom, next to the expensive reel attached to the expensive fly rod attached to the expensive
fish.

The deputy's boot pins the Colonel to the ground between his shoulder blades like a speared suckerfish, the
trooper's tail end still in the hatchery, the other half of him a
few feet away from the gently running creek he calls a river.
His forage cap hides his face until the deputy whips it off

and shines a heavy aluminum flashlight in it. The deputy, a Sioux, looks at his partner, looks at the forage cap in his hand, and says, "Good Lord, we've captured the mighty Seventh Cavalry, red-faced and red-handed."

Charlie Reynolds, now on the opposite side of Spearfish Creek, fords the river and licks Colonel on the face. Insects flit around the yellow glow of the deputy's flashlight. "Have any more scouts in there, Colonel . . . Colonel Doggett?" asks the deputy as he reads the Colonel's Montana driver's license. "By the way, I'll need to see a South Dakota fishing license. The fine for not having one is pretty steep. The fines for illegal fishing are pretty steep. The fines for trespassing are pretty steep. Randall, you bring the calculator? Now, about your scouts, Colonel."

Colonel nods, yes, then jerks his head toward the southern fencerow. "Over there, in the scrub," he says. "He's with me on this—he's my lookout . . . try not to shoot him."

They do not shoot the scout. Private waddles out of the willows in his waders with his hands high, forage cap tilted down, rod in the air like a shepherd's staff. "I'm not armed," he says. "I surrender."

"Careful with Colonel," says Private, as a deputy cinches the cuffs around his wrists. "He's got a gun."

"Why didn't you shoot in the air to warn me?" asks Colonel.

"Shoot what?" asks Private, looking Colonel in the eyes. "You're the owner of the dripping gun."

The troopers sit, hands cuffed behind them, in the caged backseat of the Lawrence County Sheriff Department Jeep Cherokee. "She must have gone fourteen pounds," says Colonel. "A fourteen-pound rainbow on a number ten elk-hair caddis. Put that in your fly book."

"That is something that belongs in your history book. It's your story," says Private, "not mine."

"This will probably mean we lose our South Dakota fishing privileges for quite some time," says Colonel. "Private, it's a good thing we live in Montana."

The engine idles and the radio squawks periodically and the deputies gather little bits of evidence from the scene of the trespassing, the slaughter. The troopers watch the deputies put the trout in a plastic garbage bag, twist it shut, and label it. They watch the deputies fish the rod, reel, and pistol from the bottom of the pool, label each, and put them in plastic bags.

The prisoners wait in the Cherokee for what seems like hours. A car pulls alongside the sheriff's vehicle, and a woman's silhouette gets out and walks over to the fence and speaks with the deputies. They show her the rainbow in plastic while she crouches, one leg in the dirt along the fence. After a moment the three of them walk toward the Cherokee. It is the Sunday-haired woman.

She looks at the prisoners. The corners of her eyes are sharp and pointed, like arrowheads, the center glassy and reflective with tears. She is going to say something and the wait for her to begin is agonizing. "They will take anything," she says finally. "They would bite on a pebble. Spit. Anything! Those fish will take a bare hook!" The prisoners see she wants to hit them, spit at them, shoot a flaming arrow through their hearts. Though she doesn't.

"Fourteen pounds, Private," whispers Colonel, then whistles for emphasis after the woman, sobbing, turns for her car. "Fourteen pounds, I tell you. I was going to have that rainbow mounted."

"Owen," says Ben Fish the scout, Ben Fish the teacher,

Ben Fish the trouter. "I'd as soon you call me Ben Fish here on out. I've gone civilian."

spearfish on monday

After nine A.M., Lawrence County Jail, Deadwood, South Dakota. The men breathe easily, adrenaline gone, in the tired relaxation when they've fully realized that fate has them and there is nothing they can do to undo all they've done. They had their photos taken with Lawrence County license plates around their necks. They have ink on their fingertips. They have called Salome for bail money, who said something to the effect of "Leave me the hell alone."

The Sioux deputy walks into the holding room, what they call the tank, says, "Your basset hound is in the pound and your wife called. She's bailing you out. See you at the courthouse in two weeks," and sets a stack of carboned forms in front of the men to sign, and hands the ex-substitute mail carrier a hastily scrawled note:

> *Owen Doggett,*
> *Come home. Be quick. Bring Charlie Reynolds and*
> *Ben Fish. I'm pregnant.*
>
> > *Sue*
>
> *P.S. You can't act as if nothing happened here. But I'm*
> *willing to work on it.*

Owen Doggett reads the note once, twice, three times. His eyes show that he thinks it over deeply. He takes a long breath, exhales, and, without looking up from the note, says, "I suppose she needs me."

Salt, pepper, and tabasco fly, and the men eat the scrambled county eggs in their cell instead of auditioning for

Pontius Pilate at the amphitheater. "These eggs need mustard," says Owen Doggett. Ben Fish chews his eggs quietly.

"Owen, things are settled between you and me. I don't want to have to worry about the three of you. Yes, the eggs do need mustard." It wouldn't take much.

Friday in october

The prairie wind is the color of winter. Mr. Fish tells his eighth-graders that on the Black Hills Expedition of 1874 Custer lost a supply wagon full of whiskey and an expensive Gatling gun in a ravine along Box Elder Creek now known as Custer Gap. He also tells them that Custer and four or five of his subordinates shot a bear. The bear was so full of lead and holes that it couldn't be eaten, couldn't be stuffed.

And he tells them this: "There was a troublemaker with the outfit, a private from Indiana. He stole food rations. He stole coffee, blankets, whiskey. He put locust thorns under saddles. He emptied canteens. One bright morning he cross-hobbled the wrong man's horse. The wrong man shot him in the chest. The chaplain said prayers for his soul and a detail buried him in the shadows of sacred Inyan Kara Mountains. Custer knew the dead man was a bad egg and judged the murder justified."

The class watches Mr. Fish and listens intently to these stories, the details once lost in the folds of history, brought to life again by the teacher, though some stories, for the sake of history, Mr. Fish just makes up.

Monday on the plains

"I have an appointment on Monday," Mr. Fish tells the secretary. "I'll need a sub." He does not tell her the blackflies are hatching on the Little Bighorn. Or that he will be there all day, with his new trouting buddy, Charlie Reynolds, fishing, reading, sucking on sunflower seeds, the two of them eating bologna-and-mustard sandwiches. He does not tell her his old trouting buddy, Owen Doggett, has to work on Monday because the packing plant never closes, never shuts down, and days off are best spent tending to legalities in Dakota Territory. The fine for fishing without a license—the teacher's only crime—can be paid by mail and doesn't show up on your permanent record. He does not tell the secretary that Sue Doggett just tied some tiny new blackflies that buzz and dance around a room on their own when a white man isn't looking. He does not tell her that Sue gave him some.

philip **gourevitch**

MORTALITY CHECK

They got Kretzky coming out of the liquor store. Two men, one blade, a sunny crowded street—he walked right into it. Three steps down the sidewalk he realized he'd stopped moving. Someone behind him held his wrist and a hand appeared before him, flashing a glimpse of steel. A skinny little white guy stood there in a limp, powder-blue sweat suit, not a person whom Kretzky, a big white guy in a black leather jacket, would have thought to fear. The man had hair the color of a nicotine stain, cut like a terrier's, and his face was red and pinched. He told Kretzky to shut up. Kretzky hadn't said a word.

The man's weapon was no longer than four inches. It looked almost dainty, cradled in his folded hand, the blade flat between his third and fourth fingers. But retract the hand into a fist, punch and twist, and Kretzky considered the prospect of survival was not good.

The mugger's eyes were all pupil, ticking from side to side in minute increments. Kretzky felt them on his chest, his groin, his throat, the bridge of his nose.

The hand of someone he couldn't see squeezed suddenly between his legs. Kretzky's guts constricted. He stumbled a half-step forward and felt his wallet slip from his rear pocket, his sack of liquor lifted from his fingers. He straightened up. The man before him jerked his hand up in a sharp salute, and Kretzky saw that what he had there was, in fact, a comb. The mugger swept it back across his scalp, grinned, and ran.

There had been time enough for Kretzky to grab his mugger, but Kretzky had never been able to count on his reflexes. He turned around. The comb-man's accomplice was also gone. The pedestrian traffic continued, as it had throughout the dozen or so seconds of the crime, jockeying along the sidewalk.

It was a splendid early April afternoon, cold and crackling with flashbulb fluorescence, that polar New York light that Kretzky loved, careening down around him—light that made even the trash look new and swift and full of promise.

"Hey," Kretzky said. He thought he saw the blue sweat suit crossing the street several blocks away. "Hey, you." He pulled his wedding band off and held it up. "Hey," he said. "You forgot this."

He found himself standing in the path of an oncoming woman in a short black plastic coat and purple tights. He held the gold ring out to her and smiled. Her green eyes appeared to darken in annoyance. She steered wide of him, clutching her collar tight at her throat.

"Have a heart," Kretzky said. "I'm the victim here."

It struck him that he did not sound credible. He turned after the woman and saw the backs of three short black plastic coats with purple tights.

His chest was wet with sweat, and his temples throbbed. He had his jacket halfway off his shoulders and was trying

to determine how to sit down on the edge of the curb between two parked cars when darkness ascended like a film
from beneath the limits of his vision. The curb came up to
meet him, and as he fell, a car alarm detonated—inside his
skull, it seemed.

Kretzky had fainted before. The previous summer, on his
honeymoon, in Valence in the Provence, he had sat on a café
terrace with his wife, Erika, and watched as an antique biplane returning from an air show crashed into a water
tower. A shout came from inside the café, and a man hurried
into the street, where he stumbled, lost his balance, and fell
forward on his knees. Events began to appear to Kretzky as
if in slow motion. The man's head smacked into a cement
planter holding geraniums. He was a mean-looking, drunken
man in a gray suit, carrying a plastic briefcase, and he took
the corner of the planter in the center of his forehead. When
he sat back up, blood lined his face and pooled behind
his glasses, which had survived the fall in place and unbroken. Kretzky believed he saw a bristling eyebrow torn and
dangling over the man's nose, and he felt the sweat start running down his chest.

In the distance, smoke poured into the sky. Kretzky told
Erika to go pay, quickly, he wanted to get out of there. He
didn't tell her that he might vomit. He pushed back from the
table, held his head in his hands, and watched as a waiter
grabbed the fallen man beneath his arms and attempted to
haul him into a chair. Nobody else paid any attention. A
woman at the next table plunged her fork into a plate of filet
tartare, a sticky mass of raw meat arranged in a swirl beneath a raw egg. Kretzky, who had wanted to honeymoon in
Maine, found himself hating Europe. His parents had fled
the Continent as children in 1940, and it appeared to him

that nothing had changed; death proliferated, and the good burghers got on with their lunch.

Kretzky realized that he did not present an inspiring alternative. He sat hyperventilating in a swirl of bitter thoughts—for instance, that his brother, a doctor, would not be such a helpless wreck. His brother had a purpose in the world of detached eyebrows. Kretzky could only be in the way. He thought he wanted to be a filmmaker, and he'd wound up working as an exhibition designer at the Museum of Natural History, a good job he would have to quit if he ever hoped to make a film, if he could ever decide on an idea for a film he believed in enough to leave his job, if he could ever be certain enough about his willingness to take on the uncertainty, if he could ever be as certain of anything as he was, at that moment, of his overwhelming uselessness.

Sweet, watery saliva flooded his mouth from the lining of his cheeks. Kretzky got up from the café, and the darkness rose with him. He heard Erika crying, "Eddie, Eddie," and opened his eyes to find her crouched over him on the sidewalk, stroking his damp forehead with both hands. The image that came to him was of Jackie Kennedy, sprawled over the murdered president's body in Dallas. The foolish grandiosity of the association made him smile. Then he looked past Erika, straight up the black skirt of a waitress with thick, strong legs and white cotton underpants, and he was overcome with desire. He began to laugh. Erika told him to be calm, but he considered the phenomenon of a quaint Provençal sidewalk strewn with the prone bodies of witnesses to a biplane explosion inescapably funny.

In the end, the wounded drunk had walked away unaided, and Kretzky, too, rose to his feet, feeling cooled and refreshed in the aftermath of his collapse. He spent the afternoon assuring Erika that he was fine, and made love to her slowly and at length to prove it. They agreed that she, who had to watch uncomprehendingly as he fainted, had been more rattled by the episode than he. They dubbed the experience a "mortality check," and told each other that she had felt cut off from him at the very moment that he had felt restored to her. But Kretzky had his doubts.

"I felt restored," he told his therapist, when he was back in New York, "but not to her. Not really. Looking up at that waitress messed up my domestic focus."

Dr. Garafollo nodded and crossed her legs.

"I don't get it," Kretzky went on. "We lived together for three years, but marriage undermines me. I haven't been so susceptible to terror since childhood."

"You've been married three weeks," Dr. Garafollo reminded him. "Such intimacy with the unknown requires some getting used to. Julius Caesar, you know, was a fainter."

"Great," Kretzky said. "And his best friend bumped him off. Plus, what I'm trying to tell you is, I'm not a fainter."

"*Who,*" Dr. Garafollo had asked, "are you trying to tell?"

Entering his apartment, Kretzky found Erika surrounded by floury measuring cups and spoons—they were expecting company—and he began to laugh.

"Honey, I'm home," he declared.

"So I hear." Erika cracked an egg and held the upturned shell halves trembling over a bowl as the white spilled, curling from the yolk.

"And don't you want to know what happened to me today?"

"Tell me," she said.

"I got mugged," he said, and watched with pleasure as she dropped the egg.

"Eddie!" she said. "Shit. You didn't?"

"I most certainly did. A junkie with a cold steel blade neutralized me right out here on Jane Street, and his sidekick robbed me blind."

Erika stared at him. She did not, Kretzky thought, look overjoyed to see him. "You're in shock," she said. "Sit down."

"I think you're the one who needs a chair," he said. He had decided on the way home not to tell her that he'd fainted, but he couldn't resist an allusion. "Mortality check," he said. "I already had the shock. You're having the aftershock."

"It's not funny," Erika protested. "You think it's funny? Right now, right this minute, I could be a widow."

Kretzky was stung by the speed with which she imagined him dead. "Sure," he said. "And Vidia could comfort you."

Vidiadhar Gandhi (no relation to the Mahatma) was the overnight guest who was due at any minute. He had been Erika's live-in boyfriend when Kretzky met her, and he was now keeping house with a man, but Kretzky didn't believe that he was gay, not as far as Erika was concerned. Kretzky disliked Vidia, and his dislike was aggravated by the fact that Vidia was immensely likable, an easy and amiable bon vivant, who treated Kretzky warmly and without a hint of competition. Even when Vidia and Erika talked shop—they both worked for National Public Radio—he would take pains to find a way to keep Kretzky in the conversation. Kretzky thought himself something of a champ for acting just as friendly in return, but he doubted that Vidia was fooled, and he knew Erika wasn't.

"A widow," he said. "How romantic."

"Back off," Erika said. "Don't you mug me now, dammit. You get yourself held up at knifepoint and come in here smiling, I'm allowed to worry. Why the hell are you smiling?"

"To protect you," Kretzky told her. "It's a reflex." He got some paper towels and proceeded to wipe up the egg off the floor. Then he asked Erika for some money so he could go out and replace the stolen wine.

Retreating down the stairs, he imagined Dr. Garafollo asking him, *Who, exactly, are you trying to protect here?*

Kretzky, who often spoke out loud when he was alone, hurried along the sidewalk, saying: "Myself. All right? I'm protecting myself. What's the alternative? Attacking myself? I shouldn't have married her. I faint to escape. Okay? Does saying it make anything clearer? Jesus, lord, give me a break. They grabbed my balls, and it's a beautiful evening, and I'm going to buy wine. Okay? Is that okay with everybody?"

When Kretzky returned from the store, Vidia opened the door, embraced him, took the wine from him.

"I feel like the guest," Kretzky said.

Vidia laughed. "After what you've been through, you should. Two muggers, a knife—and you look marvelous."

Vidia's hair had grown; he wore it tucked in soft, sleek, backward curls behind his ears. Kretzky thought he should return the compliment, but he resisted.

"I'd be a wreck," Vidia went on. "I've been burglarized, pickpocketed, had my baggage stolen. Always devastating, but always anonymous. Face-to-face with the bastards, I'm afraid I'd do something rash and wind up paying the consequences."

He launched into a story about an elderly uncle in Chicago who'd been surrounded by a pack of young punks demanding his gold watch. "He's a very tall man, but old, with a cane, and all these little bastards dancing around him."

Vidia paused to pop a cork, and Erika stood watching him with a hunk of cheese in her hands, apparently forgetting that she was going to put it on a plate. "What happened?" she said.

"The old goat puffed up to full size, waved his cane over his head, and bellowed, 'What would your mothers say if they could see you now?' They froze, the punks. They'd never seen anything like him. They scattered." He poured the wine and held up his glass. "Cheers," he said. "Here's to cool heads in a searing world."

"Cheers," Erika said.

Kretzky drank up.

"I've always called myself a happy existentialist," Vidia remarked. "But getting robbed kind of puts the kabosh on that. Getting robbed takes the fun out of existentialism. "

Kretzky savored a familiar suspicion that Vidia's lines were rehearsed, possibly stolen. Back when Erika had still been willing to complain about her ex, she had been the first to say that spontaneity was not his strong suit. Now, she laughed and repeated his words—"Takes the fun out of existentialism, that's good."

"Actually," Kretzky said. "I felt weirdly happy. I felt liberated." It was true. Rising from his faint beside the shrieking car alarm, assisted by a middle-aged woman who'd seen him fall, he had experienced an exhilarating sense of buoyancy. Spotting his reflection in a store window, he had stopped to straighten out his jacket, but it was his eyes that held him there. They were clear and bright, free of the evasiveness he often encountered in mirrors. He could not remember the last time he thought he looked so good.

"I felt like bursting into song," he told Vidia. "I came home grinning like a hurdy-gurdy monkey."

"I can vouch for it," Erika said. "You'd have thought he'd won the lottery."

"Good for you," Vidia said. "After all, you're a lucky fellow. It *is* like a lottery. Your number's going to come up some time or other, and you got off without a scratch."

"It's more than that," Kretzky said. "I felt like I was the one who got away with something. Not just my life. The relief was overwhelming. Everything seemed dispensable."

"What do you mean, everything?" Erika asked.

"I mean everything. What a load off."

"I know exactly what you mean," Vidia said. "We're so concerned with protecting our stuff, and then—pow—it's gone, and there we are, same as ever. It's very affirming, really. I know the feeling exactly."

"No," Kretzky said. "I don't think you do."

"Why not?" Erika said. "Vidia just said he's been robbed up and down. He's lost much more than you, and burglary, you know—it's like there's no home to go to after that."

"I'm not talking about loss," Kretzky said. "I'm talking about feeling like you were given something."

"Exactly," Vidia said.

"Right," Kretzky said. "Exactly."

It was during dessert that Erika noticed Kretzky's wedding ring was gone. She let out a small cry—"You didn't tell me"—and clutched his naked finger.

Kretzky bowed his head. Erika lifted his hand and stared at it. "I can't believe I didn't notice before."

"Absences," Vidia explained, "can be very difficult to recognize. When someone's just shaved off a beard, you can stare for some time before you figure it out."

For once Kretzky felt grateful for Vidia's ever ready commentary. Two bottles of wine had been drunk, Vidia had broken out a bottle of cognac, and Kretzky did not wish to account for the ring. He had long ago made his peace with the awkward necessity of keeping certain thoughts and information to himself to preserve relationships—all kinds of relationships—but he could not endure outright lying.

"They pulled it off your finger," Erika said. "What a thing. It's unspeakable."

"I was mugged," Kretzky said. "I was attacked and I didn't resist. I adopted a policy of appeasement. "

He didn't know what happened to his ring. He had waved it at the fleeing mugger, and at the purple-legged woman in black, and then it was gone. When he came out of his faint, he had forgotten about it. As Kretzky understood the event, he had taken the ring off and thrown it away.

"You must feel so violated without it," Erika said. She held his finger to her lips as if it was injured. "I'm going to get you a new one tomorrow."

"No," Vidia said. "I want to get it for him. Will you allow me? I still haven't given you two a wedding present, and replacing this ring would be perfect. It would delight me." He raised his glass. "Sometimes, as the old hags said, foul is fair. Your ill fortune, Eddie, presents an ideal opportunity for me to express my love for you both."

Kretzky watched in horror as Erika raised her glass, and leaned over the table to kiss Vidia's cheek. "What a beautiful thought," she said. "I'm incredibly touched."

What did it mean? Kretzky didn't want Vidia's love, never mind his ring. He felt like he was only now truly getting mugged.

"Maybe there's insurance," he said. He felt a light sweat rise on his forehead and chest, and got up to open the window.

"I think Eddie's drunk," Erika said. "Are you drunk, Eddie?"

"Most likely," he said.

"I don't have to give you a ring if you feel uncomfortable about it," Vidia announced. "I could understand that. I never know the right thing for weddings. I just follow my feelings, and my offer is entirely heartfelt."

"Maybe we should sleep on it," Erika said.

"Yeah," Kretzky said. "Let's give it a rest."

In the night, the crash and grind of garbage trucks emptying Dumpsters woke Kretzky from a dream of flying. He had to piss. He grabbed a towel, wrapped himself, and worked the bedroom door open silently. Vidia lay on his back on the sofa bed. He didn't stir as Kretzky tiptoed past.

On his return, Kretzky stopped to look at his wife's friend. He stood in the dim streetlight glow, with his knees against the mattress's edge, and leaned over the sleeping body until his head hovered a few feet above Vidia's upturned face. Kretzky didn't know what he was looking for. He felt excited and powerful, gazing down on the peaceful, and— yes—beautiful face, which looked as clear and unconcerned as his own face had appeared earlier in the shop window. Kretzky had always felt jealous of Vidia, but only now, see- ing him alone in the bed, did it occur to him that what he envied was not Vidia's closeness to Erika but his freedom from her.

Kretzky loved Erika, and although he was not always happy, he assumed—and Dr. Garafollo had encouraged him in the assumption—that the reasons for his unhappiness would go with him wherever he went. But he had never, be- fore his wedding, felt toward married people the furious jeal- ousy with which he eyed Vidia's solitude on the couch. He had never before felt that he was in the wrong bed, and that the only way out of that bed was a violence—not physical, though it might feel physical—for which he wasn't sure he had the strength. He had married Erika to guard against that violence. Now, leaning over Vidia, the "happy existentialist," he wondered whether perhaps separation was not a failure so much as a triumph of correction over a previous error.

Kretzky stood there for two, maybe three minutes, before he noticed with alarm that Vidia's eyes were open. He couldn't recall whether they had ever been closed. He had heard of people who slept with their eyes open, but he thought it was just an idiomatic expression. He stared at Vidia, and Vidia stared back. Kretzky had no idea if he was being seen.

He was flying again when the alarm went off. He sat up elated, still possessed of the swift, tight-limbed sensation of soaring over open fields and treetops. He rarely had such dreams, and twice in one night he had taken off and been born aloft without any effort.

"So," Erika said. "What do we tell Vidia about the ring?"

Kretzky sagged back into the pillows. He recalled the man's eyes staring in the night, and imagined Vidia telling Erika, "Your husband's a psychopath." He would not protest; he'd be relieved to be found out.

"You don't want it," Erika said. "You think the whole idea's kinky or something."

"It is kinky," he said. "Wedding rings are kinky. They're a fetish."

Erika laughed and moved over him in a crouch. "Do they turn you on?" she asked, holding her ring finger in front of his face.

"They do not," Kretzky said. "To tell you the truth, I'd rather you got rid of yours than I get a new one."

"What do you mean?" Erika said. She sat back on his thighs and gave his stomach a little backhand punch.

"What I said," Kretzky said. "Who needs rings? A ring can't seal a hole."

Erika left the bed and began to dress in quick, angry movements. "What are you talking about?" she said. "I don't understand you." She moved to the door, letting her hand linger on the knob, apparently waiting for him to call her back, to explain himself, to apologize, to make up.

"I think," Kretzky said, "that you do understand me."

There, he thought, he had done it.

But what had he done? Vidia and Erika were chatting cheerfully in the next room, and he was still lying there cozily—in the wrong bed. Nobody was going to take it out from under him.

No, he had to get up, report his credit cards stolen, and go see Dr. Garafollo. He would tell her that he'd been mugged by a man with a comb and molested by an invisible assailant; that he'd thrown away his wedding band, fainted, stood like a stalker at two in the morning over his wife's ex, and tried to derail his marriage. There was only one thing Kretzky couldn't account for. The problem, he thought, was that he was in an excellent mood.

TIM **GAUTREAUX**

DANCING WITH
THE ONE-ARMED GAL

On Saturday, Iry Boudreaux's girlfriend fired him. The young man had just come on shift at the icehouse and was seated in a wooden chair under the big wall-mounted ammonia gauge, reading a cowboy novel. The room was full of whirring, hot machinery, antique compressors run by long flat belts, black-enameled electric motors that turned for months at a time without stopping. His book was a good one, and he was lost in a series of fast-moving chapters involving long-distance rifle duels, cattle massacres, and an elaborate saloon fight that lasted thirty pages. At the edge of his attention Iry heard something like a bird squawk, but he continued to read. He turned a page, trying to ignore an intermittent iron-on-iron binding noise rising above the usual lubricated whir of the engine room. Suddenly the old number two ammonia compressor began to shriek and bang. Before Iry could get to the power box to shut off the motor, a piston rod broke, and the compressor knocked its brains out. In a few seconds Babette, Iry's girlfriend, ran into the engine room from the direction of the office. White smoke was leaking from a compressor's crankshaft compartment, and Iry bent down to open the little cast-iron inspection door.

Babette pointed a red fingernail to the sight glass of the brass lubricator. "You let it run out of oil," she said, putting the heel of her other hand on her forehead. "I can't believe it."

Iry's face flushed as he looked in to see the chewed crankshaft glowing dully in the dark base of the engine. "Son of a bitch," he said, shaking his head.

She bent over his shoulder, and he could smell the mango perfume that he had given her for Christmas. Her dark hair touched his left earlobe for an instant, and then she straightened up. He knew that she was doing the math already, and numbers were her strength: cubic feet of crushed ice, tons of block ice. "Iry, the damned piston rod seized on the crankshaft," she said, her voice rising. "The foundry'll have to cast new parts, and we're looking at six or seven thousand dollars, plus the downtime." Now she was yelling.

He had let both Babette and the machine down. He looked up to say something and saw that she was staring at the cowboy novel he'd left open facedown on his folding chair.

"I don't know, Iry. The owner's gonna have a hard time with this." She folded her arms. "He's gonna want to know what you were doing, and I'm gonna tell him." She gestured toward the book.

"Look, I checked the damned oil level when I came on shift. It wasn't my fault."

She looked at him hard. "Iry, the machine didn't commit suicide." She licked a finger and touched it to the hot iron. "Mr. Lanier has been after me to cut staff, and now this."

She closed her eyes for a moment, then opened them and shook her head. "You need to get away from this place."

He pulled a shop rag from the back pocket of his jeans and wiped his hands, feeling something important coming. "What's that mean?"

She looked at him the way a boss looks at an employee. "I'm going to lay you off."

"You're firing me?"

"Last time we had a compressor rebuilt we were down for a long time. Come back, maybe next month, and we'll see."

"Aw, come on. Let's go out tonight and talk about this over a couple of cold ones." He pushed back his baseball cap and gave her a grin, showing his big teeth.

She shook her head. "You need a vacation is what you need. You ought to go somewhere. Get out of town, you know?"

"A vacation."

"Yeah. Get your head out of those books. Go look at some real stuff."

"Who's gonna watch the compressor that's still working?"

Babette took his shop rag from him and wiped a spot of oil from a glossy fingernail. "The new man who watches during your lunch break. Mauvais."

"Mauvais can't operate a roll of toilet paper."

"We'll just be making party ice after this." She looked at him. "At least he's never let the oil get low."

He glanced at her dark hair, trying to remember the last time he'd touched it.

The next morning Iry got up and drove through the rain to early Mass. The church was full of retirees, people who had stayed on the same job all their lives. The priest talked about the dignity of work, and Iry stared at the floor. He felt that his relationship with Babette, such as it was, might be over. He remembered how she had looked at him the last time, trying to figure why a good engineer would let the oil run out. Maybe he wasn't a good engineer—or a good anything. After Mass he stood in the drizzle on the stone steps of the church watching people get into their cars, waved at a few, and suddenly felt inauthentic, as though he no longer owned a real position in his little town of Grand Crapaud. He drove to his rented house and called his mother with instructions to come over and water his tomato patch once a day. Then he packed up his old red Jeep Cherokee and headed west toward Texas.

After a few miles, the two-lane highway broke out of a littered swamp and began to cut through sugarcane fields. The rain clouds burned off, and the new-growth cane flowed to the horizons in deep, apple-green lawns. Iry's spirits rose as he watched herons and cranes slow-stepping through irrigation ditches. He realized that what Babette had said about a vacation was true.

He avoided the main highway and drove the flatland past gray cypress houses and their manicured vegetable gardens. Through sleepy, live oak–covered settlements the old Jeep bobbed along with a steady grinding noise that made Iry feel primitive and adventurous.

On the outskirts of New Iberia he saw something unusual: a one-armed woman, wearing a short-sleeve navy-blue dress, was hitchhiking. She was standing next to a big tan suitcase a hundred yards west of a rusty Grenada parked in the weeds with its hood raised. Iry seldom picked up anyone from the side of the road, but this woman's right arm was missing below the elbow, and she was thumbing with her left hand, which looked awkward as she held it across her breast. He realized that she would only look normal thumbing a ride on the left side of a highway, where no one would stop for her.

When he pulled off, she didn't come to the car at first, but bent down to look through the back window at him. He opened the passenger door and she came to it and ducked her head in, studying him a moment. Iry looked down at his little paunch and resettled his baseball cap.

"You need a ride?"

"Yes." She was pale, late thirties or so, with dark wiry hair spiked straight up in a tall, scary crew cut, and tawny skin. He thought she looked like a woman he'd once seen on TV who was beating a policeman with a sign on a stick. She seemed very nervous. "But I was hoping for a ride from a woman," she said.

"I can't afford no sex-change operation," he told her. "That your car?"

She looked back down the road. "Yes. At least it was. A man just pulled off who made all kinds of mystifying mechanical statements about it, saying it'd take three thousand dollars worth of work to make it worth four hundred. I guess I'll just leave it." She sniffed the air inside the Jeep. "It's awfully hot and I hate to pass up a ride."

He turned and looked at a large dark spray of oil under the engine. "That man say it threw a rod cap through the oil pan?"

She gave him an annoyed look. "All you men speak this same private language."

He nodded, agreeing. "You don't have to be afraid of me, but if you want to wait for a woman, I'll just get going."

"Well, I don't really relate well to most men." She looked at him carefully for a moment, and then announced, "I'm a lesbian."

Iry pretended to look at something in his rearview mirror, wondering what kind of person would say that to a stranger. He figured she must be an intellectual, educated in the north. "That mean you like women?" he asked.

"Yes."

He pursed his lips and saw the day's heat burning her cheeks. "Well, I guess we got something in common."

She frowned at this but wrestled her suitcase into the backseat anyway, got in, and pulled the door shut, adjusting the air-conditioner vents to blow on her face. "My name is Claudine Glover."

"Iry Boudreaux." He turned back onto the highway and said nothing, sensing that she'd begin to speak at any moment, and after a mile or so she did, breathlessly, talking with her hand.

"I've never hitchhiked before. I was on my way from New Orleans where I just lost my job, of all things. My car was a little old, maybe too old, I think, and it started to smoke and bang around Franklin. I just need a ride to the next decent-size town so I can get to an airport and fly home to El Paso where my mother..." She went on and on. Every hitchhiker he'd ever picked up had told Iry their life story. Some of them had started with their birth. One man named Cathell began with a relative who made armor in the Middle Ages and summarized his family tree all the way to his own son, who made wrist braces for video-game addicts with carpal tunnel syndrome. Iry guessed people thought they owed you an explanation when you helped them out.

"We got something else in common," he told her.

"What?"

"I just got fired myself." He then told her what he did for a living. She listened but seemed unimpressed.

"Well, I'm sorry for you, all right. But you can probably go anywhere and find another icehouse or whatever to operate, can't you?"

He admitted that this was so.

"I am a professor of women's studies," she said, her voice nipping like a Chihuahua's at the syllables. "It took me a long time to get that position and now, after four years of teaching, I lost it." She raised her hand and covered her face with it.

He rolled the phrase *women's studies* around in his head for a moment, wondering if she was some kind of nurse. "Aw, you'll find some more gals to teach," he said at last. He was afraid she was going to cry. It was forty minutes to Lafayette and its little airport, and he didn't want to experience the woman's emotional meltdown all the way there.

She blinked and sniffed. "You don't know how it is in academics. My Ph.D. is not from the best institution. You've got to find your little niche and hold on, because if you don't get tenure, you're pretty much done for. Oh, I can't believe I'm saying this to a stranger." She gave him a lightning glance. "Does this airport have jets?"

"I don't think so. Those egg-beater planes take off for Baton Rouge and New Orleans."

She did begin to cry then. "I hate propeller aircraft," she sobbed.

He looked to the south across a vast field of rice and noticed a thunderstorm trying to climb out of the Gulf. If he didn't have to stop in Lafayette, he might be able to outrun it. "Hey, c'mon. I'm going all the way through Houston. I can drop you by Hobby. They got planes big as ocean liners."

She wiped her nose with a Kleenex and put it into a shoulder bag. She looked as though she were willing herself to be calm. After a few miles, she looked out at the open land whizzing by, at egrets stabbing for crawfish. She sniffed and wiped her nose again. "Where are you going, anyway?"

"I don't know. Just out west. Maybe go to a couple of cowboy museums. Look at some cactus. See a rodeo." He glanced at her worried face. "What you gonna do when you get home?"

She gave a little mocking laugh. "Cut my throat."

The woman talked and talked. Iry stopped for lunch over the Texas border at a roadside café, figuring a meal would stop her mouth for a while. Their wobbly table was next to a taped-up picture window. He drank a beer with his hamburger, and she told him that she was originally hired because she was a woman and that her gender helped the college administration meet a quota. "Well," he said, wiping mustard off his shirt, "whatever the hell works."

"After I'd been there a year, the English department began considering hiring a black man to replace me."

He picked up his burger and shook it at her. "Yeah, I missed out on a job like that once. The company had to have one black guy at least on this oil rig, so they hired this New Orleans dude instead of me and put him on Magnolia number twenty-two with a bunch of them old plowboys from central Mississippi. He lasted like a fart in a whirlwind."

Claudine raised her head a bit. "When I produced evidence of my own one-sixteenth African American blood, they let me stay on." Iry looked at her skin when she told him this. He'd thought she was from Cuba.

"During my second year, the department brought in other women's studies specialists, and at that point I stopped wearing my prosthesis, to emphasize the fact that I was not only black and a woman, but disabled as well." She waved away a fly. "But they still tried to get rid of me."

"Ain't you no good at teaching studying women?"

"My students liked me. I published articles and went to conferences." Claudine nibbled at the cheese sandwich she'd ordered, brushed crumbs off her dark dress, and put it back on the plate. She looked at something invisible above Iry's head. It was clear that she did not understand what had happened to her. "They kept trying to let me go."

"That's a bitch."

She frowned and narrowed her eyes at him. "Yes, well, I wouldn't put it exactly in those words. When a search committee member told me they'd received an application from a gay, black, female double-amputee from Ghana, I reminded the committee that part of my childhood was spent in Mexico, and then I played my last card and came out as a lesbian." She picked up the dry sandwich and ate a little of the crust. Iry wondered if she was afraid that eating a juicy hamburger might poison her. "But it did no good. The college found someone more specialized, foreign, and incomplete than I could ever be."

He listened to her through the meal and decided that he'd rather spend eight hours a day with his tongue on a hot pipe than teach in a college.

The two-lane's abandoned filling stations and rickety vegetable stands began to bore him, so he switched over to the interstate. In the middle of a Houston traffic jam, Claudine suddenly asked if he was going all the way to San Antonio.

"Well, yeah, I guess." He felt what was coming and didn't know what to think. She talked of things he'd never known about: university politics, glass ceilings.

"You could save an hour by going straight through instead of detouring for the airport." The statement hung in the air like a temptation.

He shrugged. "Okay." So she kept riding with him west, out into the suburbs and beyond, entering a country that started to open up more as they glided past Katy and Frydek, Alleyton and Glidden. Claudine found a PBS broadcast and listened to a program of harpsichord music, but soon the weakling signal began to fade, succumbing to slide guitars and fiddles. To his surprise, she brought in a strong country station and listened for a while to a barroom ballad.

Claudine grabbed a fistful of her short hair and turned her head away from him to stare out into the brush. "When I hear that music," she began, "I think of my father and his Mexican wranglers sitting out under a tree in the backyard drinking long-necks in the wind. I think of their laughter and of not being able to understand any of it, because I never found one thing to laugh about in that blistered moonscape we lived on."

"You were raised on a ranch?"

"We raised cows and killed them is what we did. The place was so big, I'd go off on horseback and actually get lost on our own land. One time, I rode out at night, and over a hill from the house there were so many stars and such a black nothing that I thought I'd fall up into the sky. I felt like a speck of dust. The sky was so big I stopped believing in God."

"You had your own horse?"

She looked at him, annoyed. "You are really fixated on the cowboy thing. Let me tell you about my horse." She held up her nub and her voice took on an edge. "He was a stallion who was always trying to run under a tree to rake me off his back. The last time I got on him, I was sixteen and had a date lined up for the prom with a nice boy. When I mounted the horse, he was balky and I could tell he didn't want to work that day. I gave him the spur at the corral gate, and he bolted to a shallow gully full of sharp rocks about the size of anvils. He lay down in them and rolled over like a dog with me in the stirrups. That's how I got this," she said, pointing at him with her stump.

"Ow."

"Now, do you have some ruined or missing part you want to tell me about?"

His mouth fell open for a moment, and he shook his head. Iry didn't say anything for nearly a hundred miles. He imagined that she might be unhappy because of her missing arm, but he'd known several maimed and happy ex–oilfield workers who drank beer with the hand they had left. He guessed at the type of information she taught in her university. *Too much of all that weird man-hating stuff is bound to warp a woman,* he thought. But from what she told him, he decided she'd been born unhappy, like his cousin Ted who'd won ninety-two thousand dollars in the lottery and yet had to be medicated when he found out about the tax due on his winnings.

The sun went low and red in the face. He drove past Luling and Seguin, where she asked him to stop at a lone roadside table sitting in a circle of walked-down grass. Iry got out and pulled off his cap, pawing at his short dark hair, which in texture resembled a storm-flattened cane field. They walked around the table like arthritic old people until their muscles stretched, and then they sat down on its cement benches. A barbed-wire fence ran fifteen feet from the table, and a Black Angus stepped up and looked at them, pressing its forehead against the top strand of wire. Iry was a town boy, unused to cattle, and examined the animal's slobbery nose, the plastic tag in its ear. Claudine picked up a rock the size of a quarter and threw it overhand, hitting the cow on the flank, causing it to wheel and walk off, mooing.

"I want to drive for a while," she told him.

They stayed in separate rooms in a Motel Six, and the next morning got up early and drove around San Antonio like a tourist couple. She mentioned several times that she wanted to get to El Paso as soon as possible, but he convinced her to stop at the Cowboy Museum, and they wandered from room to room looking at pictures of pioneer cattlemen, displays of branding irons, six-shooters, and leatherwork. Iry stared at the Winchesters, leggings, badges, and high-crown hats as though he were in the Louvre. At the last display case Claudine put her ruined arm on the glass. "This place feels like a tomb," she said. "A graveyard."

He fumbled with the two-page brochure that the woman at the desk had given him. "I don't know. It's pretty interesting. All these people came out here when this place was like some uninhabited planet. They made something out of nothing." He pointed at a gallery of mustachioed *vaqueros*. "What's the difference between one of these guys and Neil Armstrong?"

"Neil Armstrong was 239,000 miles from home."

He looked at the gray in her hair, wondering how much of it was premature. "What you think it was like in 1840 to get on a horse in St. Louis and ride to the Rio Grande, maybe seeing a half-dozen guys in between? I bet the feeling was the same."

"The romance of isolation," she said, heading for the door. "A vestige of obsolete paternalistic culture."

He made a face, as if her language had an odor. "What?"

She pushed open a glass door and walked out, pausing on the bottom stone step. "How many images of women are in this museum?"

"A few," he said. "I bet not too many gals got famous for roping steers and blowin' up Indians."

"It could have been their job. Why not?"

He stepped down past her and turned around to look up into her face. He started to say something, but feared the avalanche of four-syllable words he would trigger down the slope of her anger. Finally, he brought his big, thick-fingered hand up, matching it under her thin white one. "Here's one reason," he told her. "The other's this: women are more family, that is, social-like. They're people people."

She took back her hand. "That's a stereotype."

"Oh yeah? Well, look at us. I'm heading off into the brush to look at stuff, not people, stuff. You're going home to stay with Momma." He expected a scowl, but she looked at him closely, as though he had suddenly revealed another identity to her.

West of San Antonio they took Highway 90. The weather became hotter, and the villages squatted at roadside, beaten down by the sun. Some towns like Hondo were brick-and-stucco holdovers from the last century, while some were just low and poor and could have been in southern Illinois, except for the Mexicans and the drought. The land seemed to be tumbling away from water as he drove the old Jeep west, passing through broad thickets and then open country, a dry, beige world populated by cactus and mesquite, hotter and hotter as they moved toward Uvalde, Brackettville, and Del Rio. She talked over the tinny jar of the Jeep, and he listened and looked. West of Del Rio he stopped and wandered out in the brush to look at the sun-struck plants, and Claudine had to spend twenty minutes pulling needles from his hands.

They stopped at Langtry to see where Judge Roy Bean had presided.

"Now, I've got to concede that here's a real astronaut," she said, standing on a basketball-size rock at the edge of the parking lot. "A wild man comes where there is no law and just says, 'I am the law.'" She motioned with her good arm. "He staked out his territory."

Iry pulled off his cap and scratched his head. He was feeling hot and tired. "Ain't that what professors do? Like what you was telling me in the car?"

She gave him a startled look. "What?"

"I mean, like, you say I'm going to be the Tillie Dog-schmidt scholar. She's my territory because I'm the first to read all her poems or whatever and study what all everybody's written about her. That's what you called 'carving your niche,' right? Some kind of space you claim, just like the judge here did?"

She raised her chin. "Don't belittle what I do."

"Hey, I think it's great. You invent yourself a job out of thin air. Wish I could do that." He thought about something a moment, and then pointed at her. "I read an old book called *Tex Goes to Europe*, and in it they talked about cas-trated opera singers. I bet if you found out some of those singers wrote stories, you know, about what a drag their life was, you could start up a whole department called Castrated Opera Singer Studies."

Her eyes opened a bit. "That's not how it works at all."

"It ain't?"

She stepped off of her rock. "No. Can we please get back on the road."

He pulled open the door to the Jeep and sat down, wincing at the hot vinyl.

She got in on her side. "Am I just not a real person to you?"

He turned up the air conditioner and frowned. "Am I to you?"

On the other side of Sanderson he got a glimpse of the Glass Mountains and sped up, his hands clenching and unclenching the steering wheel. The Jeep began to vibrate.

"They're not going anywhere," she told him.

"I don't get to see mountains too often."

"They're like everything else. You get used to them."

"You got a job lined up when you get to El Paso?"

"Mom knows the head of the English department at a community college in the desert. I just have to show up and sell myself."

"How you gonna do that?"

"Tell them how rare a bird I am. How I'll fill all their quotas in one shot. Aw, geez." She began digging in her bag. "I need a Prozac. I'm sinking down, down."

"Hey. We're heading toward the mountains."

She washed a pill down with a sip of hot Diet Sprite. "You bet."

"I think you ought to forget about all that quota shit. Just tell them you're a good teacher."

She seemed to bite the inside of her cheek. "The world's full of good teachers," she said.

They dawdled over the Glass Mountains and pulled into Alpine at supper. She told him that her credit card had room for one more motel, and they found a low, stucco place on the edge of downtown and got two rooms. The place had a lounge and café, and she met him for supper at eight, order-ing a margarita as soon as she sat down at a table. With his burritos he ordered a beer, and the waitress checked his ID. As the girl tried to read the little numerals in the dim light, he looked around at the other customers and the large hats the men wore. Claudine was wearing blue jeans and a white short-sleeve blouse. He looked at her makeup and smelled her perfume, which was still burning off its alcohol, and felt vaguely apprehensive, as though he was having supper out with his mother.

"You think it's all right to mix booze with your pills?" he asked.

She made a sweeping motion at him with her fingers. "Let's not worry about that." Her voice was tight.

"You think you got a shot at this teaching job?"

"Oh, they'll need somebody like me," she told him.

"You going to say to them that you're a good teacher? You know, show them those records you were telling me about? Those forms?"

"I'm a crippled black woman and a gay feminist." She put her elbows on the table. "I'm a shoo-in for the job."

He shook his head. "They won't hire you for those things."

"They'll at least need me to teach freshman English." She took a long drink. He wondered if she'd taken another pill in her room.

"Why don't you just tell them you're good with the stu-dents?"

"You have to be a certain kind of good," she said, her voice hardening.

"How's that?"

"You can't understand. They don't have people like me in icehouses."

A man in a wheelchair rolled through the front door. He wore a white cowboy hat, and his belt was cinched with a big buckle sporting a gold music note in the center. He coasted into the corner of the room behind a little dance floor and flipped switches on an amplifier. A computerized box came alive with blinking lights. Iry saw the man pick up a microphone and press a button on the box. The little café lounge filled with the sound of guitars and a bass beat, and the shriveled man in the wheelchair began to sing in a tough, accurate voice that was much bigger than he was. Two couples got up and danced. After the song, the food came, and Claudine ordered another margarita.

By the time the meal was over, she was sailing a bit, he could tell. Her eyelids seemed to be sticky, and she was blinking too much. He began to get sleepy and bored, and was wondering what was on the cigarette-branded television in his room, when she leaned over to him.

"Ivy," she began, "it's noisy in here."

"Iry," he said.

"What?"

"My name's Iry."

"Yes. Well. I'm going to get a fresh drink and walk back to my room." She looked at him for a second or two. "If you want to talk, come with me."

"No, I believe I'll check out what's on the tube," he told her.

"You'd rather watch TV than have a conversation with someone?" Her face twisted slightly, and he looked away.

"No, I mean, it might not look right, me going in your room." He felt silly as soon as he'd said it. Who, in Alpine, Texas, would give a damn what tourists from a thousand miles away did with their free time?

Claudine's face fell, and she sat back in her chair, staring toward the door. The music machine began playing "When a Tear Becomes a Rose," the beat a little faster than usual. When the old man sang, he closed his eyes as though the music hurt. Iry stood up and cupped a hand under Claudine's right elbow, right where things stopped.

"What are you doing?" She looked up at him, her eyelids popping.

"Asking you to dance," he said, taking off his cap and putting it on the table.

She looked around quickly. "Don't be absurd."

"Come on, I bet you used to do the Texas two-step in high school."

"That was another life," she said, rising out of the chair as if overcoming a greater force of gravity than most people have to deal with.

For a few seconds she bobbled the step and they bumped shoe tips and looked down as though their feet were separate animals from themselves, but on a turn at the end of the floor, she found the rhythm and moved into the dance. "Hey," he said.

"Gosh." She settled the end of her arm into his palm as though the rest of her was there. The little man did a good job with the song, stretching it out for the six or seven couples on the floor. Claudine wore a sad smile on her face, and halfway into the song her eyes became wet.

Iry leaned close to her ear. "You all right?"

"Sure," she said, biting her lip. "It's just that right now I'm not being a very good lesbian." She tried to laugh and reached up to touch her crew cut.

"You ain't one right now."

"How can you tell?"

"You dance backwards too good."

"That's stupid."

He turned her, and she came around like his shadow. "Maybe it is, and maybe it ain't." About a minute later, toward the end of the song, he told her, "I've danced with lots of black girls, and you don't move like they do."

"You're making generalities that won't stand up," she said. Then the tone of her voice grew defensive. "Besides, I'm only one-sixteenth African American."

"On whose side?"

"My mother's."

He walked her to their table, his hand riding in the small of her back. He noticed how well she let it fit there, his fingertips in the hollow of her backbone. He pursed his lips and sat down, pointing to her navy-blue purse. "You got any pictures of your family?"

She gave him a look. "Why?"

"Just curious. Come on, I'll show you Babette and my momma. They're in my wallet." He pulled out his billfold and showed her the images in the glow of the candle. "Now you."

She reached down and retrieved her wallet, pulling from it a faded, professionally done portrait of her parents. The father was blond and sun-wrinkled, and the mother lovely and tawny-skinned, with a noble nose and curly hair.

"Nice-looking people," he said. "Your momma, she's Italian."

Her lips parted a little. "How would you know?"

"Hey, Grand Crapaud has more Italians than Palermo. I went to Catholic school with a hundred of them. This lady looks like a Cefalù."

"She's part African American."

"When I bring you home tomorrow, can I ask her?"

She leaned close and hissed, "Don't you dare."

"Ah-ha." He said this very loudly. Several people in the little room turned and looked in his direction, so he lowered his voice to say, "Now I know why you really got your butt fired."

"What?"

"You lied to those people at the college. And they knew it. I mean, if I can figure you out in a couple days, don't you think they could after a few years?"

She stood up and swept the photos into her purse. He tossed some money on the table and followed her outside, where the air was still hot and alien, too dry, like furnace heat. "Hey," he called. He watched her go to her room and disappear inside. He was alone in the asphalt lot, and he stuck his hands into his jeans and looked up at the sky, which was graveled with stars. He looked a long time, as though the sky was a painting he had paid money to see, and then he went into his room and called her.

"What do you want?"

"I didn't want to make you mad."

"The word is angry. You didn't want to make me angry."

"I was trying to help."

There was a sigh on the line. "You don't understand the academic world. Decent jobs are so scarce. I have to do whatever it takes."

"Well, you know what I think."

"Yes, I know what you think," she told him.

"You're a straight white woman who's a good teacher because she loves what she's doing."

"You're racist."

"How many black people have *you* danced with?"

She began to cry into the phone. "I'm a gay African American woman who was crippled by a horse."

Iry shook his head and told her, as respectfully as he could, "You're crippled, all right, but the horse didn't have nothin' to do with it." He hung up and stared at the phone. After a minute, he put his hand on the receiver, and then he took it away again.

The next morning he didn't see her in the motel café, but when he put his little suitcase in the back of the Jeep, she walked up wearing a limp green sundress and got into the passenger seat. Five hours later he had gone through El Paso and was on U.S. 180 heading for Carlsbad when she pointed through the windshield at a ranch gate rolling up through the heat. "Home," was what she said, looking at him ruefully. It was the only unnecessary word she'd spoken since they'd left Alpine. "First time in five years."

He pulled off to the right and drove down a dusty lane that ran between scrub oaks for a half-mile. At the end was a lawn of sorts and a stone, ranch-style house, a real ranch house, the pattern for subdivision ranch houses all over America. Out back rose the rusty peak of a horse barn. Iry parked near a low porch, and as soon as he stepped out, Claudine's round mother came through the front door and headed for her daughter, arms wide, voice sailing. Claudine briefly introduced him and explained why he was there. The mother shook his hand and asked if they'd eaten yet. Claudine nodded, but Iry shook his head vigorously and said, "Your daughter told me you make some great pasta sauce." He glanced at Claudine who returned a savage scowl.

The mother's face became serious, and she patted his hand. "I have a container in the fridge that I can have hot in ten minutes, and the spaghetti won't take any time to boil."

Iry grinned at Claudine and said, *"Prepariamo la tavola."*

"Ah, *si*," the mother said, turning to go into the house.

Claudine followed, but turned and said over her shoulder, "You are what is wrong with this country."

"*Scusi.*"

"Will you shut up?"

After the lunch of pasta and salad, he asked to see the barn. The mother had leased the range, but she maintained three horses for Claudine's brother and his children, who lived in Albuquerque. Two of the animals were in the pasture, but one, a big reddish horse, came into a gated stall as they entered. Iry inspected the barn's dirt floor, sniffed the air, and walked up to the horse. "Hey," he said. "You think we could go for a little ride?"

She came up behind him, looking around her carefully, a bad memory in her eyes.

"I'm not exactly into horse riding anymore." Her voice was thin and dry, like the air.

"Aw, come on."

"Look, I'm thankful that you brought me here, and I don't want to seem rude, but don't you want to get back on the road so you can see cowboys and Indians or whatever it is you came out here for?"

He pushed his cap back an inch and mimicked her. "If you don't want to seem rude, then why are you that way? I mean, this ain't the horse that hurt you, is it?"

She looked back through the door. At the edge of the yard was the gate to the open range. "No. I just don't trust horses anymore." She turned to face him and her eyes were frightening in the barn's dark. "I don't think I ever liked them."

"Well, here," he said, opening the wooden gate wide and stepping next to the horse, putting his hand on its shoulder. "Come tell this big fella you don't like him because of something his millionth cousin did. Tell him how you're an animal

racist." The bay took two steps out into the open area of the
barn toward where she was standing, but before he took the
third step, she made a small sound, something, Iry thought,
a field mouse would make the moment it saw a hawk spread
its talons. Claudine shook like a very old woman, she looked
down, her eyes blind with fright, and she crossed what was
left of her arms before her. Iry stepped in and pushed
the horse easily back through the gate. The animal swung
around and looked at them, shook its head like a dog shed-
ding water, and stamped once. Claudine put her hand over
her eyes. Iry slid his arm around her shoulder and walked
her out of the barn.

"Hey, I'm sorry I let him out."

"You think I don't know who I am," she said. "You think
the world's a happy cowboy movie." She stopped walking,
turned against him, and Iry felt her tears soak through
his shirt. He tried and tried to think of what to do, but could
only turn her loose to her mother at the door and then stand
out in the heat and listen to the weeping noises inside.

Two days later, he was in the desert at a stucco gas station,
standing out in the sun at a baked and sandblasted pay telephone. On the other end of the line Claudine picked up, and
he said hello.

"What do you want?"

"You get that job?" He winced as a semi roared by on the
two-lane.

"No," she said flatly.

"Did you do what I asked you to?"

"No. I explained all the reasons why his English department needed me." There was an awkward pause in which he
felt he was falling through a big crack in the earth. Finally,

she said, "He didn't hire me because there weren't any vacancies at the moment."

"Well, okay." And then there was another silence, and he knew that there were not only states between them, but also planets, and gulfs of time over which their thoughts would never connect, like rays of light cast in opposite directions. A full minute passed, and then she said, as if she were throwing her breath away, "Thanks for the dance, at least," and hung up.

He looked out across the highway at a hundred square miles of dusty red rock sculpted by the wind into ruined steeples, crumpled hats, and half-eaten birthday cakes. Then he dialed the icehouse's number back in Grand Crapaud and asked for Babette.

"Hello?"

"Hey. It's me."

"Where in God's name are you?"

"Out with the Indians in Utah, I think."

"Well, I've got some news for you. The compressor, it wasn't your fault. Mauvais had put mineral spirits instead of oil in the lubricator."

"Did the shop pick up the parts for machining?"

"No. The owner is buying all new equipment. Can you believe it?"

"Well."

"When are you coming home?"

"You want me to come back?"

"I guess you'd better. I fired Mauvais."

He looked west across the road. "I think I want to see a little more of this country first. I can't figure it out yet."

"What do you mean?"

"I met this one-armed gal and she hates it out here."

"Oh, Lord."

"It ain't like that." He looked across toward a blood-red mountain. "It's pretty out here, and she don't want nothing to do with it."

"Where's she want to be, then?"

He made a face. "New Orleans."

Babette snorted. "Baby, you're liable to stop at a rest area out there and find somebody from Death Valley traveling to Louisiana to see stuff. Even around here you can't swing a dead nutria by the tail without hitting a tourist."

An Indian wearing a baseball cap rode up bareback on an Appaloosa and waited to use the phone, staring just to the left of Iry. After a minute, he told Babette goodbye and hung up. The Indian nodded and got down in a puff of red dust. Iry eavesdropped, pretending to count a handful of change. He didn't know what the Indian would say, if he would speak in Navajo or inquire about his sheep herd in guttural tones. After a while, someone on the other end of the line answered, and the Indian said, "Gwen? Did you want two percent or skim milk?"

That afternoon at sundown, he was standing on a marker that covered the exact spot in the desert where four states met. Behind him were booths where Indian women sold jewelry made of aqua rocks and silver. In one booth he asked a little copper-skinned girl if the items were really made by Indians, and she nodded quickly, but did not smile at him. He chose a large necklace for Babette and went back to his Jeep, starting up and driving to the parking lot exit, trying to decide whether to turn right or left. No one was behind him, so he reached over for the road map, and when he did, he noticed a paper label flying from the necklace like a tiny flag. It said, "Made in India."

He looked around at the waterless land and licked his lips, thinking of Babette, and the Indians, and the one-armed gal. The West wasn't what he thought, and he wanted to go home. He glanced down at the necklace and picked it up. Holding it made him feel like his old self again, authentic beyond belief.

javier **marías**

Translated by Esther Allen

WHAT THE BUTLER SAID

FOR DOMITILLA CAVALLETTI

"*During a recent short stay in New York, one of the two things
we Europeans fear most in that city happened to me: I was
trapped for half an hour in an elevator between the twenty-fifth
and twenty-sixth floors. However, I don't want to write about
my fear or the entirely justified claustrophobia that made me
yell for help every few minutes (I confess), but about the individual who was riding with me when the elevator stopped and
with whom I shared that half hour of fear and revelation. He
was a polished and extremely circumspect person (in that
tense situation he shouted only once and stopped as soon as
he knew we had been heard and located). He looked like a butler in a movie and turned out to be a butler in real life. In exchange for some incoherent and scattered information about
my country, he told me the following as we waited in that spa-
cious vertical coffin: he worked for a wealthy young couple,
the president of one of the biggest and most famous American
cosmetics companies and his recently acquired European
wife. They lived in a five-floor mansion and got around the
city in a stretch limousine with tinted windows (like the one*

President Kennedy used, he noted), and he, the butler, was one of four members of the household staff (all of them white, he noted). This individual's favorite hobby was black magic, and he had already managed to obtain a lock of hair from the young mistress of the house, snipped off while she was napping in a chair one drowsy summer afternoon. He told me all of this in a perfectly natural way, and my own state of panic was such that I listened to him quite naturally as well. I asked him how he had the cruelty to cut off that lock of hair: Did she treat him very badly?

"'Not yet,' he answered, 'but sooner or later she will. It's a precautionary measure. Because if something happens, how else can I get my revenge? How can a man take revenge in this day and age? Anyway, black magic is very fashionable' ("is very fashionable"—those were his exact words) 'in this country. Isn't it fashionable in Europe?' I told him I didn't think it was, except in Turin, and asked him if he couldn't do anything with his black magic to get us out of the elevator.

"'The kind I practice is only good for revenge. Who would you like to take revenge on, the company that built the elevator, the architect of the building, Mayor Koch? We could do it, but that wouldn't get us out of here. They won't be much longer.' They weren't much longer, in fact, and when the elevator began moving again and we reached the ground floor, the butler wished me a pleasant stay in his city and disappeared as if the half hour that brought us together had never existed."

This was the beginning of an article entitled "Vengeance and the Butler," published in the Spanish newspaper El País *on Monday, December 21, 1987. Thereafter, the text lost sight of the butler and dealt only with vengeance. It was not the right place to transcribe in detail the complete text of my traveling companion's words; moreover, I allowed myself to alter certain*

of the facts he confided in me and to leave most of them out al-
together. Perhaps I did so because the nationality of the cos-
metics queen was the same as my own. I thought there was a
possibility that she might read El País, *either on her own or*
because some acquaintance in Spain would recognize her, if
my article was too faithful to the actual circumstances, and
send it to her. I admit I was guided more by the desire not to
place my butler in a difficult situation than by that of alerting
the endangered queen. Perhaps the moment to do that has ar-
rived, now that my gratitude toward the butler has become
more nebulous, though the probability of this new text reach-
ing his mistress's eyes is infinitely smaller. But I have no other
way of warning her, or no other way that wouldn't be overly
sensationalistic. While the lady may read newspapers, I doubt
she reads literary magazines, especially not those published in
English. But that won't be my fault: the things we don't read
are full of warnings we will never hear or that will reach us too
late. In any case, my conscience will be more at ease if I offer
her the possibility, however remote, of taking precautions, but
without feeling like I've betrayed the butler, who did so much
to soothe me and alleviate the tension of waiting in the eleva-
tor. The fact I changed for the article was that the marriage
was not so recent, and the butler was not expecting future of-
fenses from his mistress, as I had him say, but, according to
him, was already enduring them continually. These were his
words, as far as I can recall and loosely transcribe them—I
feel quite unable to reproduce an ordered conversation, and
can only try to remember some of the things he said.—J.M.

The butler said:
    "I don't know if all Spanish women are the same, but the
specimen that ended up in my life is horrible. Vain, none too

bright, rude, cruel—I hope you'll forgive me for talking about a woman from your country like this."

"Go ahead, don't worry about it. Say whatever you want," I answered generously, not paying much attention yet.

The butler said:

"I know what I'm saying here doesn't have much authority or value; you might think I'm just letting off steam. I'd like to live in a world where it was possible for me to confront her directly, my accusations against hers, or my accusations against her defense, without its having serious consequences for me—I mean without my being let go. I don't think there are many families nowadays who can employ a butler, not even in New York City; we butlers aren't overwhelmed with job offers. Few people can afford to have even one servant, much less four, like they have. Everything was quite perfect until she came into the picture. The gentleman who employs me is very good-natured and was almost never home; he'd been single since I started working for him five years ago. Well, actually, he was divorced, and that's my greatest hope—that eventually he divorces her, too, sooner or later. But it could be later, and you have to be prepared. I've finished my black magic classes now; first I studied by correspondence, then I took a few hands-on lessons. I've earned the title. I still haven't done much, it's true. Sometimes we meet to kill a hen, you know. It's extremely unpleasant, we're covered with feathers, the chicken fights for its life, but it has to be done from time to time or our organization would lose all credibility."

I recall that this comment worried me for a moment and made me pay closer attention. Then, to dissipate that fear with the other, stronger one, I pounded the elevator door once more, pushed long and hard on the alarm button and on the buttons of all the floors, and yelled several times, "Hey! Hey! Listen! Hey! We're still trapped here! We're still here!"

The butler said:

"Please relax. Nothing is going to happen to us. This elevator is very large, there's plenty of air to breathe, and they know we're here. People are careless, but not so careless as to forget two men trapped in an elevator; anyway they're going to need to get the elevator working again. My employer's wife, your compatriot, is careless; she treats us all badly—or even worse, she ignores us. She has the ability, which is more common in Europe than in the United States, to speak to us as if we weren't there, without looking at us, without taking any notice of us, she talks without addressing a word to us, exactly as she would if she were talking to a friend about us instead of talking to us. Not long ago an Italian friend of hers was here, and even though they were speaking their languages that I don't understand, I know a lot of what they were saying was about us, especially about me—I've been there the longest, and I'm something like the manager or head of the entire staff. She knows very well how to say something about me right in front of me without giving away in the least that she's talking about me, but her friend didn't, she couldn't keep her green eyes from sneaking an occasional glance at me while she chattered away in whatever language they were speaking. Despite that, during the weeks her friend stayed at the house she had more distractions and thought less about me. You understand, she's spent three years here now, she still speaks English very badly, with a strong accent—sometimes I have trouble understanding her and that irritates her. She thinks I'm doing it on purpose to offend her, which is partly true, but I assure you all I do is refuse to make the effort I always have to make in order to understand her, the effort of understanding, listening, guessing. One thing's for sure, after a three-year stay you can get tired and bored even with a city like New York if you don't have anything to do. My employer leaves every morning for work and doesn't come back until late, until the Spanish dinner hour, which she has imposed on us. You might not know this, but the cosmetics business is hard work, it's like medicine, there's a lot of research and development, you can't stagnate with the same line of products. Incredible progress is made every year, every month, and you have to keep up, exactly like medicine, that's what my employer says. He leaves in the morning and works for twelve hours or more; he's only home at night and on weekends. Naturally she gets pretty bored; she has already bought everything she possibly could for the house, though she lives in continual expectation of anything new: a new product, a new appliance, a new invention, a new fashion, a new Broadway show, a new exhibit, an important new film. She consumes all new things in an instant, on the spot, more quickly than even a city like this one can supply them."

I had sat down on the elevator floor. But he, so polished and circumspect, remained standing with his coat and gloves on, one hand pressed against the wall and one foot gracefully crossed over the other. His shoes shone more than is normal.

The butler said:

"So she's usually home, without anything to do, watching TV and making phone calls to her friends in Spain, inviting them to come and visit, though they don't come very often—small wonder. When she can't talk anymore, when her tongue hurts from so much talking and her eyes hurt from watching so much television, then she has nothing else to do but focus on me. I'm the one who's always in the house, or almost always. I'm the one who knows where things are or where we can get them if we need to have them delivered.

"She focuses on me, you understand? There's nothing worse than being someone's source of distraction. Sometimes she betrays herself, I mean her contemptuous attitude; sometimes, for a few minutes, without realizing it, she hasn't been giving me orders or asking me practical questions but having a conversation with me, imagine that, a conversation."

As I recall, at this point I stood up and pounded on the elevator door again with the palm of my left hand. I was going to shout some more, but I decided to follow the example of the butler, who was speaking very calmly, as if we were on the other side of the door, waiting for the elevator to arrive. I remained standing, like him, and asked, "What did you talk about?"

The butler said:

"Oh, she would make some comment about something she read in a magazine or some game show she saw on TV; she's crazy about one that comes on every evening at 7:30, just before her husband comes home. She's crazy about *Family Feud;* everything has to stop at 7:30 so she can give it her complete attention. She turns off the lights, takes the phone off the hook; for the half hour *Family Feud* lasts we could do anything in the house, we could set fire to it and she wouldn't know; we could go into her bedroom, where she watches it, and burn the bed behind her and she wouldn't know. During that time, only the TV screen exists for her; I've only seen that kind of single-minded concentration in small children, and she is a bit childish. While she watches *Family Feud,* I could commit a murder behind her, I could cut the throat of one of our chickens and scatter the feathers everywhere and pour the blood over her sheets and she wouldn't know. Once her half hour was over she would get up, look around, and start screaming at the top of her lungs. 'Where did this blood come from? These feathers? What happened here?' She wouldn't have seen me killing the chicken. We could steal paintings, furniture, jewelry; we could bring our girlfriends or boyfriends and have an orgy in her own bed while she watches *Family Feud*. Of course we don't do it, because it's also our employer's bed and we all love and respect him. But imagine this, and I'm not exaggerating, while she's watching *Family Feud*, we could rape her and she wouldn't notice. Before I discovered this I had to watch out for the right moment to cut a lock of her hair, as I told you, or to steal some item of clothing, a handkerchief or a pair of pantyhose. Now, if I want any of her personal things, all I have to do is wait until 7:30, Monday through Friday, and take it while she's watching her program. I'll confess something to you—this is why I say we could rape her and she wouldn't realize it. Once I went up to her from behind while she was watching *Family Feud*. She watches it up close, sitting very straight on a kind of low stool, deliberately making herself uncomfortable in order to focus her attention. One evening I went up to her from behind and touched her shoulder with my gloved hand as if I had something to tell her. She makes me wear gloves all the time, you know; I only have to wear livery when there are guests for dinner, but she wants me to wear my white silk gloves all the time. You know, the idea is that the butler goes around running his fingers over everything, furniture and banisters, to see if there's any dust, because if there is, the white gloves will show it. I always wear my gloves; they're very thin; when I touch something it's as if I didn't have anything covering my hands. So I touched her shoulder with my sensitive fingers, and when I saw she didn't notice I left the hand there for quite a few seconds and started pressing down a little. Up to that point, I would have had an excuse. She didn't turn around, didn't move, nothing. So I moved the hand, I was standing up, caressing her shoulders and her collarbone, pressing quite hard, and she stayed immobile. I began to wonder if she might be inviting me to go ahead, and I'll admit I still haven't completely rid myself of that doubt; but I don't think so, I think she was so absorbed in her contemplation of *Family Feud* that she wasn't aware of anything. So I carefully slipped my (still gloved) hand inside her low-cut blouse (she always wears her blouses cut too low for my taste, but her husband likes it, I've heard him say so). I touched her bra, which, frankly, was a little scratchy, and it was that, more than my own desire, that convinced me to maneuver away from it or, let us say, to make it so that at least the scratchy fabric would only touch the back of my hand, which is less sensitive than the palm, though I was wearing my gloves. Women don't have much appeal for me, I barely have any contact with them, but skin is skin, flesh is flesh. So for long minutes I caressed one breast and then the other, left and right, very nice, nipple and breast. She didn't move, didn't say anything, didn't shift position while she watched her program. I think I could have stayed there forever if *Family Feud* had lasted longer, but suddenly I saw that the host was already saying goodbye and I withdrew my hand. I still had time to leave the room, walking on tiptoe behind her back, before her trance came to an end. My employer came home at 8:00 sharp, and the music for the end of the show was still playing."

"Are you sure they're going to get us out of here? I'm beginning to think they're taking much too long," I said, by way of response, and I started shouting and pounding the metal door again. "Hey! Hey!" Thud, thud.

The butler said:

"They won't be long, I told you. Every minute seems like an hour to us, but in reality a minute always lasts a minute. We haven't been here as long as you think. Take it easy."

I slipped back down to the floor, leaning against the wall (I had taken off my coat and was carrying it over my arm), and remained seated there.

"You didn't touch her again?" I asked.

The butler said:

"No. That was before the baby girl died, after that I'm too disgusted by her, now I couldn't caress even her finger. Twelve months ago she got pregnant. The gentleman I work for didn't have any children from his previous marriage, so this would be the first. You can imagine what the pregnancy was like, a nightmare for me; I had twice as much work and she paid twice as much attention to me as she usually does—she was continually calling for me to ask the stupidest and most useless things. I thought about giving notice but, as I told you, jobs are hard to come by. When she gave birth I was happy, not only for my employer but also because now the baby girl would be her principal source of distraction and would take the pressure off of me. But the baby was born very sick, with a terrible defect that was going to kill her after only a few months, inevitably. Don't make me talk about it. They found out right away that the baby was going to die, that she couldn't last longer than a few months, three, four, six at the most; a year would be very unlikely. I understand that this is very hard; I understand that, knowing it, a mother wouldn't want to grow attached to her baby, but it's also true that the baby, while it

lasts, should get some care and a little affection, don't you
think? After all, the only way that little girl was different
from us, from anyone else, was that her expiration date was
known. Because we all have one, that is certain. She didn't
want to know anything about it as soon as she found out
what was going to happen. You could almost say she handed
the baby over to us, to the servants; she brought in a woman
who fed her and changed her diapers, there were five of us
in the house for those months, now there'll be four again.
My employer didn't spend much time with the baby either,
but that's different, he works too many hours, he would
never have had time for anything, even if the little girl had
been healthy. But *she*, she spent a lot of time at home, as
always, more than she wanted to, but she never went into
the little girl's room, many nights she didn't even go in with
her husband to say goodnight, almost never. He did go in at
night, alone, before he went to bed. I went with him and
stayed at the threshold with the door ajar, my white-gloved
hand holding it open so there would be a little light, which
came from outside—he didn't dare turn on the light in the
room, so as not to wake her up, but also, I think, so as not to
see her except in the darkness. But at least he saw her. He
went over to the cradle, not too close, he always stayed a
couple of yards away, and from there he watched her and
listened to her breathing, a short time, a minute or less, just
enough to say goodnight. When he came out I stood to one
side, opened the door for him with my gloved hand, and
watched him walk toward his bedroom, where she was waiting for him. I did go into the little girl's room, and sometimes I stayed with her quite a while. I used to talk to her. I
don't have children, but I would talk to her, you see, even
though she wasn't going to hear me, and I didn't even have
the excuse that she needed to get used to human voices. The

worst thing is that there was no reason for her to get used to anything, she had no future and nothing was waiting for her; she didn't need to get used to anything, it was a waste of time. In the house no one talked about her, no one ever mentioned her, as if she had already ceased to exist before she died; such are the inconveniences of knowing the future. Even among ourselves, I mean the servants, we didn't talk about her, but most of us went to visit her, alone, as if we were entering a shrine. Of course my black magic was useless for curing her, it's only good for revenge, I told you. She, the mother, went on living her life, making calls to Madrid, Seville, she's from Seville, chatting with her friend when she was here, going out shopping and to the theater, watching TV and *Family Feud* from Monday to Friday at 7:30. I don't know how to explain it, after that time when I touched her without her realizing it, I'd started to feel a little affection for her, touching produces affection, even a little touching. Maybe you agree with me."

The butler paused long enough that his last comment didn't seem to be rhetorical, so I sat up and answered, "Yes, I agree. That's why you have to be careful who you touch."

The butler said:

"It's true. You don't think very highly of someone, you might even have a very low opinion of them, and suddenly one day, by chance, or some momentary impulse, or weakness, or loneliness, or nervousness, or drunkenness, one day you find yourself caressing the person you had such a low opinion of. Not that your opinion changes because of it, but you feel an affection because you caressed and let yourself be caressed. I felt a little of that elemental affection for her after having caressed her breasts with my white gloves while she was watching *Family Feud*. But that was at the beginning of her pregnancy. Because of the affection I had started to feel, I was more patient than I used to be, and I got whatever she asked me for without making faces about it. Then I lost that affection, really from the moment the little girl was born. But what made me lose it once and for all and become disgusted with her was the little girl's death; she lasted even less time than the prognosis had given her, two-and-a-half months, not even three. My employer was away on a trip, is still away; I told him about the death only yesterday by telephone. He didn't say anything, he simply said, 'Oh, it happened already.' Then he asked me to take care of everything, the cremation or the burial, he left it up to me, maybe because he realized that in fact I was the person closest to the little girl, despite everything. I was the one who took her out of her crib and called the doctor; this morning, I was the one who put away her sheets and her pillow; they make tiny sheets for newborns, I don't know if you knew that, tiny pillows. I said this morning to her, to the mother, that I was going to bring the little girl here, for cremation, to the thirty-second floor, the service there is of the highest quality, one of the best in New York City; they know their work, and they have a whole floor of the building. I told her this morning, and do you know what her answer was? She answered, 'I don't want to know anything about that.' 'I thought you might want to go with me, to go with the little girl on her last journey,' I told her. And do you know what she said? She said, 'Don't say stupid things.' Then she asked me, since I was coming to this neighborhood, to pick up opera tickets for some friends of hers who are coming in a month—not for her, she has her subscription tickets. She has a future, not like the little girl. Understand? So I came alone with the body of the little girl in a tiny coffin, white like my silk gloves. I could have carried it in my own hands, white on white, my gloves on the coffin. But that wasn't necessary, the excellent service provided by the company on the thirty-second floor had seen to everything, and they picked up the little girl and me this morning in a hearse and brought us here. She, the mother, leaned over the banister on the fourth floor just as I was getting ready to leave with the little girl, down below, with the coffin; I was already at the front door with my coat and gloves on. And do you know what her last words were? She shouted down from the top of the stairs, with her Spanish accent, 'Don't let them forget to put carnations, lots of carnations, and orange blossoms.' That was her only request. Now I'm going back empty-handed, the cremation just took place..." the butler looked at his watch for the first time since we had stopped, "just over half an hour ago."

"Orange blossoms," he said—*the flowers brides carry in Andalucia*, I thought. But then the elevator began moving again, and once we had reached the ground floor the butler wished me a pleasant stay in his city and disappeared as if the half hour that brought us together had never existed. He was wearing leather gloves, black ones, and he didn't ever take them off.

David **Mamet**

THE SCREENPLAY
AND THE STATE FAIR

It occurred to me that we were in the midst of a stock market boom. First one and then another of my friends had mentioned this or that young person who'd drastically increased the funds entrusted to them, and I reflected that, with all this good fortune going on around, perhaps it would be wise for me to buy some stocks. Further reflection suggested, however, that if knowledge of this boom had sufficient breadth and longevity to have come to my notice, the end could not be far off—that, in effect, my recognition (the first flush of greed, my call to "something for nothing") meant and must mean that the smart money was all through, and that it was time for the dumb money to pick up the tab.

Similarly with the screenplay. It is no longer an oddity, no longer a localized West Coast phenomenon, it is now a fact of life that everyone has written his or her screenplay. The butcher, the baker, and their progeny have written a screenplay. I know, because they all have tried to get me to

read them. And, if the modular, schematic nature of the
Hollywood movie is clear to all, sufficiently clear that those
daunted by the formal requirements of a thank-you note are
essaying the thriller or romantic drama, must that not mean
the end is at hand?

Yes.

The end of what? Of film as a dramatic medium.

For, certainly, these duffers, our friends the lawyers,
doctors, and bus drivers, are not writing drama. They
write, as do our betters in Hollywood, for gain, transform-
ing this broad land into one large New Grub Street. The
urge of these acolytes is not dramatic, but mercantile—to
traduce all personal history, to subvert all perception or in-
sight into gain, or the hope of gain. This work of writing
the screenplay, then, is not an act of creation, but an obeisance—it is a ceremony, a prostration, in which the individual's feelings and thoughts are offered to the golden
calf: "There is no lie I will not tell, no secret I will not re-
veal, no treasure I will not debase, if you will just buy my
screenplay."

Films themselves veer away from whatever residual
taint of drama they may have had and become celebrations
of our mercantile essence—become, in effect, pure advertisement. This is especially true of the summer film. The
summer film is, first and last, a display of mercantile triumph—it is a display of technology. Its attraction rests not
on our desire for drama (the purpose of art being to conceal
art) but on our desire for self-congratulation—on the display of technology per se. Now the highest achievement of
American postindustrial achievement, the last best claim for
American preeminence, is our technology. It is most handily
displayed in the Defense Department and in the movies. In

both we see the most shockingly novel rendition of the
human capacity for elaboration.

The summer film is not a drama, it is not even that ad-
mixture of drama and commerce, the pageant; the summer
film is an exhibition pure and simple. It is our state fair,
wherein the populace comes to be astonished, to gape at the
new delights of commerce, and to be assaulted by advertisement. The summer film has thrills and chills, as does its
cousin the roller coaster. It has the taint of the louche, as did
its forebear, the nautch show. Rather than a midway lined
by advertisement, the summer film is in itself an advertisement. Yesterday's award of prizes, "cutest baby" and so on,
has been supplanted by the announcement of the summer
film's grosses. "Number One Film in the Country," replacing
the broadcast of the winner of the greasy-flagpole climb.
And the summer film has the exhibition of the prize farm
animals, the film stars, coddled and petted and force-fed to
such an extent that we must award them all our admiration.
The summer film, like the state fair, brings us together and
allows us the delight of shaking our heads and saying to
each other, "Will you get a load of *that* . . . ?"

If we reason or accept that this is not drama, which it is
not, we need not decry the summer film's vapidity. It would
be inappropriate to criticize the pie-eating contest for lack
of a reasonable respect for nutrition. In the summer film,
drama would be as out of place as landscape design in the
state fair's midway.

The screenplay bears the same relation to the drama
that the bumf on the cereal box bears to literature. Its writing and its production are obeisance to the god of commerce. The public pays its fine and spends its two hours in a
celebration of waste in the time of abundance, the unam-

biguous enjoyment of the sun, the solstice festival, when worship of the antic god is all joy, and Nemesis is, for the moment, powerless. In this druidical observance, she is, in fact, ritualistically murdered—the hero slays her at the conclusion of the summer film, and we go on our way, out into the friendly summer night.

ROBERT OLEN **BUTLER**

FAIR WARNING

Perhaps my fate was sealed when I sold my three-year-old sister. My father had taken me to a couple of cattle auctions, not minding that I was a girl—this was before Missy was born, of course—and I'd loved the fast talk and the intensity of the whole thing. So the day after my seventh birthday party, where Missy did a song for everyone while I sat alone, my chin on my hand, and meditated behind my still uncut birthday cake, it seemed to me that here was a charming and beautiful little asset that I had no further use for and could be liquidated to good effect. So I gathered a passel of children from our gated community in Houston, kids with serious money, and I had Missy do a bit of her song once more, and I said, "Ladies and gentlemen, no greater or more complete perfection of animal beauty ever stood on two legs than the little girl who stands before you. She has prizewinning breeding and good teeth. She will neither hook, kick, strike, nor bite you. She is the pride and joy and greatest treasure of the Dickerson family and she is now available to you. Who will start the bidding for this future blue-ribbon winner? Who'll offer fifty cents? Fifty cents. Who'll give me fifty?" I saw nothing but blank stares before me. I'd gotten all these kids together but I still hadn't quite gotten them into the spirit of the thing. So I looked one of these kids in the eye and I said, "You, Tony Speck. Aren't your parents rich enough to give you an allowance of fifty cents?" He made a hard, scrunched-up face and he said, "A dollar." And I was off. I finally sold her for six dollars and twenty-five cents to a quiet girl up the street whose daddy was in oil. She was an only child, a thing I made her feel sorry about when the bidding slowed down at five bucks.

Needless to say, the deal didn't go through. Missy tried to go get her dolls and clothes before she went off to what I persuaded her was a happy, extended sleep-over, and Mama found out. That night my parents and Missy ate dinner in the dining room and I was put in the den with a TV tray to eat my spaghetti alone. If I wanted to sell one of them then I wanted to sell them all, they claimed, and eating alone was supposed to show me how it would feel. I was supposed to be lonely. Of course, they were wrong. It was just my sister I wanted to dispose of. And all I was feeling was that somehow Missy had done it to me again. She was at my daddy's elbow in the other room, offering her cheek for pinching. I felt pissed about that but I also felt exhilarated at the thought of what I'd done at the sale. I figured she wasn't worth even half the final bid.

And so I sit now, at another stage of my life, at another pasta dinner with much to think about, and I am forty years old—which is something to think about in and of itself. But instead I go back only a few weeks, to the Crippenhouse auction. Near the end of the morning, after I'd gaveled down dozens of lots of major artwork for big money from a big crowd that nearly filled our Blue Salon, a tiny, minor Renoir came up. Barely six inches square. One fat naked young woman with a little splash of vague foliage behind her. Generic Impressionism on a very small scale. Like a nearsighted man looking through the knothole in a fence without his glasses. And yet I stood before these wealthy people and I knew them well, most of them, knew them from playing them at this podium many times before and meeting them at parties and studying the social registers and reading their bios and following their ups and downs and comings and goings in the society columns and the *Wall Street Journal* and even the *Times* news pages. I stood before them and there was a crisp smell of ozone in the air and the soft clarity of our indirect lights and, muffled in our plush drapery and carpeting, the rich hush of money well and profusely spent. I looked around, giving them a moment to catch their breath. The estimate on the Renoir was $140,000 and sometimes we'd put a relatively low estimate on a thing we knew would be hot in order to draw in more sharks looking for an easy kill, and if you knew what you were doing, they wouldn't even realize that you'd actually gotten them into a feeding frenzy until they'd done something foolish. But this was one of those items where we'd jacked up the estimate on a minor piece that had one prestige selling point in order to improve its standing. Renoir. He's automatically a big deal, we were saying. In fact, though, we were going to be happy getting 80 percent of the estimate. I had just one bid in the book lying open before me—mine was bound in morocco with gilt pages—which is where an auctioneer notes the order bids, the bids placed by the big customers with accounts who are too busy sunning themselves somewhere in the Mediterranean or cutting deals down in Wall Street to attend an auction. And for the little Renoir, the one book bid wasn't even six figures, and I knew the guy had a thing for fat women.

So I looked out at the bid-weary group and I said, "I know you people," though at the moment I said this, my eyes fell on a man on the far left side about eight rows back who, in fact, I did not know. There were, of course, others in the room I didn't know, but this man had his eyes on me and he was as small-scaled and indistinct to my sight as the fat girl in the painting. But he was fixed on me and I could see his eyes were dark and his hair was dark and slicked straight back and his jaw was quite square and I know those aren't enough things to warrant being caught stopping and looking at somebody and feeling some vague sense of possibility— no, hardly even that—feeling a surge of heat in your brow and a little catch and then quickening of your breath.

I forced my attention back to the matter at hand. "I know you," I repeated, getting back into the flow that had already started in me. "You're wearing hundred-dollar underpants and carrying three-thousand-dollar fountain pens."

They laughed. And they squirmed a little. Good.

I said, "You will not relinquish even the smallest detail of your life to mediocrity."

Now they stirred. I am known for talking to my bidders. Cajoling them. Browbeating them, even. At Christie's and Sotheby's they would grumble at what I do. But they value me at Nichols and Gray for these things. And my regulars here know what to expect.

I said, "But there is a space in the rich and wonderful place where you live that is given over to just such a thing, mediocrity. A column in the foyer, a narrow slip of wall between two doors. You know the place. Think about it. Feel bad about it. And here is Pierre-Auguste Renoir, dead for eighty years, the king of the most popular movement in the history of serious art, ready to turn that patch of mediocrity into a glorious vision of corporeal beauty. Lot one-fifty-six. Entitled 'Adorable Naked French Woman with Ample Enough Thighs to Keep Even John Paul Gibbons in One Place.'" And with this I looked directly at John Paul Gibbons, who was in his usual seat to the right side in the second row. He was as famous in the world of these people for his womanizing as for his money. I said, "Start the bidding at forty thousand, John Paul."

He winked at me and waved his bidder's paddle and we were off.

"Forty thousand," I said. "Who'll make it fifty?"

Since John Paul was on my right, I suppose it was only natural for me to scan back to the left to draw out a competing bid. I found myself looking toward the man with the dark eyes. How had I missed this face all morning? And he raised his paddle.

"Fifty thousand..." I cried, and I almost identified him in the way I'd been thinking of him. But I caught myself. "...to the gentleman on the left side." I was instantly regretful for having started this the way I had. Was Renoir's pudgy beauty his type?

My auctioneer self swung back to John Paul Gibbons to pull out a further bid, even as thoughts of another, covert self in me raced on.

"Sixty from Mr. Gibbons," I said, thinking, *If she is his type, then I'm shit out of luck. All my life I've been in desperate pursuit of exactly the wrong kind of butt.*

And sure enough, Dark-Eyes bid seventy. I was happy for womanhood in general, I guess, if this were true, that men were coming back around to desiring the likes of this plumped-up pillow of a young woman, but I was sad for me and I looked over my shoulder at her and my auctioneer self said, "Isn't she beautiful?" and my voice betrayed no malice.

John Paul took it to eighty and Dark-Eyes took it to ninety while I paused inside and grew sharp with myself. *You've become a desperate and pathetic figure, Amy Dickerson, growing jealous over a stranger's interest in the image of a naked butterball.* "Ninety-five to the book," I said.

And there was a brief pause.

I swung back to John Paul. A man like this—how many times had *he* merely seen a woman across a room and he knew he had to get closer to her, had to woo and bed her if he could? Was I suddenly like him? "A hundred? Can you give me a hundred? No way you people are going to let a Renoir go for five figures. You'd be embarrassed to let that happen."

John Paul raised his paddle. "A hundred thousand to John Paul Gibbons."

The bid had run past the order bid in my book and a basic rule for an auctioneer is to play only two bidders at a time. But I didn't want to look at Dark-Eyes again. I should have gone back to him, but if he had a thing for this woman who looked so unlike me, then to hell with him, he didn't deserve it. If he was bidding for it—and this thought made me grow warm again—if he was bidding for it merely out of his responsiveness to me, then I didn't want him to waste his money on a second-rate piece. "One ten?" I said, and I raised my eyes here on the right side and another paddle went up, about halfway back, a woman who lived on Park Avenue with a house full of Impressionists and a husband twice her age. "One ten to Mrs. Fielding on the right."

She and John Paul moved it up in a few moments to the estimate, one forty. There was another little lull. I said, "It's against you, Mrs. Fielding." Still she hesitated. I should turn to my left, I knew. Dark-Eyes could be waiting to give a bid. But instead I went for all the other Mrs. Fieldings. I raised my hand toward the painting, which sat on an easel behind me and to my left. My auctioneer self said, "Doesn't she look like that brief glimpse you had of your dearest aunt at her bath when you were a girl? Or even your dear mama? Her essence is here before you, a great work of art." But the other me, with this left arm lifted, thought—for the first time ever from this podium, because I was always a cool character in this place, always fresh and cool—this other me that had gone quite inexplicably mad thought, *My God, what if I'm sweating and he's looking at a great dark moon beneath my arm?*

This man had gotten to me from the start, unquestionably, and this thought snaps me back to the trendiest Italian restaurant in Manhattan, where I sit now waiting for my pasta. There are impulsive attractions that make you feel like you're in control of your life somehow—here's something I want, even superficially, and I'm free to grab it. Then there are the impulsive attractions that only remind you how freedom is a fake. You might be free to *pursue* your desires, but you're never free to *choose* them.

And I had no choice that morning. I lowered my arm abruptly in spite of the fact I hadn't sweated from nerves since I was sixteen. But I'd already made my selling point. I'd stoked the desire of others and Mrs. Fielding took up the pursuit, as did another wealthy woman for a few bids and then another—I played them two at a time—and then it was one of the monied women against a little man who dealt in art in the Village and should have known better about this piece, which made me wonder if *he'd* had a life-changing glimpse of his corpulent mama at her bath, but that was the kind of thing my auctioneer self *rightly* ruminated on during the rush of the bidding and I had more or less put Dark-Eyes out of my mind and we climbed over a quarter of a million and my boss was beaming in the back of the room and then it stopped, with the little man holding a bid of $260,000. "It's against you," I said to the woman still in the bidding. She shook her head faintly to say she was out of it.

There is a moment that comes when you've done your work well when the whole room finally and abruptly goes, What the hell are we doing? I knew we had reached that moment. But I would have to took back to my left before I could push on to a conclusion.

"Two sixty," I said. "Do I hear two seventy? Two seventy for your sweet Aunt Isabelle? Two sixty then. Fair warning."

Now I looked to him.

His eyes were fixed on me as before and then he smiled, and the unflappable Amy Dickerson, master auctioneer, suddenly flapped. I lost the flow of my words and I stopped. It seemed that he was about to raise his paddle. *Don't do it*, I thought, trying to send a warning to him across this space. I wrenched my attention away and cried, "Sold! For two hundred and sixty thousand dollars."

I normally use the lull after the gavel, while the lot just sold is taken away and the next one set up, to assess certain buyers that I've learned to read. One woman who sits perfectly still through the bidding for items she has no interest in will suddenly start shuffling her feet when something she wants is about to come up. Another starts smoothing her hair. One distinguished retired surgeon, who always wears a vest, will lift up slightly from where he's sitting, first one cheek and then the other, as if he's passing a perfect pair of farts. But on that morning I was still struggling with an unreasonable obsession. I thought of nothing but this complete stranger and I finally realized that the only way to exorcise this feeling was to confront it, but when at last I worked up the courage to look once more to my left, Dark-Eyes had gone.

"I was relieved," I told my sister the next day at a sushi lunch. "But damn if I wasn't wildly disappointed as well."

"So?"

"So? There sat a man like John Paul Gibbons and I'm suddenly acting like his dark twin sister. "

"Is John Paul still after you?"

"You're missing the point," I said.

She shrugged. "I don't think so. You're forty, Amy. You're single. It's hormones and lifestyle."

"Yow," I cried.

"Did you get some wasabi up your nose?"

In fact I was merely thinking, *If you hadn't gone back for your dolls and your clothes I wouldn't be sitting here with you once a week out of familial devotion listening to your complacent hardness of heart.* Though I realized, trying to be honest with myself, that my alternative today—and most days—was eating lunch on my own, bolting my food, avoiding the company of men who bored me, a list that got longer every day, it seemed. I resented her stumbling onto a half-truth about me and so I leaned toward her and said, "You're thirty-six yourself. You haven't got much longer to be smug."

"That reminds me," Missy said. "Jeff mentioned he saw a poster up in Southampton for the charity auction you're doing."

"How does what I said remind you of that?" I put as much muscle in my voice as I could, but she looked at me as if I'd simply belched. She wasn't going to answer. She had no answer. I knew the answer: her loving husband was her shield against turning forty. Right. Maybe.

"Mama said she hoped you'd call sometime," Missy said.

I was still following the track under Missy's surface. Mama—still living on a street with a gate in Houston—thought that a beautiful woman like me, as she put it, was either stupid or a lesbian not to have been married when I hit forty. And she knew, as God was her witness, that I wasn't a lesbian.

"She hated Daddy by the time she was forty," I said.

"Calm down," Missy said. "Drink some green tea. It's like a sedative."

"And he hated her."

Missy looked away, her mouth tightened into a thin red line.

Okay. I felt guilty for rubbing this in. I'd arrived a couple of times myself at something like hatred for the man I was living with. In another era, I might have already gone ahead and married each of them—Max and Fred—and it would have been no different for me than for Mama.

I followed Missy's eyes across the room. She was looking at no one, she was just getting pissed with me, but there was a man leaning across a table for two touching the wrist of the woman he was with. He was talking quickly, ardently. I looked away, conscious of my own wrist. Whose gesture was that from my own life? Either Max or Fred. I twisted my mind away. Who cares which one? I thought. Whoever it was would say, Amy, Amy, Amy, you get so logical when you're angry. And yet the touch on my wrist meant he still thought I was a quaking bundle of nerves beneath the ir-refutable points I'd been making against him. All he had to do was touch me there and he'd wipe the logic away and prevail. But no way, Mister. I never lost my logic in an argument, even though sometimes there were tears, as meaningless as getting wet for somebody you're just having sex with. I'm crying, I'd say to him, but don't you dare take it wrong, you son of a bitch. It was Max.

"I've got to go," my sister said, and I looked at her a little dazedly, I realized, and we both rose and we hugged and kissed on the cheek. We split the bill and my half of the tip was six dollars and twenty-five cents. I watched her gliding away out the door and then I stared at the money in my hand.

The auction business is built on the three Ds: debt, divorce, and death. The next morning Arthur Gray sat me down in his office with WQXR playing low in the background—some simpering generic baroque thing was going on—and he fluttered his eyebrows at me over the quarter of a million I'd gotten for the worst Renoir oil he'd ever seen and then he sent me off to an estate evaluation on Central Park West. The death of a reclusive woman who apparently had had an eye for Victoriana. Her only son would meet me.

The doorman had my name and I went up in an elevator that smelled faintly of Obsession and I rang the bell at the woman's apartment. And when the door swung open I found myself standing before Dark-Eyes.

I'm sure I let the creature beneath the auctioneer show her face in that moment: the little half smile that came over Dark-Eyes told me so. The smile was faintly patronizing, even. But I forgave him that. I was, after all, making myself a gawking fool at the moment. The smile also suggested, I realized, that he had requested me specifically for this evaluation. I focused on that thought, even as I put on my professional demeanor.

"I'm Amy Dickerson," I said. "Of Nichols and Gray."

He bowed faintly and he repeated my name. "Ms. Dickerson." He was a little older than I thought, from close up, and even handsomer. His cheekbones were high and his eyes were darker than I'd been able to see from the podium. "I'm Trevor Martin. Mrs. Edward Martin's son."

"I'm glad," I said, and to myself I said, *What the hell does that mean?* "To meet you," I added, though I fooled neither of us. I was glad he was here and I was here. The only thing I wasn't glad about was that his name was Trevor. It was a name made for a rainy climate, and spats.

"Come in," he said and I did and I nearly staggered from the Victorian profusion of the place. The foyer was stuffed full: an umbrella stand and a grandfather clock and a stand-up coatrack and a dozen dark-framed hunting scenes and a gilt-wood-and-gesso mirror and a Gothic-style cupboard and a papier-mâché prie-dieu with shell-inlaid cherubs and a top rail of red velvet, and Trevor—I had to think of him as that now, at least till I could call him Dark-Eyes to his face— Trevor was moving ahead of me and I followed him into Mrs. Edward Martin's parlor—and my eyes could not hold still, there was such a welter of things, and I went from fainting bench to pump organ to the William Morris Strawberry Thief wallpaper—the walls were aswirl with vines and flowers and strawberries and speckled birds.

"I don't know where the smell of lilacs is coming from," he said.

I looked at him, not prepared for that cognitive leap. I looked back to a mantelpiece filled with parian porcelains of Shakespeare, General Gordon, Julius Caesar, Victoria herself threatening to fall from the edge where she'd been jostled by the crowd of other white busts.

"It's always in my clothes after I visit here."

"What's that?" I said, trying to gain control of my senses.

"The lilac. I never asked her where it came from, but now when I'm free to look, I can't find it."

"You must miss her," I said.

"Is that what I'm conveying?" His voice had gone flat.

I didn't even know myself why I'd jumped to that conclusion, much less expressed it. Maybe it was all her stuff around me. *See me, love me, miss me,* she was crying, *I am so intricate and so ornamented that you can't help but do that.* But Trevor clearly had seen her, and whether or not he'd loved her, I don't think he missed her much. Evidently he heard his own tone, because he smiled at me and he made his voice go so soft from what seemed like self-reflection that my hands grew itchy to touch him. "That must sound like an odd response," he said. "How could an only child not miss his mother?"

"I can think of ways."

He smiled again but this time at the room. He looked around. "Do you wonder if I grew up amidst all this?"

"Yes."

"I did."

"And you want to get rid of it."

His smile came back to me. He looked at me closely and he was no Trevor at all. "Every bit of it," he said.

That first day I sat at a bentwood table in the kitchen and he would bring me the things he could carry—a sterling silver biscuit box and a cut-glass decanter, a coach-lace coffee cozy and a silver-and-gold peacock pendant, and on and on—and I would make notes for the catalog description and I would give him an estimate and he never challenged a figure, never asked a question. At some point I realized it was past two and we ordered in Chinese and he had already

rolled the sleeves on his pale green silk shirt and we ate together, me using chopsticks, him using a fork. In the center
of the table sat a spring-driven tabletop horse-racing toy
with eight painted lead horses with jockeys that circled a
grooved wooden track. He had just put it before me when
the doorbell rang with the food.

We ate in silence for a couple of minutes, a nice silence,
I thought—we were comfortable enough with each other al-
ready that we didn't have to make small talk. Finally, though,
I pointed to the toy and asked, "Was this yours?"

"Not really. It was around. I never played with it."

"Weren't you allowed?"

"How much will we get?" he said.

"Toys aren't a specialty of mine. I can only get you into
the ballpark."

"Close enough."

"I think the estimate would be around three hundred
dollars."

"And you'd work the bid up to six."

I looked at the row of jockeys. "We've got a couple of
regulars who play the horses. And more than a couple are
still kids at heart."

"You're scary sometimes, Amy Dickerson, what you can
pick up in people." He was smiling the same smile I'd taken
for self-reflection.

"This might be true," I said. I was up to my elbows here
in mothers and children and my own mother thought the
same thing about me, expecting all the good men in the
world to be frightened away. Looking into Trevor's dark eyes
I felt a twist of something in my chest that the cool and collected part of me recognized as panic.

"I mean that in an admiring way," he said.

"How come I didn't pick up on that?"

"I'm sorry. I scare people, too."

"But you don't scare me. See the problem I'm suddenly faced with? We have an imbalance here."

"In the courtroom," he said.

"You're a lawyer?"

"Yes."

"That *is* scary," I said, and part of me meant it.

"I only defend the poor and the downtrodden," he said.

"Not if you can afford silk shirts."

"That was two categories. I defend the poor and the downtrodden rich."

"Is there such a thing?"

"Ask any rich man. He'll tell you."

"What about rich women?"

The playfulness drained out of him, pulling the corners of his mouth down. I knew he was thinking about his mother again.

"Trevor," I said, softly. He looked me in the eyes and I said, "Play the game."

For a moment he didn't understand.

I nodded to the spring-driven tabletop horse-racing toy with eight hollow-cast, painted lead horses with jockeys and grooved wooden track, estimate three hundred dollars. He followed my gesture and looked at the object for a moment. Then he stretched and pulled it to him and he put his hand on the key at the side. He hesitated and looked at me. Ever so slightly I nodded, yes.

He turned the key and the kitchen filled with the metallic scrinch of the gears and he turned it again and again until it would turn no more. Then he tripped the release lever and the horses set out jerking around the track once, twice, a horse taking the lead and then losing it to another and that one losing it to another until the sound ceased and the horses stopped. Trevor's eyes had never left the game. Now he looked at me.

"Which one was yours?" I asked.

He reached out his hand and laid it over mine. Our first touch. "They all were," he said.

There was a time when I thought I would be a model. I *was* a model. I did the catwalk glide as well as any of them, selling the clothes, selling the attitude. And off the job—when I was in my own jeans and going, *Who the hell was I today?*—I had trouble figuring out how to put one foot in front of the other one without feeling like I was still on the runway. There was a time when I was an actress. I was Miss Firecracker and I was Marilyn Monroe and I was passionate about a shampoo and I was still going, *Who the hell was I today?* There were the two times when I lived with a man for a few years. It didn't help ease Mama's angst. People actually think to get married, in Texas, she'd observe. It didn't help ease my angst either. I was "Babe" to one and "A.D." to the other and one never made a sound when we had sex and the other yelled, "Oh Mama," over and over, and I found part of myself sitting somewhere on the other side of the room watching all this and turning over the same basic question.

So what was I reading in Trevor Martin, the once and perhaps future Dark-Eyes, that would make me hopeful? After he put his hand on mine he said, "I've been divorced for six months. My mother has been dead for six weeks. It feels good to have a woman look inside me. That's not really happened before. But I'm trying to move slowly into the rest of my life."

"I understand," I said, and I did. "For one thing, we have every object of your childhood to go through first."

He squeezed my hand gently, which told me he'd known I'd understand and he was grateful.

I left him on the first evening and went to a Thai restaurant and ate alone, as had been my recent custom, though I felt the possibilities with Dark-Eyes unfurling before me. But that didn't stop me from eating too fast and I walked out with my brow sweating and my lips tingling from the peppers.

And when I was done, I went to my apartment and I stepped in and when I switched on the lights I was stopped cold. My eyes leaped from overstuffed chair to overstuffed couch to silk Persian rug and all of it was in Bloomingdale's earth tones and it was me, it was what was left of me after I'd been dead for six weeks and somebody that wasn't me but was *like* me was here to catalog it all and there was a ficus in a corner and a Dalí print of Don Quixote over the empty mantelpiece and a wall of bookshelves and I wanted to turn around and walk out, go to a bar or back to work, take my notes from the first day at Mrs. Edward Martin's and go put them in a computer, anything but step further into this apartment with its silence buzzing in my ears.

Then I saw the red light flashing on my answering machine and I moved into my apartment as if nothing odd was going on. I approached the phone, which sat, I was suddenly acutely aware, on an Angelo Donghia maple side table with Deco-style tapering legs, estimated value four hundred dollars. But the flashing light finally cleared my head: I had one message and I pushed the button.

It was Arthur Gray. "Hello, Amy," he said. "About the benefit auction. Woody Allen just came through with a walk-on part in his new film. *Postmodern Millie*, I think it is. And Giuliani's offered a dinner at Gracie Mansion. But I've had a special request, and since we're not being *entirely* altruistic here—rightly not—I really think we should do it. More later. You know how I appreciate you. Our best customers are your biggest admirers... Almost forgot. Do you need a lift to the Hamptons Saturday? We should get out there early and I've got a limo. Let me know. Bye."

All of which barely registered at the time. I realized it was the assumption that the red light was Trevor that had cleared the mortality from my head.

On that night I sat naked on the edge of my bed, my silk nightshirt laid out beside me, and I thought of Trevor, the silk of his shirt the color of a ripe honeydew, or the color— if green is the color of jealousy—of the pallid twinge I felt when I found Max, in the third year of our relationship, in a restaurant we'd been to together half a dozen times, only this time he had a woman hanging on his arm. He saw me. I saw him. It was lunchtime and I sat down at a table, my back to him, and I ate my lunch alone, which I'd planned to do, and very fast, faster than usual. I loved that Caesar salad and split-pea soup, in spite of the speed, perhaps because of it: I was furious. Only the tiniest bit jealous, surprisingly, but angry. I love to eat when I'm angry. He wouldn't talk about it that night. The one on his arm never argued with him, he said. She was just about as stupid and irrational as he was, he said, thinking, I suppose, that he was being ironic. But even at that moment I thought it was the first truthful thing he'd said in a long time.

I laid my hand on the nightshirt. The silk was cool and slick and I clenched it with my fingers like a lover's back. And then I let it go. It was Fred's shirt. It had been too big for pasty slender Fred. I looked at it. Periwinkle blue. White oyster buttons. Soft tip collar. Versace. Two hundred and fifty dollars. Who'll start the bidding at nothing? I looked at the shirt and wondered why I hadn't given it away or thrown it away from the negative provenance. But I didn't give a damn about that. It felt good to sleep in. That was a healthy attitude, surely.

I looked around the room. And my eyes moved to my dresser and found a silver tankard stuffed with an arrangement of dried flowers. I rose and crossed to it and picked it up. It was from Max. The tankard, not the flowers. It was Georgian with a baluster shape and a flared circular foot and a light engraved pattern of flowers and foliate scrolls. He'd been an ignorant gift-giver. Subscriptions and sweaters. I vaguely remembered challenging him about it and he'd bought me this for seven hundred dollars. On eBay, where every grandma and pack rat is her own auction house. And he'd gotten me a glorified beer mug. But I was grateful at the time. He wanted to use it himself, I realized. He said the silver was the only thing that would keep a beer cold in the Georgian era. Yum, he said. But I didn't let him use it even once. I put flowers in his beer mug and I kept it to this moment, standing naked and alone in my bedroom, my face twisted beyond recognition in the reflection in my hand. It was beautiful, this object, really. That's why I kept it. Both these men had vanished forever from this place. Exorcised. The objects they touched—a thing I would push like crazy in an auction if they'd been famous and dead—held not a trace of them. And I felt the chilly creep of panic in my limbs at this thought.

I put the tankard down and turned away. I crossed to the bed and I lifted this Versace shirt with soft tip collar and I let it fall over my head and down, the silk shimmering against me, and suddenly I felt as if I'd climbed inside Trevor's skin. Can you trust to know a man from a pair of dark eyes? From Chinese food and a child's game played by an adult after a lifetime of quiet pain inflicted by a mother? From the touch of a hand? Inside this draping of silk my body had its own kind of logic. These details *are* the man, my body reasoned, as surely as the buttons and the stitching and the weave of cloth are this $250 shirt. I raised my paddle and I bid on this man.

How do you assess the value of a thing? There are five major objective standards. The condition: the more nearly perfect, the better. The rarity: the rarer, the better. The size: usually neither too big nor too small. The provenance: the more intense—either good or bad—the better. The authenticity: though a fake may be, to any but an informed eye, indistinguishable from the true object, the world of the auction will cast out the pretender.

And so I turn my mind now to the fifth night, the Friday night, of my week of assessments in the apartment of the deceased Mrs. Edward Martin, mother of Trevor Martin. On this night he opened the door to the bell and this fifth silk shirt was bloused in the sleeves and open to the third button and his chest was covered with dark down and his smile was so deeply appreciative of my standing there waiting to be let in that I thought for a moment he was about to take me in his arms and kiss me, which I would have readily accepted.

But he did not. We spent the morning and the first hours of the afternoon working our way around the larger pieces in the foyer, the parlor, the library, the dining room. Then, after I'd assessed a beautiful mahogany three-pedestal dining table with brass paw feet, he said, "You're hungry." He was right. And for the second day in a row he did not even ask what I wanted but went to the phone and ordered my favorite Chinese dishes—though, in all honesty, I would have varied my fare if he'd asked—but I found myself liking his presumption, liking that he should know this domestic detail about me.

And after we ate, he took me to a small room lined completely with armoires in rosewood and mahogany and walnut, and filling the armoires was everything that could be embroidered—quilts and drapes and cushions and bellows and doilies and on and on, big things and small—and there were Persian rugs stacked knee high in the center of the floor and on top of them sat two open steamer trunks, overflowing with indistinguishable cloth objects all frilled and flowered.

"I'm surprised at her," I said without thinking. "She's out of control in here."

"This was my room," Trevor said.

I turned to him, wanting to take the words back.

"It didn't look like this," he said, smiling.

I had a strong impulse now to lean forward and lay my forehead against the triangle of his exposed chest. But I held still. I would not push him into the rest of his life. Then he said, "Let's leave this room for later," and he was moving away. I followed him down the hallway and he paused at a closed door, the only room I hadn't seen. He hesitated, not looking at me, but staring at the door itself as if trying to listen for something on the other side. I quickly sorted out the apartment in my head and I realized that this must have been her bedroom.

How long had it been since I'd made love? Some months. Too many months. One of the great, largely unacknowledged jokes Nature plays on women—at least this woman—is to increase one's desire for sex while decreasing one's tolerance for boring men. Horny and discriminating is a bad combination, it seems to me. And the situation before me—exceedingly strange though it was shaping up to be—was anything but boring. Still he hesitated.

I said, "This is hard for you."

He nodded.

He opened the door and I had no choice but to step to his side and look in.

There were probably some pots and pans, a telephone and a commode, some kitchen utensils, that were not Victorian in Mrs. Edward Martin's apartment. But almost nothing else. Except now I was looking at her bed and it was eighteenth-century Italian with a great arched headboard painted pale blue and parcel-gilt carved with lunettes, and rising at each side was a pale pink pilaster topped not by a finial but by a golden cupid, his bow and arrow aimed at the bed. The smell of lilacs rolled palpably from the room, Trevor put his arm around my shoulders, and some little voice in my head was going, *How desperate have you become?*

Then he gave me a quick friendly squeeze and his arm disappeared from around me and he said, "Maybe I'll let you do this room on your own."

"Right," I said, and I sounded as if I was choking.

An hour later I found him sitting at the kitchen table, sipping a cup of coffee. I sat down across from him.

We were quiet together for a time, and then he said, "Do you want some coffee?"

"No," I said. "Thanks."

He stared into his own cup for a long moment and then he said, "She loved objects."

"That's clear."

"My childhood, her adulthood. It was all one," he said softly. "She had a good eye. She knew what she wanted and she knew what it would cost and she was ready to pay it."

He was saying these things with a tone that sounded like tenderness. On our first evening he'd taken pleasure in my being able to look inside him, but at this moment he seemed opaque. He felt tender about her shopping? But then it made a kind of sense. I, of all people, should understand his mother. I played people like her every day.

I made my voice go gentle, matching his tone. "What she saw and loved and bought, this was how she said who she was."

Trevor looked at me and nodded faintly. "Like style. We are what we wear. We are what we hang on our walls. Perhaps you're right. She was talking to me."

He looked away.

And I thought: the buying isn't the point; it's that we *understand* the objects. We love what we understand. And then I averted my eyes from the next logical step. But I can see it now, replaying it all: we love what we understand, and there I sat, understanding Trevor Martin.

I waited for him to say more but he seemed content with the silence. I was not. I was doing entirely too much thinking. I said, "I've solved your mystery."

He smiled at me and cocked his head. The smile was reassuring. It was okay to move on.

I said, "Her pillows—and there are a dozen of them—they all have lilac sachets stuffed inside the cases."

"Of course. I should have realized. She slept in it."

I found I was relieved that even in his freedom to search for the source of the scent he had avoided her bedclothes. And he had not made love to me on her bed. These were good and reassuring things. I was free now to relax with my pleasure in the way he lifted his eyebrows each time he sipped his coffee, the way he lifted his chin to enjoy the taste, the way his eyes moved to the right and his mouth bunched up slightly when he grew thoughtful, the way—for the second time—he reached out and laid his hand on mine.

I was filled with the details of him. I could sell him for a million bucks. Not that I would. Clearly, part of me was beginning to think he was a keeper.

When his hand settled on my hand, he said, "I will sleep better tonight because of you."

I looked at him with a little stutter in my chest. I'd suddenly become what my daddy used to call "cow-simple." It was from his touch. It was from merely the word *sleeping*. It was stupid but I was having trouble figuring out what he was really trying to say.

And he let me gape on, as if I was out alone in a field, paused in the middle of chewing my cud, wondering where I was. Then he said, "The mystery. Solved."

"Of course," I said.

When this fifth workday was done, for the fifth time he walked me to the door and thanked me, rather formally, for all that I was doing. Tonight I stopped and looked into his eyes when he said this. "I've enjoyed your company," I said.

"And I've enjoyed yours," he said.

That's all I wanted to say. I turned to go.

"Amy," he said.

I turned back and my instinct said this was the time he would take me into his arms. My instinct was wrong. Was this another trend for the forty-year-old woman? Horny, discriminating, and utterly without sexual intuition? He simply said, "I'll see you down."

We went out the door together and along the hall and I pushed the down button on the elevator and a spark of static electricity bit at my fingertip. That was it, I thought. I've now discharged into the electrical system of the building elevators whatever that was I was feeling a few moments ago.

The doors opened. We stepped in. The doors closed. We were alone, and maybe the elevators did suck up the charge that was between us, because we descended one floor of the ten we had to go and Trevor reached out and flipped the red switch on the panel and the elevator bounced to a stop and a bell began ringing and he took me in his arms and I leaped up and hooked my legs around him as we kissed. He pressed me against the wall and he did not make a sound.

The next day I leaned into the tinted window of Arthur Gray's limo and faced the rush of trees and light standards and, eventually, industrial parks, along the Long Island Expressway. I never had understood what men saw in lovemaking in a standing position. Though Trevor had been strong enough, certainly, to hold me up without my constantly feeling like I would slip off him. He was silent, but he did not cry out, "Oh Mama," which would have been much worse, under the circumstances. We'd not had a proper date. We'd never even gone out for a meal. But that sounded like my mama talking. I was well fucked and unusually meditative.

When we were on Highway 27, out among the potato fields and vegetable stands and runs of quaint shops and approaching East Hampton, Arthur finally roused me from going nowhere in my head. He said, "Amy, there's one more item that I want you to put on your list. Okay?"

"Okay."

"It's the special request I mentioned on your machine." Arthur was shuffling his feet and talking all around something and he'd finally gotten me interested, even suspicious.

"What are you talking about, Arthur?"

"A dinner with you."

"With me?"

"At Fellini's. In SoHo. They've already donated the meal, with wine. Dinner for two with the most beautiful auctioneer in New York."

I was silent. This was really troubling for a reason I couldn't quite define.

"Come on," he said. "Think of the whales."

"This is for whales? I thought it was for a disease."

"Whales get diseases, too. The point is that your mystique, which is considerable, is Nichols and Gray's mystique, as well. Give somebody a dandy candlelit dinner. For us. Okay?"

There was no good reason to say no. I liked whales. I liked Arthur. I liked Nichols and Gray. But there was suddenly a great whale of a fear breaching inside me and falling back with a big splash: I was going to have to sell myself.

I looked out the window and across a field I saw a cow, standing alone, wondering where the hell she was.

We were set up in a four-pole tent on the grounds of an estate with the sound of the ocean crashing just outside. I stood on a platform behind a lectern loaned by the local Episcopal Church and I looked out at many of my regulars and some comparably affluent strangers and they were in their boaters and chinos and late spring silks and I looked at all their faces once, twice, and John Paul Gibbons was on the right side in the second row and he winked at me. This was becoming a discomforting motif. And suddenly I figured I knew whose request it was that I be auctioned off.

I began. To an ancient little lady I did not know—I presumed she was a permanent Hamptons resident—I sold the services of Puff Daddy to hip-hop her answering-machine message. I had an order bid in my book for $150 but I squeezed $600 from the old lady, invoking the great, thinking beings-of-the-deep in their hour of need. I'd gotten a cello lesson with Yo-Yo Ma up to $1,600—having ferreted out two sets of parents, each with a child they'd browbeaten into learning the cello—when Trevor appeared at the back of the tent. He lifted his chin at me, as if he were tasting his coffee.

We'd never spoken of this event during the week we'd just spent together. I didn't expect him. I felt something strong suddenly roil up within me, but I wasn't sure what. I focused on the next bid. "It's against the couple down in front. How about seventeen? Seventeen hundred? What if your child meets *their* child in a school music competition?"

They hesitated.

"Whose butt will get whipped?" I cried.

They bid seventeen hundred. But I felt it was over. The other couple was hiding behind the heads in front of them. I scanned the audience a last time. Trevor was circling over to my left. "Fair warning," I called.

There were no more bids and I sold Yo-Yo Ma for $1,700 as Trevor found a seat. Oddly, I still didn't know how I felt about his being here. I threw myself into the lots on Arthur's list and I was good, I was very good. The whales were no doubt somewhere off the coast leaping for joy. And then I reached Lot 19.

"The next lot . . ." I began and I felt my throat seizing up. I felt Trevor's dark eyes on me, without even looking in his direction. I was breathless against the wall of the elevator and all I could hear was the bell and the pop of Trevor's breath as he moved and my mind had begun to wander a little bit and he was right about how he smelled whenever he visited his mother's apartment, he smelled of lilacs—no, not of lilacs, of lilac *sachet*—and my head thumped against the wall and I said "Oops" but he did not hear and I thought about her pillows and though I was glad I was not in her bed, I figured I'd accept those dozen pillows on the floor of the elevator so I could lie down in a soft place for this.

"The next lot..." I repeated and I pushed on. "Number nineteen. Dinner for two at Fellini's in SoHo, with wine and your auctioneer."

There was a smattering of delighted oohs and chuckles.

I almost started the bidding at a measly $50. But this impulse did not come from my auctioneer self, I instantly realized. There was a shrinking inside me that I did not like and so I started the bid for what I thought to be an exorbitant amount. I'd simply go unclaimed. "Who'll open the bid for four hundred dollars?" I said.

I saw John Paul's head snap a little, but before I could congratulate myself, in my peripheral vision I could see a paddle leap up without pause. I looked. It was Trevor.

Suddenly there was something I had to know.

I said, "I'm sorry, ladies and gentlemen, let me stop right here for a moment. Before we begin, I need some more information on this lot."

There was a ripple of laughter through the tent and I stepped away from the lectern. Arthur was standing off to my right and I stepped down from the platform and I approached him.

He must have read something in my face. He blanched and whispered, "What is it? You're doing a smashing job."

"Who asked to put me up for bid?"

"Sorry, my dear," he said. "That's a bit of a secret."

"You always start sounding British when you know you're in trouble. And you are. Give it up."

He tried to wink and shrug and say nothing.

"Arthur," I said as calmly as I could. "I don't want to grab you by the throat and throw you to the ground in front of all these good clients. Tell me who."

This was convincing. "Trevor Martin," he said.

I felt a flash of anger. Why? I demanded explanations from myself as I stepped back up onto the platform: surely this was something I wanted. I wanted Trevor to pay big bucks for me and take me to dinner like he should. But what's this "should" stuff about? Why *should* he do that? And why should *I* expect—as part of me did—a sweet and gentle invitation to dinner in an elevator instead of a hot five minutes of sex? I'd been thinking about the sex, myself. I'd been wanting it. I couldn't let myself be a hypocrite.

I cried, "We have four hundred from Mr. Martin. Who'll make it five hundred?" and all the explanations vanished in my head and I was left with an abrupt realization: there was something being put before this crowd that had a value in need of being articulated. I pointed to one of the paddles in the back, some elderly gentleman whom I'd been previously pitting against Mrs. Fielding, who would want to talk about who knows what over dinner, maybe the time she'd seen her dear and pudgy aunt in the nude, after her bath. "Five hundred," I called, and that suddenly seemed way too low.

"I am not a Renoir," I said. "But I am ... not six inches square, either."

It was a start.

"I am in excellent condition," I cried, "for an object my age. Who'll make it a thousand?"

It was a big leap. But I found myself feeling ready for a big leap.

There was only a moment of hesitation and I saw a paddle go up to my right and I looked and it was John Paul

Gibbons. All right. "A thousand dollars to John Paul Gibbons. Who'll make it eleven hundred?"

And now I looked to Trevor. He raised his paddle instantly. "Eleven hundred to Mr. Martin. And this is still an unconscionable bargain. I am rare. I am. Who else knows so many of you so well? Who else has filled your homes and emptied your wallets? Who'll make it fifteen hundred?"

I turned back to John Paul and he winked again and lifted his paddle and he glanced over his shoulder toward Trevor.

I said, "I am a perfect size, thanks to my ongoing efforts. Neither too big nor too small. Who'll make it two thousand?"

I, too, looked at Trevor and he smiled that faintly patronizing smile of his and he lifted his paddle and I was caught by his smile, the smile that he gave me the first time I saw him, the smile he'd given me as we walked past the doorman last night and into the warm evening air and he said, "I think I've begun to move into the rest of my life."

His life. But what did I want in the rest of *my* life? I'd like to have seen the inside of *his* apartment by this point. I'd like to have been asked to dinner, just the two of us, without a price put on anything. He takes his first step in the elevator, when it's least expected, and he arranges to *buy* his next step. This was his mother's way. I lowered my face. My book lay open before me. I lifted my face. "I am authentic," I said. "You must look into me now, as I've looked into you." And I took my own challenge. And I looked. And I said, "Three thousand to the book."

There was a little gasp. A private tour of Dollywood, Tennessee, with Dolly Parton herself as guide had gone for $2,800, the biggest bid of the auction.

I looked at John Paul. He blew me a little kiss and kept

his paddle on his lap. I turned to Trevor. "It's against you, Mr. Martin," I said. "Thirty-five?"

The smile was gone. But he lifted his paddle.

"Three thousand five hundred to Mr. Martin," I cried, and I instantly added, "Four thousand to the book."

Now there was a great hum that lifted in the crowd, resonating, perhaps, with the one from the sea. "It's against you, Mr. Martin," I said. His face slowly eclipsed itself behind the face in front of him, a jowly man in a shirt and tie, a Wall Street lawyer who collected Stieff teddy bears.

"Fair warning," I cried, scanning the faces before me. I let the warning sit with them all for a long moment, and then I said, "Sold to the book for four thousand dollars."

And now I sit at this newest chic SoHo restaurant with the faces of Anita Ekberg and Marcello Mastroianni and Giulietta Masina and Signor Fellini himself all about me on the walls, and two places are set at the table. But I am alone and waiting for no one. And yet, I am lingering now over the linguini, eating it strand by strand, sipping my wine in tiny, dry sips. And I am feeling good. The book, of course, had been empty. I bid for myself, and I won.

CONTRIBUTORS

melissa bank is the author of the story collection *The Girls' Guide to Hunting and Fishing*, which spent fourteen weeks on the *New York Times* best-seller list and has been translated into twenty-one languages. She won the 1993 Nelson Algren Award for short fiction. Her stories have appeared in the *Chicago Tribune, The North American Review, Other Voices*, and *Ascent*, and have been performed in the Selected Shorts Program and broadcast on National Public Radio.

nicola barker was born in Ely, Cambridgeshire, England, in 1966 and spent part of her childhood in South Africa. She was the winner of the David Higham Prize for Fiction and joint winner of the Macmillan Silver Pen Award for Fiction for *Love Your Enemies*, her first collection of stories (1993). Her first novel, *Reversed Forecast*, was published in 1994 and a novella, *Small Holdings*, followed in 1995. A second collection of short stories, *Heading Inland*, for which she received an Arts Council Writers' Award, was published by Faber in July 1996 and includes stories that had appeared in the United Kingdom, the United States, and Australia. Her novel *Five Miles from Outer Hope* was published by Faber in February 2000. She lives and works in London.

jon billman is the author of the story collection *When We Were Wolves*, published by Random House in 1999. He has worked as a wildland firefighter and a seventh-grade teacher. His stories have appeared in *Esquire*, *The Paris Review*, and *The Missouri Review*, among other publications. He lives in Kemmerer, Wyoming.

amy bloom's short stories have appeared in *The New Yorker*, *Story*, and *American Fiction*, and have been anthologized in *The Best American Short Stories* of 1991 and 1992, and in the 1994 *O. Henry Prize Story Collection*. She is the author of two books, *Come to Me* and *Love Invents Us*.

adrienne brodeur is the editor in chief of *Zoetrope: All-Story* and launched the magazine with Francis Ford Coppola in 1997.

robert olen butler has published ten critically acclaimed books, including two volumes of short fiction—*Tabloid Dreams* and *A Good Scent from a Strange Mountain*, which won the 1993 Pulitzer Prize for Fiction. His stories have appeared widely, in such publications as *The New Yorker*, *Esquire*, *The Paris Review*, and *Harper's*, and have been chosen for *The Best American Short Stories* and *New Stories from the South*. He has also written several feature-length screenplays and two teleplays. He teaches creative writing at McNeese State University in Lake Charles, Louisiana, where he lives with his wife, the novelist and playwright Elizabeth Dewberry.

george makana clark is from Zimbabwe, of British and Xhosa heritage. His collection of short stories, *The Small*

Bees' Honey, was published in 1997, and his fiction has appeared in *Glimmer Train, Southern Review, Black Warrior Review, Massachusetts Review, Apalachee Quarterly, Georgetown Review,* and other publications. He is currently at work on a novel and teaches English at the University of Southwestern Louisiana. He lives in Lafayette, Louisiana.

Francis Ford Coppola is a filmmaker who has won five Academy Awards, three of which were for his screenwriting, and lists among his credits such noteworthy films as *The Godfather* and its sequels, *The Conversation, Apocalypse Now, Rumblefish,* and *Bram Stoker's Dracula.* He was the publisher of San Francisco's weekly *City* magazine in the 1970s, and launched *Zoetrope: All-Story* with Adrienne Brodeur in 1997. He lives at the Niebaum-Coppola Estate Winery in Napa Valley with his wife, Eleanor.

Tim Gautreaux's fiction has appeared in *Harper's, GQ, The Atlantic Monthly, Story, The Best American Short Stories,* and *New Stories from the South.* He has won a National Magazine Award for fiction and an NEA Creative Fellowship. A Louisiana native, he is the director of creative writing at Southeastern Louisiana University. He is the author of several books, including the short-story collection *Welding with Children.*

Philip Gourevitch, a frequent contributor to *The New Yorker,* is the author of *We Wish to Inform You That Tomorrow We Will Be Killed with Our Families,* the winner of the 1999 National Book Critics Circle Award for Nonfiction. His reportage and essays have also appeared in *Granta, Harper's, The New York Review of Books,* and numerous other publications in the United States and Europe. He has published short stories in *Story, Southwest Review, Gulf Coast, The Quarterly,* and *Ambit.*

ADAM HASLETT is a student at Yale Law School and a graduate of the Iowa Writers' Workshop. He has been a fellow at the Provincetown Fine Arts Work Center and the MacDowell Colony. He has also published an essay on contemporary philosophy in *Lingua Franca*.

PETER LEFCOURT was born in New York City and now lives in Los Angeles. His first novel, *The Deal*, was published by Random House in 1991, followed by *The Dreyfus Affair* (1992), *Di and I* (1994), and *The Woody: A Novel* (1998). His fourth novel, *Abbreviating Ernie*, spent five weeks on the *Los Angeles Times* best-seller list.

DAVID MAMET is the author of numerous plays, including *Oleanna*, *Glengarry Glen Ross* (1984 Pulitzer Prize and New York Drama Critics Circle Award), *The Cryptogram* (1995 Obie Award), and *American Buffalo*. His films include *The Postman Always Rings Twice*, *The Verdict*, *The Untouchables*, *Hoffa*, *The Edge*, *Wag the Dog*, *House of Games*, *The Winslow Boy*, and *The Spanish Prisoner*, the last three of which he directed. He is the author of four volumes of essays and the novels *The Village* and *The Old Religion*.

JAVIER MARÍAS was born in Madrid in 1951. He is the author of several novels, including *All Souls*, *A Heart So White*, *Tomorrow in the Battle Think on Me*, and *Black Back of Time*. He has also written two short-story collections, *While They Were Sleeping* and *When I Was Mortal*, which will be published by New Directions in May 2000. He has won numerous international awards for his writing, which has been translated into twenty-two languages.

LUCIA NEVAI was born in Des Moines, Iowa. She now lives and writes in New York City. Her stories have appeared in *The New Yorker*, *The Iowa Review*, *The North American Review*, *North Dakota Quarterly*, *Vignette*, *Fiction*, and other